# Praise For (

"From the very beginning I was drawn into this story and found myself mesmerized by it. It is a tale which rings with sincerity, warmth, color and depth."

~ Philip Carr Gomm, Chosen Chief of the Order of Bards, Ovates and Druids (OBOD)

"Wisewomen and clever men are in for a treat in this magnificent book; another thread in the re-weaving of our sacred wisdom."

~ Susun Weed, wisewoman, herbalist, and author

"A lively tale of ancient Druids and Irish warriors based on substantial research into Celtic history and tradition. [This book] offers and intriguing vision of a Druid path with lessons to teach the modern world."

~John Michael Greer, Grand Archdruid, Ancient Order of Druids in America

"This narrative is a beautiful glance back at pagan culture, Druidic practices and rituals, and daily Celtic life."

~ *Historical Novels Review*

"An authentically human tale of love, hope, and survival. Once I started reading, I was held captive until the very last page."

~ Christopher A. LaFond, Druid harper and professor of languages, Boston College

"Hopman' s ability to incorporate moving and beautiful examples of ritual into the narrative demonstrates a nascent talent for blending historical scholarship, modern practice, and individual inspiration into effective story-telling."

~ *Bond of Druids: A Druid Journal*

# Also by Ellen Evert Hopman

THE SACRED HERBS OF SPRING:
*Magical, Healing and Edible Plants to Celebrate Beltaine*

THE SACRED HERBS OF SAMHAIN:
*Plants to Contact the Spirits of the Dead*

THE REAL WITCHES OF NEW ENGLAND:
*History, Lore and Modern Practice*

TREE MEDICINE TREE MAGIC:
*A Revised and Updated Version Of The Old Classic
with Full Color Botanical Prints*

SECRET MEDICINES FROM YOUR GARDEN:
*Plants for Healing, Spirituality, and Magic*

A LEGACY OF DRUIDS:
*Conversations with Druid Leaders Of Britain,
the USA and Canada, Past and Present*

THE DRUID ISLE

PRIESTESS OF THE FIRE TEMPLE: A DRUID'S TALE

SCOTTISH HERBS AND FAIRY LORE

THE SECRET MEDICINES OF YOUR KITCHEN

A DRUID'S HERBAL OF SACRED TREE MEDICINE

BEING A PAGAN:
*Druids, Wiccans, and Witches Today*

WALKING THE WORLD IN WONDER:
*A Children's Herbal*

A DRUID'S HERBAL FOR THE SACRED EARTH YEAR

# Priestess of the Forest: A Druid Journey

The Druid Trilogy

Book 1: *Priestess of the Forest*
Book 2: *The Druid Isle*
Book 3: *Priestess of the Fire Temple*

Ellen Evert Hopman

*Priestess of the Forest: A Druid Journey*

Copyright © 1998, 2006, 2020 Ellen Evert Hopman

Oak Spirit Publishing
P.O. Box 219
Amherst, MA 01004

Printed in the United States of America
ISBN: 978-1-7333866-9-2

# Dedication

This book is dedicated to the Druid of the past,
to the Druid of the present and
to the Druid of the future.

Beannachd leibh.
Blessings on you all.

# Acknowledgments

Many thanks to Alexei Kondratiev for his help with Old Irish
names and terms, to Dr. Jane Sibley who helped establish
that there were Friesian raiders on the Northern seas as early
as the second century, to Maureen Buchanan Jones who
helped me give voice to the characters, to Domi O'Brien
and Daibhaid O'Broder for pronunciation help, and to
Christopher A. LaFond and Skip Ellison for their assistance.
Any mistakes are my own.

# Introduction

*To my readers:*

This book is not based on any known historical persons or events. Because it features Druids (the sacred priest class of the Pagan Celts) it will likely be cataloged as "fantasy."

Writers of Celtic History have attempted to explain the peaceful conversion of places like Ireland by claiming that Druids were subsumed into the Christian clergy in a seamless transition following the work of missionaries.

As a practicing Druid priestess in the twenty-first century I find it difficult to believe that all Druids would have chosen the new religion from the East. For female Druids in particular it would hardly have made sense. Once the Roman Christian religion came to Celtic Western Europe, women were forced to stop carrying weapons and were generally expected to conform to "proper" Roman matronly ideals, entailing an inevitable loss of freedom and power.

This novel is one woman's story that takes place at the time of the transition from the old Western European Iron Age religious and cultural paradigm to the new Roman influenced Christian era. In the ancient tradition of the Druids it is a Bardic teaching tale; hidden within it are rituals, festivals and cultural wisdom that I hope will illuminate and inspire some to follow the modern Druid path.

In writing the book I felt the breath of the Gods at my back. The characters, each with a powerful and unique presence, foreign yet oddly familiar to me, rose up one by one to tell their tale. I never knew when I sat down to write what these ancient and wise souls might do or say. They spoke *through* me, needing to tell their stories, urging me to put ancient ideas, practices and experiences into words and form, so that modern readers might understand once again the ways of old.

As I wrote, it took an extraordinary level of energy and concentration to keep up with their voices, thoughts, actions, and feelings. Images and ceremonies were revealed that I could never have thought of.

I am most grateful to the ancient spirits who were with me through my labor, guiding and shaping the process. This is truly *their* tale, and I am honored to share it with you at last.

Readers who wish to deepen their own Druid studies should consult the book list provided, especially the Carmina Gadelica which provided inspiration for some of the invocations presented in the book.

~ Ellen Evert Hopman
Herbalist and Druid priestess
Lughnasad, 2006

# Glossary (Old Irish)

*A Chara* – friend A-HAH-RUH

*Albu* – Britain ALL-BAH

*Anam Chara* – Soul Friend AH-NUM HAH-RUH

*Ard-Ban-Drui* – Arch Druidess AHRD BAHN-DREE

*Ard-Drui* – Arch Druid AHRD-DREE

*Ard-Ri* – High King AHRD-REE

*Ard-Rígain* – High Queen AHRD-REEG-AHN

*Armorica* – Brittany AHR-MORE-EE-KA

*Ban-Drui* – female Druid (*Ban-Druid*, plural) BAHN-DREE

*Bell Branch* – a Druidic tool consisting of a branch with nine bells. Depending on their rank, a Druid poet was entitled carry one made of bronze, silver, or gold.

*Beltaine* – May Day, the first day of summer
BEE-AHL-TIN-AH

*Bendacht lib* – blessings on you BAHN-DAK-LEE

*Bíle* – a sacred tree BEE-LEH

*Bíth ed samlaid* – So mote it be! BEE-ED-SHAM-LEED

*Boaire* – a freeman, a cow farmer BOO-AR

*Bothrán* – a small road shaded by trees BO-RAIN

*Brehon* – a lawyer and judge of the Druid caste, one who has memorized the ancient Brehon Laws BREH-ON

*Bricht* – charm, spell (*Brichta*, plural) BRIK

*Caledonia* – Scotland CALL-EH-DOUGH-KNEE-AH

*Ceannaire* – a leader, a guide KAHN-AIR

*Coini Sidi* – Fairies KO-KNEE SHE

*Cristaide* – Christian (*Cristaidi*, plural) KRISH-TIE-DAH

*Cristaidecht* – Christianity KRISH-TIE-DECK

*Cruitt* – a small harp KREW-EAT

*Dei* – God DEE

*Dessel* – sunwise, clockwise, to the right DEH-SELL

*Derbfhine* – the four generations of immediate family DER-VIN

*Doini Sidi* – the Faery DIN-AH SHE

*Drui* – a Druid (*Druid*, plural) DREE

*Druidecht* – Druidic art, magic, enchantment DREE-DECK

*Dun* – a fort or fortress DONE

*Fennidi* – members of a Fian VEN-NEE-DEE

*Fian* – a band of warrior-hunters FIN

*Fiana* – bands of warrior-hunters FIN-AH

*Fianaiocht* – the stories and lore of the Fiana FIN-EH-YO

*Fidchell* – a chess like game FID-HELL

*Fili* – a sacred poet and diviner FEE-LEE

*Filidecht* – the craft of the sacred poet and diviner
FEE-LEE-DECK

*Fion* – wine, imported from Gaul FEE-OHN

*Flaith* – nobles FLAY-V

*Fomoire* – forces of chaos and blight FO-MORE

*Fomorian* – an agent of the forces of chaos and blight
FO-MORE-IAN

*Gaul* – the territory encompassing modern France and parts
of Germany GALL

*Geilt* – a lunatic, a wildman/woman (*Geilte*, plural) GUILT

*Geis* – a strict obligation or taboo placed on a person (*Geasa*,
plural) JESH

*Greimm Dúr* – "hard biter" GREM-DUHR

*Imbas* – poetic inspiration, prophetic vision IHM-BAHS

*Imbolc* – the Feast of Brighid celebrated February 1-2, a milk festival in honor of the first lactation of the ewes, later termed Candlemas by the Catholic church IHM-BOLK

*Ing-* a major God of the Friesians ING

*In Medon* – the Central Kingdom EN-MEH-DON

*Irardacht* – the Kingdom of the Eagle, the Northern Kingdom EHR-ARD-AKT

*Kernow* – Cornwall CARE-NOW

*Liaig* – a Druid healer specializing in herbal healing, surgery, and magic LEE-AH

*Lugnasad* – First Fruits, a pre-harvest festival generally celebrated during the first few weeks of August LOO-NAH-SAHD

*Máthir Mór* – Great Mother MAY-VEER MORE

*Mogae*– slaves (Mog, singular) MOHG-AY

*Mudra* – (Sanskrit) a finger posture to aid concentration and meditation MOOD-RAH

*Murthracht* – the Western Kingdom, the People of the Sea MUHR-HRAKT

*Nemed* – sacred, the highest cast of society including the Druid and ruling aristocrats NEH-MED

*Nemed* – a sacred enclosure NEH-MED

*Ogum* – the ancient Celtic alphabet and script OH-GUM

*Oirthir* – the Eastern Kingdom, the People the sunrise, the people of Gold OHR-HEHR

*Pagani* – (Latin) Pagans, non-Christians, literally "country dwellers," ones who worship the old Gods (singular Paganus) PAH-GAH-NEE

*Quern* – two round stones used to grind grain KERN

*Rath* – earthen rampart, a ring-fort RAHV

*Rígain* – queen REE-GAHN

*Ruadán* – Rowan, Mountain Ash RUE-AH-DANE

*Samain* – traditional festival of the dead and the beginning of the dark half of the year, known today as Halloween or All Hallows SAH-MAN

*Samildanach* – many-skilled SAH-MILL-DEN-OK

*Siabainn* – soap SHE-BAHN

*Sith* – peace SHEEV

*Smolach* – a thrush SHMO-LOCK

*Tecosc Ríg* – inauguration ceremony of a king TEH-KOSH-REE

*Tech ind allais* – sweat house TEH-IN-AH-LESS

*Teinntech* – lightning flashes, sparks TEN-TEH

*Toirnech* – thunder TORE-NAH

*Torcrad* – the Kingdom of the South, the People of the Boar TOR-KRAHD

*Triskell* – a design consisting of three spirals rotating out of a common center representing the Three Worlds of Land, Sea and Sky (*Triskellean*, plural) TRIS-KEL

*Tuathamail* – earth-wise, counterclockwise TOO-AHV-AH-MAAHL

*Tuath* – country district, tribal area TOO-AH

*Tuatha Dé Danann* – tribe of the Goddess Danann TOO-HA-DEH-DAH-NAH-NAN

*Vettir* – Land Spirits (Scandinavia) VET-EER

# The Characters

_Aífe_ – an orphaned child in training to become a Druid
AEE-FAH

_Airmid_ – Goddess of herbcraft and healing AIR-MID

_Albinus_ – a Roman monk AL-BEE-NUHS

_Anluan_ – brother of Glaisne AHN-LAHN

_Anu_ – Land Goddess or Earth Mother AH-NEW

_Ardal_ – a monk AHR-DOLL

_Bairredach_ – a dead warrior BAR-REE-DOCK

_Boann_ – Cow Goddess of the Boyne river BOO-AHN

_Brighid_ – Triple Goddess of Healing, Poetry and Smith-craft,
Patroness of the Bards VREE-ID

_Brude_ – a shoemaker BROOD

_Buan_ – a member of the Fian BWAN

_Cadla_ – a warrior of the High King's army KAD-LAH

_Cailleach_ – a hag, a childless woman of great power, an old
woman, a crone. In some Celtic areas She was regarded as a
Goddess, the Creatrix of the world CALL-EE-AK

_Canoc_ – High King of the Eastern Kingdom, Oirthir
KA-NOCK

_Celtchair_ – a noble from the Northern Kingdom, Irardacht
KELT-CHAIR

_Cétach_ – a dead warrior KAY-TOCK

_Cian_ – a friend of Ethne in her student days KEY-AHN

_Clothru_ – a female apprentice Druid KLOVE-ROO

_Colchu_ – a member of the Fian KOAL-COO

_Coemgen_ – the Ard-Drui of the Island KEV-GEN

*Conaire* – High King of the Northern Kingdom, Irardacht KON-OR

*Corc* – a member of the Fian KORK

*Creide* – a princess, daughter of Marcan, High King of the Western Kingdom, Murthracht KRAY-DEH

*Crimthann* – High King of the Central Kingdom, In Medon, and of the Island KREM-VAN

*Cuchullain* – the greatest warrior hero of the North of Eire KOO-KUL-UN

*Dai re* – a prince, son of the High King Crimthann DAHR

*Danann* – Great Mother, River Goddess of the Celts DAH-NAHN

*Damán* – a male apprentice Druid DAH-MAIN

*Donal* – battle leader of the king's warriors DONAHL

*Duald* – Orla's brother DEW-ALLD

*Ecca* – former Arch Druidess, teacher of Gaine ECK-AH

*Ethne* – a Druidess and herbal healer EV-NEH

*Erc* – a member of the Fian ERK

*Faelchu* – a man Ethne meets at the stone circle on the hill above the king's rath HAL-KOO

*Father Per* – a wandering Coptic monk PEAR

*Fiachnae* – a noble from the Southern Kingdom, Torcrad HAK-NAY

Fidach – a member of the Fian FEE-DAHK

*Finn mac Cumhaill* – the greatest warrior hero of the South of Eire

*Fithir* – Queen of the Eastern Kingdom, Oirthir, Canoc's wife FEVER

*Gaine* – the Arch Druidess GAH-NEH

*Germanus* – the abbot JER-MAHN-US

*Glaisne* – a noble from the Eastern Kingdom, Oirthir
GLASH-NAH

*Gorm hinn Svarta* – Gorm the Black, leader of the Men of the
North GORM-HINN-SVAHR-TAH

*Gorman* – a dead warrior GORE-MAN

*Grian* – The Sun Goddess GREE-UHN

*In Dagdae* – the "Good God," patron of the Druid
IN-DAHG-DAH

*I/su* – Jesus EE-SOO

*Labraid* – a Druid healer LAH-BRED

*Liatha* – a friend of Ethne when she was a girl LIE-VAH

*Lorcan* – a warrior of the High King's army LORE-KAN

Lug Samildanach – the God Lug, master of every art LOO
SAH-MILL-DEN-OCK

*Lugnae* – a farmer LOO-NAH

*Marcan* – High King of the Western Kingdom, Murthracht
MAHR-KAN

*Máthir Mór* – The Great Mother Goddess MAY-VEER
MORE

*Miadach* – sister of Fidach, a woman who cooks for and cares
for the Fian MEE-DAK

*Mis* – a girl from the village outside of the Ard-Ri's rath

*Mithras* – a God of light MYTH-RAHS

*Morrigu* – a triple Battle Goddess often personified as crow
or raven MORE-REE-GUH

*Nessan* – battle leader of the king's warriors NEH-SEHN

*Niamh* – deceased wife of Crimthann, mother of Daire NEEV

*Nuada* – a legendary warrior king NOO-AH-DAH

*Ogma* – God of eloquence, inventor of the Ogum alphabet
OHG-MA

*Orla* – wet nurse to Ethne OAR-LE

*Ragnall* – a member of the Fian RAHG-NAHL

*Rian* – a princess, daughter of Conaire, High King of the Irardacht REE-AHN

*Rochad* – High King of Torcrad ROW-HAHD

*Ronan* – a warrior of the High King's army ROW-NAHN

*Ruadh* – red, wild, fierce one, a member of the Fian ROO-AHD

*Scáth* – (*shade, shadow*) a horse SCAHV

*Sheela-Na-Gig* – a fertility Goddess SHE-LAH-NAH-GHEE

*Snedgus* – a pig farmer SHNED-GOOSE

*Tiarnan* – a dead warrior TIE-NAHN

# PART ONE

∽

## The Waters of Life

# 1

There were no nations then. The world was a vast oak forest that stretched from sun rise to sun set, where solitary hawthorns growing on hills above sacred springs marked an entrance to the land of Faery. It was a time of bog sacrifices and of calling to Brighid and Danann, of visions and stories about ogres and sea beasts. It was a time of raids from the Men of the North, and sporadic winds of change.

Ethne felt change coming as surely as she felt the newly chill winds pushing at her back. She stood at the doorway of her hut and smelled early autumn arriving from the forest and the stream. She heard the evensong of birds and watched the hares twitch their whiskers. These were ordinary signs of life's cycle, not the cataclysm that approached. She waited for the Spirits of the land to speak. A cricket clicked behind her. Ethne turned and closed the door against the night.

Sitting down to her table, she smelled the fat bundles of herbs hanging from pegs on the wall. Among them were mugwort for the cramp, loosestrife and willow bark for fever, terrestrial sun to ward off melancholy, yarrow for the bowels, and foxglove and hawthorn for the heart. Rue and hag's tapers were for the cough. Long braids of garlic, useful for everything, swung from overhead along with the all-important comfrey, vervain, figwort and oak bark for poulticing wounds, the last hanging in dry strips from the thatch.

A cloth bag full of hazelnuts stood propped against the wall, a strengthener for the weak and debilitated, to be eaten with oats. Baskets of dandelion roots, sacred to Brighid, hung from the low ceiling; for those with an over-fondness for mead. She had wild carrot seed to prevent conception and a precious store of golden bough still wrapped in its white cloth, for the barren and those with tumors of the wasting disease.

The season of green summer was over and she had labored long and hard to gather these simples. They were the mainstay of her healing art, along with a precious crock of the Waters of Life, which she kept on a shelf. The hut was big enough for a bed, a pallet, a sturdy oaken table, two chairs, and a large carved box near the fire in which to keep oats, barley, linens and woolens from the damp. The primary feature of her home was the central hearth, which warmed her, cooked her meals, prepared her remedies and provided her with company as the flames danced and glowed on quiet evenings. The hut was surrounded by hawthorn, elder, oak and apple trees and was visited in all seasons by villagers and others in need.

On this day, the eve of Samain, Ethne barred the door long before the sun disappeared. She placed small equal-armed crosses of rowan wood, bound with red wool, in the window and against the door as protection from the mischievous *Brichta* of the Coini Sidi, the mischievous spirits sure to be about on the autumn holy night of the dead. Her gifts to the ancestors of cider, cheese and fresh bread she had lain beneath the oldest apple tree. Pulling down a cracked and weathered willow basket from a hook on the roof-tree, she hummed and stripped leaves from the branches of dried herbs, stifling an occasional sneeze as aromatic dust tickled her nose. "Brighid!" she exclaimed, as a sharp stalk pierced her finger. She heard the patter of a mouse as it snuffled across the floor looking for a drip of honey.

When the herbs were packed in their baskets, it was deep into the night and the full moon cast a hazy brightness on the bare branches outside. Ethne heard three hoots of an owl and wondered if this were a Faery spirit or a mortal bird come to bring dark tidings. The birds usually warned her within three days before someone ill or wounded arrived. This was a Spirit Night when anything was possible, and the omens were harder to read when so many of the Faery were abroad, causing mischief.

She swept the remains of the herbs into her hand with the willow broom and spread them on the embers. The fire leaped and sparked as it met the herbs then fell back to its steady glow. Ethne carefully smoored the fire, singing softly as she spread the ashes: "*May the Triple Goddess surround this house, this hearth. May the Triple Goddess shield this house this eve, this night, and every night.*"

Knowing not to venture out on this particular evening, she performed her ablutions indoors, a flick of water on the forehead, the eyes, the hands, and feet, in the name of Danann, Mother of the Waters. Yawning, she pulled back the woolen coverlet and crept between linen sheets to drift into dream-laden sleep.

In the morning Ethne ignored the first chorus of birdsong as she always did, waiting instead for the second chorus that followed about an hour after. By that time the hut was thoroughly chilled and she faced the unpleasant prospect of darting across the earthen floor to feed the fire's embers. A strip of birch bark laid on the ashes burst immediately into flame. She laid on twigs of oak and ash, and a few small branches of oak. On top of those she laid two blocks of peat and then skillfully swung the small black cauldron over to start the water boiling for an herbal brew.

As she reached for the basket of elderberries a warning "Squawk!" came from crows gathered in the trees outside. Ethne stiffened and stood stock-still to catch other sounds. Moving to the window, she pulled back the oiled sheepskin and peered through the opening. A tight knot of figures approached, two half lifting, half carrying another.

She slipped on her linen gown and deerskin belt and ran a comb through her hair.

Opening the door a crack to keep as much warm air in as possible, she waited for the figures to approach.

"Ethne! Are you home?" one of the figures shouted.

"In the name of Brighid where *else* would I be?" she yelled back. She saw the stain of blood on the leg of the middle one and began rummaging in the wooden chest for old linens to tear for bandages.

"Bring him in here," she commanded.

The wounded warrior they carried had fainted from shock and loss of blood.

"We are Erc and Buan, of the Fiana," said the one lifting the wounded man onto the pallet and removing his weapons. "The one we carry is called Ruadh."

Erc was a heavy-set warrior of twenty-eight summers, clad entirely in leather. His hair was blond, long, and tied back in one thick braid, bound with a strip of yellow deerskin. Around his neck, hanging from a leather thong, was a bronze triskell, the triple spiral that spoke of the Three Worlds always in motion. A fierce-looking dagger protruded from one boot and a sword dangled in its sheath strapped across his back. Strapped over the sword was a bronze covered, round shield.

Ethne did not immediately realize that Buan was a woman of about eighteen years. All she noticed were the blue tattoo spirals across her cheeks and nose and the shaggy brown hair ending in loose braids intertwined with strips of red leather. Then she saw the faint swell of her breasts under the jerkin. Her clothing was identical to the man's, but her triskell was gold, indicating higher birth. Instead of a sword she had a quiver of arrows over her shoulder and tied to it a bow of yew.

The wounded man also had a bow of ash wood, and a quiver of red arrows. But what Ethne noticed with greatest interest was his sword strapped to his waist and to his good leg. It was sheathed in a casing of stamped red leather, covered with intricate spirals and other markings, which she would have liked to examine. Erc stowed the weapons in a corner.

"We were hunting a boar, and Ruadh shot him," the man stated.

"It was a clean shot, but the beast wasn't dead," added Buan. "Ruadh went to finish him and set his spirit free when the pig gored his leg."

Ruadh let out low, incoherent words, something about blood and ravens.

"He's afraid he'll be food for the crows if we don't do something quickly," Erc muttered.

"He's not food for the barrows yet," said Ethne as she inspected the gash on his thigh and tore open the leg of his hide pants. "Hold him down while I clean and dress the wound."

Erc and Buan took Ruadh's arms and feet, as Ethne reached for the Waters of Life from the shelf. She poured some directly onto the wound and some onto a cloth, which she used to clean away the blood. She left another cloth soaked in the Waters of Life on top of the wound while she put oak bark, comfrey, vervain and figwort into the cauldron, which had come to a boil. Lifting the cauldron with a thick hazel rod, she carried it to the pallet. When it had cooled, she soaked another clean linen in the brew and applied it to the wound. Ruadh gasped, moaned and fainted, which Ethne considered a blessing. Now she could work in peace.

Proceeding quickly, Ethne took a thin needle and thread from a basket and soaked them briefly in The Waters of Life. She examined the wound carefully. It was not long but very deep. The boar had swung upwards with its head and caught the flesh of the leg on its tusk. Only a few stitches were needed but such wounds were deceptive, she knew. Even if the bleeding was staunched and the skin healed, the deepest parts of the injury might never repair properly. She had seen men die of such wounds.

"I'll need to apply these compresses every hour or so for the next few days" she said.

"What can we give you in thanks?" asked Erc.

"I could use fresh meat. If you could find a hare or a pheasant for the stew pot I'd be most grateful. Ruadh is going to need the broth to thicken his blood."

Erc and Buan bowed slightly to acknowledge her wishes. They were grateful and in awe of this Forest Woman who possessed the healing powers. As trained warriors they traveled in bands for protection, yet here was a woman who lived alone in the wilderness. She clearly had the protection of the Spirits, for there were no weapons in her house, except the gold covered bronze sickle on her belt. It was hard to tell if it was a weapon, or for the cutting of grains and simples, or if was for magic. Maybe it was for all three? But they wouldn't dare ask . Hadn't they heard all their lives how Druid could lay mountains flat or raise up a fog that would swallow a fleet of ships? Best to leave such matters alone. They had enough to worry about, patrolling the borders to keep out cattle thieves and the Men of the North.

Buan and Erc excused themselves and trotted off to find fresh game as payment for Ethne. "Why do you think she lives alone?" Buan asked. Erc shrugged. "She is Nemed born, the daughter of a chieftain. She could have been a wife of the first degree, with her own lands and cattle if she wanted. It is a mystery to me." Erc frowned slightly as he slowed his pace to spy out suitable brush for cover.

"The Druid are always testing themselves. They must prove themselves to the Gods, so they make a sacrifice of their lives. The greatest ones even volunteer to be buried alive so that their blood nourishes the land and the people have enough to eat. It is never wise to question the ways of the Druid. They are driven by forces none of us can understand." Buan nodded silently. She had spotted a hare emerging from a thicket of ferns and was easing an arrow out of the quiver and notching it onto her bow for the kill.

# 2

Ethne worked carefully, applying the oak bark compress, to draw the jagged edges of the wound together. In her concentration, she did not hear Erc and Buan as they returned.

"How does he?" Erc asked quietly, respectful of Ethne's craft and Ruadh's precarious state.

Ethne adjusted the compress. "His wound is deep and there is danger of blood poison, but he has the Gods to thank that he did not bleed more. I will do my best to see that he mends."

Buan held up two fat hares. "Lady, we bring you these to help you in your work."

Ethne smiled at them for the first time. "Ah, it does not require the gift of Sight to see that some stew would not go amiss for you either before you go."

Buan grinned at her hospitality. "Yes, lady, we carried our friend a good distance to find you and have as much to travel again before rejoining our band. A warm meal would be a kindness."

Ethne bid them rest while she prepared the hares. She cleaned one and placed it in the pot with wild carrots and garlic. She added fresh dandelion leaves, there were still potherbs in the fields despite the first frost. The other hare she hung in a bag from a tree limb outside the door. She carried the entrails of the first hare to a flat rock under an oak tree some thirty paces from the hut. This was her personal Shrine of the Nature Spirits, where she left daily offerings for crows and other predators, always asking that they leave her garden in peace. The skin she placed in an oaken bucket along with water and a slurry of the animal's brain for softening and preserving. She would let that sit for a few days before stretching the hide to dry on an ashwood frame she had made for the purpose.

When she returned, the stew was simmering and filling the hut with rich odors. Erc and Buan had busied themselves bringing in kindling and fresh firewood, stacking everything under the overhanging thatch on the sun facing side of the door. Erc laid a new log on the fire as Ethne ladled stew into ceramic bowls and bid her visitors share the barley bread she had baked that morning.

When the three had finished, Erc and Buan stood to take their leave.

"We are grateful for your gifts, lady. When Ruadh heals, he will find us camped to the south of the village in the Cave of the Bears. He will know where."

Ethne marked their leaving with a small prayer for safe journey, accepting their respect as was due her. She stood in the doorway and watched them depart. As she stepped inside and pushed the door closed, a moan from the pallet made her turn quickly.

In two steps she was by the wounded man's side, examining him intently. His face was pallid and beads of sweat dotted his forehead. He opened his eyes, but did not see, his pupils large and glassy. Ethne knew fever was his worst enemy and began to pray aloud in soothing song:

*In the name of Brighid;*
*Bone to bone*
*Flesh to flesh*
*Sinew to sinew*
*Vein to vein . . .*

She bathed his forehead and chest with cool water. As her hands moved over him, she carefully examined the man before

10

her. He had long brown curls and the mustache characteristic of the Celt. He was beardless, of medium build, not heavily muscled and not too thin or wiry. His jerkin was of a soft white skin – some woman had sewn it with fine stitches. His mother or a lover, she thought.

Ethne pulled the edges of the jerkin apart expecting to find the triskell that warriors wore. She jerked back with a short gasp when her hands encountered a round, golden circlet. She lifted the circlet gently and let the ends rest on the palm of her hand, examining it closely. It was a torque, a round twisted tube of pure gold, ending in elegant wolf's heads on both sides. Only the Nemed, the noble born, could wear one like that. What was such a man doing with the Fennidi? Why would a noble born leave his clann?

Ethne's training taught her to put such questions aside and attend to the body and Spirit, but she took extra care when she tilted his head to give him another drink from The Waters of Life. She would not want to be in debt to a noble family or the Fiana should anything go wrong. Even if his injury was accidental, she could be blamed if he did not survive and the fine would be heavy.

All that night, Ethne sat on a low stool by the man's side, bathing his face and chest and burning sacred herbs in a clay vessel to pull the fever away. As the first birds of dawn made their restless sounds, Ruadh's eyes opened slightly and he turned his head to the side. He stared silently, gazing cloudily at the close walls of the hut, the fire embers and at Ethne, sitting quietly beside him. His voice came rasping and low, "Tell me where I am."

"You are deep in the Forest. Your friends Erc and Buan brought you here to heal. Your leg is badly wounded, I'll do what I can to help you mend."

"You are a healer, then." He said it not as a question, but as an acceptance, giving her permission to perform her necessary tasks. He closed his eyes and let his head sink deeper onto the pallet. Ethne did not answer, but watched him closely. Just as she thought he had drifted back to sleep, he muttered gruffly, "Where is my sword?"

"Your sword and bow are in the corner. No one will touch them."

Satisfied with this answer, he turned his face away, falling into sleep again. Ethne sat for a time, watching this man who showed no fear and commanded respect even when fevered and wounded. Ethne's thoughts wandered to the life she led, circumspect and intimate within this small clearing and its surrounds. This man ranged along the seacoast, moving from village to village, and inlet to cliff. Her companions were forest birds, the voice of the brook and the stars overhead. She knew their stories well. She wondered what tales he might tell and whether she would want to hear them. With his strong jaw and straight nose, his stories were likely of conquests both martial and amorous.

Ethne spent the rest of the morning grinding meal for the evening's bannock bread. In early afternoon she made a trip to the stream for fresh water. The wind had risen and there was a snap to the air that foretold of deeper cold. The grasses by the brook turned golden in the late sun, bowing and swaying as she made her way through. At the edge, Ethne stilled her body and breath. She waited for the Goddess of the Waters to speak before she tipped her bucket. The stream rippled and sang, speaking of the deep well of abundance that the earth held, but it also sang of change as the waters tumbled over the rounded stones. Ethne heard the song more clearly today, a song of moons swelling and fading, of suns crossing the sky and of her own life as she grew in knowledge. Ethne thanked the Goddess for her blessings and filled the bucket.

As she opened the door to the hut, she heard a crash. Spilling nearly half the water, Ethne dropped the bucket as Ruadh fell full length toward her. She caught his upper body in her arms and steadied herself.

"Let me be!" Ruadh tried to wrest himself free, but Ethne was the stronger at the moment. Ruadh nearly wrenched himself out of her grasp and Ethne had to tighten her grip around his chest.

"Stop fighting! It's all right, you need to rest." Ethne tried to soothe him with her words, but it was no good.

"My sword! You're keeping my sword!" And again he swung his arms and tried to pull himself out of her grasp, nearly pulling her arms out of their sockets. His eyes were wild and his skin was no longer sweating but dry and dangerously hot. The fever had worsened, and Ethne noticed the smell of putrefaction. It was subtle, but undeniable. It was the scent of mature hawthorn blossoms, a rotting flesh smell, meant to fool the flies for pollination. Ruadh was delirious and Ethne had to act fast.

"If you rest for a moment, I'll get you your sword." She helped him back to his pallet and gave him another draught of the Waters of Life. Within minutes, Ruadh slumped almost lifeless. Ethne moved quickly. She knew his best hope was the tech ind allais, the sweat-house, where the heat would sweat out the poisons in his blood.

She went to the outer wall of the house and gathered an armful of peat bricks from under their protective covering of straw. These she carried to a stone structure built next to the stream about twenty paces from her door. The round cell was seven feet in diameter with a low wooden bench propped inside. She returned to the house for birch bark, kindling, woolen towels, a water jug, and a blanket. She placed a birchbark coil in the center of the sweat-house floor and surrounded it with a pyramid of twigs. Once the twigs were lit, she added chunks of peat until she was able to lay on entire blocks of turf. She continued this process until the fire roared and the stones were hot as an oven. When she was satisfied the heat would persist, she raked the embers with a deer antler and went to fetch the patient. Ruadh lay dazed on the pallet, almost too weak to walk. She coaxed him to his feet and guided him out the door and into the sweathouse. She made him drink fresh water from the stream, most of which he vomited.

His teeth chattered as she helped him undress. It had been a long time since she had lain with a man and this one was well made, pleasing her eye. His skin was silky and even textured for he had not known want in his youth. The muscles of his legs and arms were firm.

Ethne thought of running her hand across them. Instead, she spoke with authority. "I will remove your torque for the metal will grow hot and burn."

With vague resistance, Ruadh tried to push her hands away, but he was too weak.

"Shhh," Ethne assured him. "Your torque and your sword are safe in my care."

After wrapping him in a woolen blanket, she drew back the door covering and led him inside where she sat him on the wooden bench. She placed a jug of water next to him, saying, "Rest here until I come for you. Call on the Gods to heal you and give you peace." Ethne entered the hut every few hours to see if the fever had broken again into sweat. Ruadh was too weak to sit on the bench, so she helped him to the floor where he lay, murmuring his prayers. Outside, by the stream bank, Ethne sang:

*Oh, Brighid!*
*May I have Your skill in working with this man.*
*Fire be my friend,*
*Water be my friend, Earth be my friend, Air be my friend.*
*I call on you!*
*Out with fire and in with frost!*
*I place this charm of protection on Ruadh,*
*Between sole and throat,*
*Between pap and knee,*
*Between back and breast,*
*Between chest and sole,*

*Between eye and hair.*
*Protected shall he be behind and before.*
*The charm of the Gods above him,*
*Below him and about him.*

All the while she held the golden torque, using it to focus on the man inside the sweat-house. When the sun dropped to touch the edge of the land, she brought him out. He was very weak and leaned on her heavily as she half carried him to the water and they waded in. Ruadh stiffened at the cold and dug his fingers into her shoulder, but Ethne held them both steady. Using a piece of wool, she rubbed him from head to toe with the icy water. Back on the bank she helped him to sit and rubbed him down again with a dry blanket. "I have laid charms of protection around you, and now you must charm yourself. Find Sith within you, ask the Gods for their blessing."

Well she knew that half the healing was in the patient's desire to be healed, without which nothing would succeed. As she placed the torque on his neck once again their eyes met briefly. For the first time she saw the deep sapphire of his gaze and it held her. He smiled weakly.

"Thank you for your arts, lady." Ethne nodded and helped him back to the hut where she laid him on the pallet, covering him with blankets. As Ruadh fell into a deep, dreamless sleep, Ethne latched the door, banked the embers of the fire and curled onto her cot, her body weary, her mind sorting through the events of the day. Soon, sleep overcame her and she too breathed peacefully.

# 3

When Ethne checked Ruadh in the morning, he was still caught in the deep struggle to overcome the poison in his blood. His fever was high and he barely moved as she bathed his forehead. She had done everything she could for the man who lay hot and silent, his body fighting in the limp, strained way that bodies do when they turn in on themselves to heal.

She had left reeds and willow branches to soak overnight and now sat on the low stool by the fire to begin another basket. She decided this one would be large, wide enough to bring her clothing and blankets to the stream or to carry herbs and grasses from the meadows. She began by trimming twelve ash branches until they were the right lengths. Four were longest for the center, then by pairs on either side she trimmed the sticks shorter to form an oval circumference. These she bound together with reeds made supple from soaking, her hands moving slowly and carefully. As the ash branches were lashed one to another, the heel of her hand stabilized each stick as her fingers threaded a reed over and under. Each reed end was wound tightly and slid back on itself so that where one reed ended and another began was barely visible. The weaving process was an ancient magic; Ethne murmured prayers of healing into the basket as she plaited.

Ethne stretched. She had been hunched over her work and her back was stiff. She stood, went to the man on the pallet, spooned water between his lips and washed his face with a cool cloth. He murmured, but it was nothing comprehensible. She heard the rustle of aspen leaves and opened the door. A light breeze greeted her as well as a thin sunshine, both making their effort to dispel the morning fog. Ethne gathered up her work, threw a shawl around her shoulders and moved out of the hut to a patch of sunlit meadow. She seated herself there and set to working the rushes and branches, shaping them to the image in her mind. "Perhaps a handle," she thought, and placed thirty-two ash twigs like spokes perpendicular to the base she had made. This was the part she loved best, when the basket was really born, when it took shape and form. Her hands quickened and her face relaxed, her eyes moving over the smoothed wood and the still green silk of the reeds. She was content and felt the power of the earth beneath her and the grace of the trees in her fingers.

For the next three days, Ethne went about her work, cleaning, sorting and bundling herbs, working with increasing speed and delight on the large basket and baking small loaves of bannock bread. She tended to Ruadh at measured intervals and found no change. She knew that if he did not come out of the fever soon, he would waste away and die. On the eve of the third night she sat staring at him a long while. "He is beautiful," she whispered aloud. "A gift from the forest for one who has pledged herself apart." She eased blankets over his chest, banked down the fire and lay down on the other side of the small hut.

At first light, Ethne woke with a start to find the man staring at her from his pallet. He looked quickly away, but out of respect for her rather than shame for himself.

Ethne stood up from her cot, put her fingers through her hair to straighten the night's tangles and folded her blankets neatly. When she had attended to herself, she turned and addressed Ruadh.

"Have you been awake long?"

"Only long enough to understand that I am better. I have you to thank."

Ethne came closer and looked at him. The pallor had gone, replaced by a healthier hue and clearer eyes. Dark circles still outlined his eyes and the muscles of his face looked drawn, but the fever had broken and he would live. "I will get you some broth. It will be many days before you are well enough to return to your people."

Ruadh, as if to contradict her words, tried to sit upright. With a groan and a hiss of pain, he collapsed back on the pallet. For a few moments he lay breathing heavily, and then relaxed, opening his eyes and looking about the room. He took in the array of handwoven baskets stacked by the wall and hanging from the roof tree, the fire, and the jars and bundles of herbs neatly arranged on the shelf. His gaze came to rest on his sword in it's scabbard, and his bow and quiver stowed in the shadows. He turned his eyes upon the woman.

Ethne stood over the hearth, comfortable and competent, yet with a commanding air. Though she was dressed in simple white linen, its texture gave off a light that implied mystery. He noticed her long and loosely braided hair, the sickle at her waist which hung from a soft deerskin belt, her only mark of distinction. No clann tattoos, no triskell. She moved and spoke like a Druidess, yet not so aloof.

"Are you Ban-Drui?"

Ethne turned and gave a small nod. "Yes, I was raised in the rath of Coemgen and given the healing arts. That is why your friends brought you to me. It is my following to live apart and to heal the wounded and sick that come to my door." She faced back to her work as if the interview were over.

Ruadh felt her formality and a subtle deference towards his person. He did not know whether her reserve came naturally or if it was due to the torque she had discovered around his neck. He looked more carefully about the room and took in the hearth outfitted with iron hooks and prongs, cauldrons and fire dogs. The latter were twisted and pulled by the metal smith's art and each featured the head of a cow at its tip. He saw the thick wax candles and earthenware crockery lining the shelf, on the table was a bronze mead flagon, lined with beeswax, and two silver cups for important guests. A crockery jar of honey stood to one side. His eyes continued to scan the room and he found a mirror on one wall, and a six-colored cloak hanging on a peg beside the door. He did not need to see the set of fine combs and a torque, kept hidden in a box, to know the marks of a Druid. He decided to probe further.

"You wear no symbols of status, no rings or many-colored clothing. Is this plainness of your choosing?"

Ethne tilted her chin up and spoke softly. "I do not believe my worth or power come from breastplates or torques, though they hold the power of the artisans who work them, and of the Gods they honor. I am secure in the power of the Gods who speak through me." Ethne bent and pulled an earthenware pot from under her cot. "You are too weak to stand and make water. Be careful not to pull your stitches."

She walked out of the hut on the pretense of fetching more water from the stream. When she was several strides away, she allowed herself a smile and wondered how long he would have suffered before giving in to the shame of asking for that convenience. For his part, Ruadh scowled in embarrassment, but gladly made use of the pot.

When Ethne returned, she served him a bowl of broth and a cup of mead. His hands were unsteady, so she spooned the broth carefully into his mouth and avoided his eyes as they searched her face, taking in the line of her neck, her strong arms and the supple fingers. "He is bold," she thought. "But he must be to survive attacks from the Men of the North. She wanted to return his gaze, search his face for the person who lay within, but to do so would seem undignified and would open the way to more questioning. It had been a long time since she had shared stories with anyone. The folk from the tuath brought her children and ancients to tend, and she mended bones and cuts aplenty. But as good as these people were, they could not share her way of seeing the world. They knew about their crops and cattle, but they did not know how the trees came to be, or of the Spirits dwelling within them, or how the fish found their way or why the sun circled its patterns in the sky. She loved her solitude, she loved her own company, but this man reminded her of conversations she used to have.

"Forgive me, I never asked your name."

"No need for forgiveness. I should have offered it when you first awoke. I am Ethne."

"A name that suits you."

"And you are Ruadh, it is a strong name. It is a Nemed-born name." Ethne waited to see if he would tell her more. She did not want to pry, but his manner, his torque, the carvings on his leather scabbard all spoke of one born to a better life than the roaming Fennidi. Ruadh considered for a moment.

"Yes, I am noble born."

The silence lengthened as Ethne busied herself with the ceramic bowls and ladles.

Ruadh watched her movements.

"She is not beautiful," he thought. "Yet she has a grace in the way she carries herself. She is like a queen." He watched as she bent to stir the stew and was pleased at the roundness of her hips and the light on her skin, rosy and clear.

Ethne turned to find him staring at her again. This time she did not turn away but held his gaze, her large brown eyes luminous with inner intensity. Ruadh became uneasy.

He was used to the women of his father's rath; milkmaids, and farmer's daughters, who fell too easily into his grasp. But this was a woman of learning, a woman who lived unaided in the forest, a woman who had seen him naked and asleep. He blinked and looked away, tongue-tied.

Ethne held her ground for a few seconds more then busied herself with separating seeds from the leaves and twigs of dried herbs. The light grew stronger and Ethne put on her shawl to go outside and finish curing the hare skin. "I will leave the door open a little to give you fresh air, but don't try to walk any distance, your body still needs rest. You may have a small bowl of stew, but don't overdo that either. Even eating can tax a man." With that she went out carrying her tools with her. Ruadh lay staring at the ceiling when she had gone, wondering about this woman who could so easily command him without giving offense.

When Ethne returned, she gave Ruadh another small bowl of stew and a piece of fresh bannock. Ruadh, sitting on the pallet and leaning his back against the wall, put down his spoon and cleared his throat.

"I am not like most Fennidi."

"That much I have already discovered." Ethne chewed a piece of bannock, giving him her full attention.

"I am the older son. It should have been my duty to lead the tuath after my father's death."

"Then why are you here?"

She carefully shielded her voice from suspicion. If he was not a younger son longing to get away from his brothers and make his own mark on the world, then the reason for his flight could be ignoble. She had known of brooding and lonely sorts who didn't fit well with their clanns, some looked for new tribes. But Ruadh had been brought by comrades who treated him with respect and cared for him as a friend.

"I did not like the prospect of counting and re-counting cattle to make sure none were stolen, or settling endless clann squabbles, or repairing the dam on the river and the fish nets on the weir, or cutting mountains of firewood for winter. What I saw in my father's court was stifling. It would tie me to the land, winter through summer, spring through autumn."

"Did you give trouble to your mother as you grew out of childhood? I have heard that some mothers demand such children leave for a few years, to knock some reason into them and keep their influence away from the younger children."

Ruadh nearly smiled. "Yes, my poor mother despaired of me. But she didn't force me to leave." His face grew solemn, a shadow veiled his eyes.

"I longed to travel. But each time I put this before my mother and father they said,

'No.' They always insisted there were walls to mend, hay to cut, until it became intolerable. One day the Fennidi came to our village asking for their portion of mutton, vegetables and eggs. They were allowed to sleep in the barn on the new hay, but my father told them to leave by morning. That night in the hall they were honored guests. They told stories of Cuchullain and Finn mac Cumaill, and sang of raids along the coast, of hunting wild game, of tales from beyond the sea. I was fascinated by their adventures, spell bound by their sword work and weapons skill."

"The Fennidi are fierce warriors and skilled story weavers. They are true champions. They deserve the respect of all."

Ruadh smiled with pride. "Erc is their leader, the oldest of the lot. He asked about my training with a sword and as a hunter. Youthful as I was, I was flattered by his attention. I practiced sword-play with one or two of the younger Fennidi. They actually admired the way I used my weapon."

"Heady praise for a young man."

Ruadh made a rueful face. "Yes, and that is how the idea of leaving my father's rath was born. I needed to know if I had the mettle to be a champion, to take my place in the Fianaiocht I had heard since I was a stripling."

"But to leave the clann is deadly serious! To join the Fennidi you would have to absolve yourself and your kin of all legal obligations. You would be an outcast with no society but the Fian as your kin!"

Ruadh stared into the fire for a long moment, then said quietly, "I broke my parent's hearts." He fell silent and Ethne said nothing. Though his choice disturbed her, she knew the Fennidi did not accept lesser men into their company. They required courage, intelligence and a determined spirit. She wondered if word play was also within this man's gifts, another important Fennid trait. She would find out as he mended.

The days that followed were unusual for them both. While she was used to her own quiet company, he was used to constant movement, frequent jesting and constant planning. She worked to allow his words and presence into her cloistered sphere as he struggled to rein in his wandering thoughts and restless limbs. They found their best satisfaction in the evening, when both had grown tired of the day's struggle, she in assuring their survival and he in harboring his strength. As dusk settled around them, they opened the doors to their pasts.

"Tell me of your sword. It is beautiful and crafted with much care," said Ethne one night as Ruadh cleaned and oiled the scabbard.

"My father presented it to me when I turned seven summers. My mother taught me the use of it, as every mother does when it is her son's time. She made this scabbard with her own hands, dying it red and stamping it with triple spirals and ogums for protection. She blessed it in the name of the Morrígu and taught me to revere Her. She told me to use the sword in defense of our cattle and land. Little did she suspect that I would be using it against the Men of the North."

Ethne heard sadness in his telling, but she heard pride too. She held her words, knowing that sharing his story was as important to his healing as the poultice she applied or the sweat house he had endured.

"I was tormented by thoughts of leaving and finally, one morning I took my weapons and slipped out before dawn. I followed the King's Road in the direction of the Fennidi camp. I left it to my younger brother to break the news." A sudden spark jumped in the hearth and Ruadh looked at Ethne as if transported from a great distance.

"You have made yourself weary. Give yourself over to the night."

He stared a moment longer at the line of her cheekbones and the soft dark of her eyes. He lay back on the pallet, breathing several deep sighs and falling into a dream laden sleep.

# 4

———

Coemgen, the elected Ard-Drui of the Island, was a man of powerful presence, contemplative, wise and strong, even if the years showed upon his timeworn face. As he walked deliberately along the footpath that led from the Nemed, the sacred precinct of the Druid set within the walls of the High King's fortress, he was deep in thought. Beside him, Damán, an apprentice of seventeen years, walked a step behind out of deference.

Coemgen sniffed as they drew closer to the Ard-Ri's great hall. It was autumn, the winds were stiff, and the women had taken advantage of the weather to dye one last batch of wool for the looms they would work all winter.

"Ugh!" Damán wrinkled his nose and shuddered. "Couldn't the women find a better place to dye their wools? The stench is overwhelming!"

Coemgen's pace slowed as he considered. "This is part of our living, Damán; it is not unlike the work I do."

Damán stopped abruptly and looked at the older man in surprise.

"Can you not see it, Damán?"

Damán stood and considered the barrels of stale urine, collected from wooden buckets left outside the feasting hall each night, and placed in neat rows beside the clotheslines. Each held woad, left to ferment in the barrels for days. Fresh batches of amber-colored wool emerged from the barrels, lifted with forked sticks onto the lines for drying. Wool that had hung on the lines longest was deep blue, later batches were paler, stretching into the distance like a wave of the sea transported onto dry land. The odor took the breath away.

"You guide the people to abide by the rules of the land, to honor the ways of the Spirits so all may live in health and bounty. Your work is most sacred. There is nothing base or rank about it."

"Yes, that is what I strive to do. But are the people always willing? Do they always act in honorable ways or use their best instincts?"

"No, your holiness. They require much prodding and pushing to keep them to the old laws. Too often they act for themselves and forget the future of the tuaths. People are often base and selfish."

"Would you say the raw wools and foul smelling barrels are base as well?" Damán nodded thoughtfully.

"And do you have to push and prod the wools as well as the people to steer them in a good direction?"

"Ah, I begin to see!"

"It is the same process, and you hope the result will be like well-made plaid, the colors working together in harmony and the lines straight. You do this without thought for yourself, in service to the Gods and the sacred Land."

Coemgen grew serious. "Wool dying will continue forever without question. Women know that warm children make strong kin. But kings and warriors too easily forget that the work they do now is for the future of all, not just for personal glory." Damán nodded and they continued on the footpath, striding carefully to avoid the fetid pools of woad and stale urine.

Coemgen's thoughts were written on his well-wrinkled face. He had witnessed a disturbing lack of enthusiasm among the flaith, the aristocratic warriors, for the observance of the required round of seasonal rites. He suspected that this lack of piety was affecting the health of the cattle and the vagaries of the weather. As the task of inspiring the nobles became harder and harder, an old Druid triad repeated itself in his mind, until he spoke the words aloud. *"Three things avoided by the wise: expecting the impossible; grieving over the irretrievable; and fearing the inevitable.* That ancient saying will be a help and consolation for what we must accomplish in the days ahead, eh, Damán?"

Damán nodded. A keen student, he was aware that his primary task was to absorb all the wisdom that he could, and to observe the preparations and the execution of the upcoming festival. In later years he would be expected to know every detail of its liturgy and ritual and pass that knowledge on to another generation of Druid.

Coemgen mused; "The eve of the Samain festival is upon us and the fate of the Island hangs heavy upon my shoulders. As Ard-Drui, I must oversee the ceremonies that will honor the dead properly, and ensure the fertility of cattle, sheep, fields and women, but I am no longer young. I ache in my shoulders, fingers and knees from the damp and cold."

Coemgen had been Ard-Drui for fifteen hot summers and sixteen cold winters. His beard and hair, both once black, were peppered with streaks of white and gray. He wore a simple white tunic of linen and a six-colored cloak, held fast on one shoulder by an intricate brooch of amethyst and gold.

A golden circlet ringed his neck, a torque ending in boar's heads, the totem animal of his clann. From his belt hung a golden sickle; the soft metal was ceremonial, useless for the cutting of plants. Damán wore a dark green woolen scholar's robe, thick woolen hose and leather sandals tied up to his knees. Around his neck hung a golden triskell, the triple spiral that was a sign to all of his position in society.

The son of a noble house, Damán had shown no interest in the games and tussles of the other boys at his father's fort. Most often he was found at the foot of the house bard, memorizing the ancient tales, or pestering the Druid with questions about the exact location of the Otherworld and the personal likes and dislikes of the Gods. His kin decided early on that he be sent to Coemgen for training. It was a mark of prestige for the clann that one of their own was a student of the Ard-Drui himself. Damán was aware of the honor as he walked beside him.

Coemgen spoke as they walked. "The Samain rite is one of the two most important of the ritual year, second only to Beltaine at the start of summer. Samain inaugurates the dark half of the year. The inner working of the minds of the participants determines the fate of the next half year as much as the offerings to the ancestors."

"No one has ever explained why Samain and not Beltaine is considered the beginning of the year. Why the time when everything is dying?" Damán queried.

"It is only an apparent death. Everything that has life returns again, whether we speak of trees or people. All life begins in the dark. Seeds lie waiting under the dark soil, a calf in its mother's belly, a human child waits in the dark to emerge from the womb. All are given form in the dark. Only after the dark has given them birth do they come into the light. Thus the dark of the year is the true time of new beginnings. What is given form now will manifest in the coming season of light."

"Thus the month has a dark half and a light half, and each day begins at dusk?"

"Even so."

They reached the foot of the Bíle, in order to pay their seasonal respects and make a small offering of dried herbs to the sacred tree of the district, an oak almost a thousand years old that still produced acorns for the people. Plates of food left by apprentices were arranged beneath it on a cloth, in thanks for its gifts.

"I would like to be remembered like this oak," confided Coemgen. "As one who inspired the people for a thousand years, long after I am gone from this life."

"I am sure you will be remembered thus, in poetry and in song." Damán offered reverently.

Coemgen smiled, reached over and ruffled Damán's hair. "Good lad."

The central act of the Samain rite was the all-night vigil where the Ard-Ri Crimthann would sit until dawn with the kings of the four outer kingdoms around him, one facing each direction as protection. It was a night when Spirits were abroad and the Fomoire would do their best to disrupt the order of things. One also never knew what the Doini Sidi might attempt.

For Coemgen the problem was getting the kings to cooperate with each other, much less spend the night in reverent contemplation. Coemgen had wheedled and flattered them all day, along with their wives and councilors, to make each one feel an important and honored guest.

"You'd think they were strapping warriors of the Fiana rather than aging clann chieftains the way they defend their pride of place," Coemgen muttered impatiently to Damán as he watched them boasting and arguing in the hall. "Rochad, king of Torcrad and Conaire of Irardacht have been at each other's throats for days. Each of them thinks he deserves the choicest cut of meat at table, the hero's portion. Marcan of Murthracht and Canoc of Oirthir show a little more sense – not surprising given Canoc's fat cattle and rich pastures. His people, at least, will eat well this winter."

Then there was the problem of the Spirits. There had been a terrible omen that year when the Beltaine fire in the Nemed had almost gone out. The young Druid assigned to keep the flames were inexperienced and by the end of the day a drenching rain and stiff wind left little more than a smoky heap. By the time the runners came from the provinces with their torches, ready to take the new fire back to their people, things were in complete confusion. Coemgen relit the sacred oak flames with his own hand to prevent total blight and famine from descending on the kingdoms. In desperation, he had almost sent a novice to bring an ember from Father Per's fire.

Father Per had come from the East with other monks, Coptic visionaries zealous in their belief in writing as much as their God. He had lived within cloistered walls, shivering in his rough woollen robes while kneeling to prayer. Eventually he struck out on his own, convinced that his calling was amongst the people. After years of wandering, he eventually came to a small hillside that looked over a cluster of huts, sheds and enclosures that made the village not far from the rath of the Ard-Ri. He smelled the fires lit for evening cooking and heard the sharp direction of men leading flocks of sheep.

Women called to children who danced away for one last game in the fading light. Father Per had folded his cape about him and sunk down to spend his night at the base of a large white oak. Leaves rustled above him as he watched one after another of the clear stars show themselves to the night.

He was not a tall man, but he was an open one, a smile often playing about the corners of his eyes. His compactness made for a spring of energy that showed itself best when he worked among the stones. His hair was going to gray, small flecks in the blueblack. He walked with an easy, ambling gait, as if there were nothing more pressing than the moment. The people of the village had come to love him, but it was his voice that first drew them in. It was like a low-banked fire that pulled one close, and when sparked by a far-away tale or a rousing exchange of ideas, it danced and flickered like welcoming flames.

When he first came, he was in the last years of being young and the villagers watched from a distance. They had known others of his kind, these Coptic priests from beyond the seas who had settled in other villages to build their stone places of worship and trade stories. They were solemn and quiet men, most of them, given to low singing and a curious habit of scratching marks onto calfskins stretched so thin the sun nearly shone through.

But Father Per had come alone, dressed in rough, undyed wools and leather sandals on his feet. He appeared one spring and set about making a low wattle hut just large enough to fit his frame for sleeping or to sit in when the rains or snows came hard. Most days he kept a fire going nearby where he roasted a fish or stewed the unshapely roots he grew. As his stonework turned into a sturdy foundation for a building that could house a family, the villagers thought he meant to make himself a betrothal. But he never did. With some of the stones, he built himself an oven over his fire and it was there that he began baking the bread that lured the people to him. Soon after the bread, he found a shattered, wicker beehive, mended it and established his first colony of bees. Most of the people snickered at this lone stranger, chopping rocks out of the hard soil. They shook their heads and went their own ways. The children, however, like children everywhere, were attracted to someone who worked with a simple and skillful purpose. Children know how to watch a person's hands and see reason and possibility. Father Per knew this. He hid nothing from them. Especially not his baking.

One early spring day, a year since he had first arrived, just as the leaves of the hawthorn trees were unfurling, he set out three loaves of bannock bread, dark and fragrant. He sang songs from his own childhood as he mixed and kneaded his dough. The children could not understand his words, but they understood his voice and the smell of his bread. They both told of some place far away and of being safe at home. The loaves, set on a low wall, steamed into the air, and the children, sitting like magpies on the little hillside above his hut, crept closer. Father Per pretended not to notice and went back to wresting large stones from the earth and setting them firmly in place, balanced well so that their weight and shape added to the firmness of the wall.

Children, who are always hungry, cannot resist warm bread. These children were no different and they inched close until the oldest rushed forward when he was sure Father Per did not see, grabbing the nearest loaf. Bent over the next stone to be maneuvered, a sparkle lit Father Per's eyes and the corners of his mouth twitched. The children dove back to the hawthorn grove and divided the loaf among themselves. It was the first of many loaves they would eat from Father Per's hands.

Within half a moon's cycle, the children no longer crept forward to raid the dense loaves. They perched with legs swinging on the rectangle of walls that rose so slowly only Father Per knew they were moving skyward. With the children, he began with bread and moved on to stories, simple ones first, tales of fishing, little fables about sly foxes or clever snakes. He asked for their tales. At first the children were too shy, but

Father Per's eyes told them he would not make fun and he listened like no other grown up to what they saw and heard and the things they saw in their minds. These story swaps were always accompanied by a loaf or two of belly-warming bread.

The mothers were quick to recognize how this man occupied their children's hours, even the wildest would sit still as Father Per wove his pictures. The women were grateful and sent sacks of rye and barley flour to help keep young mouths and ears busy, though they agreed with their men that this man was foolish in his solitary struggle against the stones.

One day, however, one of the mothers pushed a barrow laden with sheared wool past Father Per's hut. Spring rains had carved deep and mucky ruts in the path and the front wheel bounced and jammed fast in the mire. The woman's efforts to pull the barrow free cracked its axle when the wheel stuck fast. The wooden device toppled sideways, spilling wool into the mud.

Father Per did not see the accident, but the woman's cries of distress brought him from around the corner of his building. He watched her for a moment then strode forward.

"It's not so bad as it looks," he said.

She took a small step back. She was about say she had no need of his help, distrustful as she was of letting him near to any real work of the village. But he was already righting the box of the barrow and piling the wool back inside. Something about the way he laid the wool in careful stacks made her ease the air out of her lungs and lean a little forward.

"That's kind," was all she said.

"Your wheel will need a mend." He bent and pulled the wooden circle from the mud. It came away with a sucking sound. He turned it over in his hands, rubbing his thumb on the place where the axle had joined the rest of the barrow. "If you would allow it, I could set this right." He said it as a question, as if it was she holding out the favor. She gave him a weak smile and nodded, following him back toward his hut. As she neared she noticed that although the hut was smaller than any of the village, it was built with great care. She also noticed that his work tools were neat and clean, nothing scattered or haphazard. This was someone who took care with his work.

He motioned for her to sit near the fire on a flat stone. "Please take a piece of bread. It may even be from your own generous flour."

She broke a piece and was surprised at its texture and flavor. His craft went beyond stones or wood. As she ate, she watched him pound out the broken peg from the barrow and clean the hole with his knife. He began to whistle and the tune amused her. It was a song the children sang to each other when they were hiding in the woods, playing at sprites and monsters. Hearing a grown man whistle it, gave her courage.

"Why did you come?" she asked in the direct way of the people.

He did not look up, but gave off whistling and said, "It is my purpose to follow my God's will."

She was not expecting this answer. She, like her neighbors, assumed he had been punished, sent away by his clann. "What God would send you alone so far from your people?" She finished the bread and sat, hands in her lap, looking intently at the side of his face as he worked.

He whittled a new peg from an oak branch and tested the size of it against the hole. At this question, though, he paused, let his hands drop a little and looked off across the hillside. "My God sends his words to any that would hear. I come so that you may hear them."

She sat puzzled as he went back to his task, blowing the dust away from the peg and fitting it into the axle. He pounded it into place with the mallet he used for settling stones. Finally, he spun the wheel and smiled with satisfaction as it rotated without hesitation.

"As good as first made, I'd say." He set the barrow upright and re-piled the wool into its box. He made to back away and resume his building, but the woman put out her hand and touched his arm.

"You have my thanks. The children call you Father Per. They say you have stories from far away."

He nodded and waited, knowing there were more questions, though she might not ask them all today. But he knew there was at least one more to come.

"I like to hear of other places. My mother was a storyteller, and I sat at her knee when I was a child. She caught a fever last winter and died. I miss her stories. I would like to come sometime, perhaps with a few of the women, and listen. Could I do that? I would sit quietly."

Father Per saw the seriousness of her question and did not smile. Instead he looked directly at her and said, "Stories are no good without ears." At that he simply turned back to his work.

It only took the time of a full moon followed by another for almost all the people to accept Father Per as someone who could keep the children quiet during a stretch of miserable damp weather, set a scythe blade at its proper angle or bake extra loaves for festival nights. The stories they exchanged were intermingled with the lives of their Gods. The people on their side told of Brighid, Danann, In Dagdae and Oghma; Father Per told of Isu. The people came to understand his Isu as a great Drui and magician who turned a few loaves of bread and fish into enough to feed a host. They heard the story of how Isu gave his body to save the people. This was a great Drui indeed, for did not their own Druid offer themselves as bog sacrifices in order to protect the tribes?

For many years, Father Per and the people of the village lived in companionship. They ventured inside his stone building once it was complete to watch his rituals and to hear his songs. They accepted Isu because they accepted Father Per. Isu they set amongst their own Gods.

Meanwhile, keeping the land whole was what worried Coemgen. The crops had not been good that year for most of the Island. The people held the Druid responsible, of course, and there was considerable resentment. It was the job of the Druid to advise the king, and if the king made bad judgments then the fields, herds and trees would suffer.

And now there was a new challenge to their authority: Roman monks had arrived from Southern lands, preaching against the Gods.

Many religions had come to the Island and most had been heard with good grace. The Druid were studious and travelers or missionaries who brought stories, new languages and fresh ways of seeing were always a pleasure. But these Roman monks, Albinus and Germanus, were different. They worked hard at building an enclosure for themselves, but sowed the seeds of dissension amongst the people. They taught that the Goddess of the river and the Spirits of the sacred trees were to be ignored. Some people of the Island believed them. Such teachings would only lead to chaos and disorder, Coemgen knew, as he faced this night of darkness and fear.

# 5

―――――

Crimthann, the Ard-Ri, was well-built, tall and blond, with midnight-blue eyes and the flowing mustache and beard of the Celt. A warrior for many years, he was uncomfortable in the elaborately colored cloaks and furs of his rank, and chose instead to wear the plaids of his native district, dyed with the distinctive colors of the herbs and grasses that bloomed in its valleys. His marks of kingship were a heavy gold torque, ending in dragon's heads in honor of his skill as a fighter, and the jeweled dirk that he kept within easy reach, protruding from a boot top. Old habits died hard.

A man of twenty-nine summers, he had been Ard-Ri for almost a year, yet still had no wife. He had been married briefly to Niamh. One summer's eve, on a night that should have brought nothing but joy, she had died in childbirth. The product of their union, Daire, was already given to the Druid for training, but Crimthann did not know if his son would inherit the throne. Such things were decided by trials and consensus among the clann chieftains, and who could tell which way the winds of favor might blow?

He relied on his reputation with the Fiana, and with the flaith, who admired his fighting prowess, to maintain his authority. The clanns revered him, for hadn't he singlehandedly beheaded three Men of the North when they came in their Long Ships to pillage the coast? He had three black spears on his wall to prove it. But this year, forces were shifting. He must choose a wife to complete the Marriage to the Land ceremony that would anoint him as regent. Without a wife who bore children, there was no way to know if the Goddess of the Land had accepted him, for She would favor only those she found worthy with a woman and an heir.

But in choosing a wife he would necessarily slight three of the four provinces. Even if he married two or more, only one would be *chief* wife. And if she allowed him to marry another – and of course that was never certain – she would rule any others he might desire. With Rochad and Conaire parading their daughters before him, it would go badly if he favored either house.

Evening was fast approaching as Crimthann climbed the wooden rampart of the dun. In the distance he could still see the warriors Ronan, Lorcan and Cadla practicing their swordplay in the fading light. Earlier he had been with them, Cadla as usual kept at it until he won almost every round by sheer force of will. All three of them were vicious, proud, the sort who might kill for the hero's portion at the feast, very useful on the battlefield but difficult to manage in times of peace.

Now it was Crimthann's duty alone to sing the evening Sun Prayer. He knew the necessity of this ritual, for the Sun must see him at least once in every day. As Her son on earth, he would be protected from the chaos of the Fomoire and if he was protected and remained without blemish, the land would stay safe from harm. He sang with sincerity and devotion so that Grian might hear him with Her whole heart.

*"Oh, Grian,"* he began. *"You who shine upon and within the waters, watch over me this night..."* He had just ended his song when Coemgen appeared at the foot of the ladder.

"Crimthann, the Land, Sea and Sky won't help you if you are unwed. You are only half a person in the eyes of the Gods. My advice is to avoid the daughters of the provincial kings and seek elsewhere for a mate. Peace and order must be maintained if the land is to give us Her bounty."

"Coemgen, your counsel is always welcome. But it is easier to fight off a pack of men with long black spears than to choose a mate."

"You must act quickly. This union will affect the future of the people, not just your own." Coemgen scowled as he left to prepare for the Samain vigil.

Crimthann lingered, gazing over the hills and savoring his quiet perch, a brief respite from the responsibilities of rulership. As he descended the evening sky was clear and a few bright stars had appeared, signaling frost by morning.

By next evening the Samain rites were officially over. The air was full of cattle sounds all day as the herds were rounded up from the hillsides and brought into the king's rath for winter. There they would be fed and protected from the cold and from rievers. Winter left warriors idle and some, house bound and bored, stole cattle for fun or for honor.

There were also those who stole from hunger, even if the Brehon lawyers had made provision for such people. The law-abiding were welcome to go door to door, and ask for food, blankets and furs if they were in genuine need, after each harvest the clanns distributed provisions to widows, orphans and the poor. But there were always those who preferred to steal what they wanted, and a prudent cattle lord locked up his herds during the season of cold.

Dust hung on the finery of the chieftain's wives and daughters and on the bronze mead flagons. It found its way onto the plates at dinner and drifted onto pillows and blankets in the guest quarters. The royal guests picked their way through piles of cow droppings just as the warriors and servants did. No one enjoyed it, but no one remarked on it either, it was simply part of the season.

Crimthann's rath was the largest on the Island, as befitted the Ard-Ri. It consisted of a huge stone roundhouse with a peaked roof of willow branches laid on top of timbers and many smaller round houses of stone, topped with their own conical willow roofs. Within the precinct of circular buildings sat an enclosure surrounded by its own smaller wooden palisade. It was a temple dedicated to the patron deities of the Ard-Ri: In

Dagdae, the great all-knowing Earth Father and patron of the Druid, Lug the ManySkilled, Grian the Goddess in the Sun, and Danann of the Rivers. Here the Druid lived and here the clergy who served the king's household made votive offerings to the fire and to the pits surrounding the enclosure.

An earthen mound surrounded the entire rath topped by a wooden palisade. Guards stood in towers at each of the four directions. A swift moving stream coursed through one side of the rath, under the wooden wall. It provided water as well as a place to cool butter and milk and to leech acorns. Dogs and chickens wandered at will in and out of the buildings. A pair of Egyptian "cats" brought by a Syrian trader as a gift for the king had already proven their value. They killed mice and all they required in return were a bowl of milk and scraps from the kitchen.

The principal building had a large round fire at its center. Smoke drifted continuously upward through the willow branches of the thatched roof, coating it with creosote and making it ever more impervious to rain. The roof was supported by thick oaken pillars, elaborately carved, with attached wooden screens that acted as room dividers. Each room featured fur rugs, woolen throws and imported fabrics hung over the walls. Every resident and guest could claim a carved wooden chest to store cloaks and other personal items. Cushions, stools and braziers stood everywhere for the comfort of petitioners, guests, and the warriors who lounged in the corners. Costly beeswax candles and torches burned all day in the smoky interior. A large room on the sunniest side of the building was used exclusively by the women. Here they traded family news, embroidered, worked their looms and listened to the household bard.

A large open area around the central hearth formed the main chamber. Before the throne was the long wooden High

Table used for feasting, with several other tables at a distance from the dais. Champions squabbled and occasionally came to blows for the honor of sitting at the High Table. At rare times someone was killed for sitting in the wrong place or for demanding a choice cut of meat. It was a busy place with little room for privacy. The Ard-Ri himself had only a small room behind a partition with a bronze brazier, a small hearth, a heather mattress on a raised platform, and cushions spread amongst furs on the floor.

Detailed carvings on the oak pillars and walls dominated the king's rath. Spirals, knot work and interlacing designs, mermaids, panthers and elephants entwined the columns. Boars marched in rows along the roof line and wolf's heads guarded either side of the door. Lions and eagles, half moons and leaping salmon protruded from carved panels. The walls were alive with unseen forces and hidden meanings within a complex pattern.

Behind the Ard-Ri's throne was a wall featuring a huge carved oak. From it hung carved bunches of the golden bough – the herb known as "all heal" for its many sacred powers, and on top of it an eagle perched, looking fearlessly into the distance, symbolic of the Imbas, the prophetic wisdom of the anointed true king or queen.

Crimthann sat on his carved oaken throne and observed the provincial kings.

"I offer a hundred head of cattle as well as grain, wool and hay," asserted Canoc, of Oirthir.

Rochad, Conaire and Marcan grimaced but said nothing, for their harvests had been bad and they knew they could not match Canoc's tribute. They felt uneasy for as they were losing stature and influence with the Ard-Ri, Canoc was gaining both. Crimthann was content to let them squabble, for as long as the provincial kings were contending amongst themselves it would result in ever greater tributes for In Medon.

Coemgen stood by his side watching, and remembering everything. The provincial kings knew that should anything befall Crimthann, they would be the most likely candidates for next Ard-Ri. Canoc's fat pastures gave him wealth and the advantage. But there was also the matter of a woman. Conaire and Marcan wanted to tip the balance of Canoc's wealth with offerings of their own.

"My daughter would be most pleased to accompany you on a walk this evening, my Lord," said Conaire of the Irardacht. "My seventeen-year-old Rian is aptly named after a river Goddess. Her beauty is matched by her steady and nurturing disposition."

"My Creide has been rehearsing a song for you all morning," said Marcan quickly. "She will be pleased to present it to you at dinner as she is most talented and has a fine voice." Marcan's Creide was a legendary charmer whom many warriors had followed with their eyes as she poured mead at her father's table. Red haired, she was as volatile and lively as Rian was calm.

Both women appeared at court dressed in the bright colors of their class, sporting gold jewelry, colorful embroidery and golden beads in their elaborately braided hair.

Each did her best to catch Crimthann's eye and to subtly monopolize his attention at table, and each was severely reprimanded by her mother afterwards when the other seemed to be winning the king's favor.

Crimthann faced the delicate task of maintaining an acute interest in both princesses while knowing he would choose neither. He permitted them to sit near him at the High Table, offering them both choice bits of meat and soft bread while their fathers and mothers followed every move of his eyes.

"*Three things which afflict the world: envy, anger and covetousness,*" he thought to himself, remembering the triads drilled into him by the old Druid at College. Aloud, he said, "I'll take both Rian and Creide with me to visit the Bíle this afternoon, and I would be most pleased to hear Creide's song at supper" Crimthann's palms sweated as he watched the faces of the mothers, daughters and kings to determine how his solution was received. There was a slight murmur of approval.

"So far, my son, you are proving yourself a true ruler," said Coemgen when the guests had gone as he and Crimthann shared a cup of mead before the fire. "I admire your tact in dealing with the problem of the princesses. How do you propose to reject them gracefully?"

Crimthann stared into the embers, thinking for a few moments before replying. "A king must be generous to gain respect; '*Meanness yields to liberality*,' as the Tecosc Ríg states. I propose to send the kings and their daughters packing with generous gifts to flatter them into silence for yet another year."

The Ard-Drui chuckled into his beard and took a long swallow of mead. Inwardly, he congratulated himself for manipulating the choice for Ard-Ri. It had taken two years of campaigning with the Druid council to convince them to make Crimthann High King. Coemgen had wanted a candidate with strong Druid ties, he did not want to risk an Ard-Ri defecting to any of the new cults on the Island. Having the king's ear, he could not resist intoning advice one more time. "My son, remember always that the Druid religion is the oldest on this Island, the only one that honors the Spirits of place and the sacred trees and rivers that have lived here forever. The new cults are strange and curious. I understand why many young people, even Druid, are attracted to the stories. But to ignore the ways of the land is to risk peril. I fear the years of bad harvests reflect the people's negligence in their offerings to and respect for the Land Spirits.

It was once the gravest of crimes to pollute water, now people dump all manner of filth into the sacred rivers. Once it was unthinkable to cut down a tree without first offering thanks and giving the Tree Spirit a new home by planting a seed of the Mother Tree. Now the people cut whole forests without ceremony."

Crimthann poured himself another cup of mead and stretched his long legs closer to the fire. Weary from the day's work, he offered no comment. Warming to the task and seeing no opposition, Coemgen continued. "The people of the Island have always been clean; our ancestors invented the siabainn, made of tallow and lye. Now they are told that bathing is unnecessary, a Roman idea brought by traders and missionaries. At the great Fire Festivals people no longer make offerings to water, trees and flames. Instead they use these occasions to eat, amuse themselves, flirt and show off their finery."

Crimthann had often heard these discourses on the fate of the Island and her people. "Coemgen," Crimthann began with a yawn and a stretch to keep himself awake. "When I was a student at the Druid center on the River Sive, my teachers taught me the ancient stories and rules of filidecht, the sacred Way of the Poets. They hoped I would learn to achieve Imbas, the prophetic trance. But instead I was interested in the Way of the Warrior. I was among the best at swordplay and could do the Salmon Leap before anyone else in my age group."

"The elders watched you, Crimthann," Coemgen said, drawing his cloak close against the chill that seeped through the walls of stone. "They noticed, but were loathe to tell you, because excessive pride is the sure path to a warrior's downfall. Remember the adage of the old charioteer: He endures life's battles and lives because he is ever vigilant. His wheels are under him because he looks ahead, behind, to the right and to the left. He looks, he defends and he is protected. He does not rest on past accomplishments."

"Coemgen, I never looked to be king. Like all boys, I heard the Fianaiocht. I longed to be one of them and to join their exploits. My chance came one winter night when they appeared, hungry and cold, at the door of the Druid College. I was on guard that night and led them to the warm stables. I bade them rest while I raided the larders for ham, sausages and blankets. After that, I offered them myself and my sword. By sunrise we were miles down the road, I with a dead sheep over my shoulders and thanking the Gods for the chance to be a hero. The Gods have given me a hard fate. I only wanted to be a warrior guarding the king and the land."

"Fate is something we all must live with, no matter our station," replied Coemgen. *"Acceptance is the beginning of wisdom.* The Gods have blessed you with talents. Use them for the good of the people. You became a warrior who prepared carefully for battle and who showed an eye for detail. You proved yourself a leader when you hid behind a rock and picked off three Men of the North one by one as they searched for food or relieved themselves. Most warriors choose to kill in view of others for the honor. But you don't need adulation; you pride yourself on a job well done. You've also kept your balance with the women who admire your blue eyes and yellow curls."

Crimthann smiled into his cup. "Thank you for your praise, Coemgen. But I beg your leave to find a little peace on this dark night."

Coemgen nodded. "I'll stay by the fire and warm my bones a while longer. Go and think on my words."

Leaving the older man gazing into the embers, Crimthann collected a cape and a staff. Fastening the cape with a simple bronze brooch and raising the hood, he headed quietly out of the royal house, hoping to remain unnoticed. The guards at the doorway were deep into a game of fidchell and barely looked up as he passed. Stepping across the flat stones of the courtyard, he inhaled sharply. What a relief to be free of the smoky dun and to breathe in the fresh night. He looked up to find the moon and nodded with satisfaction as She emerged from a bank of clouds. He would have enough light to climb the palisade and escape for a long walk in the valley. He had everything he needed; his staff, his dirk and the guard's password.

# 6

---

Before Ruadh awoke Ethne rose, stoked the fire to relieve the night's chill and stepped outside with a bowl of the siabainn she had made from deer fat and ashes. With a woolen towel over her arm, she headed for the stream. Morning was rising and though the air was chill, the sun was steadily growing in the Eastern sky. She bathed quickly, gasping as she splashed the cold water over her bare shoulders and hips. In one quick movement she dunked her head under and rubbed her hair, face and neck with the siabainn. As the foam streamed off her, she plunged her whole body into the stream and rose, pink and steaming, to the bank. She briskly dried herself with the towel, rubbing warmth back into her thighs and upper arms. She put a clean shift over her head and retied the leather girdle about her waist.

Back in the hut she added a few bars of peat to the fire and dried her wet hair, running a comb carved from antler through the tangles. Then she reached for a small wooden jar of softening cream she made each summer of snow-white suet, simmered with fresh lavender blossoms and rose petals, carefully strained, and whipped to a froth with water. In slow circles she applied the cream to her cheeks and brow, then to her lower legs and feet. She sat on her cot with one foot on the floor and the other supported on a stool, her leg stretched and bare. She was smoothing cream into her calf when she realized Ruadh's snores had stopped. Ethne's hands stilled and she raised her eyes.

"The sun finds you well, I see." Ethne removed her foot from the stool and quickly pulled her shift over her legs.

"It finds you very well, too, it seems." Ruadh, who had been leaning up on one elbow, raised himself to a sitting position. "I have slept in the arms of the Goddess herself. You are indeed a healer." Ruadh's face showed a healthy flush of pink and his eyes sparkled with curiosity and vigor.

"Don't be too quick to test your strength. You will need good eating and careful exercise before you are entirely whole. There are oats in the chest by the fire and hazelnuts in that bag by the wall. I still have a crock of butter gifted to me a several moons ago, cooling under some rocks in the stream. I'll set water to boil for an herbal brew."

Busy with breakfast, Ethne managed a quick glance as Ruadh emerged from the blankets to put on his leggings and jerkin. She had sewn the rent leg of his trousers and left them folded on a stool. "Crack these hazelnuts, please, while I go and fetch butter and water."

Ruadh was pleased to be upright on his own and glad to be useful. He liked the order of the hut, with all the tools stored within easy reach. Before he began to hammer the hazelnuts open, he stood and looked about him. His gaze lingered on the pot of cream Ethne had been using when he awoke. He gently lifted the pot, breathed in the scent and replaced the lid. The smell of flowers lingered in the room and stirred a longing he had never felt. Hearing Ethne at the door, he turned and began cracking the hazelnuts in earnest.

Ethne placed the wooden butter crock on the table, along with two steaming bowls full of oat porridge and a small dish of honey. Ruadh placed a dish of the shelled hazelnuts near the bowls. Each dipped an empty bowl into the steaming cauldron of brewed elderberries swinging from an iron hook to the far side of the fire. Ethne uttered a simple blessing: "*From the Gods to the earth to our mouths.*" Ruadh fell to his porridge with obvious hunger. After several mouthfuls he said, "This food truly is from the Gods. I have never felt such pleasure at eating."

"Food that nourishes what the body needs is a meal that tastes like no other. Your appetite says you are mending well."

Ruadh put down his bowl. "The Gods have spared me through your craft. What gift can I make in return?"

"The Gods must be thanked. Return to the land of your birth and make an offering there. The Gods of your people are surely the ones who protect you."

Ruadh flushed slightly. "I cannot go back. My father and I are not reconciled. To him I am an outcast."

"Surely your mother would welcome her son?"

Ruadh sighed softly. "You are right. For the memory of my mother I will make an offering at the shrine of the Morrígu, Patroness of Warriors. But what thanks can I offer you?"

"You are too weak yet to go hunting, but when your cure is complete, you can bring me a deer. I will need the meat and the hide to see me through winter. Hares, woodcock, trout, these I can snare for myself. The stags of the forest are a great gift and should only be taken once before the snow comes. The villagers can't often share such a gift with me."

"I will be glad of movement and action. My nature does not fare well in quiet idleness."

Ethne raised her eyebrows. "Forgive me," Ruadh added hastily. "I meant no offense. It is just that to be a Fennid means to have a taste for adventure. We seldom stay still for long."

"Tell me. I want to know what fills the days of a Fennid."

Ruadh pushed his chair back from the table and propped his wounded leg on a log drying to the side of the hearth. "We are warrior-hunters who guard the Island's borders, as you know. Mostly we are men, but sometimes women join us. We are sons and daughters of the educated class. Some of the boaire are accepted if they show skills and intelligence, and if they can afford to leave behind the plow and their family's cows. No one is given honor for leaving a family to starve."

"How do you train each other in your ways of living?"

"We have strict codes of honor and hospitality, and each must prove their zeal for battle in feats of dexterity, such as being placed waist-deep in a pit and repelling spears with only a hazel rod and a shield, or being chased through the forest by armed warriors while their hair is done up in braids."

"And if they fail?"

"If they are caught or wounded or if their braid gets tangled in a tree branch, they are dismissed. Sent home."

"So a Fennid's life is based on strength of body and also a mind tuned for battle."

"Yes, but that is not enough. A Fennid must excel in composing and reciting poems, songs and stories. These carry the message of Truth and without that a warrior does not know what to fight for and how to be inspired through long lonely watches and years of wandering. *Truth in the heart, strength in the arm, honesty in speech.* That is what sustains the Fennidi."

"It all sounds beautiful and lonely." She watched his face as he talked, his eyes seeing her but also seeing beyond the walls to the forest and seacoast he tended.

"We are loyal to one another and we roam as we like, depending upon the generosity of villagers. When we defend them from the Men of the North with their black spears, we are revered. Then the people gladly offer chickens, cabbages, and cows. They even overlook a daughter missing for a night." Ruadh's eyes flicked aside, then he continued. "But in times of peace, they grumble about our recklessness, our drinking, our demands for food. They call us insatiable and wild."

"Are you?"

"We follow the breath of the wind more than the law of the tuath. But we never forget our first duty. We are the first defense against attackers from beyond our shores. Without us, the villages would be burned and looted, their daughters carried off to bear children in distant kingdoms."

"Peace should be a time of forgetting fear and cruelty. But it should also be a time to honor those who give their days so peace can be felt." Ethne rose to clear the table.

She turned to Ruadh, "To heal completely, you'll need to let in the powers of sun and air, to build the strength of your body. And then you'll need a charm bag to protect you in battle and from the ill wishes of sorcerers."

"I have heard of these charms, but have never seen one. I am honored that you offer me such a thing." He knew only Druid were empowered to make them and had heard tales from other warriors about their powers.

"What kind of herbs do you use and how are they different from the ones you put into food?"

"The herbs of the field are part of the body of the Green Man, the male Spirit of the Vegetation. When I cut them with thanksgiving and prayer He offers His life force. That makes a powerful charm for health and protection over a person or a place. Come, I will show you."

Ethne led Ruadh outside and they walked into the meadow that spread beside and behind the hut. For a time, they walked in silence, Ethne noticing the light on the field, the height of the plants, and the smell of grasses and pollen in the air. Finally, she brought Ruadh to the center of the meadow and spread a blanket.

"Sit here and rest while I gather."

Ruadh lay gladly on the blanket and watched Ethne as she moved about the field; her thick, honey hair loosely plaited over one shoulder. She moved purposefully among the grasses, small shrubs and woody plants, but at times Ruadh could have sworn she nearly dissolved into the landscape, so much a part of this land was she. With delicate care, she placed each branch, bunch of seed heads or flowers into a basket. When she was done, she stood at the meadow's center, tilted her face full to the sun and sang a song of praise. One arm held the basket, the other she held up to the sky. The light made her skin and her hair glow and Ruadh's longing deepened. He turned his eyes away when she came back to the blanket and settled beside him.

"There are nine sacred plants that we must gather before the winter frosts. Vervain is first for the head of the God," she said pointing to each in turn. "Next comes terrestrial sun for His blood."

"But those flowers are yellow."

"Yes, but they bleed red when you crush them. The third is yarrow for His bowels because it cleans them. After that is male fern for the lower parts since it cleans out worms. The rest are ivy, fumitory, clover, and scarlet pimpernel, followed by cinquefoil to bind them. Finally, I add a small bit of charcoal from an oak tree struck by lightning and a pinch of salt to awaken the powers."

"These small herbs gain strength in your hands. I never recognized their beauty. Tell me how you came to be here, alone in the forest," he asked.

"I am trained in the ways of the Druid to be a Forest Woman, skilled as a healer and survivor in the wilderness. I am charged with maintaining this outpost for any who are wounded or sick. If I neglect my sacred duty there is a geis that could cost me my life."

"Your life! A Druidess is inviolate, a living representative of the Goddesses she serves, Airmid and Brighid and the Great Danann. None would dare harm or disrespect a living representative of the Mothers! How could your life be forfeit?"

"I am bound to sacred service. I was given to the Druid at the age of seven, upon the death of my parents. I had ten years of training in herbcraft, astronomy, natural philosophy, divination and poetry. Then I was taught Brehon Law, at least the parts pertaining to healing and the legal obligations of the Druid to the tuaths. I am trained in weaponry and hunting, enough to protect and provide for myself."

"Did you choose to come here?"

"It's a long story. I served first at the well of Brighid, pouring out the waters for the pilgrims. For five years I learned the ritual forms for the secret Druid rites as well as for public festivals. More than once I oversaw every detail of a complex ritual; from providing bed and board to visiting Druid and kings, to making sure that all participants knew the prayers, to knowing how much firewood would be needed. When I completed my apprenticeship the elders decided my specialty was herb craft and I was given the sacred geis of maintaining this Forest House."

"And were the Druid elders correct in their wisdom? Is this where you truly belong?"

"In the beginning it was a terrible burden. I was lonely and felt banished from the world. But I have learned to love this forest, these meadows, and the small hut. Those who come to be healed bring me news of the world beyond, and the stories of their lives. I am always eager to learn from them. I have the strange privilege of being a recluse who is intimate with the ways of the clanns, the provincial courts and even the dun of the Ard-Ri himself!"

"It is easy to see you as a priestess presiding over holy rituals before kings and queens. And yet, I think the duns and courts would confine a spirit that joins so readily with the power of the Land Goddess. These wild flowers and the sunlight reflect your beauty."

Pleased, Ethne looked up to smile at Ruadh and was met with the admiration of his eyes. A slight flush rose from her neck to her cheeks, but she held his gaze, secretly questioning the strength of her pledged solitude.

"You will over tire. Let's return to the hut so you can rest." They made their way back through the meadow, the way they had come. Over the course of the next few days they took many walks into the meadows and beyond, searching for the right plants, comparing those that had withered to be sure of the right ones, even though Ethne knew by heart where most of them flourished. When they had gathered all the necessary herbs, Ethne built a sacred fire in the hearth.

"Watch how I smoke these," she instructed. "I will place a small cross of rowan twigs, bound in red wool, inside the bag before I sew it shut." She then showed him how to seal the herbs with a coin in a linen bag sewn with red, flaxen thread. When she was done, she said, "Repeat after me:

*May the Green God flow in my blood*
*May the Green God shelter my bones*
*May the Green God blow in my breath*
*May the Green God live in my life."*

As she solemnly tied the bag to Ruadh's belt he put his hands lightly upon her shoulders and spoke quietly to her up-turned face, "And may you, Ethne, be blessed by all the Gods of this land."

# 7

Three weeks passed and Ethne at last judged it safe for Ruadh to venture out on a hunt alone. She had kept them supplied with the birds and hares she snared in nets, but a deer was crucial because she needed the skin for clothing as winter approached. She had watched Ruadh the day before as they strode through the meadow and she brought him onto a ridge where the path was steeper with loose stones. He had not faltered once and kept his breath on the ascent. His wounded leg did not buckle as they made their way down and he even lept playfully over a fallen tree at the edge of the meadow. She knew he was ready to honor her request.

The next morning after they had eaten she brought up the subject. "Your leg is strong now. You asked what you could do to repay me. I would have you bring me a deer to see me through the winter."

Ruadh grinned, "I 'm honored to hunt for you. I am longing to feel the forest floor beneath my feet again, and to move freely amongst the trees. I will bring you a deer to sustain you through the cold and the dark season." He stood, fastened his sword to his good leg and flexed his legs and arms. His leg was still stiff but well enough. He marveled at the strength he felt in his body, and his spirits rose as he tested the string of his great ash bow.

"I 'm not used to sitting and having others do work around me." All his life, Ruadh had thought of the good of the clann, first of his derbfhine, and then of the Fiann, his substitute family. He slung the bow over one shoulder, along with the quiver of red arrows, tied on with a strip of deerskin.

"You will need these." Ethne handed him a leather bag filled with cheese encased in wax along with several small loaves of bread. She stood back to survey him. "I see the eagerness in your eyes," She laughed. "But don't over tax yourself. Your wound can open again if you're not careful."

"I will take your caution with me. I know well what dangers wait in the forests, especially for a man alone. Your healing won't be wasted." He gave her a wry smile, thinking not only of wild boars and wolves, but also of the North Men.

Ethne understood only too well, for she too, had seen the unspeakable suffering caused by the invaders. She remembered how they came like a sudden storm, ferocious in their attacks. They had killed her father and taken her mother. The great mystery was that there were men and women of the North who came in their ships to trade amber, furs, and salt fish, who were full of kindness. They brought new dances and music and sometimes even married into the clanns. But one never knew what they would find when they met people from the North; it was wise to be cautious and prepared.

"May the forest Gods protect you and be generous in their gifts." Ethne put her hand on Ruadh's arm in blessing. Before she took her hand away, he covered it with his own, squeezed it gently and turned to go. Ducking through the doorway, he headed away from the hut to begin his quest. Hunting and killing game was a sacred task for one trained as a warrior-poet. Before the hunt began he would make an offering to the beast and explain why he needed its life.

"Spirit of the Deer," he spoke while standing under a large oak, "I ask for your life. Ethne, the Forest Woman, and I need your meat or we will go hungry. We need your fur and hide to keep us warm. I will honor your spirit at the moment of your passing. I will bring you a quick death so that your spirit travels swiftly to the Otherworld where you will dance among the stars. There you will meet your friends and kin who have gone before you. I pray you find me worthy."

He pulled his sword from its scabbard and brought it gently down on his arm, making a tiny cut. His personal life force, the only true possession he had to give, he smeared on the tree, silently imploring the Oak Spirit to accept his offering and to send his request out through its branches to the four winds. Satisfied that he had made a proper beginning, he searched for a likely spot to wait. He had called the deer and now it was up to the deer's spirit to accept his request by appearing before him.

He walked to the edge of the clearing where the grasses ended and the bracken began. The ferns were already turning yellow in the autumn chill and tufts of brown dock and wild carrot dotted the edges of the wood. A formation of geese honked and called overhead, on their way South. A faint depression on the earth and a trail of bent greenery told him that he had located a game trail, used by deer and other animals.

He followed the narrow path through the scrub until it became barely perceptible, ending at a stream. Taking careful note of his surroundings, he crossed the water, stepping gingerly over stones and a fallen tree. On the opposite bank he saw faint hoof prints, a deer had been there, drinking from the brook mornings and evenings. It was what he had hoped for.

Twenty paces from the water's edge stood a large, gnarled ash with four huge branches. His first task was to scout out fallen pine boughs and dry leaves to make a temporary shelter, in case the wait was long. He piled the boughs and leaves against the ash, a ready made burrow against the cold then digging with his fingers to find a purchase, he scaled the tree and settled into a crotch between two branches, his bow at the ready and an arrow already notched as he waited for twilight.

When the moon hung full above him, he dropped to the forest floor. Intoning a short prayer to the Gods of his people, he crawled into his bed of leaves and pine, for a short rest. At false dawn when the birds began their chorus, he was up the tree again. As the first gray light fell upon the leaves he could see wisps of fog curling up the middle of the stream, and dark shapes moving through the bushes. Five deer picked their way carefully to the water's edge. The first to the stream bank was a mature doe. He had a clear view of her but restrained the impulse to shoot. Then he saw the outline of a large-antlered buck guarding the doe against other stags.

He lifted his bow, sighted down the shaft and let fly. The red arrow found the heart of the stag. It looked up towards the tree with brief surprise and then crashed sideways. The remaining deer bolted through the underbrush and a flock of crows screamed.

He jumped from the tree and approached the fallen stag. After the accident with the wild pig he was careful to stay clear of the antlers. Using the tip of his blade he slit the beast's throat to end its suffering and begin the bleeding. He whispered into its ear. "Thank you, Lord of the Forest. May you fly swiftly to the halls of your kin in the pastures among the stars."

With one motion he slit the belly, then carefully lifted the liver out of the body to wrap it, along with the kidneys and heart, in a packet of green leaves for safe carrying in the leather bag. He removed the rest of the entrails and carried them to a flat rock near the water's edge. "Spirits of this place, I bring you these offerings. Spirits of fox and crow, be content with these gifts. Trouble not my fields nor the fields of my people."

He went deeper into the forest gathering vines, which he pounded with rocks and broke into supple strips. These he braided into a strong rope, which he used to tie the hooves and hang the carcass from a branch to drain. The effort strained the wound in his leg painfully.

As the stag's blood soaked the ground, he constructed a travois using two long branches tied together to a point and bound by the newly braided twine. He tied sections of rope along the width of the travois to keep the poles at an even distance. Easing the deer's carcass down from the branch, he slung it onto the travois and hitched the narrow end around his middle. By fits and starts, dragging and resting, he managed at length to bring the deer home to Ethne.

# 8

---

Canoc, king of Oirthir, was in a strong position and he knew it. "My Lords," he began at the council of the Samain gathering, "You see how the Eastern kingdom is blessed with cows and grain, even as the other provinces suffer. Do you not wonder why? Have the Druid of the north, south, west and center done their jobs? Why should one province prosper while the others suffer bad weather and miserable crops?"

Coemgen, appearing to doze next to the king, came suddenly awake, his eyes fixed on Canoc as a bird of prey eyes a small rodent. His Imbas told him something was awry. The wind had come from an ill direction all morning and he was poised for the worst.

"It is no accident that the East has prospered," said Canoc, facing the king and meeting his eyes directly.

"Enlighten us, then," said the king. "What magic have you used, which Gods aid you?"

"No magic. I have accepted the teachings of the monk Albinus of Gaul and his God."

Murmurs and rustling filled the hall. The provincial kings had not heard of Albinus nor did they know that following him meant denying the Gods of the Island.

"We welcome wisdom and tales from foreign lands," said Coemgen, fixing his stare on Canoc. "Truth and justice are the hallmarks of the wise in every land. What does this teacher bring to add to the Druid store of learning?

"He teaches of his God and his son, who offered himself as a sacrifice on a tree for the good of the people. That we must forswear the ways of the Druid, and let him show us a new and better way," Canoc replied.

The assembly was stunned. The provincial kings looked at one other and then at Coemgen for guidance. The queens and princesses sitting on one side of the chamber embroidering looked up, their fingers frozen, needles in mid-air.

Canoc continued, "I will hand over a hundred cattle, eight cartloads of grain as agreed, as well as quantities of wool. I will also give the High King gold, presented to me by the Abbot Germanus, if Crimthann will only accept the teachings of Isu."

Crimthann was caught. The other kings had offered little tribute this year, facing near starvation in the coming winter. If he were to keep his army and maintain the court, he needed what Canoc offered.

"Tell us more, Canoc. We cannot make such a decision lightly."

"I will bring Albinus here, he has been waiting amongst my people. He can explain everything"

Canoc dispatched a page to seek Albinus from the servant's quarters. Crimthann turned to face the Ard-Drui with searching eyes. Both men understood that Crimthann would have to accept Canoc's offer or the kingdom could face disaster. The question was how to do it without offending the Gods and disrupting the sanctified position of the Druid.

Albinus entered, following the small page. He was tall, and gaunt from years of fasting. He wore a gray wool habit with a cloak of dirty white sheepskins. His long gray hair hung in greasy strands, but for a clean-shaven circle at the top of his head. The Druid tonsure was different: their foreheads were shaved, the better to face the Gods and absorb their teachings. "Apparently this monk expects his God to drop wisdom on him blindly from above" Crimthann thought. A large crow clung to Albinus' shoulder, its beady eyes echoing the fanatical stare of its master.

Albinus planted himself squarely before Crimthann. "I thank you for this audience."

A shocked silence ringed the hall. By custom Coemgen should have spoken first, even a king kept silent until a Drui opened a council meeting. Coemgen rose and banged his staff on the dais. "In the name of In Dagdae, of Danann, Máthir Mór, and Lug Samildanach, I re-open this council that we may hear the words of Albinus, a monk of Gaul, who is unfamiliar with the customs of the court. We are pleased to hear his teachings so that they may add to our wisdom and help us to understand foreign ways."

Crimthann shot the Ard-Drui a grateful look. Things could have gone much worse.

"Tell them of Isu, and of his sacrifice for the good of all," urged Canoc.

Albinus turned slowly to hold every eye in the room. "In the Eastern land called Palestine, only one God is worshiped. Sacrifices were once made to this God of all things, the only Creator God. Animals and humans were offered until the great Drui, Isu, was born. He was a great teacher, magician and healer. His final teaching was his own sacrifice on a tree, for the good of all. His message is freedom."

"Freedom from what?" Crimthann queried, his voice rising. "We are already free and do not require Isu's magic."

"Freedom from further sacrifice. Freedom from the fires of Hell."

"What is Hell?" Marcan demanded.

"Hell is for those who do not accept Isu as their only God. They are doomed to dwell there after death."

Crimthann leaned forward. "Have you not seen the ravens of the Morrígu exulting after battle, or felt the blessings of Brighid enter your blood at the end of a sickness? Everything in nature has two sexes, even the Gods. How could there be but one male God? All beings in nature are born of a mother.

*Three essentials of poetic genius, an eye to see nature, a heart to feel nature, and a resolute courage that dares to follow nature."*

The women nodded, recognizing the old triad . They covered their mouths with their fingers as they whispered and stared at the man who ignored the Goddesses in his preaching. Only Canoc's wife, Fithir, made no sound.

"Albinus," continued Crimthann, "we will consider what you say, but we can't simply abandon our Gods and Goddesses. It may be that your Isu was a great Drui, a Sun King, who offered his life as the Druid do in the bogs, so that the people and the land may benefit from their life force."

Albinus fixed his black eyes on the king. "You must give up more than your Gods. You must give up the rituals and sacrifices the Druid would have you follow. The king-making horse sacrifice is no longer necessary. Dedicate your kingship as a follower of Isu and it will be sanctified in the eyes of the one God."

"Without the horse sacrifice, how will the people know I am their true king? How will the land know that I am wed to Her without an offering of blood?" Crimthann's deep voice filled the hall.

"Tell the people that you are a disciple of Isu. Tell them he has commanded you to end all sacrifices. Tell them Isu is the greatest of all the Druid!" Albinus' pet crow craned its neck and squawked.

Coemgen pounded his staff on the floor. "Enough! We have heard your ideas and allowed you to speak. Leave now, that we may finish our council."

The Ard-Drui returned to his seat, his eyes never leaving Albinus. For a long moment the two old men locked eyes. Finally, Albinus spun round and left the hall, his cape fluttering. The provincial kings, Rochad, Conaire and Marcan, watched the ArdDrui and the High King, their eyes shocked and confused.

Crimthann, grim faced, said, "I accept Canoc's offer of grain, cattle and gold and I ask that the traditions of hospitality be continued. These travelers may live among us and share their ideas. We know of "Heaven," and of "Judgment," from Father Per, though Albinus' would have us believe we have but one life to learn in. Our own ancient tradition tells us that one life flows into the next. We look forward to our time of games and feasting in the Otherworld before we return to another earthly incarnation, *for death is but an interval in the midst of a long life*. We value all people of learning and skill and would have them make us ever wiser. We will not, however, turn our backs on the Druid, and their teachings."

Coemgen's face betrayed no emotion but his heart thanked Crimthann for his loyalty.

"I approve your decision," said Canoc. He did not, however, announce that the people of his province were already Cristaidi in the eyes of Rome, as they were under his protection, or that that the Abbot Germanus had promised him more Roman gold and soldiers should he convert the Ard-Ri.

Coemgen closed the council with a blessing and turned to leave, holding his posture straight and strong until he had passed from the hall. Kings and queens waited for the Ard-Drui and the Ard-Ri to exit before heading to their sleeping quarters to pack for their homeward journey. They would have much to discuss in the coming winter.

Coemgen strode grimly from the hall towards the Nemed, the sacred enclosure built within the walls of the Ard-Ri's rath to house the Druid, their Fire Altar and votive pits. The Nemed was a round wooden stockade elaborately carved with spirals, interlacing knot-work, sacred animals and protective heads. A deep ditch surrounded it, crowned by hawthorn, elder and rowan hedges. The trees formed a magical shield as well as a useful source of medicines. Flowers and berries appeared in profusion from spring to fall.

Within the Nemed small stone huts with conical willow roofs made an irregular circle, just inside the wooden fence. Within the ring a circular garden contained the healing worts and magical herbs necessary for the Druid arts. At the heart of the enclosure was the round Fire Altar, a perpetual flame of oak surrounded by a low wall of stones and maintained by acolytes from sunset to sunset, in rotation. Next to the Fire Altar and slightly to one side, the Sacred Ash served as the Sky Ladder for trance journeying. An initiate could travel out through its branches to the Sky Realm and thence to any part of the world, using astral vision. A journey through its roots took one to the Underworld of the ancestors and the *Doini Sidi*.

The Cauldron of Sea, a large bronze vessel, which was emptied, cleaned and refilled daily, served as the third ritual focus for the holiest enclosure. It was a gateway to the realm of the ancestors when used for scrying, and served as a repository of the God's blessings after each ritual. The water was often distributed to the sick and to other petitioners in need.

Crossing the wooden bridge over the ditch into the enclosure, Coemgen heard the Druid chanting and smelled the herb-scented smoke. The Druid had offered herbs of peace and consecration all day, intending that the council of the Ard-Ri go smoothlly.

The Ard-Ban-Drui Gaine was unsettled. She too had read the ill wind when she went out at sunrise to sing the Sun Song. And there was difficulty maintaining the fire, always a bad sign. An acolyte had tripped and spilled half of the Cauldron of Sea. Two acolytes had been sent to the brook outside of the Nemed with buckets to re-fill the vessel and Gaine was therefore not surprised when the Ard-Drui entered looking haggard and upset.

"Gaine, a word with you," said the Ard-Drui, motioning her to a seat within the herb garden that surrounded the Fire Altar.

Gaine had been elected Ard-Druiess recently on the death of her teacher, Ecca. Younger than Coemgen, she would likely succeed him as chief counselor to the Ard-Ri, should anything befall the Ard-Drui. Born of an ancient Druidic family, she was trained by her parents before coming to Ecca at the Druid College. She possessed a wide range of skills, from herbcraft to diplomacy as well as the magical ways of Druidecht.

When at court she wore the colors of her rank - a scarlet, blue or green tunic, covered by a blue, green, white, black, red and purple plaid cape clasped by a gold brooch. On her neck was a golden torque, very thick but hollow, to keep it light. Out of court she preferred the robes of a scholar, a simple green woolen shift and perhaps a strand of amber. Her robes were scented with the lavender that she kept in the carved chest that held her clothing, blankets and ritual jewelry.

A student braided her graying auburn hair each day and coiled it in elaborate circles behind her ears. She had a habit of picking one sacred herb of the season and placing it within the plaits of her braids, to help her feel connected to the Land Spirits. This being autumn, she had tucked sprigs of red rowan berries and leaves into her tresses that morning.

"Things have not gone well at court today," began Coemgen. "The Roman missionary Albinus has converted Canoc, the only provincial king with tribute to offer this year. Crimthann was forced to accept his cows and gold in exchange for a promise to stop the Horse Sacrifice in the name of the foreign God."

There was a moment of silence while Gaine took in the news. "I feared something like this would happen," Gaine said softly. "The Roman missionaries are bringing gold to the clann chieftains in exchange for fealty to the new God. Many chieftains are glad to accept the handouts, thinking they are but adding a new God to their pantheon. It is only later when more monks arrive and settle in their district that they begin to realize what they have done to themselves. The common people are largely unaware of all this of course, and they go on worshiping as we have taught. But these new ideas are causing great divisions and unhappiness within the houses of the flaith."

"We must protect the Land, the people and our own religion," said Coemgen with a sigh.

"Let's go to the Cauldron of Sea and see if She will speak to us or show us a way," said Gaine, taking the Ard-Drui's hand. She could see how dearly the struggle was costing him, his shoulders were slumped and his face drawn with worry. Dismissing the acolytes, Gaine took the Bell Branch from a niche to one side of the Fire Altar and walked to the north of the central ritual area. Shaking it three times she spoke:

*"May the spirits of dissension and chaos leave this kingdom. May only the forces of order and good remain."*

Walking dessel, the path of the Sun, and shaking the branch with its nine golden bells, Gaine went next to the southeastern quarter and did the same, then to the southwest. Returning to the center, she took a handful of sacred herbs from a pouch at her waist and offered them to the Sacred Ash. "I ask that Earth be witness to this rite, may She give us strength and aid. Sacred Ash, mediate between the worlds and carry my prayer."

She turned and offered a handful of herbs to the Fire Altar: "May sweet smoke carry my message to the Sky Realm. May magic be quickened."

Finally she turned to the Cauldron of Sea and dropped a thin line of sacred herbs in a circle, dessel, around the base. "Help us to see clearly, O Ancestors, that we may understand Your will, and the best course for the future of the people."

Coemgen and Gaine sat down at opposite sides of the cauldron, legs crossed in the ancient posture of meditation, fingers touching in the mudra of concentration brought by their distant ancestors from the Aryan lands to the East. Having done trance work since they were children, it was no great feat for them to reach one-pointed awareness. Opening their eyes slightly and maintaining a focus in the center of their foreheads, they gazed into the dark waters of the bronze well.

They heard, rather than saw, two eagles flying high over the ritual space. The Fire Altar popped and sent a sudden reach of blue flame into the air. A gust of wind rose and made a bare-ly perceptible ripple in the waters. Gaine and Coemgen's skin prickled and the hairs rose on their arms. By such signs the Druid-trained knew the Gods were present and sending a message. Suddenly, simultaneously, they *saw*, and the instructions were clear.

# 9

Snow was everywhere. It stuck to the branches of the apple trees, settled on the ice covering the brook, and collected in the twigs of the roof. The smoke house, woven of thick wads of grass for the deer meat, was a pyramid of white. With the deep blanket of snow came a felted silence within which even the crows were quiet, huddled under overlapping pine branches, waiting out the storm.

Ethne sat on a chair near the fire pushing a needle through the deerhide breeches she was sewing for Ruadh and quietly sang to herself. *"Charm against arrow and sword and spear, charm against bruising and drowning, charm against fire and serpent, charm against death or wounding in battle, charm against Faery, charm against all hostility, against all peril . . ."*

At that moment Ruadh burst in the door, shaking off the feathered snow that cloaked his head and shoulders. "The wind has fallen off and the snow is coming down gently. You must come and see. It is as if the world has been made anew!" His eyes danced as he pulled at her arm with a cold hand.

"Ah! You're freezing!" She laughed, but stood willingly, putting aside her sewing. She let him drape her cloak about her and then wrapped an over shawl about her head and shoulders and stepped out of the hut at his side.

"Here, follow me." Ruadh took her hand and led her down a narrow track he had made. They walked single file without words beyond the first meadow and then into the woods beyond. The silence deepened as they entered the forest and Ethne realized that even the stream had stilled, mute under the ice as the cold snow fell. Every tree branch was furred in white and a bluish canopy of snow shadowed the forest.

"Come softly." Ruadh moved carefully beside an ancient hemlock whose massive limbs swept the ground. He pulled one long limb aside and pointed. It took several moments for Ethne's eyes to adjust and then she gave a small "oh." A doe knelt under the shelter of the huge tree. Beside her were twin fawns, spring births about to test their strength against the dregs of winter. The deer's breath steamed in the tent of branches and warmed the air. Her young were well hidden beneath the covering of dark boughs. The deer's breath steamed in the tent of branches and warmed the air. The mother had cleared the ground then pushed soft leaves and needles together to form a nest for her young. Ruadh softly let the branch fall back into place and he and Ethne stepped again into the larger world of the forest.

"They are beautiful!" She exclaimed when they had moved down the path.

"Yes, I wanted you to see how the Gods provide. They gave us the stag to sustain our lives and now they give new lives back to the forest."

"Now I know how to find a doe and her young in winter, but how do you find a stag when the leaves are turning? Do you follow the tracks to their hiding places?"

"Yes and no. I follow their tracks and their rubbing marks on trees to the deep part of the forest where the older deer roam. Then I climb a tree and wait."

"Climb a tree?"

"Yes, you see deer will never look up. It's a strange thing but if you sit there long enough, and you have the right spot, say near a stream, they are bound to come sooner or later. It only requires patience and the ability to remain very still."

"You are so much in tune with the forest and its ways."

"My mother taught me when I was very young to honor all life around me and to watch the animals carefully. They never take more than they need to survive. I hear my mother's sayings when I am in the forest."

"She must be very wise, tell me more of her."

Ruadh turned and looked about for a place to sit. An outcropping of rocks stood just off the track, and he brushed the snow away for Ethne and himself. "She is most content when she is making something. Her honey cakes are the best I've ever tasted."

He caught the look on Ethne's face. "I know every son says that about his mother's cooking, but this happens to be true. She has a way of blending the grain, fresh milk and honey to make the cakes light, soft and even on the inside, and just crisped on the outside.

When they are warm, right from the hearth, they'll make you groan with pleasure."

Ethne watched his face as he talked and saw on it the happiness and the fire of life that had been so absent when he first arrived. He was full of the air around him, the scent of pine and the brisk cold. His spirit could never be cooped up in a tiny hut no matter how severe the winter. He had busied himself for weeks with chopping wood and stacking it neatly to one side of the small house. He had told her stories of how his family managed their large land holding with its animal and human populations. She asked him to tell her yet more his history and of his corner of the Island.

He did not hesitate, offering memories, family lore and descriptions of the land where he grew up. For his part, Ruadh asked her to teach him more about healing plants and the charms and spells to bind bone or mend fluxes and fevers. Ethne, too, held nothing back, happy to share her knowledge with someone who readily comprehended the importance of small details and showed reverence for the meaning of each ritual.

They talked during walks, over meals, well into the night. Neither tired of the other, and each knew that it was long past the time when Ruadh could have left. He reasoned that she needed someone to hunt for her, at least until spring. She reasoned that he needed conversation and lessons in the proper observance of ritual forms.

A squirrel overhead loosened a blob of snow, which fell directly on Ruadh's head as he finished his latest story. "Ah! Even the animals have heard enough of me. Tell me, Ethne, about your life before you came to the forest. You must have tales of your novice training."

"Actually," she said laughing, "seeing you with snow in your hair reminds me of when I was quite young. I was given the simple task of mixing the siabainn for the Druidesses. Though all the ingredients were set out for me, I put in too much lard. When the women took the cakes to bathe, it was the same as bathing with the pig's grease for cooking. They scrubbed and scrubbed, but their hair remained stringy and smelled of animal. My friend Liatha and I giggled and giggled as we watched, but I was sent to grind grain for weeks after. I didn't mind, though, because I love the smell of the seeds as they crack between the stones and I love the fine yellows, greens and browns that sift and mingle together as you work." The same squirrel skittered further up the tree and a larger mound of snow fell, this time on Ethne, sliding down her collar.

"Ah! Oh that's cold!" Ruadh burst out laughing. Without thinking Ethne grabbed a handful of snow and flung it at him. For a second he froze then he too grabbed a fistful and threw it with perfect accuracy, hitting her on the nose. With shouts and laughter, they fought furiously, she dodging behind tree trunks and he ducking and spinning as her missiles came. As one huge snowball from Ruadh caught her squarely in the chest, Ethne slid on a hidden patch of ice, skidded down the path for a second, then landed with a thump on her back. Ruadh, still laughing bent over her and put out his hand to haul her back to her feet. She came up in one swift motion and he put his hand on her shoulder to steady her. Ethne was still laughing and giving off great steaming puffs of air, her eyelashes frosted with flakes and her cheeks red, when he bent and kissed her hard on her open mouth. Ethne drew in her breath and stiffened slightly. Ruadh stepped back and they eyed each other steadily, warily, each one hunter and prey, ready to spring. Then Ethne raised her hand and drew it gently down Ruadh's cheek. He covered it with his own and then brought it to his lips. Neither moved their gaze. Ethne tilted forward slightly when they both heard the sound.

Turning to listen, they heard again the distinctive cough of a horse, followed by the metallic clink of its bridle as it shook a dusting of snow off its forelock. Ruadh instinctively reached for his absent sword, meaning to draw it silently from its scabbard.

Ethne spoke softly under her breath, *"May we be surrounded by a triple ring of protection, and may all evil be returned to the sender in the name of all the Tuatha de Danann"*

They saw a rider approach the hut, dismount and stand before the door. When he knocked, it was the "three times three" code of the Druid, three sets of three raps in succession. Ethne sighed with relief. "It is safe."

She called a greeting and the rider turned in their direction. When they stood before him, he placed three fingers on his palm, a secret gesture to communicate with the Ban-Drui. Ethne responded in kind, knowing that the secret sign language would reassure the visitor that all was safe. "Ruadh, this man is a Drui." To the man, she said simply, "Please enter and warm yourself at my hearth."

Ruadh was mystified as he followed them both into the hut.

"Welcome stranger, to my hearth. You must be cold and tired after your ride. Won't you give me your cloak and sit by the fire?"

"Thank you Lady. I have been riding these three days to bring you a message from His Holiness the Ard-Drui Coemgen and the Lady Gaine."

"Take off your boots and put them near the hearth to dry, I'll put a cauldron to boil. I expect you would appreciate a drop or two of the Waters of Life as well?"

The stranger had entered wearing a thick gray cape. The hood, coated with ice and snow, had all but obscured his face. He proved to be a red haired man, bearded with a ruddy complexion. A fierce looking dagger hung from his belt and another was stashed in his boot. A bronze torque of the flaith was visible beneath his tunic. He eyed Ruadh with curiosity while Ethne prepared a posset of elderberries, rose hips and spirits.

"Thank you, Lady, that would be most welcome. Is it safe to speak in front of this man? My message is urgent."

"Of course. He is a Fennid and a friend. I would trust him with my life," she said, realizing the truth of it for the first time.

"My Lord Coemgen and the Lady Gaine bid you to return to court, as soon as the weather turns. You have been in this house these five years and they say your term of service is done. Another healer will be sent to replace you and to serve as you have here."

Neither Ethne nor Ruadh spoke, nor could they meet each other's eyes. Ethne felt as if a veil had been torn from her beloved world of forest, stream and fields. In these past weeks it had been especially easy to believe that she and Ruadh encompassed the entire world. Her eyes widened as she sat frozen between the realization of how much Ruadh had entered her heart and the recognition of her duty.

Ruadh sat stiff-backed trying to will away the moment. He had tried to regard Ethne as nothing other than a healer and priestess; now his feelings were engulfing him like a tide. An overwhelming sense of loss pounded in his ears. In desperation, he made himself speak, his voice coming low and hoarse. "Ethne, if you must go, you will be safer with someone to escort you. I would be honored if you would accept my protection."

She turned and stared, blank-eyed, masking her confusion. She was on a knifeedge. The stranger spoke before she could formulate any words. "Protection on the road would be wise, Lady. Much is changing and there are dangers none would have thought could befall a Ban-Drui "

"What do you mean, much is changing? What is happening?" Ethne demanded.

"It seems the Ard-Ri has turned Cristaide. Many of the our ways are being questioned. Perhaps that is why they need your presence back at court."

"That's not possible!" exclaimed Ethne. "The Ard-Ri was hand picked by the Druid council. They pressed mightily for Crimthann precisely *because* of his loyalty and devotion to the Gods."

She knew that his popularity with the people rested mostly on his reputation as a warrior, but the kingship was a sacred office as well as a political one. What could possibly have gone so wrong in the order of things for such a calamity to befall? This made the Ard-Ri an oath breaker of the worst sort, the kind who turns his back on his word and on his Gods. What terrible retribution could they expect from the spirits of Earth, Sky and Sea? These thoughts were too frightening to contemplate.

"Nevertheless, the ancient wisdom is being challenged. Others than the Druid have the ear of the Ard-Ri."

"If this is true, it is a matter of great sorrow for Druid everywhere, and for the people of the Island. The Druid teach that foreign religions are to be studied and respected, but I have never heard of an Ard-Ri actually adopting a foreign faith! He is sworn to uphold the religion of the ancestors and of this land. What sort of man would go back on his word like that?"

The messenger looked at the floor, ashamed. There was nothing he could say in defense of the Ard-Ri. "I am sorry to bring you such evil tidings. The Ard-Drui and the Ard-Ban-Drui will tell you more when you return."

"Then I must leave as soon as the weather clears." She turned to Ruadh, her back straight her chin tilted up. "I would be pleased to have your company on this journey as a warrior and protector."

Ruadh gave a curt bow of the head as his answer.

"If that is your plan," said the messenger, "then I will retrace my journey, since you have no stable for my horse. I have made camp several miles from here in a cave. If I build a fire, he and I can keep warm and out of the snow."

Ethne remembered her courtesies and said, "Thank you for your message, your long ride, and all of your trouble. May I gift you with a store of smoked venison for your homeward journey?"

"You are most kind, Lady, I thank you for your hospitality. I'd best be on my way before my poor horse goes lame with frost bite."

Ethne wrapped a few thick strips of venison in birch bark and bound the package with a length of wool. The man's horse was stamping impatiently outside, so the messenger hastened to put on his boots, now warm and almost dry. "Poor Scáth wants to be off. I'll tell the Ard-Drui to expect you within a fortnight."

Ruadh handed him his cloak. "May the Gods you worship protect you this night and every night. May the road rise to meet you and the winds be soft and at your back."

"Bendacht lib," said the messenger. "Nine blessings on you and on this house." As Ethne and Ruadh stood in the doorway, he pulled himself into the saddle and turned his horse to go.

# 10

———

Ethne and Ruadh sat across from each other at supper. Small whiffs of steam rose from the stew and the only sound was a gust of wind rounding the walls of the hut. Ruadh fiddled with his bread, tearing it into small pieces, but not eating. Finally, he pushed back his chair and growled.

"Must you do as they command?"

Startled out of her reverie, Ethne stared at him, trying to make sense of his words.

"Of course I must go! I am of the larger Druid tribe, part of a tuath that encompasses this land from North to South."

"But you have made this hut yours. You said yourself this place gives you happiness."

Ethne's anger softened as she looked into his eyes. "Yes. I am home here. But Druid have no possessions of their own. What we have, we have in common. We are one family. From my birth to my death all my needs are met. In return, I owe my faith, my duty and my gratitude to those who taught me, healed me and helped me. I am bound by my oath to go where I am needed whether to heal the sick, settle disputes, guide the leaders or supervise offerings to the Gods. We Druid are bound by vows of hospitality and pledges of mutual support. I cannot turn away." Then more softly, "You knew it was time for us to take leave. Our time together is done."

"We can't leave until the weather clears." Ruadh's voice was gruff. "When the Sun shows Her face, enough snow will melt for us to leave safely. Two, maybe three days." His words gave only a hint of the turmoil he felt. The day of returning to the Fian had seemed sensible but distant, a choice he could put off by attending to Ethne's needs as payment for her care. Now, with this strange and shocking news, he was no longer certain where his allegiance lay. His father's tuath might need him or the Fian might require his skills all the more. A third possibility lay in the depth of his heart, a small flicker that he was afraid to acknowledge, lest it be blown out.

Ethne stood, gathered the bowls of unfinished stew and returned their contents to the simmering pot. Turning her face away from Ruadh, she surveyed the hut, considering what to leave behind. She would certainly take the jewelry and clothing, the mirror, her mead flagon and silver cups, and some of the more elaborate ironwork with which she had been gifted. Otherwise everything would remain for the benefit of the next healer and his or her patients. With these thoughts, Ethne dipped the bowls in the wash bucket, splashed her own face in a bucket of clean melted snow and snuffed the candle. Her heart was heavy as she thought of leaving this shelter of so many years. Perhaps an offering to the Spirits at each of her favorite places would soften her sorrow. As she smoored the fire, she intoned, *"May the Three surround this house, this hearth, this night and every night."* She crossed the floor to her bed and sank into a fitful sleep.

It was past midnight when Ruadh woke, full of questions, longings and misgivings.

He tried to will himself to sleep, but gave it up with a sigh. His eyes found Ethne's face in the ember-lit hut. Quietly, he stole across and sat beside her, watching as she dreamed, following the line of her cheek as she breathed. One of her hands lay open, palm up. On impulse he took her fingers and folded them gently in his hand. Her eyes opened and she pulled away as if to brush off some living creature. She half raised and saw Ruadh sitting close, knees drawn up to his chin.

"What is it? Did you hear a noise?" Her eyes were huge and shining.

He faltered. He saw before him the holy priestess that had used her gifts to heal him and teach him. He saw the sister that had sported with him in the fields and the snow. He saw the woman whom he desired with every rise and fall of his breath. He wanted only to hold her and lie with her, she the embodiment of all that he held holy. If she, a Druidess, had chosen to walk onto a battlefield in the heat of conflict, all hostilities would cease, yet he wanted to shelter her in his arms and whisper his protection into her ear.

Ethne, now fully awake, sat up slowly and returned Ruadh's gaze. Her fingers felt hot where he had held them and she realized the tingling extended up her arm and into her chest. Suddenly her eyes filled with tears and she bowed her head. Not once had she faltered in her oaths and geasa, though many men had entered her house. From the day of her initiation she had understood that she was expected to set an example, counted upon to represent the Gods. When urged by the Ard-Ban-Drui, she had given herself to a man at the Beltaine festival. But it had not been her choice. Ruadh was here because she wanted him to be. She looked up again into his eyes and the room swam, a whirlpool with them at its center.

"I want to be near you," was all Ruadh's answer, his eyes full of torment.

"You are shivering. You will give yourself the fever again." Ethne drew a long breath and steadied herself. "Come then, lie next to me. We can do no more than that. Bring one of your blankets for the night is cold and the fire long out."

Ruadh eased next to her on the cot, telling himself that to ask for more was to dishonor her. He carefully stretched his length next to hers and reveled in the closeness of her face, her warmth, her scent, but to touch without her consent was to break the sacred laws they had both vowed to keep. How could he ever tell her that among all women she was dearest? He clenched his eyes shut against the lost possibilities.

As the cot warmed with their two bodies, Ethne uncurled her legs and fitted her back against Ruadh's chest. Feeling his breathing slow, she used her meditation skills to steady her thoughts, contain her desires and move her mind toward the Druid truths.

Neither warrior-poet nor Druid priestess slept that night. Both lay nestled in each other's warmth without hope of crossing the impossible chasm between them.

The next two days passed quickly enough. As Ruadh had predicted, the Sun smiled broadly on the mounds of crusted snow and the steady drip of melting ice was heard. Even the stream broke free, sending a soft mist swirling over its banks as the warm air met the chilled water. Neither Ethne nor Ruadh spoke of their night on the cot, neither daring to split their hearts again.

Ethne cloaked herself in the offices of a Druidess, enacting the ancient rituals in perfect detail. She also washed every bit of crockery, dusted corners and polished the furniture with beeswax and oil. She left offerings of herbs and honey at each of the places she had used for meditation or to gather necessary herbs and simples. At each spot she sang a song of thanksgiving, leaving a blessing on the Spirits of the place.

*Power of raven be here*
*power of eagle, power of the Fian.*
*Power of storm be here,*
*power of Moon, power of Sun.*
*Power of sea be here*
*power of land, power of heaven.*
*Each day be joyous*
*no day by grievous,*
*honor, compassion and love to all who walk here.*

Ruadh watched her with a heavy heart, spending his time whittling an elaborately carved serpent staff. He had two rock crystals in his pouch, which he intended to use for the eyes. When Ethne returned from a trip to the field for early spring roots, he showed her his work.

"See how the serpent climbs the stick, coiling around and around? That is the search for truth."

"It will be a beautiful staff and an honor to the one who carries it." Ethne meant it as a double compliment.

"I mean to offer it to Coemgen, who has dedicated his life to Truth. I made the serpent to symbolize rebirth and the way we shed old realities when we learn something new."

"You are going, then, to Coemgen's rath? What of the Fennidi or the help your family may need now that allegiances are changing?"

Ruadh bent his head and continued to work the stick as his only answer. Ethne set her face to show no emotion. "I'm sure he will appreciate the staff, both for its magical meaning and for its practical use. He's getting on in years and can certainly use such a staff to negotiate the snow and ice." Her voice was soft, but held only officious approval.

As a Druid priestess, she knew Coemgen would need strong allies. She would not turn Ruadh aside.

On their last morning in the forest the air was sparkling and clear under a full sun, and only small patches of snow remained in the shadows of banks and stones. An early morning mist rose from the stream and the fields, a sure sign of good weather ahead. Ethne bundled her possessions inside a woolen blanket and strapped it to her back. On each arm she carried a large woven basket filled with a crock of the Waters of Life, a tinderbox, a cooking pot, and some extra bedding. All that remained was to put out the fire, take apples from the underground cache pit, and collect fresh cresses from the stream.

As she cut the cresses with her sickle, Ruadh piled rocks against the door to keep out wild animals. He would leave with his weapons and the new leggings Ethne had sewn. He had a leather bag of smoked venison wrapped in bark, a basket filled with herbs, Ethne's best cauldron, and the staff intended as a gift for the Ard-Drui. The bulk of the medicines they left behind.

Ethne wore a simple wool tunic bound by a belt of soft deerskin from which dangled her sickle. Over that she wore a blue cloak and a gray wool peasant's cape.

Ruadh's bow and sword were hidden under a brown wool cloak that Ethne had stored in her carved chest. Moving on foot and dressed humbly, they were less likely to attract the notice of brigands should any be near the road.

They crossed the apple orchard and followed a muddy track through the grass which led to a dirt bothrán that snaked over the mountains to the main road of In Medon, and the rath of the Ard-Ri.

The days were still cool and the nights hovered just above freezing, cold enough that the road had not yet melted into a sea of mud. Ruadh's leg was healing, yet the steady pressure of brisk walking on the track awakened a deep pain. He ignored it for most of the morning, but by late afternoon the throbbing was nearly unbearable. Ethne noticed his stiff gait and the sweat that had broken on his brow.

"You are pushing yourself too hard. We'll get nowhere if your wound becomes inflamed again."

Ruadh stopped, wiped his forehead and nodded. "The Cave of the Bears is just past this hill. We can stop there."

They walked up a steep incline bordered by a rushing rill, stopping once to drink the sweet, clear water. A stiff breeze wove through the treetops, a good omen for travelers. Ruadh's pain was evident, but he refused to stop until they gained the shelter of the cave. Night would fall quickly and he did not relish the idea of making camp in the dark. Slowly, and limping badly, he led Ethne through a small break in the undergrowth, following a thin path around the back of the hill. Just hidden by a stout oak was an opening in the rock.

"You must let me go first," said Ruadh. "It is called the Cave of the Bears for good reason." He took an arrow from his quiver and notched it on his bow. "Even if the messenger and his horse were here only days ago, the bears may have smelled food." He handed Ethne his sword and made a booming call to frighten off any animals. When nothing moved he stepped into the dark, adjusting his eyes and moving through the recess as quickly as his leg would allow. As he reemerged, Ruadh laughed at sight of Ethne.

"You look more frightening than any bear! You can save your valor, the cave is empty. Bring in the baskets and let's make camp for the night."

Ethne let out her breath and lowered the sword. "Let me look at your leg out here in the light first." Ruadh removed his arrow quiver and his scabbard, and then hesitated. "I have seen your bare leg already, Ruadh. Remove your leggings and sit on this rock." He did as he was told, avoiding her eyes and wincing as she probed and kneaded to find the source of his pain. "The stitches I have made are still tight. I see no bleeding, can feel no swelling, nor any smell of rot. The wound was deep and the healing may take more rest and time than you've given it."

Ethne sank back on her haunches, feeling her own weariness. The last hours of the journey were especially hard. Neither of them was used to steady marching with so much baggage, and the road ascended at a constant incline for miles. By the time they reached the cave the shadows had grown long and sunset was fast approaching.

Ethne swept the cave floor with a pine bough and prepared soft beds of pine twigs and dried leaves, which she covered with their blankets. She poured out a portion of the Waters of Life into a silver cup as an offering to the Spirits of the place in thanksgiving and to her patron Deities as a petition for their continued safety.

Ruadh brought in armfuls of dry branches from the forest floor. These he alternated with twigs and dried leaves to form a conical pyre. The cave was transformed into an inviting shelter for the night. All that was needed was a spark to set the branches aflame. Ruadh reached into his pouch, searching for his flint and steel. His fingers groped in vain. He checked the folds of his bedroll and the contents of the baskets.

Ethne, pausing in her work of setting out bowls and food, asked, "Did you lose something? Can I help you find it?"

"I've lost my flint. All I have are my steel and a wad of wool to catch the spark."

Ethne reached into a nearby basket and fished among her belongings. "Here, I have a flint in my tinder box." Opening the intricately carved box, she drew out the flint and held it out to him. As he grasped it, his hand overlapped hers on the cold stone. She disentangled her fingers and lifted her eyes to meet his. As he looked at her, she shook her head gently.

He turned away and knelt before the piled branches, pausing slightly before striking flint against steel with one abrupt motion, the outline of his face hard in the dim light of the cave. A spark struck and caught, singeing the wisps of wool. He bent and eased his breath out slowly, fanning with his fingers until hungry tendrils of flame licked up the edges of the twigs and branches. The sudden fire pushed the walls of the cave back and brought the two travelers into a close circle of light and radiating warmth.

*"Brighid of the flames, Goddess of inspiration and healing, we thank thee for bringing us safely to this shelter."* Ethne said, lighting a few candles and placing them around the cave on rock ledges. The cave grew and settled into a soft glow. She poured a small stream of The Waters of Life onto the fire, saying, *"Spirits of this place, thank you for your presence here and for your many blessings to us in our time of need."* She flicked droplets of the sacred liquid onto the cave walls and the floor in a sun-wise circle.

She dipped her cup once more into the Waters of Life and held it up towards Ruadh.

"Will you share a blessing with me in this new home the forest Spirits have lent us?" She sat beside the fire and waited until he had done the same. Then she passed him the cup and watched his face as the flames made shadows that deepened the blue of his eyes. They sat quietly, letting the crackling fire speak for them, and feeling its warmth sink into their stiff and tired arms and legs. When Ethne rose to prepare dinner, Ruadh made to stand and help her.

"No," she said. "Let your leg soak up the heat. I can have a meal ready with little effort."

She moved about the cave, unwrapping smoked venison and placing it on stones near the fire, Ruadh watched her as the light and shadows accentuated the curve of her hips and the soft roundness of her breasts under the woolen shift. He wanted to grasp the long, honey-colored braid that fell over her shoulders and feel the weight of it in his hands. He wanted to be close to her and knew he would never smell herbs or siabainn again without knowing the longing he felt now. "She is my priestess, my friend and my playmate," he thought, "and oh, Brighid help me, it is not enough!"

Ethne moved quietly, focusing her mind on the simple tasks before her, stirring, slicing, and pouring. If she let her thoughts go, they would burst and crackle like the fire over which she crouched. She recited bits of prayers, silently reminding herself of her status as High Priestess. She turned the venison on the stones and watched the pieces sizzle, knowing her hunger had as much to do with the man across the fire as it had to do with the meat before her. What judgment would the Gods give if she transgressed this night? Her chest felt tight and she forced her hands to be steady as she served venison, bread and watercress in wooden bowls.

Ruadh set his bowl down. "When we reach the court you will disappear into the Nemed. You will be a dream I once had, a dream I will never forget."

"Ruadh, don't," Ethne whispered. "We are meant for other lives, not for each other."

"Perhaps, yes. But I must tell you so you understand." He shook his head as she raised her hand in protest. "I am a wretched man, a wounded warrior who has left his family and his people to wander the world. I am not worthy of you. I am ashamed that I have nothing to offer, no land or possessions. You saved my life, you taught me, befriended me. But I am even more ashamed because I want to hold you. I want to feel your heart beating against mine as it did for one night. If I could feel that again, I could carry the dream with me."

Ethne had not taken her eyes from him. She was afraid to breathe; afraid she would speak, afraid of what her words would say.

"I have only my love to offer you," Ruadh continued.

Ethne's eyes spilled over. "Ruadh, I am but a woman. I am not a Goddess or even a holy image of one. I too have failed the Gods and my family."

Ruadh set down his bowl and came around the fire to sit beside her. "Tell me, Ethne. Tell me who you are."

"I bear the scar of death, the death of one who was not meant to die. When I was younger, I and some other novices sneaked out one night beyond the confines of the school. We wanted to see what people did in the village, what sport they had. On a byroad at the edge of the village we were set upon by robbers. We struggled and were nearly free of them when one of the robbers grabbed me and put a knife to my throat.

Cian, a novice I had cajoled into joining us, threw himself on the man, tearing at his hair and eyes, trying to defend me. The robber became enraged and stabbed him, killing him instantly. Cian gave his life that I might follow the Gods and learn the Druid truths. If I dishonor those truths, I dishonor Cian who died in my stead." She stared bleakly into the fire, tears streaking her face.

"Do you think your friend died so that you could feel no love?" Ruadh asked softly.

Ethne turned her face to him, her eyes confused. "I have no right to feel ordinary joy. I was given a sacred gift and I must repay it by living up to the highest truths of Druid teaching."

"Ethne, joy is never ordinary. It, too, is a gift from the Gods. To turn aside when it is offered is an insult and dishonors their love for us." Ruadh picked up Ethne's hand and brought it to his lips. "Your young friend never had the chance to feel this kind of joy. Don't you think you owe it to him to let it into the life he saved?" Ethne did not pull her hand away, but searched his face.

"I see no scar on you, Ethne."

Without a sound, she drew down her shift to reveal the top of her breast. A thin scar, the length of his first finger showed pink in the firelight. "That is where the robber cut me before Cian saved my life."

Ruadh drew her to him, bent his head and gently kissed the scar. A rosy flush fanned over Ethne's chest and neck. She tilted her head until it rested on Ruadh's.

"Oh, love," she whispered. "You are a dream I would never wish to wake from," and she put her hand under Ruadh's chin and lifted his face so she could kiss him as he had kissed her in the snow. This time their kiss lingered and grew stronger until they sank upon the soft pine bed, he touching her face as if to be sure she was more than a vision. As they kissed again, Ethne loosened her soft leather belt and Ruadh pulled at the folds of her gown.

"By Brighid's light!," he exclaimed as he saw the true lines of her body in the firelight. Gently, he pushed her back onto the leaf bed and pulled off his shirt. Ethne held up her arms to encircle him. He stayed one moment to look on her, then lowered himself to bury his face in her neck. A forgotten cup lay tipped, spilling its contents on the floor, the Waters of Life spreading a pool at their feet.

# 11

═══════

The morning found them very hungry. Ruadh soon had a small fire glowing as Ethne pulled more smoked meat from their birch bark wrappings. She set the cauldron to boil next to the flames and turned to Ruadh.

"Come with me into the sunlight. I want this day to bless us."

He took her hand and they stepped beyond the mouth of the cave. Ethne breathed deeply, making her salute to the Sun:

*Hail to thee, Grian,*
*as you fly on the wings of the Heavens,*
*you are the Great Mother of the Stars.*
*You have lain in the deep of the ocean without fear,*
*you have risen again, like a queen in bloom,*
*we sing you our praise.*

They walked hand in hand to the tiny rill and washed with a cake of siabainn. Laughing and shivering, they ran to the cave to warm themselves and eat a breakfast of dried venison, watercress and a rosehip brew. As Ethne reached for Ruadh's cup to wash it, he caught her wrist and held it tight against his chest.

"How am I to let you go? How can I look upon you at court and pretend we have not been made one?"

Ethne put her hand to his face and smiled. "You have freed me from myself, love.

I am no one's prisoner even if all the Druid disapprove. I'm sure I can escape the Nemed from time to time; after all, I managed to escape my old teacher, Ecca, at the Druid College."

Ruadh took her by both wrists and kissed them each in turn. Ethne laughed and tried to pull away, but he held her wrists tighter. "You may be able to escape the Nemed, dearest, but now you are the prisoner of my cave." He released one wrist and grabbed her round the waist, lifting her off the ground and holding her to him. Ethne freed her other hand and pummeled his chest, laughing harder.

"Shall I use my valor now, brave warrior?" and she slithered out of his grasp. Surprised, Ruadh lunged for her, tripped on a stone and fell headlong onto the pine bed, just managing to catch her arm as he went down. She fell in a heap on top of him, and before she could rise, he rolled her over and pinned her to the bedding.

"I have no doubts about your valor, lady, but I would not have you doubt my desire."

Some hours later they were packed and on the road once more toward the Ard-Ri's dun, but they progressed slowly. Ruadh's leg continued to give trouble and they could walk only several miles in a day. Most nights they found shelter in a barn or shed, relying on the generous hospitality of the boaire. They repaid their hosts by telling stories and singing songs of the Tuatha Dé Danann. Occasionally, Ethne used her healing skills to still a cough or offer simples for a woman's aches. But they were careful to keep their identities and weapons hidden. On the last night they built a fire in an abandoned stone cottage, reveling in the privacy and silence, so reminiscent of their days together at the house in the forest. Ethne, ever careful to prevent conception, drank a strong cup of wild carrot seed brew each morning. The love they made this last night was gentler, with the light of a bright moon spilling across them as they lay, entwined in each others' arms.

"This is how I will see you: with the silver night touching you as I would." Ruadh bent and breathed in the luxury of her hair.

"And I will see you shining in the Sun. My warrior, no longer lost."

The next morning, Ethne unwrapped her court clothing, her torque and manycolored cloak. Walking to a nearby pond, she washed her hair with lavender scented siabainn and scrubbed as much road grime as she could from her hands and feet using silt from the bank. Ruadh coaxed a fire to blaze in the cottage and took his turn at the pond.

Both came in, shivering over the fire until the cold of the pond had dried from their hair.

Ethne selected a robe of crimson fleece, which she belted with a gold studded cincture of pale green leather. Her small golden sickle dangled, as always, at her side. She placed the golden torque upon her neck, and draped the six-colored cloak over her shoulders, fastening it with a large, golden brooch. Ruadh watched as she braided her hair into four separate strands, plaiting golden ribbons into each and finishing every one with a strand of tiny gold balls. She attached the braids to the crown of her head with tortoise shell pins as Ruadh held her small mirror. As she pushed the last pin in place, Ruadh stepped back and grew very still.

"You look as you did when I first saw you."

Ethne laughed then saw how serious he was. "But you have never seen me like this!"

"I have seen your beauty and your virtue, lady. You are truly a Rígain!"

"If I am a queen, then you shall be my loyal warrior and my lord," she answered, offering her hand for him to kiss. He knelt and lifted her hand in mock gallantry, but the attempt failed. He rose, still holding her hand and placed a solemn kiss on her forehead.

"Forgive me, I can't play lover's games so near to parting," and he went outside to retie the bundles before they set off again.

They walked in silence along more well traveled roads. Neither could find words to comfort the other. Finally, out of compassion for Ethne, Ruadh tried to cajole a smile.

"Won't you be happy to see old friends?"

Ethne shrugged then nodded. "There are some I will be glad to see. And there is much news to be heard after being away so long." But there the conversation died, each aware of the oaths Ethne had made and the sanctity of her honor.

Nearing the top of a rise, they saw the dun of the Ard-Ri sprawling on its hill across the horizon, beyond a broad valley. The fence posts of the outer rampart gleamed brownish red in the light of the setting sun, the black silhouette of the leafless ancient Bíle etched sharply before the gate. A low lying pall of smoke from cooking fires and from the Fire Altar of the Nemed hung over the rath, scenting the wintry air. A steady stream of people on foot and on horse and cart moved in and out of the fortress. It was nearing Midwinter and preparations were underway for the great fires that would be set inside the dun and on the surrounding hilltops.

As they watched the activity, Ethne wondered. "How do you suppose a Cristaide king will celebrate the return of the Sun?"

"I have heard that the Cristaidi celebrate in the manner of the worshippers of Mithras, the Roman God of Light," said Ruadh.

Ethne shivered, her nerves showing at the thought of entering the rath of an oathbreaker. But then she, too, had broken a promise by loving Ruadh. A Ban-Drui should only mate with a man chosen for her by her kin, or by the Ard-Drui himself.

"Who knows how a man without honor will celebrate," said Ruadh. "It seems that in these days anything is possible." He saw Ethne's tense face. "Here, love, stay a moment."

He drew her off the track and into a small stand of evergreens. "I did not mean to frighten you. I will never be far should you need me, and every breath I take will have your name woven into it." They held each other in the slight shelter of the trees, she with silent choking sobs, he looking unseeing over her head toward the busy crowds of the dun.

"You are the dear love of my heart," murmured Ethne as their lips met. But her heart shattered with the loneliness to come.

# 12

─────────

Gaine instructed the acolytes to perform the traditional Midwinter observance. The youngest children gathered in a circle around the Sacred Ash with bowls of milk, honey and oats. The Druid stood in a solemn circle at the perimeter of the herb garden.

"Why do we leave offerings for the Antlered God at this time of year?" asked Gaine, uncovering a small statue with detachable antlers she had propped at the base of the tree.

Daire, son of Crimthann, responded; "They are a gift for the Spirits of the Land, who feed and clothe us and give their lives so that we may live. And for the Green Man, the antlered spirit who lives within the vegetation."

"What happens to the Antlered One on this night?"

Little Aífe of the golden curls spoke up: "He loses his antlers!"

"Correct!" said Gaine, removing the tiny clay antlers from their sockets.

"Why does he lose his antlers?"

Daire piped up eagerly. "In the Spring, His antlers bud like new plants, in the summer they grow and branch and in the winter they drop off, just like the plants that die in the frost!"

"Well said." Gaine smiled. "Now everyone, place your offerings beneath the tree."

As the offerings were laid beneath the ash, a Drui initiate distributed red ribbons to the children. Each child was lifted in turn to bind a ribbon to a tree branch. They whispered blessings into the ribbons, for the land and for the people, before they made the knots.

"The tree will send your blessings down to the earth and up to the sky," said Gaine, presenting each with a sweet honey cake as a reward. The older acolytes attending the fire looked on hungrily, and Gaine surprised them with a second plate of sweet meats.

"It is time for the little ones to go to bed!" Gaine clapped her hands, and the youngest students fell into a ragged line to follow one of the adolescent acolytes to the girls' and boys' houses.

Only a handful of the youngest Druid apprentices attended the Druid College. Such children were normally raised and trained by their Druid parents in the ways of tradition. As son of the Ard-Ri and without a mother, Daire was being fostered at the Nemed. This arrangement was a source of consternation to Bishop Germanus, who did not want the boy in the Druid' care.

Aife was of the Nemed class, her Druid parents had died in a fire after a raid by the Men of the North. The other four children came from similar situations. By tradition the Druid strove to represent every age group in the Nemed and other Colleges. They believed that every person, no matter their age, carried sacred Truth within and that it was wise to consult with all manner of people to understand the nature of the world.

Tying ribbons on the Sacred Ash was a facet of training for young Druid. This act, performed in the privacy of the Nemed, taught them to bless the people and thank the Land Spirits. But the lighting of bonfires on every hill was the most important public observance of the Midwinter festival. Preparations had proceeded for weeks as huge piles of sacred woods – ash, oak, rowan, birch, hazel, willow, elm and pine – were collected. Dried leaves, pine cones, smaller branches and coils of birch bark lay beneath each pile as tinder, ready to explode into light at the touch of the sacred fire from below.

"Coemgen" said Gaine as they gathered the last bits of ribbon scattered on the ground. "We must make the fires extra bright this year to purify the land and the people and to drive away all evil spirits that beset this place."

"Our magic will encourage the Sun in Her return to the summer cycle of growth" said Coemgen. " It will also be good to see the common folk and warriors in their straw costumes, burning effigies of 'winter.' The cold and their fears will diminish as they drink mead and dance. Merriment is always good, it nourishes the land and the Spirits."

Coemgen called to runners who waited with cloth-bound branches soaked in fat and wax.

"Prepare to light your torches in the sacred fire and to carry the flames to every hilltop!"

He began the traditional rite, singing the Sun Song as he poured oil from a chastened silver beaker onto the flames: *"Light of grace, pour upon us from season to season. Gentle and generous art Thou. Glory to Thee, glorious Sun, Goddess of Life!"* Then he poured The Waters of Life from a golden cup decorated with tight spirals, amethysts and emeralds. *"Strength to Thee, Mother of the Stars. Return to us in the fullness of Thy glory. Blaze forth from the fires like a queen!"* The stream of liquid turned the flames blue and a shout went up from the Druid around the fire. Coemgen raised his arm to signal the runners to dip their torches into the flames and carry the sacred fire to the hills.

"No!" A shout came from the outer darkness beyond the robed priests and priestesses. Albinus burst through the ranks of the robed Druid. "On your knees to worship the newborn Isu! These fires and this drunkenness is blasphemy! Coemgen, you are only leading these people into the fires of Hell!"

Coemgen froze. He was sworn as Drui to judge fairly and maintain equanimity when provoked. Angry retaliation was not permitted. But it would be hard to compose his thoughts and recover from this insult to his Gods. Coemgen slowly lowered his arm and let his breath go in and out of his body three times.

"Though the Roman emperor has become a Cristaide and has influence in Gaul and Albu, the Romans have no presence here on this Island. We do not accept your religion or your threats. You are free to worship as you please. But you have no right to disrupt our ceremonies."

Albinus hissed, "You forget that your king has banned these sacrifices. He has come to his senses and now worships the one God. So too, Canoc, of the Oirthir. You have lost, old man!"

"Remove him from this sacred ground and post a guard. Neither he nor his followers are to set foot here again!" Coemgen's words held as much sadness as anger.

Two young Druid carried Albinus by the arms from the Nemed as he screamed of Hell's fires. The crow on his shoulder rose above his head and circled, cackling above.

Coemgen looked into the faces of the assembled Druid and saw shock, fear and tears.

This unprecedented confrontation was the worst possible omen; the spiritual heart of the king's household and had been crudely violated.

*"Three signs of a bad man: bitterness, hatred, cowardice"* he said aloud so all could hear, intoning the ancient triad. "A man of true wisdom wins by discourse and reason. These Roman Cristaidi seek to win through fear and disruption. They are as destructive as the raiders from the North and show as little respect for our people and ways. Let us pray to the Gods that they leave us in peace. Let us burn herbs of peace and purification around the perimeters of the Nemed and in the sacred fire. Let each one purify their feet, hands, heart, eyes and forehead with water from the Cauldron of Sea. We must not allow them to win. We *will* retain our faith."

The Druid obeyed his words, and Coemgen offered again the oil and Spirits to the flames. "Mother Sun," he whispered, "I remain constant as you. This day and every day, forever." He raised his arm and the runners took the holy fire to the hills where the people were waiting.

# PART TWO

~

## The Fire Altar

# 13

Ethne and Ruadh approached the main gate of the dun. People swirled around them, many were making their way back to their homes after a days work in the fields. Some called greetings to each other, some sold wares to passers by, and some were travelers like themselves seeking kin or friends to welcome them. Carts, cattle, and shuffling feet blended with the faces, clothes, baskets and unmistakable smells of human habitation. Knots of people stood about talking animatedly, some pointing, but all looking tense and clearly upset. Ethne, long used to the silence of the forest, felt the noise as an assault and shrank within her cloak as the preparations for the festival swirled about her.

Suddenly a series of shrieks cut through the cacophony and Ethne's raw nerves jolted into panic. Ruadh grabbed her arm, pulling her to the side as both craned their necks to find the source of the screaming. A man was being wrestled out of the dun by the Ard-Ri's guards. It was the monk Albinus, but Ethne and Ruadh saw only a strangely dressed traveler being roughly escorted toward the gates.

"Something is very wrong," Ethne murmured. "I have never seen such chaos during the Midwinter festival. Where are the dancing, the celebration fires, and the merriment? These people look confused and wary, not expectant and happy."

Ruadh, too, was perplexed. "This bedlam bodes ill for the coming season, if this is how the Midwinter festival is observed.

I suspect the answer lies in why that man is being thrown out of the rath."

Both knew the Ard-Ri's rath as a ritual focus of the Island from which prayers and directives were sent to every part of the Island. "The Land Spirits will be happy only if this ritual is observed correctly," Ethne commented. "These unhappy people won't bring the right feelings to their celebrations. I fear for the results. Sickly lambs and failed crops could follow."

They pushed through the bunched groups that were talking and pointing and headed for the Nemed. As they approached they heard laughter, singing, and the music of flutes and drums issuing from the royal house where every window was ablaze with light.

The sights and sounds contrasted strangely with the uneasy clots of people outside.

"Can the king be unaware of the distress and disturbance outside his hall?" Ethne wondered.

"Perhaps he is aware but unconcerned."

Ethne shot Ruadh a worried look, her fears at what had befallen her people and her land rising.

"Look," Ruadh pointed, "there are people inside the Nemed, let's see if they can tell us what is happening. Surely not everyone here is in confusion and distress."

They crossed a small footbridge into the sacred precinct and approached the central fire. Two figures stood conversing beside the flames. As Ethne and Ruadh neared, the smaller of the two turned.

"Ethne! My dear child!" Gaine folded Ethne in her arms and held her. "We have waited for you, worried that storms had made your journey difficult." The older woman held Ethne now at arm's length and looked at her, smiling, "You look tired, but well. Tell us of your travels."

Ethne smiled back at Gaine, feeling at once a sense of homecoming and affection.

"I am well. The journey was uneventful and no longer than a fortnight. It is good to see you after all these years apart and to hear your voice again." Ethne then turned and gave her hand to Coemgen, who was standing next to Gaine. "I am honored to be in the Nemed with you again, Coemgen."

Coemgen bowed his head briefly to her and patted her hand. "Ethne, you are a most welcome sight. We have need of every Drui, and you have gifts that we must draw upon in this difficult time. But we will talk of that later. Tell me now of your companion."

Ruadh stood respectfully at a distance so as not to intrude on Ethne's first greetings with her teachers. Now he stepped forward into the firelight.

"Ruadh, son of Canoc, please be known to the Ard-Drui Coemgen and the Ard-Ban-Drui Gaine."

At the name of Canoc, Coemgen stiffened and darted a glance at Gaine. Neither Ruadh, making his obeisance, nor Ethne, watching him, saw this exchange. She continued, "Ruadh has been my protector and companion these several weeks since he came wounded to me at the forest house."

Gaine smiled at Ruadh as he straightened. "Tell me how you came to be wounded and how you found your way to Ethne's care."

As Ruadh began his tale, Coemgen turned to Ethne. "Forgive my abruptness, but recent matters require immediate action. I must speak with you in private." He took her arm and pulled her away from the fire into the shadows. When there was no chance of being overheard, Coemgen tightened his hold on Ethne's arm and turned her to face him.

"I forbid you to have contact with this man."

Ethne went cold, withdrawing her arm. "I have honored you and the Druid in every way. What threat is my friendship with this honorable man?"

"It is a matter of gravest spiritual and political concern. Do *not* disobey me in this."

Ethne tried to keep her voice from rising, tried to keep her knees from turning to water. "Coemgen, I would follow your wishes in all things. But in this I need more than your command. Forgive me, but I need a reason."

"Ethne, you do not know what has befallen us since you have been in the forest. I cannot speak of it all now, but as you observe the Ard-Ri and his court, you will understand why I must insist upon this."

Remembering Ruadh's words, Ethne asked, "Does it have to do with that man we saw being forced out at the gate? I have never witnessed such a disturbance during the Midwinter festival. He screamed terrible curses and people were frightened."

"He is a Cristaide monk called Albinus. He demands that the people follow no God but his. These Roman monks are moving through the land, trying to force everyone into their beliefs. They are unlike the Egyptians such as Father Per who live like us close to nature, honoring the sun, the moon and earth." Coemgen's shoulders were bent and his face was gaunt with concern.

"Ruadh is of our faith," Ethne said softly. "No one need fear him."

Coemgen put a hand gently on her shoulder. "There is more you need to know, child. Ruadh's father, Canoc, is a Cristaide."

"But Ruadh does not follow his father's ways!" Ethne blurted, desperate to extract her love from the tangle she saw tightening.

"Ethne, listen. Canoc connived and manipulated the Ard-Ri into banning the Horse Sacrifice at his king making and the Abbot Germanus will officiate beside me at his consecration. Neither I nor the Druid council could dissuade Crimthann from this."

"Ruadh knows nothing of this! He is a Fennid and has been away from his clann for many years."

"Would you trust a man who abandons his clann to join a wild band of warriors? He could be a spy. He must be kept out of all matters at court and *especially* from you."

"Me? He has been nothing but honorable to me. You must hear me. You tell me I don't understand what is happening here, well, you too, do not understand. Let him prove his worth and he will repay you tenfold, I give you my word."

Coemgen drew himself up and folded his hands before him. "Obey me in this, Ethne. I wish you to dismiss him. We will recompense him with gold for the service he has done you and there the matter will close." He turned and walked stiffly back toward the fire. Ethne stood like a stone, her heart like a poor fluttering bird. She made her feet move and followed Coemgen into the circle of light at the Fire Altar.

"I was just thanking Ruadh for the way he has looked after you on the road," Ethne heard Gaine say as she came closer. "I offered him a meal and a place for the night before he returns to the FiaOirthir to his clann." Gaine's tone was final.

Ruadh, without a look at Ethne, bowed with polite correctness, turned and strode into the dark. Ethne, tears blurring her vision, walked around the fire and deeper into the Nemed enclosure.

"By the Gods, I hope this goes according to plan," said Coemgen and gave Gaine his arm as they set out to circumambulate the fires on the surrounding hills.

Ethne found Ruadh at one of the guest houses. Furthest from the central fire and closest to the palisade, it was a small round hut with a circular hearth. A red leather door stamped in knot work and spirals distinguished the hut from dozens of others huddled within the Nemed. Few of the huts had windows and this one was no different, lit instead by beeswax candles of varying sizes. A bedstraw pallet covered in sheepskins, linens and woolen blankets lay against the wall. A carved chest for clothing and personal belongings stood beside it. A bronze water cauldron, clay cups and a mirror were the other amenities.

Ethne stood just inside the doorway, willing herself to be the Drui priestess she was. She had turned Coemgen's words over and over in her mind all that night. She mentally sorted through her days with Ruadh, remembering their conversations and the look in his eyes. She could not reconcile the two. Yet Coemgen could not be ignored and the seeds of doubt had been planted. Ruadh reached for her hand and she felt a dread come over her.

"Have you been given everything you need?" she asked stiffly.

"All but what I need most." He put his arm around her waist and Ethne felt a hot rush of conflict. She stepped out of the circle of his arm.

"Ruadh, I must tell you..." she had to swallow and could not go on.

"Tell me, love, what you have to say. I'd rather hear it at once since it causes you such pain." Ruadh clenched his fists to keep from touching her, giving her the time she needed.

Ethne raised her eyes and spoke directly at him. "I am forbidden to be in your company."

"But why!" Ruadh burst out. "What reason could they possibly give? What do they know of me?"

"It is the Ard-Ri," Ethne spat. "I *hate* him. He has broken his oaths and now everything has gone wrong. Coemgen needs me and every Druid to bring things right again."

"But we are free people, Ethne." Ruadh's voice was deep and full of anguish. "It's our choice whom we love."

"You are free, Ruadh. But I am bound by my sacred duties. I am forbidden to see you after tonight. To do so could cost me my life." She did not tell him that she knew of Canoc's treachery to dishonor the Ard-Ri. Ruadh must show her where his allegiances lay. She tried to see him as a wraith, a passing specter in her life, a dream without material substance. In her mind she chanted: *Three excellences of wisdom: to be aware of all things, to suffer with all things, and to be detached from all things.* She let the ancient triad fill her mind.

Ruadh stood stunned, then slowly knelt at her feet. "I would walk into the winter ocean if it would keep you safe. Tell me what I must do." His hands were upturned before him in offering. With a small wail, Ethne crumpled beside him and put her arms about his shoulders.

"Ruadh, I must do what is asked of me. I healed you in the forest, but now the Land and the people have greater need for my healing. I cannot turn away. I do not mean to abandon you!" Her tears ran over his hair and he reached around to hold her, pressing her against him fiercely. Crouched together, they held on against the dissolution of their world, Ethne crooning softly to comfort them both.

After a time, she untangled herself from his arms and sat back. "You must be very hungry, and have they brought you a bath?" When Ruadh shook his head, she stood and left the hut to order hot water and a meal. She soon returned with five mogae bearing an oaken tub and buckets of boiling water. Ethne herself carried a platter of roasted meats, bread, mashed turnips and carrots and a beaker of crimson fion.

Dismissing the servants, she set the tray next to the fire and poured the fion into the clay cups. Music from the Ard-Ri's feasting drifted through the village and made its way faintly into the hut. Along with the profusion of candles, it gave their small supper an almost festive air.

"Nearly everyone is making merry around the fires," mused Ethne.

Ruadh watched the candles burnish her skin and give light to her hair. "You are the fire of my joy." And he raised his cup to her. Ethne smiled and raised her cup in return.

"Come, finish your bread and then soak in the bath." She stood and poured the last cauldron of heated water into the tub. "Get in and I will scrub your back." Ruadh undressed and slid into the water with a sigh.

"Quite different from a dash to the stream, isn't it?" Ethne laughed as she knelt behind him. She lathered his arms, legs and chest with lavender-scented siabainn and scrubbed him with a woolen cloth, pausing as she went over the scar on his thigh. A lump the size of a walnut had risen just under the skin.

"Does is it give you pain when I press it?" she asked.

"No, I wasn't even aware of it until you touched it."

"Perhaps it is the last of the healing, knitting itself together." She touched it tenderly thinking of how this wound had brought them together. Ruadh caught her hand and pulled her toward him. Ethne was perspiring in the warmth of the fire and the steaming water, but at the touch of Ruadh's hand a flood of heat washed over her. In one movement, she pulled off her shift and stepped into the tub, not caring at the water sloshing over the sides. Ruadh pulled her down to him, moving his hands over her shoulders, her breasts, and her legs. The water swayed around them as they kissed, Ethne's mouth trembling as tears spilled over.

In the short weeks since Samain, word had gone out to the kingdoms that the ArdRi was now Cristaide. The effect on the lesser nobility and the clann chieftains was immediate. They perceived that the Roman ways were now the fashion and each vied with the other, acquiring Latin crosses and baptismal fonts to be stylish and correct. Foremost were the courtiers seeking favor with the Ard-Ri. Canoc and Queen Fithir became the darlings of the petty kingdoms, those rulers too inconsequential to participate in the official Samain rites and in the High Council. These did not know the true nature of the king's "conversion." Canoc and Fithir did nothing to correct the impression of their status, both waiting for the Ard-Ri to stumble. Canoc was a strong contender for the throne.

While the Druid supervised the people in the Midwinter ceremonies, Roman Cristaidi priests moved amongst the nobility. Families of the Warrior class now regarded the clerics as entertainment for their elegant dinners. The foreign clergy told fantastic tales of miracles, a heavenly kingdom and of Hell. Their Isu was certainly a great ArdDrui, who knew magic and had sacrificed himself for the good of the people, elevating himself to the status of "Sun King." Hadn't the greatest Druid of old done the same, for the good of their tribes?

The symbol embroidered on the priests' mantles, an amalgam of the Latin cross and the Druid Sun glyph - a cross with a circle laid over it, gradually became the rage among the flaith. They wore it as a necklace, displacing the triskellion, now seen only on backcountry dwellers ignorant of the latest fashions. Of all this Ethne and Ruadh knew little, having spent the last years in forests and among the warrior-poets of the Fiana.

The next morning Ruadh emerged from his hut to find Ethne, the Ard-Drui and a fine horse standing by his door. "I am presenting you with a strong mount and gold, in thanks for your service to Ethne," said Coemgen stiffly.

"I do not need gold, but I accept the horse for my journey," said Ruadh, his voice even.

Ethne's face was impassive, belying the searing pain in her heart. "Will you accept bread, cheese and apples for the road?"

Ruadh bowed his head. "Lady, I will accept *any* gift from your hand."

Ethne placed her hand upon his head, intoning a prayer of protection for the traveler:

*May Brighid shield you on land and sea.*
*May the Three succor you,*
*the Three follow you,*
*the Three uphold you.*
*May you proceed in peace*
*as to the immortal garden of the Gods,*
*By earth, sea and sky may this be so.*

Ruadh gathered his few belongings and mounted. Coemgen gave the horse's rump a slap and Ruadh was gone through the gates to re-join the Fiana.

The Abbot Germanus sat on a hill beside the road to the Ard-ri's rath and preached the virtues of building a new monastery to a group of farmers and laborers. His gray robes spread on the grass about his knees and his long gray hair fell loosely about his shoulders. Albinus sat beside him, calling to passersby. "Those who help build win a place in Heaven! Your salvation is assured! We will also pay you in good Roman gold, when the project is done."

"But a monster attacks the stones each night. The walls tumble once they are built!" a red-faced pig farmer insisted.

"Many are the enemies of the True Lord and Satan is ever about, but he will not deter us from our sacred mission. Who will put up the walls?" replied Albinus.

Not one hand rose.

"He goes about with the *Morrígu* on his shoulder" Snedgus the pig farmer shuddered as he and others made their way back to the fields.

"The Battle Crow is a terrible omen. Perhaps it's what keeps the Cristaidi priests from wanting a woman!" answered Lugnae, a thickset farmer from the neighboring district.

"The flaith follow those monks and worship the God called Isu. But *I* won't give up the faith of my fathers," said another.

"Who are those monks anyway?" Snedgus snorted. "I don't trust them, *or* their ways. They will cut down our circle of oaks, cut down the hawthorn trees on which we hang our prayer cloths. They will fill our holy well and divert the water for a 'baptismal font.' I've heard their plans. Father Per built his chapel himself. He never made us lug stones."

"He didn't offer anyone pay either. They've kept the Sheela-na-gig to put over the doorway of their new chapel. Do they want Sheela to bless their building?"

"I think it's a trick to get us inside."

"We have enough work with our own beasts and fields, we needn't help these foreign monks."

A few local men were following Albinus and Germanus, hoping to avoid family obligations, military service and taxes. They also led a handful of monks from Gaul who had fled north for a purer spirituality. Several, like Father Per, knew how to read and write and hoped monastery life would give them access to a library and a scriptorium. The abbot had plans to erect a monastery, three miles from the dun of the Ard-Ri, now that the king had officially adopted the new religion. Germanus assumed that all souls in the district were his to command, even if the common people were unaware of their conversion.

"The problem of the stones is baffling," said Germanus to Albinus privately. "The architect of the monastery is a respected builder from Gaul. There is no sand or mud in the area and the foundation is built on dry land. There have been no high winds or disturbances to account for the collapse each night of work done during the day. After thirty days of lost labor I have enlisted the locals to build thicker and higher walls. But there is obstinacy amongst them. Don't they want quick gold? It is deeply puzzling."

"They are a stupid lot, Germanus," said Albinus when the search for workers had again failed. "Illiterates, all of them. All they think about is brawling, mating and the drinking of ale, while we bring them civilization to save their miserable souls."

"What can you expect from Pagani? I'll double my offer of gold tomorrow."

The next morning Germanus inspected the rubble of their previous day's work. "I believe the mysterious monster who overthrows the stones has a man's face, Albinus. See the footprints at the base of the wall? Are they not human?"

Albinus inspected the mud and found clear footprints.

"I have a way to put a stop to this nonsense. Come with me to the preaching hill."

Albinus and Germanus settled themselves again on top of a hillock in full view of passing tradesmen and farmers, letting it be known that an important spiritual revelation was at hand. Small children were sent as runners to the nearby village to collect more people.

When a crowd was assembled, Germanus spoke. "A fearful monster has attacked the stones of our monastery each night. Aided by Satan, the beast has thrown down our labors and gloated in his triumph. But we have a way to combat this monster through divine revelation!"

A murmur went through the crowd, but many looked unimpressed. Albinus's crow ruffled its feathers and peered out from behind the monk's head.

"By divine guidance the walls will stand if a sacrifice is offered. A human sacrifice as in days of old!" Now Germanus had the attention of the townspeople. "The sacrifice of a son or daughter of this land will appease the Spirits of Place. In this way your blood will bind the building to your ancestors and to your children and your grandchildren, for all time. Whoever is sacrificed is guaranteed a place in the Heavenly Kingdom. All sins will be forgiven! I have the approval of the Ard-Ri and the warriors in this. Select one of your own or we'll do it for you!"

Germanus and Albinus descended the hillock, heads held high. Albinus's crow clung tightly to his neck calling out, "Gaak! Gaak!" The crowd parted like wheat in the wind.

"These monks have us by the hind parts," said Lugnae the farmer. "First they make it illegal to own slaves, then our women may no longer use weapons to defend themselves and their families. Now they actually want a human sacrifice for their cursed building! Why don't they offer one of their own if they are so pious?"

Snedgus the pig farmer snorted, "I hear they hate women. One of them threw a woman over a cliff because he was attracted to her. They are mad-men, and I don't doubt they will kill to get their way."

Brude the shoemaker, spoke in a low voice, "They believe that dying in a pool of blood is the ultimate honor. Their God died thus and they think it a great privilege to follow His example. We had better stop throwing down the walls and let them have their way."

"I agree. We are not warriors with swords to defend ourselves against these *geilte*," said Lugnae.

"Our best course is to lay low and leave them be. We can perform our rites as we always have. So what if we have to go to the church on their High Holy Days? Old Sheela is still there to bless us, and sometimes I like the songs. But they can't expect us to pay them in coin, just for the show." Everyone nodded in agreement.

From that day, the building of the monastery went without hindrance, and Germanus sent letters and envoys to foreign lands, seeking a piece of the True Cross or a drop of the Lord's Blood to establish his house on the Northern pilgrimage trail.

Father Per sat at the doorway to his hut; his tiny stone church was long finished and being used for Matins, Angelus and Vespers. He said his Masses with simplicity, passing out bits of consecrated bread to those who gathered. He knew they were there because they believed that another God added to their store was a blessing, not because they were abandoning the ones that had accompanied them thus far. He knew too, although he would not have used these words, that they came because they trusted him. They found comfort and hope in the way he touched a shoulder or listened to a grief. At this moment he was mending once more the frayed edges of his cloak. His needle moved with a relaxed rhythm and his mind was carried along with it, away from the troubles that were unfolding. He was drawing the thread through when the long, narrow shadow of Albinus fell across his hands.

"Have you spoken to the people yet?" Albinus asked in his rasping voice.

Father Per continued his work, letting his thoughts re-gather around the question. He had expected the visit and had known he must answer before long. "I speak with them almost daily."

"Don't evade the question!"

Albinus was by far the larger of the two men, his ungainly shape and boney head towering over Per. But Per's contentment and competence with the small things that made life worth living put Albinus at a disadvantage. He felt it every time he was with Per and he felt it now as an insult to his authority. It was for that reason and because Albinus had seen the smiling children as they handed him a sack of flour. Albinus also saw the small earthen jar pass from Per's hands to the oldest boy, Daire.

"Do you give away the Lord's work so freely, Father Per?" Albinus' voice boomed too loudly off the stones of the hut.

Per laid the sewing beside him and greeted his visitor properly. "I give you welcome and peace, Albinus. Your presence honors my home." Per gestured with one arm wide as offer for Albinus to sit near the open fire where an herbal brew was steaming. When Albinus was settled with a thick mug between his long fingers, Per said, "They are good people, Albinus. And children anywhere are a blessing."

"But honey!" Albinus erupted. "Giving away honey is wasteful!"

"It is God's own gold I share," answered Per. "Is Roman gold a better way to secure their souls?" It was said softly, but the words had their effect, as Per intended. "Rome defends itself wisely. Coins can waylay warriors and prevent bloodshed.

Would you have more battles?"

Per shook his head, but not as answer. "You ask the wrong question, Albinus. No one wants more fighting. The question is what will each side allow to save what they most love? I have heard the stories of the people, listened to their tales of Brighid and of Grian. At the heart of each telling is the same wish the Christus brings: be kindly to those of this earth, all creatures. We need each other to live."

Albinus gripped his mug tighter and growled, "Never say the name of the Christus in the same breath as those Heathen Gods. I came to see if you still followed Scripture. I fear there is no room to reason with you. I warn you, Per, Abbot Germanus will not be pleased."

Per rose as Albinus stood to leave. He took the mug from the monk and said, "With such meager fare did our Lord lure people to his table."

Albinus turned down the corners of his mouth and strode away.

# 14

―――――

Crimthann paced the floor of his sleeping quarters. The moon, nearly full, made his windows glow and he found it hard to sleep. He had listened to Canoc, Germanus and Albinus until Cristaidi demands rang in his ears. Germanus said that to earn esteem from foreign kings and become part of the "civilized" world he would have to make the new religion the official faith of the Island, just as the emperor had in Rome. He insisted that women be prevented from using arms or being educated. A "good" Cristaide woman obeyed her men, in the Roman manner – her only duty to bear children and maintain a household. He said the Celtic warrior-women were an abomination and doomed to Hell.

"The Fennidi are unruly outlaws," Germanus complained. "They obey no laws but their own. They must be stopped!"

At the same time Crimthann received lectures and pleas from Coemgen and the Druid council not to abandon *their* ways, not to abandon the Land Spirits. They reminded him daily that he embodied the land and the correct observance of ritual was his highest responsibility. To do otherwise made him an oath-breaker, a man without honor.

The Ban-Druid also brought their complaints. The women of the villages told stories of the Gaulish monks advising their husbands to "beat them into submission," because a woman named "Eve" had caused the "downfall of men." If the women should not use weapons, how could they hunt or defend themselves? Who would teach the children the use of arms? These monks feared women and preached to lower women in the eyes of the law.

"*Three candles that illuminate every darkness – truth, nature, knowledge.*" The old triad ran through Crimthann's mind. "I am split in every direction by these factions and am stiff with tension. I will seek answers from the Goddess who has never failed me."

Slipping into a simple, gray cloak and taking up his wooden staff and dirk, he swung wide the leather door to his chamber and stepped into the great hall. Warriors and dogs slept by the fire, snoring off their mead and feasting. Making his way to the entrance where two guards played fidchell, he exited without comment. Once safely beyond the palisade, Crimthann slowed his pace. This time the stroll was more than a respite from the smoky halls of the rath. He engaged in a walking meditation, in hopes of finding a solution to the morass in which he was trapped. Using concentration combined with night vision, Crimthann let his mind go quiet so inspiration could surface. A swath of moonlight led up the side of a hill.

"Thank you Moon, my night guide. Thank you Moon, beauty of the heavens, sister of the Sun. My knee bends to the Queen of loveliness."

Crimthann let the Moon lead him. Cresting the rise, he understood. Before him, facing the Moon and slightly below the hilltop, rose the ancient stone circle used by the Druid for their Moon rites. It appeared deserted. The stones cast black shadows upon the moonlit grass and a light mist circled their base. An owl called and a cowbell tinkled as some sleepy kine shifted her weight in the valley below. The stars shone like embers in the black cauldron of the sky.

"I am stirred like the stars in transformation, by the Goddess' hands. Where does She lead?" Crimthann's wondered. Heavy in body and spirit, he dropped to the ground in front of a stone and leaned against it, facing the Moon. As his eyes adjusted to the dark, a shiver of movement at the base of one monolith arrested his attention: a trick of light, a Faery of the night, a shift in the stones. He peered, keeping still and straining to make out the cause. The movement came again and this time he knew it for what it was, a hooded figure, barely perceptible in the mist. Crimthann pulled his dirk from his boot. His staff lay across his lap, his hand tightening around it as a woman's voice sang:

*Moon whom I love, you bless all creatures.*
*You make each thing holy that you illumine.*
*You reveal every good deed.*
*You guide those in need.*
*Shine your light on everyone who is wanting.*
*Come, as through black clouds,*
*to everyone in tribulation.*
*Be a helping hand to the people,*
*Moon, jewel of the night.*

Strong and clear came the words. As the song finished, she turned and nodded her head towards him, unafraid. He recognized her as Ban-Druid, singing for those in need. He knew too that she was protected by magic.

The figure in the hooded cloak raised her arms in invocation, gathering the moonlight in her palms. Quickly she dropped them to send the Moon's energy to earth, and then knelt to kiss the sod. After a moment she rose, exited the circle and returned with a beaker and bowl. She poured liquid into the bowl, which she placed at the center of the ring. Next, she walked to the inner perimeter of the stones, stopped before each one, touched it, kissed it and dropped a handful of herbs before it.

"An offering for the Faery," thought Crimthann, watching as she came near.

Finally, the woman stood in front of him, motionless and silent. After some seconds, Crimthann realized she was waiting for him to get up so she could complete the circuit of offerings. He stood and moved to one side, embarrassed. When she finished, she exited the circle only to return again, this time bearing another beaker, a cup and a loaf of bread.

"I always finish blessings with bread and fion." Her voice was fluid and rich, though she spoke in a near whisper. "Will you share with me? You are part of this offering and it will make the celebration complete."

Crimthann bowed his head in acceptance. "You honor me, and I accept your bread and fion. Please forgive my intrusion. I did not mean to interrupt your Moon ceremony." He too kept his voice quiet.

"You need not apologize. The Moon welcomes all who seek Her company."

"It was my understanding the Druid only used this circle at the New Moon. I did not expect to find a priestess." Crimthann tried to see into the depths of the cowl, but the shadows were too deep and only the melodious voice came forth.

"Your understanding is correct, but I find comfort coming to the circle alone. I too seek solace of the Moon."

They sat cross-legged before the stone, sipping the fion and enjoying the textured bannock. Every stone around them had a presence, as if it listened. As if to speak for them, Crimthann said, "These stones have witnessed many seasons and many offerings. They are a constant when so much is changing."

The hooded figure said quietly, "I will be here for the next two days. The Full Moon is tomorrow night and the Third Day of the Moon will be the night after. I will make offerings and pray for the people on the three nights of the Full Moon."

It was as if the Goddess herself had invited him to return. "My heart needs guidance. I will gladly join you and bring offerings as well as food, if you do not object."

"This ancient circle belongs to all. These stones gather what we give them and radiate power to the country beyond. One

Ban-Drui is not enough to honor these stones or offer prayers to the Moon. I am pleased at your devotion."

"Bíth ed samlaid" said Crimthann, draining his cup. She took it, showing long fingers and a narrow wrist. Without a word she left the circle, disappearing into the folds of mist. Crimthann kept company with the silent stones and the Moon riding in the clear night air.

In the morning the great hall was full with the stale smell of sweat and too much breath. Villagers had come bringing their complaints and gone away either satisfied or grousing. Germanus observed all afternoon from a stool near the far wall, watching and reading from his Psalter. As Crimthann stood and stretched, Germanus rose and walked toward the dais.

"My lord, Crimthann," he said with a bow. "Will you walk in the air with me?"

Crimthann's relief at the invitation was evident. "Air would be most welcome." He stepped down and the two walked the length of the hall to the door. They veered left at the bottom of the stairs of one accord and began a slow amble round the perimeter of the dun. Crimthann filled his lungs and relaxed his hands. Germanus looked to the far hills and noticed the cloud shadows tracing across them. He was patient. They strolled past the smithy and felt the curls of heat and still neither spoke. As they reached the far side of the dun, they came upon a small boy struggling to bring a lamb back to the pen.

Crimthann laughed. "Here's a task with no recrimination." He lifted the lamb and dropped it gently over the fencing. The boy stood with eyes like new coins.

Crimthann tousled his hair and did not embarrass the child by waiting for thanks.

"You are easy with your people," said Germanus as they continued. "You are a good king, fair and intelligent."

"I would be what the people deserve," replied Crimthann.

"I find it strange that you do not raise your kings or train them," Germanus commented.

"In what way strange?"

"In Rome, as in other countries of high culture, kings are taught from birth within dynastic families. Would you trust your sword making to a man who only learned the art yesterday?"

Crimthann slowed his pace at this question and looked directly at Germanus. "Go on."

"Men are educated to understand the law, the principles of policy and the history of their kingdom. They read and write so ideas may be shared and passed on. In books the wisdom and power of the ages are protected, and reading is the key to both."

Neither man was moving now. Crimthann, with forehead creased, said, "Our Druid keep our history and our laws in their heads. From one generation to the next it is not forgotten. How is your way better?"

"If you could read our Latin writings, you would be connected in spirit to the Roman Empire, and respected by men who wield great power. You would be more than Ard-Ri of this small Island. You would be a sovereign among great kings."

Again they began to walk. After a moment, Germanus added, "Do your people deserve less?"

Crimthann's head came up and caught the other man's look. "Can you teach me?"

Germanus opened his Psalter and pointed to a word. "*Dei.*"

Crimthann looked long at it and repeated the sound. "*Dei.*" He looked up questioningly. "It means God."

Crimthann was an eager student.

# 15

The cave of the Fennidi stood near a rocky promontory on the coast where any ship would be visible. Ruadh sat on an old tartan in view of the sea, one leg crossed over the other, his scabbard resting on his knees. A wooden keg of goose fat stood beside him into which he methodically dipped a cloth to work oil into the leather. Buan, Erc and the others sat similarly, some on tree stumps, some on the grass. Erc had a double bladed ax captured from raiders from the North, and was sharpening it with a stone. Buan inspected a bundle of throwing spears for cracks in the wood. Fidach looked over the wooden handles of a pile of throwing axes to make sure none was splitting. Colchu checked the bows, to insure the wood and bindings were sound, the strings properly braided. Ragnall scanned arrows for cracked wood and frayed fletchings, and Corc sharpened and oiled the point of every arrow that had passed Ragnall's inspection.

The band of Fennidi had greeted Ruadh joyfully on his return. Miadach, Fidach's sister who didn't fight but did most of the cooking and sewing, was especially glad to see him, for many times she had shared his pallet under the stars. She searched his face when he was occupied, to read his thoughts. She offered him extra blankets and inquired after his leg. She lingered near him on the night of his return, and offered her own palette, but he smiled and shook his head. It was as if half of him was left behind, elsewhere.

"Why this distance?" she thought as she offered him a bowl of seaweed soup with choice bits of shellfish.

"In a few weeks it will be Imbolc," said Erc who was oiling the pommel and cross guards of his sword "Teinntech."

"The Men of the North may reappear at any time. It is good to get the weapons in order. We must also gather provisions and smoke the meat we have hunted."

Ruadh laid his sword "Greimm Dúr" across his knee and oiled its blade thoughtfully. "It is unwise to assume they will wait for the frosts to break. We should redouble our guard and expect the worst." Ruadh was hoping for an encounter soon. Anything was better than the ache in his heart. He had stunned Corc and Ragnall by his ferocity during sword practice.

The morning, which had been fair, suddenly turned dark. "I see rain headed this way!" declared Miadach.

"Grab the weapons! Into the cave!" yelled Erc as a fierce gust of wind rolled in from the sea. Each grabbed whatever was nearest. After all their careful oiling, they did not want the weapons ruined by water.

Soon the wind was howling and thick drops of freezing rain pelted the rocks and ground. Buan built up the fire at the front of the cave and hung a rough patchwork of skins over the entrance. A coating of grease made everything rain proof.

Inside, the cave grew warm. Pallets of grasses and heather covered by blankets were scattered by the walls. Shields, scabbards and quivers hung from iron spikes driven into the rock above the beds. One section of wall supported bows, spears and axes, which leaned in neat rows, ready at a moment's notice. Miadach swept discarded pieces of flint, bowstrings and metal shavings, the detritus of a warrior camp. A large cauldron of seaweed soup purred over the fire full with limpets, mussels, fish and the flesh of a sea bird newly added to the salty broth.

"Who will watch tonight in this foul rain?" asked Ragnall, dipping a wooden bowl into the cauldron, grateful for the warm liquid.

"I will," said Ruadh. He volunteered for every unpleasant task, regardless of the time or weather.

Fidach and Miadach exchanged looks.

"When is the last time you had a full night's sleep? You wander in and out of here at all hours," said Erc, who felt responsible for the safety of the Fian.

Ruadh did not answer, but gulped a mouthful of soup and pulled on a double cloak. He took up a stout stick and hung a horn around his neck. If a raiding ship appeared, he would blow it and a Fennid would run to the nearby town to sound the alarm while the others followed the ship, unseen, from the forest lining the coast.

The Fian attacked when raiders came ashore for fresh water or an assault. The trick was to wait until they were out of their boats, and best was to catch them after a meal when they were sure to be drunk. After a raid they were always drunk.

Ruadh scrabbled up the side of the hill, slipping on a pile of wet leaves and cursing. In his fall, a rock broke open his wound, lancing the knot under the skin.

Reaching the top, he turned his face into the rain and let the pain sear through him. He thought of Ethne and the days they shared. Bracing his weight with the staff, he peered out to sea and saw nothing but thrashing waves and one storm-tossed bird. He saw the ocean swell and he saw a gray mass. In the fading light it was hard to be certain. But then, unmistakably, the pale gray of a woolen sail emerged from the surrounding darkness of the ocean as the sharp prow of the vessel cut a swath through the water, making for the sandy beach.

Ruadh, choosing not to blow the horn, slid down the wet hill to the cave entrance and threw back the skins. "Douse the fire! Put out the candles! A ship approaches! It is headed for shore!"

"Corc! Run to the village and alert the townsfolk. Everyone else, with me!" called Erc, slipping on his boots.

Miadach saw the red stain through Brain's pant leg, opened her mouth to speak then seeing the hardness of his face, kept silent. She gathered the bowls and turned away. The Fian dressed and armed with the precision of long practice. This time the ship would land in their territory so there was no need for Miadach's usual provisions. The warriors crept from the cave, crouched or crawling as they went, made invisible by the trees.

The ship came steadily for shore. As the Fian watched, it dropped anchor and lowered a thin rowing boat over the side. Twelve armed men dropped from the ship into the boat, slid into their seats and plied their way to shore.

Erc looked at Ruadh for signs of recklessness. He looked at the others. "Listen!" he hissed. "Stay close until the last possible moment. Our advantages are surprise and our bows. Shoot on my signal. Aim for their legs!"

They notched their arrows silently. The boat beached and the raiders jumped into the frigid shallows, pulling the boat after them. Once the boat was on the sand, the leader barked a command and the men sprinted for the forest and the town.

Erc held up a hand. "Hold . . . hold . . . hold . . . "Now!" he cried.

Arrows sang and found their targets. One by one, the Men of the North dropped, howling as their dark blood poured onto the ground. The Fennidi closed in like a pack of wolves forming a ring around fresh prey. The fallen raiders floundered helplessly, arrows through their calves and thighs. When a raider raised his shield arm to repel a Fennidi arrow, he exposed his back or belly.

Eight of the Men of the North were down, dead in the sand, eyes staring. The Fennidi swung axes and swords, finishing the rest. Yet one still staggered on his feet. Before Erc could reach Ruadh, the raider had stabbed him in the leg, slicing upward with a vicious stroke. As Ruadh fell, the man aimed his sword at his throat. A swift arrow from Erc stopped his arm in mid stroke, the flat of his blade falling harmlessly against Ruadh's cheek. The raider crumpled and became the last to die.

As the Fennedi collected weapons, Erc found Ruadh laying on the sand, his body stiffening in shock. "Ruadh is down!" he called to the others and they gathered round.

Miadach, who had seen everything from the height above the cave ran to the beach bearing a vial of the Waters of Life and powdered herbs to staunch bleeding. She rapidly tore Ruadh's clothes and applied herbs to the wound in his leg. He was delirious, babbling, his eyes wild, his skin hot.

"Get him back to the cave." barked Erc.

Fidach and Colchu carried Ruadh, the task made more difficult by his thrashing.

In the cave, Buan built the fire to a roaring pitch while Miadach bathed Ruadh's wound with compresses of oak bark and the Waters of Life. Several of the men held him down while she stitched the wound. The fever grew worse.

Townsfolk arrived bearing gifts of gratitude: blankets, chickens, barley flour, apples and roots, a barrel of cheeses pickled in salt brine, and a fat pig. Men walked to the beach to claim the ship's planks for their houses and any other prizes. The rowing boat they would use for fishing. They burned the bodies of the raiders in a communal funeral pyre. The women looked at Ruadh and shook their heads. "He's got one foot in the barrow already, mark my words," clucked an old hag.

In the morning, Erc had made up his mind. "Tie him to a cart and I will take him to the rath of the Ard-Ri. The Forest Woman is there. If he survives the journey maybe she can heal him again."

# 16

Coemgen and Gaine spent their days and nights with the Ard-Ri. Ethne suspected it had to do with the Gaulish monk, Albinus and the Abbot Germanus. As a result, she was left on her own in the rath. She had seldom been idle in the forest, so she found ways to busy herself: preparing healing ointments, bandages, candles and other necessities. She kept her vigil at the stones, worshiping by moonlight with the man called Faelchu. Some nights she wandered over the hills, and several times met him, though she never saw him in the village daylight. She liked his piety and desire to meditate in the great stone circle. His delight at leaving gifts for the Faery and praying to the Earth, Water and Sky spirits endeared him to her. Though she never spoke of it, her grief at Ruadh's departure was deep. Faelchu, with his honest words, gave her the attention she needed.

No news came from Ruadh. She hoped he would get a message to her somehow, and wondered at his silence. She imagined everything: Ruadh dead in battle, Ruadh sick from the poison of his wound, Ruadh giving his love to another. The last, though not the worst, caused her terrible pain. With each image she turned to her Druidic training for balance and impartiality of mind. As a Ban-Drui she could not leave the dun without permission; she could not follow and find the man she loved. To stave off despair she sank herself into tasks.

On this particular day, she made fresh batches of siabainn. Ethne appreciated the luxury of the Ard-Ri's dun. It was well stocked with fragrant herbs; chamomile, lavender and rose-buds, preserved in wooden drawers in the storehouse. Ethne gathered ashes from the Fire Altar of the Nemed and from the Ard-Ri's hearth. These she had sifted and poured into buckets, then covered with water and left them to soak. Ethne put her finger into a bucket and touched it to her mouth. The water tingled and bit her tongue. She nodded, knowing the ashes had reached the correct acidity for making siabainn.

Next she lay dry blossoms in wicker baskets upon the oaken worktable that stretched down the middle of the storehouse, expertly powdering them a handful at a time with a bronze mortar and pestle. Soon there were three full bowls, one with crushed red roses, one of golden chamomile flowers and one of powdered lavender blossoms and leaves. She covered each bowl with a linen cloth and carried them outside on a tray.

In the courtyard several mogae tended three fires. Over each fire hung an iron cauldron in which acid water was coming to a boil. Ethne instructed the mogae to add bits of tallow. A woven straw mat in the bottom of each cauldron would strain any solid particles of suet and ash. After the straw mats were lifted out and the mix was reduced to a gelid mass in the bottom of each cauldron, she added roses to one, chamomile to another and lavender to the third.

The mogae, at her direction, poured the thickened liquid into wooden bowls to mature and harden. Ethne was carrying the last bowl to the storehouse for drying when she saw Coemgen and Gaine approaching. She set the bowl down, watching their faces as they came nearer, her stomach tightening. "*May the Sun find you whole,*" she greeted them, offering a respectful nod, but watching them warily.

"And you, child," answered Gaine. "We need your attention in a very serious matter. Will you leave your work and come?" It was a polite command and Ethne knew better than to resist. She handed the tray to the nearest mog and instructed her to take it into the storehouse.

Gaine opened her arms wide to Ethne, "Come to the herb garden, we would speak with you in private." The three walked in silence to the seat nearest the Sacred Ash.

Ethne felt the tension but held her questions, waiting for them to begin.

"We have told you how the Cristaide planted their ideas in the Ard-Ri's mind, how the flaith accept their stories and their God as superior to other religions of the Island. The Cristaide have weakened the connection of the people to the Land Spirits and the connection of the Ard-Ri to the people. We risk losing our way."

Ethne bowed her head as she listened, and her foreboding grew. Gaine took up the thread of the Ard-Drui's thoughts, "You, child, can be a powerful force in the pattern of these things. We need your assurance that you are loyal to the Gods, the Druid and the Spirits of the Land."

"Do you doubt me? I have done everything you ask, and I have done it with love for the Land and all Druid teachings in my heart!" Ethne sat wide-eyed, her fists clenched in her lap.

"We do not doubt you," Coemgen continued, his voice low and rolling. "We now must ask you to make a difficult offering."

Ethne looked from one to the other, guessing this task would cost her more than her years in the forest, more than her loss of Ruadh.

"The Ard-Ri's king-making will not be complete until he takes a wife. We ask, Ethne, that you be that wife."

Ethne's breath stopped. The wind in the trees stopped, the travel of the Sun across the sky stopped. This request was beyond what her mind could make itself see. She saw instead her hut in the forest, the path to its door, wood stacked under its eaves. She held that still, clear picture a moment and her heart again beat in her chest. The sounds of life came back to her, the scrape of Coemgen's shoes on the stones under their feet.

Ethne turned to him and made herself say, "I know that political marriages are thus arranged. But I do not know why

I have been chosen for this honor. I have no wealth, no land or title."

"Ethne," said Coemgen "you are a priestess, a mediator between the Land, Sea and Sky, between the Spirits and the human beings who walk the earth. You offer the entire Island and beyond."

"Your face shows no joy," added Gaine, "do you foresee trouble with this union?"

"I fear I cannot respect him, though Ard-Ri he may be. I know he was once a great Fennid fighter, but he is now forsworn, an oath-breaker. How can I, who have been trained to revere and uphold the Druid truths be allied to such a one?" Ethne kept her voice even, kept her hands in her lap.

"Things are not always what they seem," responded Coemgen. "The patterns of life are more complex than our human minds can comprehend. Can you rely on your faith, the same faith that sent you to the forest, to believe this union is the answer to the most difficult question the Druid have faced?"

Ethne bowed her head. She was loath to let them see her face. While taking in these words, her thoughts had been of Ruadh. If she remained faithful to him, she betrayed the Druid. If she followed her faith, she abandoned her love. She could not conceive that he was no longer alive, and everything collided within her like a gale wind that ravages the sea cliffs. Tears she could not let fall burned in her eyes and throat. Coemgen's voice rumbled again beside her.

"Ethne, the king has grave need of a consort who is unshakable in her faith. He must be allied with one who holds the health and happiness of the land and of the people above all things. You proved yourself in the forest with inner guidance and strength of character."

"No! It's not so!" Ethne screamed inside her head. "I am not who you believe me to be!" To say the words aloud would condemn her. Worse, to say words of truth would condemn Ruadh. She clenched her teeth.

"The Druid Council respects and admires you. All believe you are most suited to what we ask," Coemgen finished.

They sat in silence, letting the questions and answers unfold, and Ethne let the storm blow and rage, seeking a sheltered place within.

"We will give you time, Ethne," said Gaine at last. "We know what we are asking of you. Stay here, in the peace of the Nemed. Meditate with the fire, scry into the waters.

Ask the sacred Ash for counsel; She will give you wisdom." With these words, Gaine and Coemgen rose, laying their hands on Ethne's head as blessing.

Long after they had gone, Ethne sat, neither praying nor asking for wisdom. She thought only of chamomile blossoms sinking and held in the chilled gel of the siabainn.

# 17

Ethne slept and dreamed of a bird circling the village, of pathways leading to the Nemed gate, of Ruadh. It was a vision dream, its colors bright with figures and objects clearer than waking life. Ruadh came to her with hands outstretched. In each palm burned a flame and another spouted from his head. From the wound in his thigh coursed a yellow liquid. Ethne woke with a start.

"He is coming!" she said aloud to the stone walls. "The fever has taken him again." She drew on her cloak and stumbled outside towards the glow of the central fire, her mind racing. She approached the light and made her way to the Cauldron of Sea. Steadying herself with several deep breaths, she sat before the Cauldron, calming her mind for further vision. The acolyte in charge of the fire withdrew, leaving her alone. Ethne stilled her hands and straightened her back, following the path of her breath and releasing her will. Images would come if she opened her mind to Truth. This time she did not see but *heard* the guidance. A voice from the depths of the Cauldron matched a voice from the depths of her heart. Twined in unison, she heard from within and without: "You and Ruadh are forest-joined. Your union cannot be divided, no matter the path you take."

Ethne put her face in her hands and murmured a prayer of thanks, then stood and stretched, returning to her hut for a bag of vervain and a jar of honey. The sky was clear as she walked to the stone circle to make an offering to the megaliths, and the waning Moon rode high over the village.

The ancient stones gave her comfort. She felt their weight as they pressed into the earth and she drew on them for resolve. Stepping into the circle, Ethne saw faithful Faelchu leaning against a stone and staring across the valley. His hood, like hers, was pulled forward to obscure his features, but he tilted his head and raised his hand in greeting.

"*May the stars find you well*, Ethne."

"And you, Faelchu. Do I disturb your prayers? I come with an offering to the Spirits and for answers."

"You told me these stones belong to everyone. I hope our prayers mingle and lend each other strength. Make your offerings in peace. If you need, I am here to listen." They kept their voices muted, barely above a whisper.

Ethne bowed her head in answer, and then made a circuit of the stones, offering vervain and a kiss to each. Lastly, she placed a small dish of honey at the center, food for the ancestors and nature spirits. When complete, she settled herself cross-legged next to Faelchu and gazed with him over the valley.

They sat in silence, hearing the small scream of a field mouse as an owl snatched it up and watching shadows turn and rise over the hillsides. Faelchu stretched his legs and refolded them and Ethne realized how long they had been sitting, side-by-side matching each other's vigil.

"Faelchu, something weighs on your heart also."

"Yes. I need the clarity and peace these stones offer. But my worries won't end; yours, I sense, have overtaken you. There is anguish when you speak. We have met here for almost a moon cycle. I would hold your confidence an honor."

"Your devotion is evident, Faelchu. Though you are not a Drui, I know you are sincere. I trust you as a man who loves the Gods and cares deeply for the land."

"I am not a Drui as you say, but I *am* Druid trained. I studied the ways of Filidecht. My parents hoped I would be a poet

148

and a seer, because words came to me from the trees, the wind, and the stones in the hills. But I wanted to fight."

"Are you a warrior, then?"

"Yes." He said firmly.

"I suppose I am a warrior too. All my life has been a call to do battle. When I lived alone in the forest, the battle was to survive. When the sick and wounded came to me, the battle was for their lives. But my hardest battle is with myself. My Druid vows demand that my needs and feelings not interfere with the work I am called to do. It is the cruelest battle of all."

"I have known many warriors, and what you say is true. There are those of the sword, mighty in their strength of arm, cunning in their strategies. There are also those who guard our ways with their words and tasks. I have sometimes thought the latter require a greater strength of heart and endurance of spirit because their battles are often unseen and they often battle alone. I think you are in such a struggle now." He reached to her and placed his hand gently on her arm.

Ethne turned towards Faelchu and placed her hand over his. The touch grounded her and gave her courage. "I spent five lonely years in the deep woods. I night-watched over dying men. I told women their children would not live. These are nothing to what I now face."

Faelchu kept his hand on her arm. "Name it. Place it before you like an object."

"You must swear on these holy stones to keep your silence."

"I swear by the sword at my side and by this ancient circle, the Gods be my witness."

Faelchu's cloaked body sat still beside her. She had not yet seen his face, nor he hers, and yet their whispered voices had found each other in the dark as they listened to each other's questions and prayers. If trust was to be found, she found it in his stillness.

"I am asked to marry the king."

Faelchu stiffened and pulled back his hand. "Who asks this?"

"The Ard-Drui Coemgen and the Ard-Ban-Drui Gaine. They ask this to protect the ways of the Island."

Faelchu sat silent, turning over her words. He had offered his help, sworn his trust. He must give her his friendship. "Is this a terrible thing, to marry the king?"

"Yes!" Ethne nearly choked. "The Ard-Ri is an oath breaker. He is forsworn and become Cristaide, deserting the Gods of the Island. How can I join such a man?"

Stunned, Faelchu said nothing. Finally, groping for direction, he ventured, "Perhaps it is not as bad as you say. You cannot know the inner workings of his mind, maybe things are not as they appear?"

Ethne pulled at a blade of grass and gave a derisive laugh. "You are right, I have never met the Ard-Ri and I cannot know his mind. You sound like Coemgen just now."

"Ethne, you are free. Ask for a meeting with the king, converse with him, spend time and determine for yourself what manner of man he is. You may find that you judge him differently."

Ethne pulled at a few more blades of grass, then leaned back, her head thrown back against the stone. "That sounds so reasonable. I could ask the elders to arrange it. But I can't ask for a private meeting, so I don't know how well I will be able to judge him."

"You are a seer and a Drui. You are also a woman. Women have a keen sense of these things. If you spend time in the king's company, even briefly, you will know his heart." Faelchu kept his voice light and reasonable as his mind raced.

"I am free, Faelchu, but not as free as you think. We Druid are sworn to uphold the traditions and religion of the Island. If I *am* called to marry this king to preserve those traditions, it would break my vows to refuse him. But a meeting will tell me with whom I am dealing."

"It will also let him know the measure of you," said Faelchu, a note of laughter in his voice. "The Ard-Ri must have as many questions about you."

150

For the first time, Ethne's smile came through in her words. "You speak like a Drui, more, you speak as a friend. I am grateful for your listening and will count on meeting you here again."

"I assure you, the gratitude is mine." They clasped hands as the first birds of morning began to stir.

In the morning Ethne dressed in rich clothes and ornaments to project her rank. She found Coemgen in the Nemed instructing the acolytes for the Imbolc festival, sacred to the Goddess Brighid. Coemgen rarely got the chance to address the youngest students and he was clearly enjoying the lesson.

"What are the three provinces of the Goddess Brighid?" asked Coemgen.

"Poetry, smithcraft and healing," the children replied, in chorus.

"Who is Brighid's mother?"

"Boann of the cows," said Aífe.

"Correct," said Coemgen, pleased. "White heifers are sacrificed to Her in thanksgiving when the golden bough, the medicine for the wasting disease and for the barren, is gathered from the oak trees. What other animals are associated with the Goddess?"

Daire spoke. "The snake, the white mare, the red eared dog, the cat and the oystercatcher!"

"Why the oystercatcher?"

"Because it is a black, white and red bird."

"Correct again. Black, white and red are the colors of the Goddess in Her three forms: black for the coals of Her forge of creation, white for poetic inspiration, and red for healing and the Fires of life. Whenever you see the oystercatcher know that Brighid is with you, guiding you and lending her support to whatever you do. I have brought threads of three colors for you to wear in remembrance of the Goddess."

Coemgen reached into a willow basket at his side and took out three balls of yarn.

"I want each of you to take a length of black wool, a length of red, and a length of white." He passed the balls of wool sunwise around the circle.

"Twine the threads together so, tie them together with nine knots and make yourself a necklace." Each child did as instructed. "Such a necklace can be bound around a wound or tied around the neck of one who needs healing. When you tie the threads sing a charm like this one:

*May you repel every ill, every ill wish, every evil.*
*As this thread goes round thee may you be well forever.*
*In the name of Brighid, in the name of the Three,*
*in the name of all the powers together.*
*Power of air be with you, power of fire be with you,*
*power of storm be with you.*
*Power of Moon be with you, power of Sun be with you,*
*power of Stars be with you.*
*Power of Sea be with you, power of Earth be with you,*
*power of Stone be with you.*
*I appeal to Brighid, cast off every harm!*

Seeing Ethne waiting in the background, the Ard-Drui ended the morning class.

He rose and clapped his hands. "Now it is time for lunch!"

Ethne watched the children troop off for their midday meal. She swallowed hard and approached Coemgen, arranging her features to appear calm and controlled. She was determined to honor her vows.

"Coemgen, may I speak with you?"

"Of course, Ethne. Have the spirits given you answers, or are you come with more questions?" His voice was gentle as he saw the struggle in her face.

Ethne wet her lips. "I know, teacher, that you and Gaine would never propose a union unless it was necessary. I trust your guidance. I also know my own will is nothing before the wishes of the Druid and the needs of the Land. But I ask first, before the union, if I may meet the king, speak with him, learn what manner of man he is."

Coemgen frowned slightly. "You are a Drui and, therefore free. But you have also pledged yourself in sacred oaths. What do you seek to know of the Ard-Ri?"

Emboldened by Coemgen's opening, Ethne spoke firmly. "I have been taught to trust my inner spirit and to read the strengths and weaknesses of those around me. If I am to embark on a life-long journey with this man, I would use my own skills to determine whether we can travel well together... or not." She tilted her chin up slightly as she ended.

"I am sure this can be arranged. When would you meet him?"

"Now."

Coemgen's eyes crinkled at the corners and he patted her softly on the shoulder. He saw the woman before him as priestess, choosing her time and working her energy to gather the forces she required. "My child, you have the right to your own mind in this. But do not judge the king too harshly. There are matters here that go far beyond what you may understand. He struggles to keep the throne and hold fast the well being of the Island. His heart is steadfast and good, I assure you."

Ethne's eyebrows rose, "Those are promising words. I've rarely heard you bestow such praise."

"Praise is given where it is deserved. Now come and walk in the sun with an old man. We will see if the Ard-Ri has a moment to meet his intended."

Coemgen and Ethne walked arm in arm out of the Nemed and toward the king's rath. The morning's white sky had given way to streaks of bright blue, and the children, let loose from their studies, whooped and called as they raced each other around the inner yard. Across the small expanse they saw Gaine instructing the mogae to inspect and polish the Ard-Ri's plows, harrows and scythes for their re-consecration at the coming Imbolc festival. Coemgen raised his arm in greeting and Gaine joined them.

"Ethne would meet the king. Today." Coemgen waited as Gaine looked quickly from one to the other.

"Today?"

"Now." was all Coemgen's response.

Gaine considered their faces carefully, then slowly nodded. "Yes. Yes, maybe that's wise. Ethne, you use your arts well. Wait here and I will tell him that you would speak with him immediately." Gaine walked swiftly across the yard to the steps of the king's rath. At the bottom step she glanced back at Ethne and nodded again. Then she disappeared into the hall.

Coemgen and Ethne continued their slow walk around the village, but Ethne heard little of Coemgen's comments on the animals in their pens or the women's weavings hanging to dry. Nor did he expect her to. For now, he was merely an old man keeping the company of a very anxious and determined woman. His conversation was meant to cushion her fears not erase them.

As they turned to repeat the pattern of their steps, Gaine reappeared, somewhat out of breath.

"He is waiting." And held her arm up pointing as if Ethne did not know where her future lay.

Upon entering the rath, Ethne was struck by the filtered light and trails of smoke clinging to the rafters. It had been many years since she had been at court and the interior of the building felt cavernous. All eyes were upon her as she made her way up the center of the hall. She wondered what these warriors really knew of her or of the Druid' intentions. She was not used to men watching her, she felt them look her over, taking in her size and shape, and she knew they saw in her a pleasurable and unexpected attraction in the middle of the day.

Coemgen and Gaine led her to a seat outside the great chamber and left her there alone as they cleared curious courtiers and warriors from the room. They wanted as much privacy as possible for this first meeting between the Druid priestess and the Ard-Ri.

Crimthann sat on his carved chair, his back stiff and his palms wet. He shifted and rearranged himself several times, trying to find a position both commanding and welcoming, but soon gave up and sat with his hands on the arms of the chair, his fingers drumming. As Coemgen came near, he whispered tensely, "Are you sure this is what the lady wants? She is not under your orders to do this, is she?"

Coemgen shook his head. "The request came from the lady herself."

"She is not to be forced. I would not have a consort out of obedience to you."

"Crimthann, she is here of her own will. But she is a Ban-Drui, pledged to honor and protect the ways of this Land. If she sees her path as one with yours, she will consent to uphold her vows."

Crimthann pressed his lips into a thin line and nodded, then turned and ordered refreshments from one of the mogae: wine, sweet cakes, dried fruit and an herbal brew.

"Let her enter," he said at last.

The far door opened and Ethne stepped into the inner chamber, her red gown flaming under a six-colored cloak. Her golden torque gleamed against her skin and her braided hair shone richly with intertwined ribbons. Crimthann felt slightly faint as he rose from his seat and made a small bow with his head.

Coemgen spoke first, as was proper. *"May the Gods bless your meeting. May the Ancestors look with favor upon you, and may the Nature Spirits give you sustenance all your days."*

Coemgen and Gaine retreated tactfully to their seats behind the throne.

Crimthann stepped toward Ethne and put out his hand. "You honor this house today, Ethne. I welcome you and bid you share in a small repast."

Ethne's mouth was dry and her hands felt cold. "I thank you for your welcome and am pleased to share your food."

They stepped toward the table. A silence followed while Ethne and Crimthann tore pieces of sweet bread. It could have been winter straw for cattle for all that either tasted it. Crimthann filled her cup and she noticed the tremor of his hand. "He is nervous!" she thought and realized he was concerned for her feelings. She took a breath and studied his features. He was solidly built with a thick head of long yellow hair, his beard salted slightly with gray. He wasn't the arrogant man she had imagined. She took the cup from him and looked directly into his eyes.

"The color of larkspur," she breathed.

"Excuse me?" Crimthann turned red in confusion. He had expected to be impressed by this woman's determination to do what was asked of her, he had not foreseen that she would turn his world on end by the spirit in her face. She was a queen whether she held the name or not. No one could doubt her noble intentions or her royal rank. She would be respected and admired wherever she went.

"Blue," said Ethne, pointing at the blue dye in the pottery. "Blue is for optimism. These days require that we look for hope in unlikely places." Ethne's thoughts were colliding. This was not the meeting she had envisioned.

"Do you think hope so scarce we must search for it at the bottom of tea cups?" Crimthann asked, intrigued.

"No. Well, yes. I mean so much is changing and I hear the fears of the villagers."

"You are worried, aren't you, that my conversion to the Cristaidi God will bring ruin to the ways of the Island." Crimthann put down his cup, and faced her.

A deep flush spread over Ethne's neck and face. "My lord, Crimthann, as a follower of the Gods of this Island, I cannot imagine being intimate with one who is forsworn." She did not look away from him.

"You have every right to question me. I am Ard-Ri, yes, but I am the servant of the people and the steward of this Island. I will *never* cease being loyal to the Gods of this Land." He spoke the words in a low rich voice full of pride.

Ethne startled. His voice shook something within her. "Your people do not think so. Everyone believes the Abbot Germanus guides you. Haven't you renounced the Horse Sacrifice, our ritual of a thousand years?"

"I will not lie, Ethne. There are forces in this land which are troubling, and I fear the direction in which we will be pushed. Canoc's was the only kingdom to pay tribute this year. He has become Cristaide and threatens to withhold his cattle and gold unless I concede to the Abbot. I can't pay my warriors nor maintain this household without Canoc's payment. For the good of the kingdom I compromised. But I am no oath breaker."

Ethne frowned. "Those are logical words. But they ring like one one who seeks dignity while conniving to betray the people."

Crimthann flushed red at her accusation and he looked hard at her. Then, just as suddenly his features softened and a small fire lit his eyes. "Ethne," he said so that only she could hear. His whisper caught her and her head came up so her eyes met his. "Do you see these cakes before you? Take another bite."

Confused, Ethne was nevertheless transfixed by the sound of Crimthann's whisper. She lifted a cake to her mouth and bit, letting the crumbs slowly dissolve on her tongue.

"These cakes are made with a spice from the Orient, the bark of the cinnamon tree. The spice is rare and costly, and they are only made on my orders for very special occasions."

Ethne's heart began to race, "Cakes like these are good enough to leave as offerings for the Moon Goddess," she ventured.

He searched her face and smiled. "Good enough for a Moon Goddess and a Drui priestess."

"Faelchu!" she breathed.

"My lady of the midnight stones." Crimthann gave her a deep bow and began to laugh. Ethne, unbelieving, took his hand and closed her eyes. She felt his steady pulse and the trust he gave so freely. She knew him as the friend she had found in her dark grief. She opened her eyes and laughter bubbled out of her like water from a spring.

Mystified, Coemgen and Gaine came to see what had so changed this visit. But in answer to their questions, all Crimthann would say was, "The lady and I share a common love for sweet cakes."

At the king's request, they left the hall, still wondering what had transpired between Ethne and the Ard-Ri. For their part, Crimthann and Ethne spent the rest of the afternoon in a windowed alcove, drinking mead and comparing their early lives. He told her of his early days as a Drui scholar and poet, of his exploits with the Fiana and of his hopes for the Island. She told him of her upbringing in Coemgen's care, of her first years in the forest house and of her knowledge of the royal families, knowledge she had won by healing their sons and daughters over the years. She answered everything about herself but the deepest secret of her heart.

# 18

———

Erc and Buan lifted Ruadh onto a cart filled with straw as Ruadh's horse stamped and waited to pull the cart along the track to the Ard-Ri's dun. Ruadh's arms and legs were secured to the rails to prevent him from hurting himself or falling off the cart. His delirium was constant now, his skin so hot he tore at it as if to rid himself of clothes. Miadach sat with him in the cart, swabbing his face and arms with cool water. Erc and Buan walked before the cart, leading the horse.

On the third day of their travel, they reached the dun of the Ard-Ri, and Ruadh was near death. Miadach wept, moaning and praying to Brighid as she covered him with blankets. She only untied the cloth straps when she saw he was too weak to struggle.

Buan ran ahead to alert the gatekeepers and ask for help, calling "A healer! We have need of a healer!" A gatekeeper came forward and asked who lay in the cart. "A Fennid is wounded, nearly dead. Direct us to a healer so he may be tended," cried Buan.

The guards opened the gate and sent a runner to the Nemed to find a Drui skilled in herbcraft. Ethne was within the Nemed garden, teaching the children how to purify a charm stone for healing. The children had been given an egg-shaped crystal a Moon before and had buried it for one Moon cycle.

"Now that your stone has been cleansed by earth, it is time to charge it in a tree. Dig up your stone and leave it in the hollow of the apple tree for another Moon. After that, we will charge it under the Sun and Full Moon. Then it will be ready to use." The children dug furiously with their sharp sticks.

"How will we use it?" asked Daire, the Ard-Ri's son.

Ethne now thought of herself as the boy's stepmother. Though her marriage to the king was months away, she took a special interest in his questions and found that he was bright and unassuming, much like his father.

"Once the stone is prepared we can use it several ways. It can be dipped in water to be given to those who are sick. Dry, it becomes an oath-stone to swear upon. As you grow older you will take many oaths and your stone will remind you of your duty and honor."

"Someone is coming!" exclaimed Aife, pointing towards a runner fast approaching.

"My lady, we need a healer. The Fennidi have brought one of their men. He appears near death." The runner spoke between gulps of air.

"Bring him to the sick house outside the Nemed and I will tend him," said Ethne.

Leaving an older acolyte in charge of the children, Ethne walked briskly to the storehouse for bandages, needle and thread, healing herbs and a jug of the Waters of Life. Her movements were swift, her mind moving ahead to what she might find. As she ran toward the sick house she saw figures around a cart and recognized with dread the broad shoulders of Erc, and Buan's lithe grace. She knew who lay on the straw.

Ruadh's face was pasty white. His hair hung in clumps against his clammy skin, his eyes barely open. A moan escaped his lips as they laid him on the pallet in the sick house. Ethne betrayed none of her feelings, but the sight of him again so near death froze her heart. "Bring peat and kindling," she ordered the guards outside. "Prepare the sweat house." Then she focused on Miadach and saw her tear streaked face and anxious eyes.

"Have you looked after him?" Ethne asked Miadach gently. When Miadach nodded, Ethne urged her, "Tell me what happened. Was he wounded in battle?"

Miadach responded to Ethne's kind eyes, swallowing her grief to answer, "We do not know what happened. He was wounded by a Man of the North, it was only a slight cut. But Ruadh was like a wild man, out of control. We thought the blade was poisoned."

Ethne's dream came back to her: yellow liquid coursing from an old wound. "Tell me," she urged, "was he wounded in the leg?"

"Yes. You can see where I stitched up the cut and purified it with the Waters of Life. There is no rot."

Ethne took a small dirk from her basket and cut open his trouser. The wound was clean and well stitched. Probing the skin, she found no trace of the walnut-sized lump.

Placing her hands on Ruadh's thigh, she went into a trance, asking her Imbas to give her an answer. As her mind settled she saw wavering images and then one became clear. She saw Ruadh's body as if transparent, but infused with a yellow blood that gave off steam.

She took three clarifying breaths and opened her eyes. "His blood is poisoned. A knot from the old wound has burst, filling his body with rot."

Miadach, Erc and Buan looked to her with gratitude. Only a Druid of exceptional skill could have named Ruadh's sickness.

"Carry him to the sweat house," said Ethne in a firm, quiet voice.

They wrapped him in woolen blankets and bundled him to the Tech ind Allais. Ethne instructed the mogae to prepare a strong bath of vervain, yew, figwort and comfrey, and told them to place the bath next to the sweat house. First the heat would open his pores and let the poison run freely then the cool waters would soothe the fever.

Ethne felt sobs rising as she looked on Ruadh. She fought her grief and rage as she moved about and talked to distract herself. "Yew is the herb of Immortality and Regeneration," she said aloud as the mogae stoked the peat fire within the sweat house. She saw Erc, Buan and Miadach look to one another and continued. "Have you noticed how an ancient Yew will send up shoots before she dies? She lives forever, constantly regenerating herself over the ages. We plant her in graveyards and use her in baths to bring the sick back from the gates of the Otherworld."

"We are privileged to hear your words, lady," said Buan quietly.

Miadach stood again at Ruadh's side, placing cool compresses on his forehead while they waited for the peat fires to glow. A curl of jealousy coiled in Ethne's belly as she watched Miadach, but she smiled in encouragement when Miadach looked to her.

Ethne knew she owed Miadach much for tending Ruadh, yet a small inner voice asked if Ruadh would look to Miadach if he recovered. Ethne stared fixedly on Ruadh's closed face and put all her energy into healing his body.

# 19

Gaine gathered the girls of the rath and village around her, in preparation for the Imbolc procession.

"You girls will carry this straw image of the Goddess from house to house, bringing the blessings of Brighid to every door," she explained. "The face of Brighid is hard after Winter Solstice when She wears the hag face of the Cailleach. When She shows this face the winds are bitter and the plants die. But on the eve of Imbolc, the sheep give milk again, and She transforms herself into a young maiden. Right now She is walking across the land, spreading Her green mantle and breathing warmth into the hills. Notice how the ice is melting and the sun feels warm at your backs?"

The girls nodded. The weather had thawed as it always did for the Brighid Festival.

"Imbolc is when the snake comes out of her hole and sheds her skin. This shedding symbolizes the renewal of the Earth Goddess, for She brings forth the new green every year. This is why we say: *"Brighid puts Her finger in the icy water and takes the venom out of it."* Snakes are sacred to Brighid and must be shown all honor."

The girls moved in a solemn line, their white frocks glowing in the soft morning air. Father Per stood with the other villagers, smiling at the simple beauty of the spring ritual. He had baked soft honey breads for the girls' feast and offered them to the women, saying, " *He broke bread with those he cherished.*" They knew it was Father Per's blessing on their daughters and they accepted the breads with both hands. Germanus stood watching too. He saw the breads change hands and the easy talk between Per and the villagers.

The girls, dressed in white gowns, walked solemnly. For the youngest it was a great honor bestowed on them, to be in the parade of the milk festival. The greatest thrill would be stopping at the hall of the Ard-Ri. Crimthann had ordered that a milk feast be prepared in honor of the girls. Golden egg puddings and curds sweetened with rose water lay on the High Table, along with beakers of foaming, fresh milk and soft, white breads.

Reaching the king's rath the girls circled it three times, bearing the basket with its straw effigy of the Goddess. The older girls carried white candles, symbolic of the Fire of Life that was re-kindled in the herds and in the soil. Finally, the girls lined up in front of the Ard-Ri's door and asked to be let in. The guards admitted them with a deep bow, holding back their smiles until all the young ladies were inside.

As the girls approached, Crimthann, the warriors and his councilors stood at attention as they would for honored dignitaries. Mis, the eldest of the girls and their designated leader, walked at the head of the line. She approached the king with dignity, bearing snow drops, a flower sacred to the Goddess.

"My Lord Crimthann, we present you this token of Spring. *We ask that Brighid bless this household; all herein, their kindred and their substance.*" She handed the flowers to Crimthann with a curtsy.

"Do not curtsy, young maid. You personify the Goddess and the Land. You honor *us* by your presence. Please be seated and accept our repast."

The girls sat, each with a warrior or a Drui behind her, like a great lady of the realm. After their meal with the Ard-Ri, the girls walked to the forge to bless the fire and tools of the blacksmith. Their fathers blessed the plows by pouring The Waters Of Life over them for the first ground breaking next morning.

Gaine then took the girls to a house outside the gates where musicians and a storyteller entertained them until dawn. After the parade the boys of the dun sulked a bit, not liking to be left out of the merriment. More than one got his ears boxed for teasing his sister until a few warriors were enlisted to occupy the boys with fencing practice.

Upon the low hill overlooking the dun, Father Per retired to say his Vespers. He had expected to say them alone.

"You are too familiar with these people." Germanus leaned on his staff and looked solemnly down at Father Per. When he got no answer, he went on. "It is one thing to share a bit of food with the children and to weave Scripture into the tales you tell them around your fire. I would never say against that. But baking bread for their rituals is heresy!"

Father Per let out a breath and brought his gaze up to look directly into the Abbot's eyes. He saw a touch of anger there, but what he mostly saw was a doubt, a kind of fear at something the older man did not understand.

"Did the Lord not give loaves of bread to the people?"

The question sounded rhetorical, but Germanus heard it as a clever dodge. He squinted his eyes and pointed a strong finger. "The maiden's feast of Imbolc is a Pagan rite. The Church of Rome forbids any participation by its clergy. I will not be disobeyed in this." He clamped his hand heavily on Father Per's shoulder then walked away, his staff punctuating the scuff of his footfalls on the road.

Per resumed his prayers, including the Abbot as one who needed them most.

Ethne and Crimthann also retired after the festival. "I've been thinking about the children," Crimthann confided to Ethne as they sat sharing a meal. "What will become of them after we are gone? Are we right to teach them only Druid ways?"

"You have a son, Crimthann. Don't you want him to be what he loves in you? What would you have him learn besides the teachings of the elders?"

"The world is changing. I am not certain the clann teachings are enough. Germanus tells me how children are taught in the South lands. Our children need to understand those ways, perhaps they fit the children of today better." Crimthann let out a long sigh and looked at Ethne, a question in his eyes.

Ethne had hoped for light conversation, a friendly dinner from which she could absent most of her cares. She needed time to gather the wild longings that had risen since Ruadh's return. She picked distractedly at the salmon that Crimthann had ordered. It had been spitted on a green stick and roasted slowly over the fire coals. A queen's meal.

"Are you unwell?" asked Crimthann, watching as her fingers pulled the slender bones from the flesh only to leave the pink meat scattered before her.

"No, I'm sorry and do not mean to ignore your efforts to please me," she answered.

"Then tell me what is filling your mind. I would have you share all your troubles no matter how small."

"It is a healing matter. A man, gravely ill was brought to the dun. I have been attending to him."

"Yes, I have had news of him. But why must you attend to him, surely there are others who can do the work?"

"I was first to answer his need when they brought him, so I have continued to watch his progress." Ethne sensed that Crimthann was not certain of her answer so she added, "there are others to see to him, but I can learn from his strange illness."

Ruadh had been sweated and bathed in yew and put to bed, wrapped in blankets and sheepskins. The danger was that having been unable to eat for days he would grow weaker from the sweating. Miadach was at his side, forcing liquids into him whenever he roused enough to swallow. Ethne made a bitter drink of vervain to purify his blood, which Miadach spooned into his mouth. Ethne thought of the mulled elderberries and the chicken stock she had told Miadach to feed him if he showed any hunger. There was nothing more she could do, but her thoughts and heart stayed beside Ruadh. She dragged her attention back to listen as Crimthann turned the conversation to its start.

"I hardly see my son. He is occupied with his studies at the Nemed, as it should be. But he does not learn of the world beyond."

"Perhaps the world beyond does not suit the life of *this* land, Crimthann. What would you have him know? What do you lack from your Druid learning?"

"That leaders and clanns can order their people and lands differently. For example," he went on seeing the skeptical look in her eyes, "in the Gaulish lands, daughters are taught to obey their fathers' wishes and stay by their elders until they are wed. They do not roam with warriors or learn politics or law. They are the caretakers of the home, the children and the elders. That would be a great comfort in one's old age. Would it not?"

"Crimthann!" Ethne blurted, "Don't you want your daughters to have an education like Daire's? Do you want docile daughters who cannot think for themselves? You have listened over much to Germanus and his Cristaidi notions of women."

"Of course I admire educated women. You are the life of this Island and have woven your strengths into the blood of our sons. But a daughter or a wife who stayed at home, singing to me in my old age, listening to my stories, I would cherish her."

Ethne was now thoroughly distracted from Ruadh's sick room and the salmon before her. "Crimthann, such a girl would be unsuited to face life. Can't you see that Germanus is pulling apart the very fabric of what makes our Island and its people strong?"

Crimthann chuckled and helped himself to a second portion of roasted salmon. "I see why Coemgen and Gaine think you are a match for me. You oppose the Abbot's views on nearly every subject."

Ethne did not like this turn in the conversation. Her stomach clenched. It was very clear what kind of ally Crimthann needed to unravel what Germanus daily presented to him.

Crimthann was a good man with good intentions, but he was too willing to consider Cristaidi ideas, too ready to adopt their philosophy. She had hoped he would be more adamant in protecting their own ways. She heard his desire to appease the powerful newcomers. Her heart ached.

Crimthann reached for Ethne's hand, but she drew it out of his reach.

"The Abbot Germanus does not understand that docile women would leave this Island undefended," Ethne said coldly. "Docile women are no better than sheep." She put her hands in her lap and stared fixedly at the table.

"Forgive me, Ethne. I did not mean to anger you, but to let you into my thoughts. I am sorry I upset you during our supper. It's not fitting that we argue before we are even married."

"I also mean no rudeness." Ethne answered. She longed to be out of the king's chamber. She had no patience to argue religion, policy or child rearing.

"We need air," offered Crimthann. "Shall we walk to the Bíle? We can stroll together through the gate now, for we are openly betrothed."

"I am weary, Crimthann. Forgive me; it would be best if I returned to my hut in the Nemed."

"I will escort you." Crimthann stood to accompany her out of the hall.

"I prefer to walk alone. I have little chance to be by myself, and after years in the forest, I crave the reflection a solitary walk can bring. Do you understand?"

"I understand how rare one's own company is. One day I will visit this forest house of yours. Hearing you speak of it brings a vision of peace."

"It is like no other place I know. A part of my heart will always dwell there."

"Go then and rest, and the Gods protect you, my sweet."

"And you, my Lord."

Crimthann helped her put on her cloak and fasten her golden broach. He kissed her gently on her forehead, and she slipped quietly out of his hand.

Albinus strode into the king's hall, smudged cape flapping behind him like the wings of an untidy goose, and battle crow clinging to his collar. He pushed past others waiting for an audience. "Crimthann, a word!" he boomed from the back of the hall.

The Ard-Drui Coemgen stood behind the king, ready to advise on the law and record in his memory the kingdom's petitions and decrees. He moved as close to the king as possible, to mitigate any influence the abbot might exert. "Crimthann, tell him to wait his turn with the others. He has no privileges here," whispered Coemgen.

"I demand to speak with you in private!" declared Albinus, from the back of the hall.

Crimthann held up his hand to silence a pair of beekeepers pleading their case before him. A colony of bees from one farmstead had swarmed and taken up residence at another. Both farmers now laid claim to them.

"Albinus, take your place at the back of the line with everyone else. You are welcome here, but everyone has pressing concerns."

"My Lord, this matter is *most* urgent! It concerns the woman chosen to be Rígain!"

Crimthann scowled. "If you have something to say about the Lady Ethne, say it when it is your turn."

Crimthann turned his attention back to the beekeepers with deliberation.

Albinus persisted. "She sleeps every night in the House of Healing with a Fiana warrior. That woman is immodest and unseemly!"

Crimthann rose from his seat. His voice was low and deadly. "Speak no more! She night watches because she is a skilled healer. The man was brought here near death."

"You are a fool, Crimthann! She will outwit you and *ruin* you."

Crimthann instinctively reached for his sword, his face a deep red though his expression remained unchanged. "Guards! Accompany the intruder to the gates of the rath. He has brought his message and I have other business."

"Hear me . . !" Albinus began as guards lifted him by either arm and ushered him away.

# 20

━━━━

Ethne slept nightly in the House of Healing, enduring sleepless hours, all her being trained on Ruadh and the shallow path of his breathing. To explain her actions, she named herself Anam Chara, his guide through sickness and even to the gates of death if that were his fate.

She would not bring shame on Crimthann, herself or her Druid teachers, but she could not abandon Ruadh, not after losing him once. As the future Rígain, her movements were watched by everyone. She conducted herself in a manner beyond reproach, but she yearned to cradle Ruadh in her arms, kiss his burning forehead and whisper prayers of love into his fevered thoughts.

Miadach, who slept curled on a straw mattress at Ruadh's feet, brought a bowl of cool water to bathe his face and chest. As she did so, she crooned words of comfort and kissed him gently on the cheek. Ethne stood rigid as Miadach whispered, "Do not leave me, my love. Return so we may roam the Island's shores once more."

"He will heal more readily if you say prayers for the sick while you bathe him," Ethne said more sharply than she intended. When she saw the stricken look on Miadach's face, Ethne softened. "Here, let us tend him together."

She sprinkled fresh herbs into water, lit candles and called in the Spirits of healing. With slow caresses, she rubbed Ruadh's arms, legs, chest and back to keep energy moving throughout his body. Miadach followed her lead, wondering at the devotion Ethne showed. She noticed how Ethne stared at him with lips moving in silent invocation.

Ethne left the hut to gather more herbs from the store-room and Miadach sat again on the floor next to Ruadh, holding his hand. She had just begun to drowse when he suddenly called out.

"Ethne! Where is Ethne?"

"Be easy, my love. Miadach is here. You are safe."

"Ah, Miadach. Tell me of Ethne."

She answered his confused questions until he slept again, she would not let him see the hurt she felt. "Of course he asks for Ethne," she assured herself, "she is a skilled healer and in that knowledge he finds comfort." When Ethne returned, however, Miadach did not tell her of Ruadh's waking.

"Miadach," said Ethne, considering the young woman with her head bowed over the pallet, "get some fresh air or you too will be under my care. Walk through the village or onto the hills. Take in the sky and the greening trees and bring their life-giving spirits back to Ruadh." Miadach stood and reluctantly left the hut.

Alone with Ruadh, Ethne lifted his head in her arms and rocked him gently. "You are my forest love, my trees, my air, my wild silence. You and I are twinned trees, with our roots, our branches dancing together in the wind. I am yours freely, and the love I give you is as constant as the waters of the stream near the forest house, flowing ever from the well of my heart. With you I am my own as well as yours and we are free to grow stronger towards one another. Please, dearest love, do not travel without me to the Otherworld. I could not bear the loneliness of my life."

She was weeping, her hair and tears mingling as she held him to her, when she heard steps outside the hut. She lay him back on the cot, smoothed her hair and wiped her face.

Crimthann appeared in the doorway, squinting to adjust to the dim interior.

"I have come to look on this Fennid under your care."

He stepped further into the room. He saw that Ethne had been alone with the man and he saw her eyes swollen and red. Doubt thrilled about his heart.

"You make yourself ill caring for him day and night," he said, trying to sound merely concerned. "This night watching is bad for your own health. Come away, Ethne.

You have duties elsewhere and we must prepare for the king-making rites."

Crimthann watched her closely as she wrung out a cloth and rearranged the simples on the oak chest. She looked thinner and her hair disheveled. Ethne looked at Crimthann, and saw Miadach standing behind him in the doorway.

"Ah, there you are! I must leave with the king. Please change his linens and give him the elderberry brew." Ethne's voice sounded false even to her own ears. She went to Crimthann and took his hand. "Walk me to my hut, Lord. I have overstayed my care."

The following day, Crimthann sent a runner to Ethne with a formal invitation to dine at court. Crimthann invited Gaine and Coemgen to be there also, to ensure that Ethne could not refuse. When Ethne made her entrance there were deep gray circles under her eyes and creases across her brow. Gaine saw the signs of worry and wondered.

When she commented to Coemgen, he dismissed them as anxiety over her coming marriage combined with the duties of healing.

"Once she is Rígain, she will let others assume duties over the sick. It is natural for her to be uneasy before this union." Gaine was unconvinced, but said nothing.

The four gathered and ate roasted pheasant, buttered turnips and fion. When they were nearly done, Coemgen spoke to all four saying, "The king-making rites have three primary components. Ethne, you, of course, embody the Land Goddess and will on the first night sleep with Crimthann's sword. It is being forged even now. On the next night you will sleep with Crimthann after you have both bathed in the holy well outside the gates. I have commissioned a golden cup from which you both shall drink when you arise the following morning. You will drink from this cup again when you take communion at the church."

"What do you mean by 'communion,' Coemgen?" The official rites pressed on Ethne like a stone rolled over the top of a well.

"Communion is the most solemn part of the Cristaidi ceremony. It involves drinking from a chalice so that the Cristaidi God can enter your body."

"I do not want the Cristaidi God to enter my body!" Ethne's voice was sharp. She did not meet Coemgen's eyes for fear her anger would spill over. She did not want to hear his voice. She did not want to hear anyone's voice, but Coemgen continued.

"Their God is but one of many, Ethne. Think of it as an honor to Him and a way to keep the Abbot and Canoc happy. We are dependent on their gold and cattle. It is a small gesture to keep peace in the kingdom."

"Can you not think beyond gold and cattle? I had thought you, Coemgen, would look past these difficult days and keep the Island's Gods before you. It is communion with our own Spirits of the water, the rocks, the wind, and the growing crops we need."

Ethne's throat felt raw.

"I have not forgotten, child. But Canoc makes threats we cannot ignore. Germanus goads him and we'd best avoid conflict if we can." Coemgen turned to Crimthann. "You will prepare yourself by three days of purification in the wilderness. You will fast on water and hazel nuts, to build your store of Imbas, the poetic inspiration you will need to face the problems of state. You will be asked three questions by a Druidess. After you answer correctly, she will take you to your marriage bed with Ethne."

Crimthann listened studiously. "If I do not answer correctly?"

Gaine smiled, "Don't worry, Crimthann. We will coach you. The most important answer is your willingness to guide your people. We will begin the rite at the new Moon closest to Beltaine. It is fitting to begin a new reign at the start of summer when all the earth is celebrating with flowers." No one disagreed.

For weeks Ruadh slipped in and out of consciousness. Faces and fragments of faces loomed before him, then disappeared into a mist. Erc, his parents, Ethne, Miadach all swam before him, trying to tell him things. Sometimes he strained to hear, other times he did not care. At times he was sure someone was really there, but mostly the faces wavered and flickered.

Then everything he saw was bathed in red. He was in a river of red, red wounds flowing, red salmon leaping from red pools, red spotted mushrooms hiding under dark logs. Red as the ruadán berries from the Faery Tree. Red as a deep sunset or the rise of the blood Moon. Red as the thread used to bind luck into an amulet of power. Red as the first blush of sunrise, red as the roses in his mother's garden, as the buds on the trees in early spring. Red as fion, hot and sweet in the cup.

Ethne bound red threads around his arms, legs and neck, in invocation of Brighid the Fire Goddess. Miadach forced red elderberry brew into him to fortify his blood. Ruadh lay on red blankets, at Ethne's insistence, the color of life. "He is in the Goddess's hands now," Ethne sighed as she unfolded a clean blanket over him.

On a late morning when the sun had finally fought its way through a mass of bruised clouds, Ruadh opened his eyes.

"I am In Ruad, the Red One."

Miadach fumbled with the ewer she was holding and stared. "Ruadh!" She rushed to his side and knelt. "Ruadh. What are you saying?" She searched his eyes and face. He was gaunt, thin beyond belief and his eyes were hollow, but there was no wildness, no sign of a mind lost in the flames of fever. Miadach looked around, but Ethne was being fitted for her coronation gown.

"I am the Red One, In Ruad," Ruadh repeated.

"In Ruad? You are Ruadh, my love, come back to me!" Miadach brushed his matted hair back from his forehead then brought a cup of clear water. "Take a sip. Steady yourself." She knelt again and held the cup to his lips.

He drank greedily, gulping the water as if he had trudged across dry lands.

Miadach took the cup and wiped his face with a wet cloth.

"Ruadh, do you know me?" she asked.

He looked at her so long she was certain his mind had been burned by the fever.

"Miadach, I would know you and the touch of your hand in the darkest forest. Have you been here with me since the struggle on the beach?" He reached out and touched her cheek.

Tears started down her face and she nodded. " I thought you were lost to me! You lay here burning for so many, many days."

"Miadach, dear friend, I must tell Ethne. Is she close?"

Miadach blinked, her tears abruptly halted. "Ethne? Yes, she will be back momentarily. But tell *me* Ruadh. I would share your journey."

He put his hand again against her face. "Miadach, I must share this with Ethne. She will understand." He let his hand drop and closed his eyes, exhaustion overcoming him. He slept again and Miadach sat by, silently. She had heard in his words a farewell.

When Ethne returned, ducking into the hut as she turned aside the leather door, she sensed a change. She dropped the armful of wood she carried by the hearth and faced Ruadh and Miadach. "His breathing has slowed and deepened!"

At the sound of her voice, Ruadh opened his eyes and turned his head. "Ethne," he breathed.

In one movement she was at his side, tears coursing down her face onto his. "Ruadh! Oh, my love. The Goddess has answered my prayers. You were lost to me, wandering where I could not find you. I dared not hope. Oh Ruadh, I was so frightened!" She held his hand and laid her head against his chest, letting the tears fall, wild with delight at the sound of his chest rising and falling beneath her.

"Ethne, please listen before I sleep again. I am so very tired."

"Yes, Ruadh. Tell me, I am here."

"The Gods gave me a vision and a new name. I am In Ruad."

"The Red One? The color of life!"

"I have been to the shores of death and back. My life is new."

Ethne's tears came again in gratitude, for the Gods showed her he would not die. "Rest now, love. I will sit beside you while you sleep. Close your eyes with no fear. You are safe here with me."

Ruadh smiled and touched her hair, her chin, her hand, then closed his eyes and drifted to sleep. Ethne pulled the blanket over his chest and sank back beside him. As she pulled a damp strand of hair off her face and hooked it around her ear, she looked up and locked eyes with Miadach.

"You are lovers."

Ethne saw the grief and loss in the young woman's eyes. She saw the strain of willing Ruadh not to die. She nodded, giving Miadach the honesty she deserved. "We did not mean it to be, but it is so."

Miadach looked down at Ruadh's sleeping face, his ashen skin, his hands weak and limp on the blanket. She looked back at Ethne and saw it was no use.

"Ruadh never once allowed me into his bed since he returned from the Forest House. He was ever friendly, but he turned aside every advance I made." She bowed her head as tears came.

"Miadach . . ." Ethne began, but she could not find the words.

Miadach raised her head. "You needn't comfort me. I should have recognized the signs. Your love for him is in every spoonful of soup you give him, in every fold of these blankets. I saw but I did not want to see."

"Miadach," Ethne began again. "Your love is easy to see too. I am grateful you are here to care for him, to help call him back from the Otherworld. My prayers, my voice alone could not have brought him back. He needs your friendship as well as mine." They sat on either side of the cot.

"Miadach, our love is dangerous. It cannot be. I am to be Rígain." Her eyes were bleak.

"You and Ruadh found each other in the freedom of the Forest, no one can take that away. Do not fear for your secret. I love Ruadh, but I honor and respect him, as I do you. I would not see harm come to either of you. I have no love for the Abbot or his ways. But I would ask that you do not bring Ruadh to disgrace."

Ethne rose to put her arms around Miadach and they held each other, holding each other's grief and love as they had shared the fears and labors of the sick room. Finally, Ethne put Miadach at arm's length and looked into her eyes.

"I would send him back to the Fian, back to you, back to his clann before I would see him stripped of his honor. He is more than my love, he is a warrior for our people. I cannot keep him for myself and I must follow my own duty to protect the Island." She kissed Miadach on the forehead.

"I will give you a moments of privacy, lady." Miadach left the hut.

Ethne offered a silent prayer of thanks and protection for Miadach as she gently shook Ruadh awake.

"Ruadh, we have only a little time. I must tell you something."

Ruadh came out of his sleep with a sigh and turned to look at her. "What is it, Ethne? What must you tell me?"

"Oh Ruadh, my heart aches to say it. I am to marry Crimthann. I am to be the Rígain of the Ard-Rí."

Ruadh lay still, his eyes roving her face. Then he looked at the candles flickering against the far wall.

"You have always been a Rígain, Ethne. This will change nothing."

"But I will be wed in the Cristaidi church!"

"Is that the Druid strategy? Is Crimthann such a weak man?"

"He is a good man, Ruadh, but Canoc is powerful and has allied himself with the Abbot. The harvests have been bad and Crimthann needs Canoc's tribute this year. He has no choice.

I was chosen as Rígain to keep Druid ways alive in the king's hall. To persuade him not to abandon the people and the Land in the face of Canoc's strength and wealth." " Then there can be nothing more between us. I will return to the Fian when I am strong."

A shard of ice went through her, but she said nothing. Neither knew the words to open a way.

"You won't be well for many, many weeks," Ethne ventured.

"I can ride again in the back of the cart."

"If you think that's best . . ."

"Best? Best is to stay with you, protect you, serve you. But you know it's impossible. How long could we avoid each other's eyes, pretend we are only queen and warrior? We both love truth. Lies and pretense would poison our love. We must be who we are: Ethne and Ruadh of the Forest." He reached for her and she bent and kissed him slowly, their hands clasped tightly.

"One thing," he whispered, "I would have you promise me."

"Anything, love. Ask me."

"Will you handfast with me in the Stone Circle in the ancient way? Will you be my Goddess and my Lady for all my days and beyond?"

Ethne looked into his eyes and saw the partner of her soul, the joy of her heart.

"Yes, Ruadh, I will handfast with you under the stars, you and me alone." The words took the clouds from her sky, the fear from her heart. She pressed her mouth again on his and he held her face in his hands. Suddenly she sat up.

"Ruadh, I have heard of great chiefs having more than one wife, but never of a woman to have more than one husband! Are we blaspheming the Gods?"

"You are the Drui priestess, Ethne. Search your heart and tell me if you find it wrong to serve your people and honor your love at the same time?" he smiled.

Miadach coughed politely in the doorway, bringing a tray from the kitchens and fresh candles from the storehouse. Ethne stood, smiled at Ruadh as she put on her cape.

"Thank you," she said softly to Miadach.

"May the Gods go with you both," was her reply.

# 21

A vessel of the Men of the North was harassing the coast-al settlements. One of the largest ever seen, it's belly dis-gorged no less than thirty fighting men when it stopped along the shore. Equipped with strong blades, bows, and double axes, the raiders landed five times in six days.

The leader of the crew, Gorm hinn Svarta, was a wily and capable commander.

"No man celebrates immediately after a raid. I apportion no beer until every warrior is back on deck" was his command.

The pickings had been easy and fast. Terrified villagers gave up their goods with little resistance, the few who made a stand were quickly slain, their flayed bodies left in town squares and holy places as a warning.

Gorm hinn Svarta knew of the Fennidi patrolling the beach-es. Day and night he posted watchers to look for movement amongst the trees, and he kept his ship beyond arrow's reach.

A messenger rode to the Ard-Ri's rath to sound the alarm, but it would take three days yet for the king's army to reach the coast. Another messenger rode to the Fennidi cave.

"They are a giant bull and we are gadflies," said Buan when she caught a glimpse of the enormous vessel.

"A bull may be large and strong, but we're lighter of foot and have our wits," said Erc, grimly.

A meeting convened to determine a plan. A collection of arms stood stacked against a wall. Every weapon was shiny and clean and in superb working order, Erc had seen to that. The pig still rooted in its makeshift enclosure, it had not been slaughtered because no had found the time to build a smoke house for curing.

Erc spoke. "This raiding band does not behave like the others. They avoid the beaches. But they will have to come ashore soon to take on water."

"I know of a way to trick them, if you're all willing to give up your rations of bacon and ham," said Fidach.

"Enlighten us, friend" said Erc.

"What if we put deadly nightshade, henbane, thornapple and wolf's bane into a sausage and feed it to the pig? The pig will feel nothing until the poison is digested.

Then we can let it loose near the Men of the North when they came ashore for water.

They will kill it and eat it. For men long at sea it will be a treasure."

Buan clapped her hands and laughed. The Fennidi were famous for such tactics. It was why they were tested for intelligence and strength when admitted to the Fian. It would make a fine tale to tell other bands next winter. The plan was irresistible.

"How do we smuggle the pig as we follow the raiders and still have it stay quiet?" asked Buan.

"Tie a cloth around its snout and feet and carry it on a litter. We can untie it once a day to drink and eat." replied Erc.

The following morning the band left at first light, heading South, towards the ship. The pig slowed them considerably, especially when they had to negotiate rocky places or areas tight with trees.

"We'll be legends!" declared Ragnall with a grin.

After two days of hard marching, they spotted the ship. Gorm hinn Svarta had chosen a deserted stretch of coastline to bring the raider's ship close to shore, to take on water. They untied the pig except for a leather belt around her neck with two stout ropes attached. They fed the sausage to the pig mixed with apples and carrots, which she ate greedily. Then they put the cloth around her snout and held her for more than an hour, enough time to ensure that the food would be at least partly digested.

Erc took off the collar and slapped the pig's rear, sending her toward the raiders. Barely containing their merriment, the Fennidi scrambled up nearby trees, the better to get a view. A few well-placed stones kept the pig moving on the right trajectory and her squeals soon brought the raiders running. Mercifully, the herbs began their work and the pig was dazed before the first arrow pierced her side.

Gorm hinn Svarta's men could hardly contain their joy at finding fresh meat so near at hand and gave thanks to the God Ing for their luck. After the pig was gutted and cleaned, they offered a horn of beer in honor of the beast and of the Land Spirits that had fattened the hog for their use. Gorm hinn Svarta judged the coast clear enough to hazard a fire on the beach. They poured out another horn in honor of their Gods, spilling the amber liquid on the soil and the fire.

With fresh meat on hand there was reason to celebrate, the men had been chafing at the close quarters on board. The raiders gathered wood and built up the fire, singing songs and jesting, their bellies full. The Fennidi watched from the trees, keeping their heads low and moving little.

Not long after ingesting the pig, the Men of the North showed the effects of the poisonous herbs. They sweated and walked as if dazed. Six of them stripped off all their clothes and perched naked on the rocks, mumbling. Others wandered up and down the strand, talking to no one. One walked calmly into the fire and stood there, feeling no pain. The sentry, who had not yet eaten, tried to pull him out, but his clothes had already ignited and the smells of burning flesh mingled with smoke.

As the raiders became stranger and wilder, Erc gave the signal to launch the attack. Only the sentry had enough presence of mind to fire back, but he was soon lying dead on the sand with his face to the stars.

"It's a pity we don't know how to pilot the ship," Erc commented. "I would enjoy sailing into port with this trophy. Let's alert the villagers. They can board her and take the cargo."

News of the Fennidi victory spread far and wide. Details of their daring plan reached the king's ears before his soldiers returned to court. The villagers divided the spoils as was the custom, books, candlesticks and chalices they left for the monks to claim.

# 22

The Ard-Ri was deeply angry, but he would not reveal it. Only Coemgen heard Crimthann's rage when they met in the Ard-Drui's stone house within the Nemed.

"Why does news of the raiders come so late? The people will think the Fennidi are their only protection on the coast. The people must think *my* army the strongest force on the Island."

Coemgen sat by the fire stroking his beard, watching Crimthann pace.

"You were a Fennidi warrior once, you know their cunning. Often they are the only force standing between the people and chaos. Why this displeasure?"

Crimthann stilled his body. "The king-making will be upon me soon. I want the warriors to respect me and look to me as their champion. How can I be seen as a great warrior when Erc and the Fennidi are celebrated in verse and song from one end of the Island to the other?"

"Ah, so it is jealousy, Crimthann? This small emotion is unworthy of you."

"I may be jealous. But I am also concerned for the people. Hasn't Germanus brought complaints from the villagers who feed and supply the Fennidi? In times of plenty the people give willingly of their stores, but in hard times like this it is an unbearable burden."

"A burden you have taken advantage of yourself when you needed sustenance."

"These times are different . . . and, there is another matter. The Abbot teaches the women to give up arms and their fighting ways. His goal is to create refined women in the Roman style. The Fennidi encourage women to fight, making them coarse and rude."

"Would you have the women give up their warrior skills? What would Gaine and Ethne say to that?"

"The Abbot says it is man's natural place to rule women. Most of our leaders are and always have been men, so I see the rightness of it."

"My son, if you pursue this reasoning, you will make a very disappointing ruler and husband. Island women have always been equals to their men, when they are born of equal status. The Abbot is a foreigner and does not understand."

"Many of our people have adopted his views. I owe it to them to honor both points of view, don't I?"

Coemgen sighed. Crimthann was being obstinate.

"As your advisor I must tell you what I see. My Imbas tells me that if you seek to abolish the Fiana, as Germanus wants, you will lose favor with the common people. If you control the women you will lose favor with half the kingdom *and* you will lose Ethne's respect." Coemgen stood and shook out his robes. "However, you are free person and must do as you think best."

Coemgen wondered what had caused such a change in Crimthann. Something more was bothering him than the recent notoriety of the Fennidi. Why did he speak so hotly of controlling women? Did it have to do with Ethne?

Crimthann nodded, turning for the door and stopping briefly to put a blanket around the older man's shoulders before he let in the damp night air. Coemgen smiled to hide his mounting concern.

Weeks passed and Crimthann's mood did not improve. He forbade stories and songs of the Fian's exploits in the feasting hall. In conversation he referred to the Fennidi as "rebels and outlaws," not protectors of herds and villages. These words were repeated in the monastery chapel and outdoor meeting places on the Abbot's instructions.

One morning Ethne could bear it no more and took her place in line to petition the king.

Crimthann, startled to see her, bade her walk to the dais.

"My lord," she replied. "I would not usurp the rightful place of anyone here. I will wait my turn like the others."

"You are the highest Lady in the land. If you have something to tell us, then by rights step forward and speak," insisted Crimthann.

Ethne waited until all eyes were upon her. "I will speak from where I stand. I am not yet queen and have no place by the throne. I give thanks to those ahead of me for their indulgence. I hear rumors of a movement to abolish the Fiana. I have personally served their needs as healer and priestess for a decade and I tell you this would be a grave mistake."

Crimthann reddened, his knuckles gripping the arms of the oaken throne, but he uttered not a sound. Ethne had his permission to speak and he was honor bound to allow her to finish. As Ban-Drui her words were sacrosanct; no one but another Drui could interrupt according to ancient law.

Coemgen watched from behind the throne, feeling the king's tension rise, repeating magical verses to dissipate the king's mounting anger.

"Every person on this Island knows the service the Fennidi perform," Ethne continued. "They defend our coastal towns and guard our cattle from thieves. Who among you has not been touched by their protection? Some say that their very existence guards the land from the brichta of the Fomoire who would blight the crops and the new born calves and render the women and land barren. They also make a haven for the misfits among us. Young men and women of high spirits and mischief are taken in and turned into skilled, intelligent fighters. If they return to their tuaths they are the better for it, sober and responsible.

Germanus and his monks teach that women are evil and a danger to men. They would forbid women the use of weapons and afford them the same legal status as children, dependents to the men of their clanns. They say that the Fennidi women are the worst examples of all: living wild upon the land, choosing their lovers, and becoming expert fighters. They say the mere existence of such women taints all other females, making them uncontrollable.

But consider what we see in other creatures. Deer are led by an older and experienced doe. The she bear is alone to defend her cubs. Female wolves and great birds of prey are skilled hunters. No female of any species waits passively for defense or provision. The triads state: '*Three essentials of poetic genius: An eye to see nature, a heart to feel nature, and a resolute courage that dares to follow nature.*' Minds much wiser than ours composed these ancient triads. We ignore them at our peril.

Crimthann was silent, refusing to give her words further weight by a response.

Instead, he said simply, "Thank you for you views," and looked past her to the next petitioner.

There was an awkward silence. The assembly had expected a judgment from the Ard-Ri. Ethne flushed red as she realized she was dismissed. Holding her head high, she turned her back on the king and walked to the door. Only when she was well away from the dun, hidden by a clump of blackthorn, did she allow her rage to escape in an angry oath.

# 23

————

Ruadh stood in the sunlight, in the doorway of the Healer's House. The busy village sounds and the warm light that crept under the leather curtain had lured him outside. His strength was nearly returned and the darkness of the hut oppressed him. Though not well enough to take up the more taxing tasks of the village, Ruadh felt he could help tend cattle, sort grains, and weed gardens.

This morning he headed for the herb garden near the Nemed, hoping for a glimpse of Ethne. He was rewarded to see her on her knees, thinning a bed of irises near the gates. As he watched, she straightened, sat back on her heels and wiped the back of her hand across her brow. She looked pleased with her work and sat surveying what she might do next. As Ruadh neared he cleared his throat. Ethne looked up, shading her eyes with her hand and squinting into the sun. At first all she could make out was a man's shape standing in the blinding light.

"The flowers do well under your hand, lady."

She dropped her hand and smiled. "These flowers have always been happy here. Even before I came to tend them. You look well, this morning."

He glanced about before kneeling beside her. " I am well and very soon I must leave. When may we be handfast?"

She took in the smell of him, the feel of his shoulder so close to hers, the sun warming both their backs as they knelt before the blue flowers. "Tonight, Ruadh." Then she laughed

201

with delight. "It is the Full Moon nearest the Spring Equinox, I can think of no better night for a wedding."

He touched a smudge of dirt on the side of her face then pulled his hand back. "I will meet you on the far road near the old cattle sheds with a cart and horse. I would carry my lady to the ceremony in some style. Is there an offering I should bring for the spirits of the ancestors?"

"For other ceremonies it is the custom to cast a small statue or piece of jewelry into the waters. But on this occasion, we ourselves are the offering. We give ourselves in our union to the land." Laughing squeals from a group of children made her raise her head. "Go now and I will meet you on the far road when the Moon has climbed half way to the top of the sky."

He walked away, and Ethne turned back to the irises before her. As she separated the bulbs, pulling their tangled roots apart, she pictured Ruadh and Crimthann in her mind. They were very different men and growing ever more dissimilar as the pressure of Canoc's influence weighed upon the village.

Crimthann was dutiful and cautious, seeing Ethne as his consort, a beautiful queen to ornament his court. Ruadh had left all doubts behind, his confusions burned away by the fire in his blood. His only desire was to serve Ethne and the land, and it burned in him like a flame lit from within.

She went about her tasks, preparing simples, attending to the weaving of cloth and helping to preserve some early peas for next winter's larder. She kept her mind on the tools and materials before her, leaving the chatting and gossip to the women around her. One old woman teased her, saying her mind was wandering toward a marriage bed. Ethne laughed at herself with the rest and could admit the truth of it freely. She did not clarify *which* marriage bed.

As evening drew on, she excused herself and went to her own hut to rest before the night's ritual. She knew sleep was impossible, but she also knew that it was essential to calm her spirits and enter the handfasting with a clear, untroubled heart. Lighting a candle, she made her prayers to the Goddess, stepped out of the clothes she had worn that day and then lay down, letting her mind drift where it would, focused on the rise and fall of her own breathing.

When the moon had broken free of the horizon and the stars sparked overhead, she put on a simple shift of green and belted it at the waist. From her oaken chest she took a silver cup and from her table she took herbs, honey and a jug of fion. Lastly she gathered woolen towels and a blanket. She threw her cloak about her, pulling the hood down over her face and walked solemnly across the Nemed courtyard towards the circle of stones.

Once outside she made sure she was alone. Then sliding slightly on the damp grass, she rounded the shoulder of the hill and saw Ruadh standing next to a cart.

"Quick, let me help you in." He offered her his hand and she swung up into the seat, placing her bundle beside her. He climbed up next to her and they set off, leaving the rath behind. They rode in silence, but Ruadh held Ethne's hand tightly in his own as if to bind her to him before the night grew any older. The moon rose, obscured by only a few streaked clouds, and the horse stepped briskly along the track.

Before long the sacred hill of the Goddess rose before them. It was a mound of earth covered with soft grasses and violets, deep within it lay the holy well. A large hawthorn tree hung protectively over the entrance, growing from one side of the knoll. Strips of tattered cloth hung from its branches, each strip a prayer from a visitor who had beseeched the Goddess of the Spring to answer their need.

The entrance was a steep stairway carved out of stone that led straight into the center of the hill. On either side of the stairway, issuing from cracks and holes in the rocks, were spleen worts and ferns. Tiny blue and white flowers peeped from amongst the shadows of the stones and thick clusters of shamrock hung from the edges of the opening over the narrow pathway. In the moonlight the greens took on a rich bluish hue and the white blossoms glowed like fallen stars.

Ethne took Ruadh by the hand as they walked sun-wise three times around the mound, then stopped at the entrance. Gazing into Ruadh's eyes, Ethne undid the tie at her waist and pins from her shoulders. Her shift fell past her hips and pooled around her feet.

Ruadh stood drinking her in, then removed his shirt and leggings. Naked, Ethne led Ruadh down the steps into the heart of the hill. Holding hands, they stood beside a dark pool, listening as unseen freshets trickled and made soft plashing sounds. They breathed in the moist air and felt the peaceful pull of the earth. Ethne intoned:

> *The shelter of Danann,*
> *Mother of the Gods, be nigh our hands and feet*
> *as we enter the waters may we come safely home.*
> *May Lug the Bright Warrior aid us,*
> *may Brighid the Healer preserve us,*
> *may Anu, Earth Mother, bless us.*

"We have entered the Mother to be twice born," Ethne said softly. She handed the silver cup to Ruadh who took it and dipped it into the dark pool, saying:

> *With this water may we enter a new life,*
> *a life of greater love and wisdom.*
> *May the five streams of knowledge be increased in us.*
> *May we together achieve the perfection*
> *of our five senses.*
> *May the Ancestors, the Nature Spirits and the Gods*
> *direct our purpose and twine our lives together*
> *like the heather and the bee.*

Ethne smiled with joy. He had spoken the words of her heart. Ruadh held the chalice while Ethne sipped from it, then

Ethne held it in turn and offered him a drink. Without a sound, they moved, again clasping hands, into the depths of the pool until even the tips of their heads were covered. After several seconds' immersion, they rose, gasping and laughing at the cold and ran quickly back up the steps. With shaking fingers, Ethne pulled the woolen towels from the bundle and threw one over Ruadh's shoulders and drew the other around her own. They rubbed themselves vigorously to put off the damp and cold, then pulled their clothes back on. Clambering into the cart, Ethne covered them both with the blanket as Ruadh turned the horse back toward the stone circle.

As the Moon rose near its zenith the Hill of Stones reappeared on the crest of the hill overlooking the Ard-Ri's rath. They left the pony and cart tied to a tree below the rise and walked up the grassy slope, stopping outside the circle to greet the stones and make offerings around the outer perimeter. Ethne took pinches of vervain from a deerskin bag and placed a bit at the foot of each menhir while Ruadh poured out a thin stream of honey. "For purity and sweetness," said Ethne as she smiled at him.

After finishing their round of the outer area, they stood at the entrance briefly and then entered the circle, their hands tightly clasped. Ruadh spread the red blanket in the center of the ring while Ethne poured bright red fion into the silver cup. Ruadh sat watching while Ethne invoked the five directions, facing each one in turn:

> *Powers of East, of prosperity, of earth.*
> *Powers of the Salmon, the Wise One*
> *who knows how to return to the Source of all things.*
> *We welcome you into the circle, please be with us now.*
> *Powers of South, of the dark mystery,*
>
> *of the Waters of the Goddess,*
> *of music, of arts, of the great Boar and Sow.*

*Show us how to root into the dark of ourselves*
*to find Truth and Inspiration, be with us now.*

*Powers of West, history keepers, poets,*
*and those who transport us*
*across the Nine Waves to the Otherworld,*
*in life and in death, in song and in story.*
*Great Stag who heralds the changes of the seasons,*
*be with us in this circle.*

*Powers of North,*
*bright spear of Lug and sword of Nuada*
*fire from the place where the Sun never sets.*
*Mighty Eagle who teaches us courage and vision,*
*be with us in the circle.*

And finally, returning to the center and facing the man she loved, Ethne spoke:

*Powers of the Center of Sovereignty and firm rulership,*
*teach us mastery and judgment,*
*balance and true-seeing.*
*Be with us in this circle.*

Ruadh took both of her hands and gently pulled her to her knees until they were face to face, embracing in the center of the Sunwheel. He kissed her gently on the mouth, his hands cupped about her face, drinking her in as he had drunk from the pool of the Goddess's well. Then his kiss deepened and he folded her in his arms, pressing her to him and holding her as if his arms would never let go. Slowly, with small kisses at the corners of her mouth, near her eyes, at the base of her throat, he pulled her shift from her shoulders, kissed the mound of each breast and then her belly as her dress fell away. He then rose, removed his clothing, and tied a red ribbon around their two joined hands, kissing the insides of her wrists. Their bare skin gleamed softly as the Moon rode high overhead.

He drew his hand over her hips, over the swell of her bottom and then pulled her fiercely to him. This time their mouths joined in a hunger that had been left too long and they fell back onto the earth, tasting the salt of each other's passion. Ethne clung to his shoulders, circling his waist with her legs. She pulled him in, but he held himself above her, gazing at her in the moonlight:

*Your flesh is the Earth. I worship you as one.*
*Your bones are Her stones. I worship you as one.*
*Your blood is Her water. I worship you as one.*
*Your thoughts are Her clouds. I worship you as one.*

Looking up, Ethne finished the ancient verse:

*Your face is the Sun. I worship you as one.*
*Your eyes are the stars. I worship you as one.*
*Your breath is the wind. I worship you as one.*
*Your soul is the Sky. The Sky is my self. We are one.*

Then he sank his flesh into hers with a moan that echoed off the stones. They rocked and grappled until Ethne cried out to the stars. When their breathing came no longer in gasps, Ruadh raised himself and sat beside her. He untied the red ribbon from their hands and retied it around Ethne's braid. "I have a gift for you," he said as he placed a soft kiss on one breast. "It is not much, but it is all I could manage here at the dun."

Ethne rolled to her side and leaned up on one elbow. She took the parcel he offered and with a questioning glance unwrapped it. Four small bundles, each wrapped in red cloth, fell into her hand. She sat fully upright and began to peel away the cloths one by one. As she did so, Ruadh explained, "Salt, to purify our home, whenever we may be together. Bread, that we may never go hungry, wood, that we may always be warm, and a silver coin, that we may never go without. Keep them safe until we can live together as husband and wife. In this world or the next."

Ethne gathered the bundles to her heart and wept. "We will always be as one and my inner guide tells me we *will* live together." She did not tell him that she could not say if it would be here in this world. "A cup of fíon, love, to close the rite," she added, and they drank another blessing to the Goddess and to each other.

Ruadh stood and thanked the directions and the powers for their presence in the circle while Ethne remained seated at the center. When he returned to her, he kissed her tears and they joined their love again, sweetly, gently this time, holding each other against the leaving they must make. And though Ethne would have held him until the whole kingdom found them there at the center of the stones, Ruadh quietly urged her to dress. With a last kiss that split both their hearts, she turned and made her way on foot toward the Nemed while he descended the back of the hill and walked to the tree where the horse stood patiently waiting.

# 24

The following night, in a pouring rain, a man arrived on horseback from the East, demanding to speak to Crimthann. The messenger had ridden for two days and nearly collapsed as he was led into the Ard-Ri's chamber. The king was asleep when the knock sounded at his door.

"My Lord, I bring evil tidings," said the messenger who, in his haste, had not removed his wet cape and boots.

"Fetch this man a hot posset and food and make a bed by the fire," commanded the king.

"My Lord, Canoc is marching from Oirthir. He intends to take your throne by force."

Crimthann reached for his belt and sword and pulled on his boots. "Guards! Call Coemgen. I am calling a war council!"

He turned back to the messenger. "When will he be here and what force has he gathered?"

"About five days with the assembled tribes of the Oirthir. No others have joined him. He says he has *paid* for the right to the high throne."

"Arrogant cur without honor," Crimthann growled.

"My Lord, he claims that you are not yet consecrated as Ard-Ri, that the throne is vacant because you are not married. He says the Island needs a Cristaidi king, who will champion the new ways."

Crimthann stared into the fire, his mind caught up in Canoc's daring claim. A movement from the messenger brought him back and he looked at the man. "The mogae will feed you and take care of your needs."

The king's warriors assembled before the throne as did Gaine, Coemgen and Ethne. When the king emerged from his chamber, he was in full battle dress, his face already painted with the blue markings of the sacred warrior.

Coemgen, as was the custom, shook a golden chain for silence then invoked the Gods with ringing voice; *"In the name of the Morrígu, Great Raven Queen and Goddess of Battle, in the name of In Dagdae, He of the Mighty Staff of Death and Rebirth, I open this council of war."*

Crimthann stepped closer to the warriors. "You have heard the threat of the Oirthir. Canoc has no honor. He seeks to upset the balance of the Island. If he subdues In Medon and binds it to Oirthir as he threatens, the ritual balance of the kingdoms will be undone.

"He claims to come in peace, following the ways of his Drui, Isu. Instead he brings chaos and bloodshed. I need you to ride to your clanns and return with your best men. Canoc and his army will be here in five days. You will fight for me and the legitimate kingship, and you will fight for the ancestors and the patterns set upon this land since the beginnings of our people."

One warrior, face painted in triple spirals of red and black, stepped forward from the assembled circle. "My lord king, I am Ruadh, the Fennid made well in the House of Healing. Your generosity restored my life. I would now use it in your service. Let me ride to the coast and assemble the Fennidi to aid in your defense."

Coemgen stepped forward, peering intently. "What is your clann, Ruadh? What is your father's name?"

Ruadh hesitated only a moment, knowing the truth was best put before them. "I am Ruadh, the Red One. Once known as Ruadh, son of Canoc."

Crimthann stepped toward Ruadh. "You are a strange man. Where does your *true* allegiance lie?"

"I broke with my clann and with my father when I was very young. My allegiance is to the Fennidi, and the people of this Island, to serve them and protect them as I am needed. I claim no further ties or obligations with my clann and they have no claim on me."

"Why should I put my trust in one who has broken ties with his clann? Are not kin ways the life blood of this Island?" Crimthann growled.

"My loyalty is with the Fian. I pledge to keep the sacred balance of the Spirits and I do *not* accept the Cristaidi religion. I don't want to see my people and their ways destroyed." Ruadh held his head proudly, speaking so all could hear.

"Son of Canoc," Crimthann retorted, "You speak with smooth practice. How is it that the son of our greatest foe enters this rath for a *second* time? You say you will defend the people, but your father is the enemy. I find your presence here more than curious."

A few men standing near Ruadh grumbled and nodded their agreement.

"I defer to Coemgen in this," Crimthann continued. "But I am inclined to take you as hostage and send a message to your father. You are not an ally of this dun."

Crimthann's voice rose as he spoke but Ethne's voice overrode his.

"Crimthann, you don't know what you are saying!"

Crimthann spun about and faced her as she made her way into the circle of men. The tremor in her voice and the passion in her eye reminded him of the day he had found her weeping in the House of Healing. A flame of jealousy shot through his chest and he clenched his teeth against her words.

"This man escorted me from the Forest House last autumn. He shielded me with his sword and his life. He is an honorable and a sacred warrior who has risked his life again and again for the people. Listen to him. He offers you the best fighters of the Island. Do not turn him away!"

Ethne's words only fanned Crimthann's anger. "I need no wild Fennidi to come to my aid. These warriors here are loyal to me and trained by my hand. Our defeat was a defeat of time, not arms. On our own soil, with the dun at our back, we will defend our territory with valor. Coemgen! What say you?"

The Ard-Drui, not wanting to undermine Crimthann's command, made his judgment. "Place the son of Canoc in the Hill of the Hostages and post a guard that no person may speak with him."

The guards seized Ruadh who did not struggle, but kept his gaze on Crimthann. Crimthann turned to look at Ethne, who's eyes focused on the ground to hide her emotions. She turned to leave the hall but Coemgen stopped her.

"I have something more to say. The Marriage to the Land Ceremony must be performed *immediately*. Crimthann and Ethne, you must prepare at once. We will need three days to do the ritual properly and in that time the warriors can ride out to their clanns and bring back their fighters. If we act quickly, none can claim the throne save Crimthann.

"So be it!" said Crimthann, his eyes still on Ethne.

She tilted her face up and spoke; "My fate is yours, Lord. I would take up my duties as Rígain as soon as I am needed." She made herself smile and was relieved to see Crimthann's shoulders relax. In moments he was deep in conversation with Coemgen and several of the clann chiefs. The warriors dispersed, each in the direction of their homeland to gather tribesmen. Gaine made her way through the crowd to Ethne's side, seeing her troubled look.

"I know it is a disappointment to have a hasty marriage. You should have a month of feasting to celebrate properly. But the people will celebrate you in their hearts. You will be a Rígain they love because you understand your duty and their need."

Ethne gave Gaine a thin smile. She needed no celebration to know that her Marriage to the Land was complete. Her thoughts were with Ruadh and the lives of those suffering under a false king's greed.

# 25

Crimthann left the rath under cover of night to spend three days alone in the wilderness. Not even Coemgen knew where he had gone. Secrecy was imperative to see if the Spirits would protect him if he were attacked by man or by beast. Gaine gave him a sack of hazelnuts and three questions to ponder. He would find answers in the stones, the water, the birds and the trees.

"Whom do you serve? Where is that which you serve? What is the secret that you serve?" was Gaine's three-part riddle.

"The Druid taught me to revere nature as the source of Truth, for only if a thing is revealed by nature can it be said to be real." Crimthann replied. He tried his best to put thoughts of battle out of mind. The long siege would come soon enough.

The first morning of his retreat Crimthann built a small shelter near a stream against the changeable Island climate. He used his dirk to cut twelve saplings then dug a ring of six holes and placed the end of a sapling into each hole, bending it over to make an arch. He bound the tip of each sapling to the butt end of another with vines and tied them to join at the ends. When he had a rough beehive structure of bent trees, he interlaced supple branches and vines around the whole, covering it with oak and hawthorn branches. He lined the interior with hemlock boughs. By mid afternoon he had a waterproof shelter from which he could listen to the voice of the stream nearby.

Everything about this sojourn would be significant: the animals he encountered, the birds he heard, the configuration of stars and planets. By abstaining from food and speech his senses would sharpen and attune to the sounds of trees, of the water and the rustlings of living things.

On the second day a pair of wood pigeons appeared, cooing and preparing to mate. Crimthann watched fascinated as the male spread his feathers and danced to charm the female. "I must do the same to win Ethne," mused Crimthann. "I see how he follows her ceaselessly."

Towards evening a tiny wren appeared on a branch above the king's shelter. It sat under a large oak leaf, ready to spend the night. "An excellent omen," thought Crimthann. "As the wren is the king of birds, I too, shall be king." The birds showed no inclination to leave, a further indication that these were Spirit animals sent as messengers for Crimthann's benefit.

On the third day, Crimthann's last, he cracked the hazelnuts between two rocks and ate a few. His hunger sharpened at the taste of the nuts. He chewed each one slowly, savoring it. The rest he pounded into coarse meal and spread on the ground as a gift for the pigeons that soon pecked at it greedily. They were nearly finished when a raven suddenly dropped from the sky and speared the male pigeon's neck with its strong black beak. Crimthann watched as the black bird pierced the pigeon again and again until it fluttered and died. The raven tore at the pigeon until Crimthann intervened, shouting and stamping to frighten it off. The wren watched from its perch in the overhanging branch.

The female pigeon watched too.

"This is a strange and evil omen. I will consult with Coemgen or Gaine," thought Crimthann, inwardly shaken. After he buried the pigeon, covering it with a small cairn of stones, he sat for a long time, his thoughts centered on the image of the raven's bloody beak.

That same evening, Ethne began her part in the ritual sequence. Tradition demanded that she sleep from sundown to sunup with her future husband's new sword under her bed to imbue it with the feminine forces. The assumption was that a bride-tobe was not already wed and Ethne did nothing to dissolve this notion, but she wondered at the outcome of the rite. Any revelation of her true status would mean her death or Ruadh's or both. These thoughts circled her mind as she dressed in an embroidered white linen smock for the Sword Blessing ceremony. She propped herself against down pillows and waited for the Druid to bring the sword into her house. At dusk she heard a bard approaching, singing songs of battle and of wooing, while another played on a willow Cruitt. A line of Druid and acolytes followed, joining in the choruses. They carried lit torches, bowls of sweet herbs burning on coals and strings of bells, which they shook in time to the music.

Coemgen and Gaine, walked side by side, carrying the newly forged sword between them, each holding one end. It was wrapped in a heavily embroidered red cloth with a sheath of chastened red leather nestled beside it. Despite the coming battle, there was an air of celebration and joy.

On entering the small house, Gaine and Coemgen stood at the foot of Ethne's palette while acolytes sprinkled rose water and lavender flowers around the room. Daire carried a tray with spiced fion and sweet cakes, which he placed at Ethne's side. The bard remained outside her window to sing wedding ballads, for there was much luck in these songs.

Coemgen and Gaine slowly unwound the cloth from the sword and scabbard.

Ethne gasped involuntarily when she glimpsed the red leather; it was so like the scabbard Ruadh had brought to her house in the forest. Coemgen held the sword aloft while Gaine knelt to lift the mattress, and then Coemgen slipped the bright weapon underneath.

Coemgen and Gaine chanted the ancient Rest Benediction in unison:

*Blessings of the Moon above you*
*Blessings of the Earth below you*
*Blessings on your kin*
*Blessings on everything upon which your eye does rest*
*Blessings on everything on which your hope does rest*
*Blessings on your thinking and your purpose*
*Blessings on your bed companion*
*Blessings on your hand's work Sky,*
*and Sea and Gods defend you.*

Gaine poured a cup of fion and handed it to Ethne. "Drink this and sleep deeply. Gird yourself for Crimthann's coming. Gods willing, he will join you in the morning, and you shall both be twice born at the Sacred Well."

Ethne drank, tasting more of its bitter essence than its sweetness. The man she truly longed for was held fast in a cold earthen mound, beyond her reach. Finally, the Druid extinguished the beeswax candles and backed out of the doorway, leaving Ethne alone. The music of the bard drifted in through her tiny window. Ethne stared for a while at the dark walls then drifted to sleep, dreaming of birds nesting.

# 26

Crimthann returned to the gate of the rath before daybreak on the third morning. A guard, posted to keep a lookout for him, raced to alert Coemgen and Gaine.

"Crimthann is back! Awaken the Druid!" The excited call was passed from house to house in the Nemed. Everyone flocked to the central fire to hear Gaine intone the ritual questions and to hear Crimthann's replies. Only a High Priestess could ask the questions and only a High Priestess could say if the answers given were correct. No ears save those of the Druid would ever hear the questions and responses.

Gaine held a chalice covered by a royal purple cloth, the golden cup Coemgen had commissioned for the coronation.

Crimthann knelt before her, light headed but firm of heart.

Gaine spoke, "Have you answers to the riddles?"

"I have."

"Answer then, whom do you serve?"

"The Goddess, who is the land."

"Where is that which you serve?"

"Everywhere I walk, sit and breathe."

"What is the secret that you serve?"

"The land and I are one."

Gaine smiled. "You have spoken truly, Crimthann. I find you worthy." At this pronouncement Gaine uncovered the golden vessel and handed it to the king.

"Drink the Waters of Life; you have consecrated yourself to the highest service in the land."

Crimthann drained the cup and returned it to the Ard-Ban-Drui. Coemgen approached with a plate of apples, freshly sliced, and handed it to Crimthann saying: "Eat of the Apples of Immortality, food sacred to the Gods and the Otherworld, and welcome back into our midst, O Sacred King."

Crimthann ate the apples sparingly, the first food he had taken save hazelnuts in the last three days.

"Go now to the house of Ethne, who holds your new sword. You will need it much in times to come."

Crimthann turned towards Ethne's house, followed by the Ard-Drui and Ard-BanDrui, witnesses to the handing over of the blade and its scabbard. Ethne had heard the cries of the Druid and was awake, standing in the doorway of her house, holding the sheathed sword in her arms. Crimthann knelt before her, understanding now how this woman embodied the earth and that his sword and his power were given through her. He would serve her as a living representative of the Earth Goddess for the rest of his days.

"Welcome, Sacred King," Ethne said. "Here is your weapon, freely given from my hand to yours. Use it with justice, in defense of the kingdom and the people."

"Lady, I thank you for the new blade that you have given from your hand to mine. I will use it to serve the land, the people and you, for as long as I have life."

Crimthann stood and turned to face the gathered Druid who sent up a loud cheer.

Coemgen's voice rose above the shouts, "Crimthann, sit now with the sword and divine its true name. At noon present it to the Sun and after dark present it to the Moon. It will then be consecrated to your spirit."

Crimthann was led to the Cauldron of Sea at the heart of the sacred precinct. He was given a strong drink of the herb artemisia to prepare him for scrying into the waters. Several Druid sat silently around the perimeter of the ritual space, burning dried artemisia and wafting the smoke towards the king with fans made of eagle's wings.

Sitting cross-legged before the Cauldron of Sea, Crimthann stilled his mind and peered into the waters, allowing inspiration to surface. Coemgen sat nearby, silently lending encouragement. When his mind became like still water, a single word surfaced: "Toirnech is the sword's name!" said Crimthann.

"Tell it to no one." said Coemgen softly. "Now you and Ethne must prepare for the trip to the Holy Well of the Goddess and then to Germanus' chapel."

Crimthann, startled, looked hard at the Ard-Drui. "I don't understand. Why placate the Cristaidi now?"

"My son, Canoc cannot have the advantage. If you are anointed a Cristaide king as well as married to the land, who can stand against you?"

Crimthann understood the pattern of Coemgen's thoughts but remained troubled.

His doubts he kept to himself. "Coemgen, as always I defer to your wisdom."

The next morning the marriage procession moved slowly down the king's road towards the Holy Well. At the head Crimthann stood in a chariot twined with holly, sacred to warriors, and ivy, sacred to women. He wore a rich tunic of fine blue wool with a golden torque glistening at his throat. Ethne stood beside him, in a red gown overspread with her six-colored cloak. She too wore her finest jewels, her hair carefully braided with ribbons, flowers, and golden ornaments. Heralds and musicians went before, calling the clanns and villagers to witness.

A retinue of warriors flanked the party at a distance, keeping a lookout. Bards and Druid came last, chanting blessings on the new king and queen. By the time they were half a mile from the rath people lined the road, throwing flowers and greenery. The closer the cart came to the Goddess's mound, the louder the cheers became. In the din of merrymaking and singing,

Crimthann turned to Ethne. "I am overwhelmed, Ethne, at this, our marriage day."

She looked to him and met his eyes, but her heart was quaking as they approached the hill.

"I do not mean the ceremony only, I mean the marriage." Crimthann stumbled on his words and frowned.

"Ethne, you are asked to represent the Land and the Goddess in the king's hall. But I am here because I would not have any other for my wife. You give me the greatest honor." He bowed his head to her and she took his hand, steadying herself at the feel of his warm palm against hers.

"The honor is mine, Crimthann. Let us be a comfort to each other as we fulfill our duties and uphold our traditions. We began in friendship as shadows in the dark. Let us build our marriage on that trust."

"I am committed to the land and to the Gods, and though our duty will come first, I would have our differences be a source of learning so we may grow closer."

"My sincerest wish is that it be so."

The chariot drew up before the Well and the Druid formed a protective circle around the mound, keeping the crowd at a distance. Ethne took Crimthann's arm as they circled the mound sun-wise three times. Then Gaine stepped forward to help Ethne unclasp and remove her cloak and gown, while Coemgen did the same for Crimthann.

Finally, they walked into the hill and descended the stairs. At the lip of the pool, Crimthann turned to Ethne, "We will submerge ourselves in these sacred waters to be born anew. Just as we are naked here, we will share our thoughts and hopes, leaving nothing concealed in our marriage. I am yours Ethne, in mind, body, and spirit." He kissed her gently on the lips then pulled her slowly into the depths of the pool.

Rising out of the icy water, Ethne held to Crimthann's shoulders and returned his kiss. He held her briefly then they scrambled out of the pool and up the stairs to Gaine and Coemgen holding thick woolen towels at the well's mouth.

"You have been reborn in the Holy Well. Your royal wedded state is now sanctified!" Coemgen intoned. A series of cheers went up and a rain of blossoms fell around them. The pair dried and dressed then stepped into the sunlight in view of all.

Coemgen asked the Gods' blessing:

*Today you gird yourselves with the triple power of the Ancestors, the Nature Spirits and the Gods. You take unto yourselves the bounty of the inexhaustible Cauldron of In Daghda, the precision of the Spear of Lug and the strength of the Sword of Nuada. You bind yourselves to the Stones of the Mother and are consecrated to the service of the Land.*

*From today forth, you pledge yourselves in selfless service to the people, to the service of the Doini Sidi and to the honor of the Mighty Dead. You must display at all times the wisdom of the wise, the courage of the strong, and the trust of the young.*

*Today you are girded with the power of the Heavens, the brilliance of the Sun and the light of the Moon. Let these be set on your brows. Today you are girded with the speed of Lightning, the subtlety of Wind, the depth of Sea, the firmness of Rock and all the powers that lie below the Earth.*

*May the Goddesses direct you in all your ways. May the Gods' wisdom enlighten you. May you be shielded from the snares of dark spirits, from weakness of will, from sloth and indifference and from all who wish ill upon you.*

*May you be equal to the challenge when any enmity threatens your body or your spirit or that of the people you serve. I place a ring of protection above you and below you, behind you and before you. In the eye of all who behold you, in the ear of all who hear you, in the heart of every being, may it*

*be known by all that you are anointed Ard-Ri and Rígain of
this Island. Bíth ed samlaid!*

Gaine handed Coemgen a golden bowl filled with scented
oil. The Ard-Drui dipped his finger into it and traced triple spirals on Crimthann's brow and then on Ethne's. Gaine took back
the bowl and handed Coemgen a golden circlet. Coemgen lifted
it to the sky, invoking Grian, and placed it upon Crimthann's
head. Next he held a second circlet aloft, showing it also to the
Goddess and then gently placed it on Ethne's brow.

A cheer went up from the Druid, warriors, and common
folk. It was mid day; Crimthann unsheathed his sword and held
it aloft, presenting it to the Sun Goddess and silently invoking
its True Name. When it was securely in the scabbard, he turned
to Ethne and kissed her, long and hard as befitted a warrior king
and his new queen. The people laughed with delight.

"Let us go to the chapel. The Abbot is waiting!" said
Crimthann with a joyous grin. Not even the prospect of stand-
ing within those dark stones could dampen his spirits. He was
Ard-Ri in the eyes of the Goddess, the land, the Druid and the
people. He was wedded to Ethne, noble, graceful, and wise.
Who dared oppose him now?

Germanus sullenly watched the wedding party approach
the tiny stone chapel.

"I had hoped to crown Canoc, and give this Island its first
Cristaide ruler. He and I could extend the power of Rome.
Instead the Ard-Drui thinks he has outsmarted me. Coemgen
may know about the approaching army, but he will not prevail."

Germanus saw the golden crowns set upon Crimthann's
and Ethne's heads. He turned to an Albinus, "Those two will not
receive the blessing of communion without baptism."

One small window over the altar illuminated the chapel,
alligned to capture the Easter sunrise. Beeswax candles burned
in stone niches and in golden candlesticks. A precious copy of
the Bible, inscribed on calf skin, lay on the altar cloth beside a

golden cross, a golden chalice and a reliquary of gold encrusted with pearls and one ruby, which held a drop of Isa's Blood. The Blood had been dearly purchased from a broker in the Levant, and had already attracted pilgrims from the southern lands who made donations for the upkeep of the monastery.

Only a dozen of the Druid fit into the chapel, most of the space was already filled by priests and monks. Casting her eyes on the crowd, Ethne whispered to Crimthann,

"None but men. Where are the women?"

Crimthann squeezed her hand to still her nerves.

Germanus cleared his throat and addressed Crimthann to begin the rite. "We are gathered here in the sight of God to join in holy matrimony this man and King, Crimthann, and this woman and Queen, Ethne. Who gives this woman away?"

There was confusion amongst the Druid. No one there was capable of "giving a woman away," unless she were a mog. Coemgen finally spoke. "Ethne has no parents or kin present. I then 'give her away,' though she is a free person." His words came out in a rush followed by an embarrassed cough. Germanus ignored Coemgen's discomfiture.

"Crimthann, in the presence of God and of the holy cross do you take this woman, Ethne, as your legal wife?"

"I do."

"Do you swear to join your people with hers, your future with hers?"

"I do."

"Do you swear to be the sire of her children, the companion of her house, from this day forth in the name of Isu?"

"I do."

"Ethne, do you swear to give this man your loyalty and obedience, your love and your possessions now and forever in the name of Isu?"

With only the barest hesitation, Ethne's "I do" followed.

"In the name of the Father, the Son and the Holy Ghost, and by the power invested in me by the Holy Church of Rome, I pronounce you married."

The brevity of the service relieved Ethne, and only Coemgen gave a thought to its meaning. Germanus apparently placed less weight on this union than he had believed. In his delight at out-maneuvering Germanus, Coemgen smiled at the Abbot. "Here Germanus, take this day's golden cup and keep it for your altar."

Germanus gave a curt nod as the company left the chapel. Messengers were sent to all the kingdoms to announce that Crimthann and Ethne were married in the eyes of all the Gods, including the new one. Father Per stood on the slope below the Abbot's chapel, offering a silent blessing.

As the evening sky drew its mantle over the rath, the wedding feast unfolded in the king's hall. Roasted meats and piles of honey cakes weighed on the tables and the fion flowed freely. It was an odd celebration filled with battle tension, for the warriors were already preparing for a siege, gathering in sheep and chickens from the countryside. The cows had not yet been sent to their summer pastures, so there would be plenty of meat. The bards added to the strange atmosphere, as they sang alternately of marriage and war.

Ethne listened and was oddly comforted by the juxtaposed themes. Her life was a kind of battle, whether peace returned or a siege prevailed. She was duty-bound to one man and bound by all she held sacred in her heart to another. The stirring words of the bards strengthened her resolve to serve the Gods, the people and the king.

Blessings and well wishes came from all sides of the hall along with the usual bawdy jokes. Ethne and Crimthann smiled, bowed and led the merriment in a traditional dance. As the candles grew short and the noise of the courtiers grew, Gaine rose and took Crimthann and Ethne each by an elbow and led them towards the king's private chamber. At its door they turned and gave a deep bow to those whom they would serve. A rousing cheer went up as the door swung shut.

With the congratulations still ringing through the closed door, Crimthann leaned against it, resting his back in relief. "Being a groom is hard work!" He smiled down at Ethne. "How are you fairing?"

"I crave a cup of cold water and the light of the stars through your window."

"Let's abandon the trappings of royalty. We will return to Ethne and Crimthann." He removed his fillet and hers, and she took off her brooches and armbands as well as his. Crimthann pulled her to the wide, soft bed and sat her gently down. He held her by her shoulders and kissed her. She pulled away at arm's length and looked into his face.

"What do you seek?" he asked. "If you are looking for the man you found at midnight on the Hill of Stones, he is here. I am ever your friend, Ethne. Do not be afraid." His voice was low and kind. Ethne closed her eyes and heard the tones of those nights when they had sat side-by-side, and found each other's comfort. She leaned her forehead against his chest and he gathered her to him. With easy caresses and warm, slow kisses Crimthann made his way into her heart. Undressed, they slid under the blankets and furs and he took his time to kindle her answers to his desire. As he mounted her and made her his queen, he groaned her name, "Ethne!" And again, "Ethne!" Surprised at the joy she felt in his arms, she whispered "Faelchu!" and he tightened his grip around her.

The stars sparkled in the window frame, mimicking the jewels entwined in her hair.

Morning found them still in each other's arms. a Crimthann woke, felt the woman beside him, and a joy he had never known. Not waiting for Ethne to rouse, he began to kiss her from head to toe, tickling her behind her knees, at the small of her back, on the bottoms of her feet until she awoke laughing and wriggling. In one motion he pulled her on top of him and they made love again before either had spoken a word.

"Do you wake thus every morning, my lord?" Ethne asked, as they lay sprawled across the bed.

"Only when my bed mate wears a crown," he answered laughing. Then growing more serious, he added. "Ethne, I want to give you a gift for our wedding. What would please you most?" He sat up, pulling the covers around his waist. Ethne, too, sat up and faced him. She thought deeply before replying, knowing what her first answer would be, knowing too that it was a dangerous request. But it was an opportunity she could not waste.

"You have given me more than I knew I wanted. You are indeed the Faelchu of my nights."

A beam of pure pleasure broke out on Crimthann's face. "Name something, my sweet. I would give you every star to wear."

Ethne touched his hair, his ear, and his cheek. "There is only one thing I would ask. I would have you release the man being held in the Prisoner's Mound." She put her hand lightly on his lips to stop his protest. "I've labored twice to bring him back from death. It pains me to think of him suffering in the cold, dark of that place. Release him after the rath is closed and fortified, so there is no possibility of his escape."

Crimthann watched her closely as she spoke, but he saw no signs of dissimulation. "You are a strange woman, Ethne, my Rígain. Jewels or fine white horses are not the proper adornments for you. You would deck yourself in truth and fairness. So be it. I will set the man free as soon as the gates are blocked and the guards positioned on the ramparts."

Ethne rewarded him with a brilliant smile and a kiss that took his breath away.

# 27

The next evening, Coemgen was in the Nemed, making his own preparations for battle. He ordered neophytes to gather twigs and branches of ruadán from the hedges around the Nemed's stockade and pile them on a bed of aged birch logs, leaves, and bark.

By his side, Gaine held Coemgen's great headdress of eagle, swan, owl, and crane feathers. As the smoke from the green ruadán branches poured forth, Coemgen sang, inhaling smoke as he chanted:

*By those who are above me*
*By those who are below me*
*By those who surround me; Spirits hear me!*
*For our side I wish for death without pain*
*If it comes may it be death without fear*
*Death without horror or grieving I ask,*
*In Dagdae bring it to us!*
*Power of Moon have we over Canoc*
*Power of Sun have we over Canoc*
*Power of Rain have we over Canoc*
*Power of Thunder have we over Canoc*
*Power of Lightning have we over Canoc*
*Power of Dew have we over Canoc*
*Power of Sea have we over Canoc*
*Power of Land have we over Canoc*

*Power of Stars have we over*
*Canoc Power of Planets have we over*
*Canoc Morrígu, bring us to victory!*

Coemgen's body swayed as he moved into trance. Gaine stepped forward and placed the headdress on him. It was her job to stand by and make sure he didn't fall into the flames as he went deeper into the working.

Gradually, Coemgen lost sense of his body. In his mind he saw twelve stars, one on top of the other, stretching over his head. He had eagle's wings and flew from one star to the next, moving in wide spirals, arching higher and higher with every round.

When he saw his human form below it was a mere speck and the smoke from the great pyre a smudge against the ground. He soared over the rath, looking down at the countryside, searching for Canoc and his forces. He flew over seven hills and one river before he saw them, advancing in a shimmering tide of shields, helmets and spears glinting in the sun. There were so many of them! Having seen, Coemgen wheeled back to the rath. He found the pathway of stars and spiraled down again to the smoke of the ruadán fire as his human form slumped next to the flames.

"Gaine?" croaked Coemgen hoarsely.

"You are among us once more. What did you see?"

"An army, more men than I imagined, well armed and provisioned. They are about two days march from here . . . I don't understand. There was metal everywhere." Coemgen coughed.

A knot of fear grew in Gaine's belly. "Canoc has more wealth than we knew. No wonder he is emboldened to claim the kingship."

"Crimthann . . . cannot win."

Coemgen went very pale, raising Gaine's concern. Spirit-flight was draining, some seers died, their hearts giving out after the journey.

Gaine put a hand on is chest as he tried to rise. "No, Coemgen. Two of the young Druid will help you back to your house. You must rest and eat. I will deliver the message to Crimthann."

Only when Coemgen was safely settled in his hut did Gaine cross the distance from the Nemed to the king's hall. With so many people and so many cattle shut in for the siege the ground was a sea of mud. It took longer than usual to reach the royal house. She found Ethne and Crimthann in their private chamber, Crimthann in an oaken tub before the fire with Ethne seated on a low stool combing his hair.

"There is dire news," said Gaine.

"Tell me," said Crimthann as he rose, pulling a towel about him.

"In spirit flight, Coemgen saw Canoc's army with more men and weapons than any of us suspected."

"We can wait. It will take him time and work to feed a large army. We have our stores and cattle. We will survive."

"I leave these things to your experience," continued Gaine. "But you should also know that Coemgen is weak and taken to bed."

"Shall I make a healing bath of pine and oat straw for Comegen's recovery?" Ethne asked.

"It has been done," Gaine answered lightly, touching Ethne's cheek. She hurried back to the Nemed, cursing the thick globs of mud clinging to her boots and skirts. The dun was filled with the sounds of metal crafting, wood hewing and the clanking of swordsmen practicing. Canoc's army was a day away and there was still time to fletch arrows, to repair and manufacture weapons and armor. There was not enough fodder for the cows, therefore many were slaughtered, and the meat smoked, packed in salt or ground into sausage.

Ruadh had sat within the Prisoner's Mound for eight days, the dampness and cold seeping into his bones. His shoes and pants were wet and no person had spoken to him since his incarceration. As a Fennid warrior he had spent many lonely watches in trees and caves; this was not so different. In the past he had watched to defend his tuath, his tribe. Now he was kept from fleeing to the coast and sounding the alarm. That night long after a mog had left a plate of cold food, Ruadh lay shivering in a thin blanket on the stone floor. In his mind he made his way to the coast, towards the Fennidi.

He heard the guards' conversation suddenly interrupted by the higher tones of a woman. He knew her instantly the cadence of her words but, straining to hear, he could decipher nothing. Within moments a guard stooped through the doorway and gestured him to follow. "Move it, you. The Rígain is waiting."

Ruadh stepped into the night and took a deep breath of clear air. When his eyes found Ethne's he lowered them respectfully.

"Release this man into my care. Your watch is no longer needed," she commanded and motioned with her hand for Ruadh to follow. When they were out of hearing, Ethne turned and handed him a hot posset. "Drink this. You must be cold to the bone." Her face betrayed no emotion, but her eyes were moist and shining. He gulped the warm drink gratefully, letting the elderberry brew laced with cinnamon, ginger and the Waters of Life work as antidote to the dank stones of the mound.

"Ethne, I won't be released if it puts you in danger." said Ruadh hoarsely.

"It was my wedding gift from Crimthann."

Ruadh nearly choked on his drink. "How original! How did he come to be so generous?"

"There's no time for that." Ethne led him further from the guards and handed him his sword. A wild thought to carry her off raced through his mind, but her courage caught at his throat and he looked away. With stiff fingers he belted the scabbard and tied it to his leg.

Ethne continued in a low voice. "We have a report that Canoc's army is huge. Coemgen is ill and Gaine has assumed the duties of Ard-Ban-Drui. Now that you are free, you can take your place among the warriors defending the palisades."

"Ethne, now that I am free I will do whatever it takes to protect the people and yourself."

"Go with the Gods, Ruadh, may they keep you safe." She put a hand on his arm, but withdrew it as a small band of men came into view. Ruadh made a deep bow and turned toward the soldiers' quarters to find a meal and a warm bed for the night. Ethne watched him disappear into the dark and made her way back to the royal hall.

Shortly after cock crow, Crimthann scaled the palisade to sing the Sun prayer. As he gazed towards the east he noticed a flickering light, in and around the trees at the perimeter of the fortress. Peering closely he saw that the lights were the first rays of sun glinting off armor; helmets, shields, and spearheads.

"Oh Grian!" he exclaimed. "Now it begins." He slid down the wall quickly. As of now anyone exposed on the ramparts could be felled by an arrow.

Crimthann ran to the warriors' quarters to alert the cean-naire who had brought their kin groups to fight for the Ard-Ri. The ceannaire in turn woke their kin and gave them orders. Every warrior traced patterns of blue, the color of protection, on face and arms. Some were permanently tattooed with blue spirals on their bodies.

"All archers to your posts in a circle around the rath!" commanded Crimthann. "Perch behind the oaken beams of the fencing. The remaining warriors within the fort will continue to butcher and salt meat. Everyone, make your prayers to the Morrigú." Crimthann paced restlessly up and down the pali-sades, overseeing everything. Canoc did not strike that day or the next, or the next. When the attack came it was with fire as the Oirthir shot flaming arrows over the walls. A few arrows found their mark in the willow roofs within the enclosure, but the flames were quickly smothered with blankets. The outer fence caught fire in one section and villagers formed a line with buckets and cauldrons filled from the stream, dousing the flames. Only one man was killed, shot in the chest by a flaming brand. Day and night the rain of arrows continued. Some were firebrands; some wounded a child, a warrior or an animal. Many landed harmlessly and were collected to be shot back.

Days passed, and Canoc stormed at the pace of the campaign. He conferred with his battle leaders; Donal and Nessan. "Too much time is spent searching for food. We make no progress in capturing the fort."

"They have water," said Nessan.

"That's not news," Canoc barked.

"With water they can contain the fires. They can't live long without it, nor can their cattle."

"Do you mean to poison it?" asked Donal.

"No, that would be too difficult. We should divert the stream away from the dun with a barricade of logs and stones. They won't last a fortnight."

A half-smile spread across Canoc's face. "Get the men to it immediately."

The order was given to fell trees, and to collect rocks and boulders, and pile them in the swift running stream. A channel dug at right angles further altered the river's course.

# 28

Coemgen lay fevered on his palette, muttering and describing islands in the Western sea. "Who can say if he sees dream or Truth?" asked Gaine. She sat with him daily now.

"He is slipping from this world," Ethne stated calmly. "A portion of his Self was left behind in the Spirit world. I fear he cannot live much longer."

Gaine scanned Coemgen's body with her inner sight. The shining aura that she saw around healthy bodies was but a feeble glow. In places the light was missing altogether and in others it had given over to gray patches. She understood those dark places as an absence of light, of will, of spirit.

Ethne held one of Coemgen's hands, and Gaine the other. They each worked to strengthen the man's fire of life and both understood it was likely futile. From time to time they looked up and searched each other's faces for hope. They had sat thus a long time when a warrior knocked at the door.

"Your majesty, your holiness!" He bowed. "Disaster has come!"

"What is it?" Ethne kept her voice under control.

"The river has dried up. The Ard-Ri asks both of you to come to the stream bed and pray to the Gods for the water's return."

Ethne looked at Gaine. "You are Ard-Ban-Drui. All magic working for the kingdom is in your hands."

"I accept that it is so. In a time of peace an election would have been held but I must lead for now. Let us see what can be done."

The women left Coemgen in the care of a young Drui and picked their way across a sea of mud. A crowd stood at the place where the river should have been, and Ethne and Gaine were greeted by weeping women and frightened children, by Crimthann and the warriors looking grim. Everyone understood that without water they were doomed.

The two Druidesses knelt at the edge of the riverbed, "Water spirits, speak to us. Tell us what has happened," Gaine said aloud. With eyes closed, they stilled their breathing and brought their attention to their brows, just slightly above and between their eyes. Gaine was more gifted at "seeing" and soon had a vision. Ethne, who often "heard" the spirits, was told where the water had gone. Emerging from their trance, they looked knowingly at each other.

"We have seen the problem. The river is directed away from its bed by tree trunks and stones," said Gaine.

The people hunched together and some put their hands over their mouths. There was no hope without water. Seeing people's fear, Crimthann stepped forward. "It has not rained for some days now, but eventually there will be a storm. Scour the houses for pots, pans, bowls and barrels, anything that will hold rainwater. Place these where they will catch the rain. As soon as it begins to rain, take your linens and cloths and spread them on the rooftops and in the trees. We can wring them out to capture the water. If we are diligent we will survive."

The frightened folk took strength from his words and dispersed to put out their barrels and cauldrons, and to pray to the Gods for rain. Ethne returned to the royal hall and Gaine to the Nemed to supervise the setting out of pans and dishes. Crimthann retired to the barracks to confer with the ceannaire about strategies should the walls be breached.

Days passed, and there was no rain. Every available vessel was set out doors. Prayers and offerings were made at every altar. A dog and horse were sacrificed, both beloved and healthy animals in their prime, offered to In Daghdae in hopes of protection. They were buried whole and untouched just inside of the walls of the Nemed. The worst problem was the cattle that needed watering daily, so more were butchered.

Ruadh watched the growing fear of the people and made up his mind to act. Telling no one of his intentions, he got himself posted to a section of the outer palisade for night watches. On the sixth night, the moon was a mere sliver, and the ground a sea of mist. Using a stout rope knotted and wedged between two timbers, he lowered himself over the side of the outer wall, dropping soundlessly onto the turf below. He had watched the enemy's fires for days and now headed for the darkest patch in the surrounding trees.

By dawn he was miles away, towards the coast.

# PART THREE

~

# The Sacred Tree

# 29

<hr/>

"Ethne," Crimthann spoke as they dressed for the day. "Is there anything the Druid can do? If Coemgen were well, he would make magic to aid us."

"Gaine and I are waiting for a sign from the Gods before we exercise our magic. We want to see if the people's prayers will be answered. Every magical working has a backlash: look at what it cost Coemgen. He will not live out the week."

"I understand the consequences of Druidecht, but that is the burden of leadership. We have to do something or the people will demand surrender."

"Very well . . ." Ethne pulled on her cloak. "I'll speak with Gaine."

She walked to the Nemed deep in thought. She knew that if the Druid enacted a battle spell to oppose the surrounding army it could recoil and cause equal harm to Crimthann or his followers. The laws of the world were impartial, and balance would be maintained. It was impossible to know how and when streams of magic might turn back on the sender, or how to protect oneself fully from them.

She found Gaine at the Fire Altar making offerings of butter and mead to the flames. Tears of supplication wet her cheeks, her face red from the fire's heat.

"In Dagdae, save us! We are your people. We seek to preserve your ways and your honor. Brighid inspire us! Show us the way. Morrígu, Bran, help us! Bring your ravens of war to

our aid! We need you! Lug! Give us your skill and brilliance!"
Ethne waited in the shadows and then stepped closer to the fire.
"The king asks that we do a working to bring back the water.
He believes the people are losing heart."

Gaine stared, glassy-eyed and distant. Not fully grounded, she was still with the Gods. "Prayers and offerings are one
thing, Ethne, but the ways of Druidecht are dangerous. There
are always consequences and any request we make of the Gods
returns to us three fold. Perhaps the Cauldron of Sea will show
us a way."

The women approached the Cauldron, sat before it cross-
legged, and focused their breathing. Their fingers, placed in
the ancient mudra, thumb to forefinger, symbolized wisdom
and of the circle of life. They searched within for inspiration
and a life-enhancing, powerful spell. Acolytes wafted artemisia
smoke with eagle wing fans and save for the crackling fire, there
was no sound.

A sudden gust of wind rippled the Cauldron's waters as a
smolach called from the Sacred Ash . "More wet, more wet,
more wet!"

The smolach ate berries from the golden bough and carried
them from one tree to another, spreading the sacred herb. It was
a powerful symbol of protection and of the power to ward off
misfortune. And it was the best possible omen because when
it sang, it presaged rain.

"Ecca taught me that Nature is the greatest magician of all"
said Gaine. "Now that the smolach has predicted rain, we can
rouse the Druid for an impressive show. The people will believe
that we ourselves made the clouds come, but in truth it is the
will of the Gods. The bird is never wrong."

By evening a line of Druid wound across the open space of
the dun to the empty riverbed. Three of them held the iron lids
of cauldrons in their hands. Three more carried "hag's tapers,"
dried mullein stalks dipped in melted fat and bee's wax and
dried for later use. Three others carried tree branches and a

small pot of water. Several more had drums and rattles. Ethne held a handful of silver coins and jewelry, offerings for the water Spirits, while Gaine led the procession bearing a staff of ash and a wand of oak, both known to attract lightning.

Gaine invoked the powers:

*Ancestors, hear us! You, who lie beneath the soil and bless it with your bones and blood, you are welcome here! You, who lie beneath the waves, come to us. You, whose wisdom has been our guide and inspiration through many lifetimes, be with us.*

*Nature Spirits! You, who help us every day of our lives, join our circle! You, who feed our bodies, clothe us, warm us, and shelter us. You who give your love and whom we love in return, we honor you and ask you to join us now!*

*Gods of our people! Our need is great. We honor you with songs and offerings. Be with us now! Danann, Great Mother of the Rivers! Send forth your bounty on this small patch of earth. We are your children and we are thirsty. We need your living waters!*

The Druid, in unison, began a chant punctuated by the rhythm of the drums:

*Come storm, come lightening*
*Showers like a mighty river,*
*Heavy clouds, thunder bearing*
*Wash the hills and feed the trees,*
*Cheer our people with your music*
*Winds sweep o'er the strath and plain!*

Three Druid stood at the highest point of the palisade and clanged their iron lids, simulating thunder. Other Druid lit the hag's tapers and swung them in great arcs across the open space of the riverbed, mimicking lightning, or dipped the tree branches into the pot of water and sprinkled the ground, the fence and each other, making rain.

The chant continued unbroken while Ethne danced, spinning dessel, in the middle of the riverbed. In rhythm she stooped and placed a silver offering on the rocks, a gift for the water Spirits. Gaine sang, and pointed her oaken staff to the heavens and then towards the soil, directing streams of water to descend from sky to earth.

As the dancing and chanting reached its crescendo, a deep rumble shook the sky. The singing quickened and the drummers increased their pace. Everyone danced now, moving in sun-wise spirals, their will in harmony with the heavens, welcoming the Spirits of rain and weather.

The wind picked up and black clouds approached from the South, the Goddess direction.

"Danann is with us! Rain clouds approach!" the Druid exulted.

Fat drops of water pelted the ground. The people cheered and ran to hang out cloths, gathering the water and wringing it into vessels. Dogs barked and cattle lowed.

The smolach sang from the dripping branches of the Sacred Ash at the heart of the Nemed: "More wet! More wet! More wet!"

# 30

---

C oemgen was dying. Gaine declared herself his Anam Chara and prepared to stay with him as he made his transition to the Otherworld. A harper played as Crimthann sat in the death-watch, waiting in silence should his mentor speak.

The Druid circled Coemgen's hut, singing and praying for his easy passage. They wore green funerary robes, the color of immortality and rebirth. In the Nemed, Ethne supervised the digging of a grave and the collecting of stones for a cairn.

A round cairn rose over every grave in the Nemed, and each burial included articles associated with the life of the deceased Druid: torques, mantles, golden jewelry, drinking horns and magical staffs, branches and leaves of oak or sprays of the golden bough.

The people of the rath gathered to pay their respects and sat on the ground near Coemgen's hut, praying, waiting for news. In late afternoon Coemgen tightened his grip on Gaine's hand. She sang of walking into the sunset, into the Western Sea, of meeting family, lovers and friends. Coemgen's eyes lost focus and his breath rattled. Gaine dipped her fingers into a golden bowl and drew out a few drops of water, which she dripped onto Coemgen's tongue. "Go easy to the land of the ancestors. Let the waters bear you to the Blessed Isles."

Crimthann wept for the loss of his teacher and friend. When it was certain that Coemgen's spirit had departed his form, Gaine addressed the assembled Druid, who would take the news to the waiting people. Damán, Coemgen's apprentice, recited a praise poem he had composed. It compared Coemgen to a mighty oak that fed and sheltered the people and kept alive their Spirit fires. The people wept openly as they listened.

Coemgen's corpse was lifted, placed on a wooden stretcher and carried to the center of the sacred precinct. Flanked by an honor guard of Druid, the body was viewed by every person living in the rath. They brought flowers, leafy sprays, and food for his use in the next world, including a small jar of honey brought by Father Per. When all had said farewell, the Druid carried him in a slow procession to the place of burial.

The interment would take place at dawn. That night would be spent in vigil, every Druid sitting near an existing grave and several sitting in a circle around Coemgen. The vigil was kept to give Coemgen company, for spirits lingered, sometimes giving messages, near their bodies for three days. Other spirits also came near when someone new passed over.

Gaine sang:

*Come spirits across the ocean*
*Join with your brother who waits here*
*Take him across to the bright land*
*Take him across moor and meadow*
*Take him across a calm sea*
*Take him across the blissful ocean*
*Peace and joy on his day of death*
*As he finds his path to the white Sun.*

Crimthann held vigil with Ethne as she waited for a spirit vision. He held his grief, praying for guidance to lead the people to safety. Ethne had been occupied with ritual duties and the royal household and this was her first moment to fully feel the loss. The death of her life-long teacher and friend shook the earth beneath her for he was the foundation of her knowledge, the leader of her Druid kin.

She remembered the first time she had seen him. She had been nine and he had been more rugged than the north cliffs of her clann home. She heard his first words to her, "In you, the Nemed grows a new branch." And then the sobs came.

In her loss, her thoughts groped toward Ruadh. With a start, she realized she had not seen him during the days of Coemgen's death vigil. She put her hand into the small pouch at her waist, searching within until her fingers found the red ribbon of their handfasting. Smoothing and re-smoothing the cloth between her fingers, she focused her mind and saw an expanse of water. She smelled the salt spray on the breeze and heard gulls crying. Was she seeing Coemgen's crossing or the place where she would find Ruadh? As she struggled for answers, a wave if nausea engulfed her and the vision disappeared. She wavered as she stood, Gaine saw beads of sweat break out on her brow.

Ethne broke from the huddled Druid to be alone. Without warning, she vomited behind a clump of bushes. No one else had been ill, no one had complained of stomach cramps from food or tainted water. She retched again, steadied herself against a tree and walked further from the gathering. When the chants of the Druid were a mere hum in the background, she lowered herself against a trunk. Gaine came up beside her and sat down.

"Are you ill, Ethne?" Gaine's face was full of concern.

"I am better now. It is worry and fatigue. The air was so close, I could hardly breathe."

Gaine smiled and put her hand on Ethne's hair. "There are no small accidents on such a night, child." She placed her hand on Ethne's belly and focused her awareness, asking her Imbas for answer. She saw a tiny light peeping from the folds of Ethne's womb.

"You are carrying a life, Ethne. It is no coincidence that this child is revealed on the eve of Coemgen's passing."

"What are you saying, Gaine?" Ethne asked, the implications filling her like the sun filling a room.

"This child may be an ancestor to replace Coemgen, a helper for the tribes. This child may be Coemgen himself, returned to lead us as he has always done. Let me take you back to the hall."

As they walked back, Crimthann strode towards them. "Ethne, are you unwell?" His face creased with concern.

Ethne put out her hand to him and he put an arm around her shoulders, bending over to hear her words. "I am with child, Crimthann. I am only faint from this new life that makes its way through me."

Crimthann held her and kissed the top of her head. "My sweet, Ethne. Over and again you bring me joy!" Tears filled his eyes. He and Ethne knew this was the Gods' final confirmation of his kingship and of his union with the Land. They had bestowed full sovereignty upon him through Ethne's fertility. As Ethne's face paled again, Gaine took her arm and led her toward the kitchens where she would make a brew of raspberry leaf and peppermint along with toasted bread. From the royal kitchens, news of the queen's pregnancy traveled quickly to every corner of the dun.

Emboldened by Ethne's pregnancy, Crimthann asked Gaine for a battle spell at the council meeting. "Gaine, you and the Druid brought us rain, but we can't hold against the siege forever. Though the ways of Druidecht are dangerous, I must request another working to defeat Canoc's army."

"My Lord Crimthann, we'll do as you ask. But the working will be done in your name only to spare the tuath any ill from the magic."

"I would have it no other way," he replied.

Gaine exited the hall, filled with determination. The people were calm for now because the archers were keeping Canoc's men at bay, but pressure was mounting. The spring crops were not yet planted and soon the herds should be moved to their summer pastures. The fodder was running out.

Ethne refused to participate. Harm to her unborn child had to be considered, and she was already tired. Gaine addressed Damán and Clothru under the sacred ash of the Nemed.

"A battle spell is the most dangerous of all workings, and we don't know what shielding Canoc's Druid are using. We three will perform this magic, no one else is to be involved. I have been clear that we are working strictly on the king's behalf.

"Clothru and I prepared the lead tablets," said Damán. He produced three tablets, pounded, rolled, and ready to be inscribed with sharpened and fire-hardened ash sticks."

He had matured during the siege, from a gangly-armed, uncertain boy to a selfdirected young man anticipating the needs of the tuath. Perhaps it was Clothru's influence. He and the young Ban-Drui were of equal age and rank, but Clothru possessed an assurance that Damán had lacked.

Gaine nodded, pleased. "The waning moon is a good time to do what we have been bidden. Meet me here tonight after all are asleep."

They convened in the still of midnight, exiting the Nemed without sound, and processed to the ditch surrounding the sacred precinct. Working in its depths they would be obscured by the hawthorn, elder and ruadán hedges. Gaine inscribed a circle in the air, using a gold wand with nine bells attached. They tinkled lightly as she walked a tight circle defining the perimeter of their working. *"In the names of Land, Sea, and Sky, I cast a circle of protection around us, around the king and queen, around the people of the tuath, and around the dun. May magic sent against us be repelled. Gods of our people,"* she continued in a hoarse whisper, moving dessel, inscribing a second circle with the bell branch and then a third, *"Be with us now! Crimthann the Ard-Rí asks for a spell against our enemies. Help us do his bidding!"*

Clothru and Damán held the lead tablets and the ash sticks. Each tablet to be inscribed and then buried. Gaine carried a small barrel of red ale, flavored with ruadán berries, an offering to the earth as a sacrifice. She whispered as they wrote upon the tablets, squinting in the moonlight.

"Inscribe the tablets thus." she directed. "Three showers of fire will fall . . . the flames shall diminish our enemy's courage . . . the urine in their bodies and their horses bodies shall be stopped . . . every inhalation our warriors take shall strengthen them . . . every exhalation our warriors make shall weaken the enemy . . . the trees, stones and sod of the earth shall appear threatening to our enemy . . . our spear points shall be as numerous to them as leaves in a forest . . . fever and chill shall take them until they die."

They incised the curse deep into the tablets. Using an ox bone, they dug deep into the loamy soil and buried the tablets, carefully replacing the sod so none would find the spot. Gaine poured the ale upon the ground as they finished the spell with a dance, a tuathamail spiral, that sent their curse into the night. After thanking the deities of Land, Sea and Sky, the three returned silently to the Nemed. They would not speak of this night to each other or anyone else, and no one would be foolish enough to ask.

# 31

Canoc's Druid wanted to cast a wall of protection around his troops, but Germanus forbade it, declaring it superstition and unfit for a Cristaide king. He assured Canoc that the sign of the Holy Cross had brought the Roman emperor victory. Canoc put his trust in the new God and forbade his Druid to act. Many a Drui grew impatient and returned to Oirthir, believing their effort was better placed among those who served the Island's Gods.

The Cristaide monks woke the troops each dawn with chanting, and all were obliged to assemble for Mass. The rest of the day the men combed outlying areas for game, an increasing problem with so many to feed. The people of the nearby towns were sheltered in the Ard-Ri's dun, and had taken their livestock with them along with stores of grain and root crops. There was little left for Canoc's army.

Heavy thunderstorms now soaked the tents, bedding, clothing and the fodder for the horses. Swords and knives had to be greased with goose fat continuously to prevent rust. Everyone's boots were moldy, the campfires were powerless to dry them no matter how long they were left by the coals.

A strange sickness was attacking the horses. It began with bloating in the belly until the creatures writhed on the ground and had to be put to death. They lost half of the cavalry to the malady. Fever also raged among the men of the camp. As one returned to duty another would fall ill, only to have those who had recovered begin vomiting again, unable to void their bowels.

The Abbot ordered a second Mass at twilight. He walked among the sick with a flagon of holy water – spring water in which a bible had been dipped. Every stricken man was ordered to drink.

"Healing herbs will do little against this sickness. They need faith in the healing power of Isu," Germanus declared. "Pray!"

Crimthann was unaware of conditions outside the rath. His biggest concern was how to feed the remaining sheep and cattle and how to plant the summer crops. He knew a direct assault would have to be made, else more than warriors would be lost.

Reluctantly, he broached the subject with the ceannaire.

"My archers report that fewer and fewer arrows come from Canoc's men each day. Either they hold back in preparation for battle or they are losing strength. Now is the time to act before their men and arms are re-supplied from distant kingdoms." said Fiachnae, a ceannaire from Torcrad.

Celtchair of Irardacht agreed. "My men have said the same thing. Their archers are fewer and fewer. I say we attack before they build up their forces again."

Crimthann looked into each face. "Who says 'Aye' for battle?"

"Aye!" was the shouted reply.

"Then hear me. We go forth tonight while they sleep."

"Aye!" came again the reply.

The men turned to each other, excitement in their faces, making battle plans and eager to finish with Canoc, the sooner to get back to their herds and farms.

# 32

Ruadh agreed to lead the assembled Fennidi from every part of Island, joined in a loose confederation to aid the Ard-Ri. They came together out of respect for Crimthann's status as a warrior and anger at the Cristaidi preaching against their ways.

"I need no recognition from any king, nor will I take orders from one. I fight for our honor," said Erc to Ruadh as he sharpened his sword.

The Fiana warriors moved expertly through mountain passes towards the rath of the Ard-Ri, with Ruadh in the lead. He had strapped his sword and shield to his pack, slid a dirk in his belt, and kept his bow ready as he walked, scouting where Canoc's guards were posted, not wanting to penetrate Canoc's perimeter prematurely.

Ruadh habitually moved through the underbrush like a fox even through dry leaves, but this morning his footsteps rustled the forest duff. He paused and looked up for the sun's position. It was then he heard a noise. He walked on deliberately, stopping at random to listen. Each time he did so he heard footfalls for an instant after he stopped. He knew that deer would sometimes follow a hunter, sensing that behind the hunter is the safest place. But deer have a distinctive pattern of footfalls caused by four feet. The other possibility was a bear or wolf. But no creature other than a human moves one foot at a time. Ruadh felt a tingle of fear. He was being hunted.

He dropped behind a log and rolled onto his back, knife drawn. There was no sound, only the green smell of crushed fern. He waited, sprinting to a nearby tree to put the tree's girth between himself and the hunter. A twig snapped, the hunter moved closer, well hidden behind holly shrubs. Ruadh dove into a clump of woodbine and fern, crouching low, his knife held before him.

To evade his pursuer, he darted from undergrowth to trees to fallen logs. With each step, he became more certain that the hunter was one of Canoc's guards, and that he had reached the outer edge of Canoc's forces. The problem was getting back to warn the Fennidi, a day's march behind.

Ruadh darted behind another tree. An arrow whizzed past his ear and sank into the tree behind. He dove for the under-brush again, hearing a waterfall in the distance. Moving from side to side he worked his way towards the sound, doing his best to be an erratic target.

A rocky outcropping came into view and Ruadh sprinted towards a boulder a quarter of the way up the rise, next to the waterfall. An arrow sliced the dirt to one side of the stone just as Ruadh dove behind. He now had the high-ground advantage. He fitted the arrow into his bow and crept from behind the rock; seeing his pursuer crouched behind a low juniper. Ruadh shot and heard a muffled scream. Someone staggered from behind the bush and Ruadh let fly another arrow, splitting the man's skull.

Kneeling next to the body, Ruadh saw the distinctive tribal tattoos of the Oirthir on the arms and face. He took the man's bow, arrows, sword and dirk, and sped back towards the West to alert the gathered bands moving through the wood.

Crimthann's warriors assembled behind the gates of the rath as women and children moved among them, passing out bowls of stew, fion and ale. Gaine and the Druid made offerings at the Fire Altar. Her voice rose above the others. "We beseech you, Morrígu, Triple Goddess of battle, and Lug Samildanach, the many-skilled one, bring skill to our fighters! We beseech you, Brighid, for protection over every warrior.

Spread your mantle over them, in the coming battle." Gaine worried about Canoc's Druid and their battle spells, as she waited anxiously for the backlash from her own magic.

Crimthann, face painted red and black, banged on his shield for attention. "We wait for the dark, then we can drop over the walls invisible and unheard. We will move in bands like the Fennidi, using our wits and skill. Surprise is our best weapon. Stay low and move like shadows."

The men nodded, muffling their buckles, chains and armor.

"Disappear into the trees or crawl along the grass. Speed is essential. Once the attack begins, do not hesitate. Find a fire and sleeping men then kill and retreat immediately. Nothing more." Crimthann surveyed the men before him, seasoned warriors, ready for a fight. None of them held allegiance to Canoc.

In the dark of night the men dropped over the walls by twos and threes, using stout ropes to lower themselves over the palisade. In dark clothing and with faces blackened, some headed to the trees for cover and some crawled on their bellies towards Canoc's camp.

With lethal swiftness the warriors crept in and killed dozens of Canoc's men as they slept by the fires. They worked efficiently with a determination born of anger, their hands bloodied and the smell of death on them. A blast of trumpet split the night, an alarm from Canoc's guards.

Crimthann's men sped back to the safety of the trees and from there raced to the wall where ladders and ropes had been lowered by the women and children to help them scale up. A few were killed as Canoc's men followed, but archers on the ramparts held most of Canoc's forces at bay.

When it was clear no further retaliation was coming, Crimthann led the men to the great hall. A fire blazed, and Ethne ordered the mogae to pour glasses of fion and mead. She opened her arms to embrace Crimthann, running her eyes over each man as he shuffled to get near the fire. But none showed the face she was seeking. She did not ask if Ruadh had gone over the wall with the rest. She held her questions and fear, unwilling to betray him.

Gaine began the meeting according to tradition. "In the name of the Three Worlds, Ancestors, Nature Spirits and Gods, I declare this assembly open. Let us give thanks to the deities that inspired and protected us this night, The Morrígu, Lug and Brighid." She stepped down from the dais holding two beakers and approached the center fire.

"I offer butter to the flames in thanks to the Ones who made our way smooth – the Spirits, deities and forces who helped us move swiftly through the night to accomplish our task." She poured the butter in a circle sun-wise around the edges of the fire.

"I offer the Waters of Life to the flames in memory of the dead – Bairredach, Gorman, Cétach and Tiarnan. May their spirits rise like the essence of these waters to travel the Western ocean and find the Islands of the Blessed. May they return to us again in the wombs of their loved ones."

As she poured the liquid in a sun-wise circle onto the fire the flames turned blue causing gasps of surprise. Ethne let out her breath when Ruadh's name was not spoken. She had not yet told him of the child she carried, as likely his as Crimthann's. A messenger, flanked by Crimthann's guards, appeared in the doorway.

"Lord," said one of the guards. "This man asks to speak to the assembly." "Let him come forward," said Crimthann.

The man looked weak and tired as he spoke his message. "My lord, Canoc challenges you to single combat to spare the lives of husbandmen, fathers and sons."

Crimthann kept his eyes on the man. "There is justice in what he asks, messenger. I will confer with my warriors and give my answer. Let the rules of hospitality be observed. Bring this man food and drink and give him a place near the door, out of earshot of our conference."

Fiachnae, a ceannaire of the Torcrad spoke first, "Sire, did you not mark how little resistance there was among Canoc's men? And where were the horses? Did they eat them?"

"This messenger appears ill. I saw fresh graves near the camp. Do you think they suffer from a plague?" asked Celtchair of the Irardacht.

Gaine's eyebrows rose, but she kept silent. This was the first intimation that her spell had worked, but it still didn't explain the lack of resistance from Canoc's Druid. "Whether they suffer from sickness or starvation, Canoc's offer is fair. As battle leader I must honor his challenge or lose face. I will stand for the good of the rath and all the Island's sons and daughters."

"My lord Crimthann," Ethne said, "our fates are in the hands of the Gods as are the kingdom and this child within me. Do as your honor requires." She held him with her eyes.

The messenger was sent back to answer Canoc's challenge: single combat on the morrow for the Ard-Ri's crown.

Crimthann's men spent the night polishing his shield and oiling his spear, which they fitted with feathers and bright ribbons. The women pressed his plaid and brushed his boots. Others saw to his horse, which they outfitted with a bridle of worked bronze. They cropped its mane, braiding it with ribbons and feathers, combing its tail carefully.

Ethne ordered a bath for the king, a wave of tenderness moving through her as he lowered himself into the warm water. She dismissed the mogae, knelt and lathered his powerful shoulders and strong back. She kissed the back of his neck and tears started in her eyes.

"Crimthann, I would be the consort you deserve."

He turned in surprise, putting a wet hand to her face. "Ethne, you have been my queen since the moment I first heard your voice. You have been my love since the first day you stepped into my hall. I could have no better wife."

She put her arms about him, ignoring the damp that soaked her shift. "My love for you deepens and grows. It took root when we shared our fears and dreams on the hill of stones. Your voice comes to me in my dreams when I am uncertain, and I would protect you from this terrible battle if I could." Her tears fell freely as she thought of his life given for the people, for the child he might never see.

Crimthann rose from the bath and lifted her in his arms, water streaming over them both. He carried her to their bed and softly drew off her gown. Kissing her neck, he whispered, "Your face is dear beyond measure." Then he kissed her breasts. He put his face on her belly, kissing the unborn baby within. His kisses were soft, but urgent. "This child of ours will tell you of my love every time you look upon it."

Ethne reached to him and kissed his forehead, his temples, his nose, and his wide mouth. She tangled her fingers in his hair and pulled him down to her, joining her body with his as they strained and clung, neither wanting the least thought or distance to separate them. At long last, they fell asleep, locked within each other's need, tangled in a knot of linens and furs.

In the stillest hour before dawn, Crimthann woke and lay watching Ethne as she slept. Her hair swirled away from her face and lay spread across the bed. He took a handful and brought it to his face, breathing in the smell of her. His heart constricted and a sob shook him. He pressed her hair to his eyes and to his lips. "You carry the Island within you, my love," he whispered, then extricated himself carefully from her arms and legs. As he stood beside the bed, Ethne opened her eyes and looked at her husband from his knees and thighs to his broad chest and shoulders to his clear, fierce eyes. She sat up and drew the blankets around her shoulders.

"It is time, Ethne," Crimthann said before she could question or argue.

She pressed her mouth into a tight line and nodded. "I will be the one to comb your hair today."

Crimthann put on his tunic and leggings and sat on the edge of the bed. Ethne took up the set of combs she had brought from the Forest House and carefully untangled his long thick hair. When it was smooth and shining, she made two braids in front, to keep any strands from his eyes while he was fighting. These braids she finished with strips of red leather. She tied an eagle feather bound with red thread to a gathered strand of hair on one side of his head. "The eagle's Spirit will give you clear vision. It will help you anticipate Canoc's movements." She stood back to survey her work and her eyes rested on his. They stood taking each other in, until Ethne's eyes and throat burned.

"Don't, Ethne. There is no separation for us. You, as Ban-Drui know this. Promise me to hold this day in your memory. Remember how I looked with my bright shield and my plaid and my horse. Remember that I rode out for the people of the Island."

"I will tell our child that you fought bravely, that you did it for all the children and for honor." Her tears fell unheeded. "I will hold you within my heart, and the bards will sing of you for generations to come." She had no chance to kiss him once more, the women had come with his plaid. Ethne stood while the men handed him his shield and spear and strapped on his great sword. Through it all, his eyes stayed on her. As he stepped past her to move into the great hall he heard her whisper;

"I promise."

# 33

Half of Canoc's men and nearly all his horses were dead from sickness and Canoc was no fool. To everyone it looked as though he had compassion for his warriors, but fighting Crimthann in single combat was really his only hope, he couldn't even call upon his Druid to aid him; the Abbot had driven them away.

"Germanus!" he called, his voice cracked and dry. He repeated the call several times before the Abbot appeared.

"I was at prayers, Canoc. Devotion to our Lord comes before all else."

Canoc grimaced and pointed a finger at the Abbot's chest. "Ask your Drui, Isu, to put a magical ward upon my weapons and upon my horse. Give me a veil of protection from Coemgen's magic."

"Canoc, the one God fights for those who believe in him. We surrender ourselves to his will. Isu will lend your sword strength. If you but trust in his power, you will easily overcome Coemgen and his Druid spells."

"Does this religion have no battle magic?"

"I will pray to Heaven while you are in combat. I will beseech the Almighty to make your weapons swift and deadly. I will entreat him to give you victory this day." These words did not match the elaborate Druid incantations Canoc had known all his life, but Germanus stood firm. With a curt bow of his head, Canoc swept past the Abbot toward his horse. As he neared, he saw Albinus sprinkling holy water on his horse and sword and the monks wafting incense and intoning prayers in Latin.

Germanus joined them, holding Canoc's spear wrapped in a cloth to keep the damp from the sharp metal. He slid it into the saddle thong saying; "I have placed a special blessing on your spear. It will find its mark if you follow your faith."

In the early hours of dawn, before any in the rath save sentries were awake, Gaine, Damán and Clothru buried another lead tablet. This one spelled death for Canoc and promised a wise, valiant and devout ruler for the Island, one who honored the Island's ways.

As the sun breasted the treetops, a messenger approached the gates of the dun.

"Canoc marches this way!" he shouted, spurring his horse on the track back to the enemy position on the hill. The people of the rath stood on the walkway of the palisade, their clann banners flying, their plaids and battle-painted faces bright in the sun.

Ethne stood to one side of the gate, watching as Crimthann clasped hands with his chieftains then mounted his horse. Her heart hammered her chest and she clenched her fists by her side as the great gates swung open. She raced up the steps to find a spot near Gaine overlooking the gates.

As Crimthann appeared on the field before the dun, a roar went up from the people. He marched his horse, in a long zig zag up one side of the palisade and down the other, the horse's hide shining in the morning light, its tail held high, Crimthann's weapons gleaming, his back straight and proud.

"People of the tuaths!" he shouted. "I ride this morning in the name of the Spirits of the Island!" A roar arose. "I ride in the name of Lug! In the name of Nuada! In the name of The Morrígu!" Roar after roar followed his shouts. " I ride for honor, for justice, for the soil of our birth!" His voice crested the thunder of the crowd. "I ride for *you*!" He raised his spear, gave a mighty war whoop and pointed his horse to the top of the rise.

The people on the palisade saw Canoc approach the rath with his warriors, startled to see how few they were. Crimthann sidled his horse within shouting range of Canoc. "I salute you as a free person!" he yelled.

Canoc spurred his horse a few steps forward from his line of men. "We can end this peacefully if you will surrender your weapons and the rath."

Crimthann's charger took a step sideways and Crimthann twisted his torso to face Canoc. "I am the anointed Ard-Ri of this Island, married to the land in the ancient manner. My wife is with child, the Earth Mother Anu has accepted my reign, and I have been blessed by the Abbot Germanus in the monastery chapel. Swear your fealty to me now, before it is too late!"

Canoc spat in the dirt. "This is a new day, Crimthann, your Gods have no power. The new religion and the forces of Rome are behind me."

"What has Rome or a foreign God to do with *us*, Canoc?"

"You are a fool, Crimthann! It is Rome's gold that bought these weapons, these horses, these shields. Do you think a large crop of oats and a few head of cattle can raise such an army? Germanus brings *gold* to pay my warriors, gold from the Romans!"

"You are more than a greedy man. You are a traitor, Canoc, leading men who fight because they are paid. *My* warriors stand ready to give their lives out of loyalty to their kin and to me. Will the bards of Rome sing your praises when you are dead? Will generations to come know your name?"

Canoc's eyes burned, his face crimson as he ground his heels into his horse's flanks. "In the name of the new God Isu, I will *kill* you for those words!" His horse reared and spun. Crimthann backed his horse for the charge.

The horses' hooves pounded as they galloped towards each other. Mud sprayed as they met and swerved, the two warriors colliding in a clash of spear and shield as a roar went up from the palisade. Then circling again in an ever widening spiral, the two men waited for their moment, steadied their horses and charged anew, Crimthann nearly knocking Canoc's shield from his hand. Again they charged and again, grunting and gritting their teeth as they lunged and jabbed with their spears. At the next charge Crimthann turned abruptly to lodge his spear under Canoc's arm. Canoc blocked the thrust with his own spear, which glanced off Crimthann's shield, slicing his arm.

Canoc's men beat their shields with their swords and yelled curses at Crimthann.

The crowd on the palisade screamed insults at Canoc and beat the drums to rekindle Crimthann's courage. Ethne stood motionless, her face taut and her hands white as she gripped the wood of the palisade.

The next attack brought the two men into a grappling embrace, neither able to drive their spear into the other. Their sweat and mud-stained bodies churned and twisted over their horses until Canoc wrenched himself free. Crimthann drove his horse directly at him, but Canoc outmaneuvered and knocked him loose, sweeping him from the saddle.

As he rolled clear of his horse's hooves, Crimthann jumped quickly to his feet and threw his spear with deadly force. Canoc dodged and the spear sheered past his head to lodge quivering in the ground. Canoc brought his horse to a standstill, spurred it to a trot then quickened to a gallop, aiming his spear at Crimthann's heart.

Crimthann stood his ground, holding up his shield, his sword cutting an arc before him, the light glinting off the blade like a lick of fire. Canoc leaned low over his horse's neck and charged, seeing only the small point on Crimthann's chest standing between him and victory. The distance between them shrank until Canoc raised his arm to send the spear home. Just as he let loose the shaft, an arrow whistled toward him and sank into the bone above his eyes. He swayed slightly, slipped off his horse, and crumpled to the ground. The spear missed Crimthann's heart, but pierced his arm to the bone.

A man charged out of the trees, followed by a host of others, each brandishing a sword or bow, notched and ready to shoot. Ruadh led the advance, screaming and cursing as they ran at Canoc's men. Then the gates of the rath opened and painted warriors streamed forth, screaming the name of Morrígu and joining ranks with the Fennidi pouring from the forest, women and men alike dressed in skins and leather, with blue painted faces and bits of totems, plant and animal, tied onto their clothing and caps.

Ethne, frozen when Crimthann was unhorsed, shouted wildly when she recognized the Fennidi and their leader, Ruadh. She saw them over match the enemy and cheered with the crowd as they swept up and over the crest of the hill.

The leader of the Fennidi parried and struck with the speed of Lug. He danced his way in and out of Canoc's warriors, charging and thrusting tirelessly, working his way through the knots of fighting warriors.

When Ethne looked for Crimthann, she could not find him. Gripping Gaine's arm, she cried, "Where is the king? Do you see him?" She searched for his tartan and for the feather she had tied in his hair.

"There!" shouted Gaine. "He is down!"

With her heart pounding, Ethne watched several warriors defend Crimthann as he tried to rise, stumbled and fell. The warriors covered him with their shields and half dragged, half carried him off the field. Ethne all but slid down the stairs as the gate opened and Crimthann was brought in, his chest heaving and the color draining rapidly from his face.

"Bring him to the hall!" Ethne commanded, turning to Damán. "Run to the Nemed and get needles and thread and a flask of the Waters of Life. Clothru! Run to the kitchens and fetch the pot of brew I ordered this morning, oak bark, figwort, vervain and comfrey. It should be well steeped and cooled by now. Bring fresh linens for bandaging!"

She followed the men as they carried Crimthann to the hall on their shields. There they laid him on his bed and stepped back. Ethne knelt beside him and tore off his tunic to examine his wound. Gaine was by her side.

"This is strange, Gaine. It is a sharp cut and deep, but he should not be so stricken by it." Crimthann's eyes rolled and foam bubbled at the corners of his mouth.

"The raven circles!" he screamed. "I feel the talons in my flesh!"

Ethne looked at Gaine over the king's twisting body. "Poison?" The look in Gaine's eyes told her she was right. "Damán! Fetch comfrey and pound it with a mortar and pestle. Make a paste and smear it on a cloth. We need a poultice to draw out the poison." She took a breath to steady herself. "Clothru, find men to hold the king while I wash and stitch the wound."

When they had bound him by the arms and legs, Ethne worked skillfully to wash the cut with the herbal brew and then with the Waters of Life. Crimthann moaned, thrashing his head from side to side. She closed the wound with small deft stitches and covered it with a cloth soaked in the herbal mixture. Damán arrived with the poultice of mashed comfrey. As Ethne placed it over the wound, Crimthann whimpered and called out, "The raven's beak tears my heart!"

"Shhh, Crimthann. I am here," Ethne crooned. "The raven is no more. Let your mind be at peace." She bathed his face and chest and gestured to the warriors to leave them. She cradled his head in her lap, caressing his hair and singing a quiet song. Soon, his eyes closed and his breathing eased.

"Gaine, will you stay with him while I go to the palisade?" When Gaine gave her consent, Ethne went to the gates and ascended the stair once more. Bodies lay strewn about the field before the dun and Crimthann's warriors and the Fennidi were collecting weapons and jewelry. Men of the rath, wounded or dead, were being carried back into the fort. Overhead the crows circled.

"Take my blessings to your queen, the Morrígu," Ethne called to them. "Give her thanks for our victory today." As she climbed down, the men held out their arms to help her, concern showing on their faces. She pushed through the confusion of the inner yard where knots of warriors stood or lay in exhaustion and pain. Women, along with Father Per brought bread, ale and blankets, and children rushed about to find their fathers, uncles or brothers. The one face she sought was not to be found and she dared not ask. Turning back towards the great hall, she nearly collided with Gaine.

"Ethne, you must return to Crimthann." Ethne heard her urgent tone and fled across the yard, up the steps and into the chamber where he lay. As soon as she saw him, she commanded everyone to leave save Gaine and one warrior as witness. All color had drained from Crimthann's face, his lips were gray, his eyelids streaked with blue veins. His hands clenched and his teeth chattered. His body jerked in spasms as if a great bird pulled at his flesh.

Ethne kneeled beside the bed so her face was even with his. "Crimthann, my king. I am here, your Anam Chara. Be not afraid."

Crimthann's eyes flew open, but he saw nothing. Froth spilled again from his mouth and his breath came in panting heaves.

"A chara, my dear one," said Gaine, "it is time to cross the Western ocean to join your kin. Your ancestors are waiting with open arms. They long to greet you, to hold you again."

Ethne, eyes streaming hot tears, bent over him. "You have given your life for the people and now it is time to go with joy to the next world. My love, I set you free, My Faelchu."

Crimthann opened his eyes once more and saw her. In a voice of wonder he whispered, "You are my wren, my Drui, my queen. Fly to me!" His voice faded and his head lolled. Blood and foam gushed from his mouth, and as Ethne cried out, his breathing stopped. She put her hand over his eyes to close them, raised him in her arms and held him, rocking and keening.

She mourned the loss of Faelchu, her true friend of secret rites in the moonlit stone circle. She mourned for his guileless true heart, given so completely to her and to the people. She mourned his bright hair and strong body, without blemish, that had held her in the night. She mourned too the loss of the family that she had imagined with him, while gazing into his eyes, the weight of her grief an anvil, cold metal in her bosom, rendering her immobile.

She would have stayed with him thus all night, her head resting on his, arms clasped about his shoulders, but Gaine gently pulled her away. Gaine straightened his legs and folded his arms across his chest, then held Ethne to still her weeping.

"Ethne, you must listen. Now that Crimthann is dead, *you* are Rígain!" Ethne raised her head, staring blankly at Gaine.

"Think of the people. There is no time for grief." Gaine turned to the warrior, a ceannaire from In Medon, "You heard him call her *queen*, did you not?"

"Yes, lady." He turned and bowed to Ethne.

"Tell the warriors," Gaine continued, "and the people that their king has given his life for them. Ethne will greet them as their queen when she has finished her prayers for Crimthann."

The ceannaire stepped quickly out of the room and moments later the two women heard the keening of the rath begin. Gaine left quietly, while Ethne sang the blessing for one who has crossed the waters of death and reached the farthest shore, her love following him across like a tide.

# 34

The Ban-Ard-Drui stood before the shocked crowd gathered before the door of the royal hall, rattling her golden chain for silence.

*Land, Sea, and Sky, protect the people! Fire, Water, Wind and Stone protect the people! Those who are above and those who are below protect the people! Ancestors, Gods, be with us now!*

*We have suffered, yet we have not been defeated. One who would usurp our ways and traditions has killed the Chosen One of the clanns and of the Druid. The champion of the Oirthir has also met his death; he lies in the field, food for crows and ravens.*

*But the Gods have not abandoned us. We are blessed this day with a new ruler, an Ard-Rígain. Anointed in the old way and also the new, she is the one chosen by the Land Spirits. We mourn with her now as she buries her king.*

Ethne emerged from the royal enclosure. Six warriors followed carrying Crimthann's body. They laid him on a pallet with his arms crossed over his sword, his hair combed and his face washed. Except for a bloody patch on his shirt, he was unblemished. Ethne willed herself to speak.

"My people, I salute you. Look your last on your beloved Ard-Ri. He fought with valor and honor, but he did not die by the spear-thrust of a skillful champion. His death was made in treachery and deceit. The blade that cut him was poisoned."

The crowd moaned as one, and several warriors called for vengeance on this dishonorable deed, but there was no enemy left to fight. Canoc and his men were dead.

Ethne waited for silence. "My first act as Ard-Rígain is to appoint Glaisne, ceannaire of In Medon, as high king in Oirthir, to replace Canoc."

Glaisne fell to one knee and bowed his head before her, placing his sword at her feet.

Ethne took up the sword. "Glaisne, your task will not be easy. There was a strange sickness among the men and horses in Canoc's army. I don't know what you will find when you get to Oirthir. You will be challenged by the followers of the new faith who chose Canoc as their champion. They will tempt you with their beliefs. Do you swear to remain loyal to the Gods and ways of the ancestors; Land, Sea and Sky as your witness?"

"I do."

"Do you swear to remain faithful to the Spirits of the land, the River Goddess, the sacred trees and all who help the crops to grow and keep the herds healthy, Land, Sea and Sky be your witness?"

"I do."

"Do you swear to honor the ancient tribal laws of our people, Land, Sea and Sky be your witness?"

"I do."

"Do you offer your life in sacred trust, in defense of the people of your kingdom and of this Island, Land, Sea and Sky be your witness?"

"I do."

Ethne returned his sword, and Glaisne stood and faced the people, who shouted their approval.

Ethne continued; "Warriors, carry Crimthann to the Nemed where he will lie in state for a day and a night. Bring your gifts of devotion to him there. He will be buried with all honors as a sacred king of this rath, next to the cairn of Coemgen, his advisor and friend."

Six warriors raised the palette. Led by keening women, they processed to the Druid enclosure while Ethne's eyes followed Crimthann and the cortège. Her heart spoke; "Goodbye, my love, there is so much left unsaid, so much left undone. Our time was too brief. May we meet again on the Other shore."

Beyond the gates crows circled the battlefield, settling upon corpses, pecking hungrily at eyes and tearing flesh. Canoc's men, stripped of their weapons and clothing, lay in rows atop the rise, exposed to the elements, birds, and foxes. In a few weeks, when the bones were picked clean, they would be carried back to their kin in Oirthir.

Ethne began the daily ritual obligations of her new station, taking a moment to face the setting sun. *"Oh, Grian,"* she intoned. *"You who shine upon and within the waters, watch over me this night..."*

The Fennidi melted back into the forest, to wait around campfires for a word from the queen, nursing her grief in her chamber, or from Ruadh, who walked amongst the dead. Ruadh found the corpse of his father, a broken arrow protruding from its skull. Bending to pull it out he wept.

"Why, father? Why did you abandon the Island? For *gold*? For *power*? Was it worth it to go against everything we believe, that your father believed, that your grandfathers believed, and everything you taught me? Did you turn your back on our Gods?"

He knelt to place his forehead on his father's heart, dropping tears onto his chest. Out of deference for Canoc's rank the body was untouched, still clothed with weapons and jewelry. Ruadh lifted the body over his shoulders to carry it into the rath and away from the marauding crows.

The warriors of the rath assembled in the great hall. One by one the ceannaire of each province pledged his support and men to Ethne. Each laid his sword before her, and she handed it back in token of her acceptance of fealty. Everything was exhausting, in her gravid condition she could hardly get through a day without a nap, but now she must ordain each warrior then sit through the night by Crimthann's body.

"Forgive me," said Ethne, moving towards the oaken throne, "I must sit."

From the back of the hall a familiar voice called. "Your highness, will you accept the pledge of the Fennidi who wait outside the gates?"

Ethne looked toward the door as she sank onto the throne, feeling a wave of nausea and willing it to subside. Her eyes played over those assembled. The tribes stood in distinct groups around the room: there the dark-haired, black-eyed clann; there the taller, broader, blonde clann; there a kin group where every one had red or chestnutcolored hair. Each clann wore a distinctive plaid dyed with native plants from mountain, bog or forest.

One man stood out because he was clad in skins, with feathers tied to his braids and clothing. His shirt had a cowl attached, drawn over his head, concealing his face. He looked like a geilt, a sylvan spirit who ate squirrels, nuts and ferns in contrast to the wellarmed warriors of the flaith.

"Your Highness, the Fennidi have fought bravely for you, and it was a Fennidi arrow that pierced the brow of Canoc. We stand ready to defend you, your kingdom, and the people."

"Come forward, sir, and give me your weapon," answered Ethne.

The man stepped forward and withdrew his sword from its incised leather sheath. The leather was dirty, stained with mud and sweat yet retained patches of a bright red coloring. Ethne could hardly contain her joy. "Remove your cowl, sir, that I may see your eyes."

The strange warrior uncovered his face. He and Ethne locked their gaze. Gaine, observing silently beside the queen, cleared her throat to speak. "Your face is familiar, stranger. The people of this rath watched you with great admiration today as you fought.

What is your name?"

The spell of silence broke as the Fennid turned his face towards Gaine. "I am Ruadh. I served this rath during the siege. I left one night and traveled to the coast to alert the Fennidi. The warriors who came out of the trees to defend the Ard-Ri are under my command."

"We are grateful for your help. Ethne, as your Ban-Ard-Drui, I advise you to accept the fealty of the Fennidi. Ruadh, aren't you the son of Canoc?"

Ruadh stood tall. "I am Canoc's son. But I left my father's rath years before he was influenced by the monks. I am loyal to the Gods and to the traditions of this land."

His voice grew quiet. "I have brought my father's body into the fort; it lies beside the palisade, just inside the gate, to keep it from the crows. After I swear fealty to the Ard-Rígain, I will take his body back to my homeland for burial."

Ethne spoke. "We are grateful for your service to the kingdoms. Tomorrow you may carry your father to rest. Glaisne is the appointed king of your province, he and his men will travel with you. Tell your kin that the bones of their relatives will be returned to them when they are clean, that will give them time to prepare a fresh barrow. Tell the warriors waiting outside the gates to come in, I will accept their pledges." To the mogae, she said, "I want food and drink for every man, woman and child and all of the Fennidi this evening. Let no one go cold or hungry."

"My lady, you are gracious." Ruadh knelt and handed Ethne his sword. As she looked at him it seemed as if the last year had been a dream. Even if her duty held her to the rath and the council hall, her heart was in the forest with this man. She smelled the bracken, woodsmoke and the sweet clear scent of wild waters emanating from him. She yearned to embrace him and wrap those memories around her heart.

"Rise, Ruadh, and take your weapon. It is sanctified to defend me and the kingdom."

Ruadh took the weapon and looked deeply into Ethne's eyes. "Your Highness, my sword is yours until I die."

Ethne blushed. Gaine wondered, but said nothing.

That evening there was merriment such as had not been heard or felt in months. The bards brought out their cruitts and drums and sang songs of victory. Fires burned around the royal hall, a circle of Fennidi around each one, regaling the children and the warriors with heroic tales, embellishing their prowess and skill. The story of 'The Poisoned Pig and The Men of the North' was a favorite. Ragnall acted the part of the pig with wonderful squeals and grunts. The mogae served platters of roasted roots and meats and there was enough for everyone to have their fill.

Warriors carried Crimthann's body to the burial ground within the Nemed and placed flaming torches around it as the people of In Medon and the Fennidi came in groups to pay their respects. A Druid recited his life history and genealogy, and a bard sang praise poems long into the night. Ethne and Gaine sat through it all propped on pillows and blankets on the grass. As a concession to Ethne's condition and at Gaine's insistence, a small platter of food and drink was brought for her comfort. The Druid fasted, meditating on their philosophy of death. Their sorrow was for the grieving kin of the departed. They knew that the dead were past pain unless they had committed evil acts, in which case, they would be tormented and unable to move freely into their next life. The Druid knew Crimthann was a good man, loved by his people, and therefore did not worry for his well being now that he had left his body.

Ethne sat hunched and drawn. Ruadh approached and sat near her, choosing to kept watch with her rather than with his own father. Ruadh thought of Canoc, covered with a blanket of royal purple but otherwise unacknowledged. His mother and kin would bury him with honor when he returned the body to the Oirthir.

When the folk of the tuath had said their last goodbyes it was time for the all night vigil. The Druid, covered in capes and cowls awaited a message from Crimthann. Now the only sound was the occasional pop of the small fire kept going to light artemisia, whose smoke aided visions. Acolytes also handed out cups of brewed artemisia to all.

Towards dawn, a form materialized out of the smoke and mist. The Druid saw it first, Gaine and Ethne roused as the form congealed and drifted towards them. The vaporous figure paused before Ethne then turned toward Ruadh. Ruadh, however, could not see it. He had not drunk the herbal brew, but he felt a current in the air as his hair stood up and his arms prickled.

As they watched, the shape expanded to encompass Ethne and Ruadh in a smoky embrace. Within seconds, it faded.

"Crimthann!" called Ethne, feeling the longing and love she had experienced when he left to combat Canoc. But he was gone.

"He has left us, Ethne," said Gaine softly. "He leaves us for the Western Isles."

Everyone's eyes turned to Ruadh. To their herb-altered vision he glowed with Crimthann's blessing.

"Ruadh, stand before us," said Gaine.

He stood where everyone could see him. Streams of colored light emanated from him, gossamer threads of magenta, green and yellow. He had been blessed by the Otherworld and all the Druid could see it.

"Speak to us Ruadh," commanded Gaine.

"I say this: I am the queen's champion."

"Crimthann has chosen you, Ruadh," said Gaine.

Ethne wept openly. Crimthann had given her his love *and* what she desired most.

The Druid carried Crimthann's body to an open barrow where he was laid on a wooden cart embellished with golden ornaments, his hands folded over his sword. They arranged food and beakers of fion around him with furs, blankets, dirks and kilts. Crimthann wore his golden torque and slippers embroidered with gold thread. Everyone shoveled a spadeful of dirt and piled stones to make the cairn.

By the time all was finished, the sun was high in the sky. Ethne, worn and spent, leaned heavily on Ruadh's arm as they walked back to the royal enclosure. Some wondered to see the queen on the arm of a stranger, but the Ard-Ban-Drui was there, lending approval. Too much was changing, and few had answers.

# 35

―――――

"Your highness there is trouble!" Damán spoke through the Ard-Rígain's private door. It was late afternoon and Ethne had slept for almost an hour. She stood up, straightened her shift, smoothed her hair and opened the door.

"What is it, Damán?"

"We went this afternoon to look on the dead warriors of the rath, those that are still lying beyond the palisade. When we got to the walls, we saw it."

"Saw what, Damán? Speak up!"

"Someone cut off the heads of the enemy and impaled them on spikes outside the fort." He hung his head in shame.

At that moment Ruadh approached from his seat in the hall.

Ethne looked at Ruadh over Damán's bowed head. "And Canoc?" she asked holding her breath as the reply came.

"Canoc too."

Ruadh moved toward the great door of the hall.

"Ruadh!" Ethne called, fearing what he might do. He stopped, rigid, as his voice echoed across the room.

"Do I have your permission to recover my father's head?"

"Take some of the men with you. Take down *all* the heads."

He bowed his head and left. Ethne turned to Damán. "Who did this?"

"We don't know. It must have been last night when the village was feasting and paying their respects to Crimthann. We only discovered it now."

"Bring Canoc's remains to the royal house and post guards around his body. I want to speak to the warriors now, *all* of them. They are to come immediately!"

Ethne understood the tradition of displaying the heads of defeated warriors. It frightened potential enemies and proclaimed a conquest. If a head was captured, the victor had that warrior's mind, spirit and body in his control. But with none of Canoc's warriors left, the beheadings were an insult that demeaned the victors.

Guards dispersed to every section of the rath to round up the warriors and Damán alerted the Druid that an assembly had been called. Ruadh returned to the hall with a grim face. Ethne spoke to him in her chamber with tears in her eyes.

"You have my apology and the apology of my people for dishonoring your father so. He deserves respect as chieftain in his burial and I will see that he is given a place of honor outside the royal hall."

Ruadh put his arms around her. "It is not your fault. Nor is it the fault of the warriors. Their battle rage is not easy to control and these traditions are in their blood. But I grieve to bring my father's broken body back to his rath and to my mother."

"We have had too much of death and grief," said Ethne. "I send my respect to your mother." She reached up to touch Ruadh's face, but stopped short with an, "Oh!" of surprise.

When Ruadh looked puzzled, she took his hand and placed it on her belly. His eyes grew round as he felt the rolling within.

"This baby is ours," he whispered to her. "I know the night this life was made."

Ethne held his hand in place a moment longer then looked up at him. "When you return, we will be together, the people of In Medon will see us planning and making decisions. They will accept us as one."

"Will you marry me again?" Ruadh asked, smiling.

"I will marry you over and over, my love," said Ethne, smiling in return. But now you must go. Make preparations for your journey." They kissed lightly and then Ruadh bent to give her another long, deep kiss. He went out the door as Ethne prepared to dress and braid her hair for the assembly.

Ethne entered the feasting hall wearing her royal jewels and robes. Purple dominated her cloak of seven colors, which was fastened with a gold brooch; over a gown of purple. Around her neck was her golden torque and she wore shoes of red suede. A golden crown covered braids twined with red and gold ribbons, from which golden balls hung in clusters. Large golden hoops hung from her ears and she carried a golden branch from which dangled nine golden bells, symbolic of her status as a Ban-Drui of the highest grade. It was a magnificent display, meant to reinforce her station in the eyes of the warriors. The crowd hushed when she appeared.

Gaine, looking pale by comparison in simple saffron robes, stood before the throne to open the assembly. "Ancestors, be with us as we listen to the words of our queen. Nature Spirits, be with us and give us strength, Gods of our people, be with us. May we have ears to hear, eyes to see and heart to feel the truth of the message she brings." Gaine retired to her position behind the throne as Ethne stepped before the dais to address the crowd.

"My people, I am pleased to see you all here looking fed and rested. We have much to be proud of. We have bested our enemies in a fair fight, and the lives of most of our warriors have been spared. Thanks are due to the Fennidi, our allies. They and their leader, Ruadh, are ever welcome here as honored guests."

The warriors and people cheered, acknowledging their debt to the Fennidi. Ethne raised her hand for silence. "Despite our victory, we have reason to be ashamed. Someone has dishonored our kingdom. Last night, our enemy's dead were beheaded, including Canoc, the sacred king of the Oirthir. Why was this done?"

The warriors made no sound. Most had no knowledge of the desecration and were shocked by it. Women stared wide-eyed, wondering if Ethne would exact retribution from the men.

"This cowardly act was done by those who could not control their lust for blood and so vented their rage upon corpses. There is no honor in this for our people or for those who committed this deed. The heads will be taken down and placed beside the bodies at once. The Druid will go amongst the dead with sweet herbs to purify and consecrate. Guards will be posted around Canoc's corpse until a retinue of warriors is ready to transport him to his homeland. Gaine and the Druid will insure that the bodies are treated with respect. I am ashamed for those who did this deed, and I will have no more retribution!"

Everyone in the hall gave a somber "Aye," though some of the fighters looked sullen.

Ethne continued. "I want every able-bodied man and woman to go to the river and clear the stones and timbers that divert the stream. Clean water must flow again through this rath!" Ethne rose from the throne in a swirl of color turning her back on the assembly and returning to her chamber.

That night, after restoring the river to its course, the tired warriors of the rath gathered to drink, and reflect. "This is what comes of having a *woman* for a leader," Cadla muttered darkly.

"If Crimthann were alive he would have understood why we cut off the heads. He was a warrior, not a Ban-Drui. She had us cheering for the Fennidi, alright. But where was the praise for us? *We* defended the fort!" added Ronan, spitting on the ground for emphasis.

They had both been drinking heavily.

"I think a *true* Rígain should be a battle leader" added Lorcan. "This one knows everything about stitching a wound but nothing about how to make one!"

"That's right!" said Cadla. "I say we call for an election!"

"Or one of us should marry her. We know she's fertile!" said Lorcan with a snicker.

They smirked as each tried to imagine her in his bed, but none dared voice the fantasy. She was a Ban-Drui, and surely the Gods would hear their words.

In the field before the rath, the Druid were preoccupied with very different matters. The bodies of the slain enemies had to be censed. Vervain and the foreign resin known as "frankincense" were burned in a small black cauldron and wafted over the cadavers with eagle's wings. Damán, Gaine and Clothru sat vigil all night with the remains, though at a distance to avoid the smell and to avoid interfering the foxes and crows. They wanted the bones picked clean as soon as possible.

The crows and ravens fed until dusk when the full moon illuminated the work of foxes. Clothru fought off nausea and Damán ran to the bushes once or twice, overcome by the sight.

"This night," said Gaine "teaches you the impermanence of flesh and form. The body is ever changing; one moment a bawling infant, the next an adolescent seeking the opposite sex. Later it grows to full strength and births other bodies. In the end, it weakens and dies, only to reappear in a womb to begin the cycle anew. Throughout, the soul remains constant. Each body is a vehicle as the soul migrates from form to form. Life is a cycle of darkness and light, of death, birth and rebirth, like the changing seasons of the year and the sinking and returning of the sun."

Clothru ran for the bushes to vomit as a large dog trotted by with someone's foot.

# 36

The time came for Ruadh to depart. In the early morning Ethne went with him to visit the Fennidi camped in the forest, to give them her personal thanks. A train of mogae followed, bearing gifts of cloth, iron tools and dried meat. Ethne brought a selection of dirks and swords she had hand picked from the dead and handed one to each Fennid leader.

"This is hardly fair recompense for the service you have done the kingdom. Had we not been in a state of siege, there would have been more."

"Lady, we will always defend you and the kingdom wherever we are, to the best of our ability," said Erc.

Ruadh and Ethne stood together as the Fennidi put out their fires and gathered their few belongings. Within minutes they were packed, melting into the trees, an entire army moving in silence. "It's like watching a herd of deer or a pack of wolves, more than an army of people," Ethne observed.

"We are half wild, a foot in both worlds. It's why we are respected and feared. But any wild creature can be tamed."

Ethne raised her eyebrows as Ruadh took her hand and kissed it. The mogae saw the gesture and tittered. Ruadh and Ethne returned to the road where Glaisne waited with a few warriors and a cart where Canoc's body, reunited with its bloody head, rested. The corpse was wrapped in a purple blanket out of respect for his royal rank and covered with herbs to mask the smell and repel flies.

Too soon for open displays of affection, Ruadh and Ethne contented themselves with a stiff hug and a handshake.

"Bring your mother my sorrow at her husband's death. Tell her she is welcome at court." said Ethne."

Ruadh bowed and started the procession eastward, under a clear sky and on dry roads. He spent the days telling Glaisne of his family's history, the politics of the region and the particular characteristics of its crops and weather. Glaisne asked good and relevant questions, which reassured Ruadh that Ethne had chosen wisely in naming him the next king of Oirthir. Ruadh enjoyed Glaisne's company, realizing with pleasure that he was a man with whom he could confer on Island matters. The two men talked together over the evening fire, comparing experiences of leading men and sharing knowledge of land stewardship.

One night as their talk meandered from cattle husbandry to sword skills, Glaisne looked hard at Ruadh.

"You are the rightful king of the Oirthir. Why did the queen appoint *me*?" Ruadh gave a rueful laugh before answering. "I have no desire to be king in Oirthir. I severed my clann ties to join the Fennidi long ago." He threw a glance at Glaisne. "Before you protest, I have no regrets."

They sat in companionable silence, watching the firelight spark and flare. Ruadh stretched his legs, yawned, and put his hand on Glaisne's shoulder. "It is my brother Anluan you will have to contend with. He will be furious to find himself not only fatherless but usurped as well. He and the priests."

"The priests?"

"Albinus and Germanus. The Cristaidi were my father's allies. I understand it was they who convinced him to challenge Crimthann."

"Do you believe they have also influenced your brother?"

"Anluan was ever the dutiful son. He obeyed my father's plans like a goose. I suppose he tried to fulfill my father's wishes all the more once I left."

"But how can anyone accept what these priests are saying? Our ways have kept the people alive on the Island for time beyond memory." Glaisne shook his head.

"The priests' stories are new and exciting. They hold a different kind of magic."

Ruadh shrugged his shoulders. "They also offer gold from Rome."

Glaisne eyed the man sitting next to him and put his thoughts into words. "Do you think the Rígain can withstand such a force? She is a powerful Ban-Drui, but she is not a warrior."

Ruadh sighed. "I know what the men are saying, and I have heard these doubts. The queen knows what the people and land require to survive. But I too wonder at the strength of these missionaries from Rome. Across this land our ways are being questioned, even scorned, and new thoughts are taking the place of our beliefs. I don't know the answer to your question, my friend. I only know that she holds our ways and our people in the stronghold of her heart."

The next morning they sighted Canoc's rath. High on a hill it was surrounded by ancient earthworks but no palisade. At the base of the hill ran a river with its dam and weir. Ruadh was dismayed to see how they had deteriorated. The weir was rotted and near collapse.

"One of my duties when I was young was to see to the weir. My father impressed upon me the importance of mending it and checking it almost daily for fish. I can't imagine why it has been neglected so."

As they moved closer, the smell of rotting flesh assailed them, several fish and a duck hung in the netting. Ruadh's concern mounted. The silence troubled him most for he heard no cows lowing in the fields below the rath . It was too soon to have the herds on higher ground beyond the fort.

"Something is very wrong," Ruadh said to Glaisne. "I remember herds of cattle. I and other boys tended them and counted them. I see no cattle and no boys." The desolation brought uneasiness with it. The seat of the provincial high king should be the best provisioned and guarded in the area. "This was a refuge where people assembled in times of danger. It bodes ill if this center fares so poorly." A sense of foreboding settled over the small group.

As they neared the entrance, heavily armed men appeared on the earthen embankment and another group emerged from the gate.

"Halt! State your business!" came the shout from the gate.

"We are from the rath of Crimthann, the Ard-Ri. We are sent by his Rígain," Glaisne answered.

This announcement was met with consternation, and the men at the gate turned to one another, arguing their response tersely. One finally stepped forward. "I am Anluan, son of Canoc. In my father's absence I lead this stronghold."

"Anluan," said Ruadh stepping toward him. "We come with news for this rath and the tuath beyond. The battle is done; Crimthann has won."

Anluan stiffened. "What news of my father?"

"I bring the body of Canoc to his Rígain. He and Crimthann are both slain."

"Liars!" Anluan cried out.

"Anluan, look at me. Don't you recognize your brother?"

Anluan's mouth twisted in rage and disbelief. "I have no brother."

"Anluan, I bring our father's body from the battle field to give him all honor in his departure from this world. I bring him home to you and to our mother."

Anluan looked long at Ruadh, struggling to see beyond his grief and anger.

Eventually he recognized the man before him. "Ruadh? Why were you at the battle for the crown of Ard-Ri, and why do you bring these men?"

Ruadh sighed and began. "Much has happened that will take long to tell. I fought with the Fennidi to protect the Island

and the king. These men are appointed by the Rígain to restore peace within her kingdom. She has appointed Glaisne king of the Oirthir."

Anluan stood speechless, staring first at Ruadh then at Glaisne.

Ruadh went on, hoping something of his explanation would penetrate Anluan's dismay. "Our father slew Crimthann with a poisoned spear and was then killed by a Fennid arrow."

"Canoc was an honorable king!" Anluan exploded. "He needed no *poison* to win his battles!"

"I was there when Crimthann died and know this to be true, though it brings me no honor to tell you. Crimthann's queen is now Rígain and we come at her command.

"Anluan," continued Ruadh softly, "let us enter the fort and bring our father's body to its rest. Let us give mother the news that he is dead."

"I would meet with Canoc's Rígain and offer her my sorrow," said Glaisne, but Anluan gave him no heed.

Anluan signaled to the men on the earthworks to lower their bows. He walked slowly towards the gate, with Ruadh, Glaisne, and his father's retinue. Anluan's mind was a turmoil of shock and rage, all his adult life he believed he would take his father's place as king. Now two men stood beside him with older and stronger claims.

Canoc's fort held numerous small round houses with thatched roofs, a large round barn and a rectangular feasting hall and throne room. Unlike the rath of the Ard-Ri, which depended on the river, this rath had several deep wells to provide for the people and cattle. As the group neared the feasting hall, Canoc's widow, Fithir, appeared at the door. Her hair was tightly bound and hidden under a dark cloth, which matched her dark clothing. She stood twisting her hands, straining to make sense of the voices she heard.

As the voices came closer, her face paled and her mouth dropped open.

"Ruadh!" she exclaimed, running towards the men and the cart. Ruadh caught her in his arms and she clung to him, calling his name over and over. At last, she pulled herself away and looked him over, noticing the calmness of his eyes and the sureness of his bearing. He in turn took in the mother he had not seen for many years. She had aged, of course, but it was the dullness of her eyes and manner that shocked him most. Gone were the bright colors of her rank and the sparkling jewels and hair ornaments she had worn so proudly. Gone, too, were the carefully plaited braids and the flashes of wit and humor. Ruadh understood that his father's conversion to the Christaidi religion had done more than set him at war with the Ard-Ri. Ruadh let go one of her hands and turned her to face Glaisne.

"Glaisne, may I present Canoc's Rígain, Fithir, my beloved mother."

Glaisne gave Fithir a bow. "I am honored and I give you my respect, but I come with dread news of your king and to offer you my sorrow for your grief."

Fithir looked from one to the other, then looked back at Anluan. At the look on his face, she knew the meaning of Glaisne's words. Her legs went weak and her eyes clouded. "No. No, it can't be," she whimpered, shaking her head. She put a hand out to Anluan who caught her and supported her as she turned her back on Ruadh and Glaisne. Her wailing brought the rest of the villagers to stand about and wonder, all of the women looking as drab and subdued as she.

Suddenly she turned back and pointed a finger at the cart. "He is there, isn't he?"

Her face was wrinkled with misery and she broke loose from Anluan and ran to the cart. Before Ruadh could stop her, she lifted the purple cloth to look on the face of her husband. At sight of him, she let out a scream. Ruadh, this time, gathered her up and gestured to the men to help him bring her into the feasting hall.

When Fithir was restored with warm drink laced with spirits and a seat by the fire, Ruadh began the tale of Canoc's battle with Crimthann. Quietly, with head bowed she listened, never looking up or asking questions, not even through the revelation of the poisoned spear. Only when Ruadh told her that Ethne was ruler of In Medon did Fithir raise her head.

"She sends her deepest apology, Mother. She would have stopped the warriors from such brutality, but they acted on their own. The high queen bids you visit her at any time and will welcome you with all honors." Ruadh turned to Glaisne.

"Madam, I have been sent by the Ard-Rígain to be the new king of this province," said Glaisne. "I will serve this kingdom and honor its traditions. You will be cherished under my command."

At this, Fithir blushed a deep red. "I would not be under the same roof with that Heathen! She has no right to be Rígain. She is without wealth or warrior status. She is a Fomorian she-devil! And *you*," as she turned on Glaisne, "You are nothing to me. My son rules and no other!" Fithir's wails spiraled to the rafters.

"Anluan, put mother to rest," said Ruadh. "I will speak with the Druid about Canoc's funeral."

Anluan gave a dry laugh. "No Druid live here, brother. We are Cristaidi. I will ask Germanus and Albinus to perform the burial service." He left with Fithir on his arm, and Ruadh watched as they exited the hall with halting steps.

That evening Anluan shared a meal with Ruadh and Glaisne, leaving Canoc's body in the great hall guarded by warriors. It was a simple meal with fíon, not the feast Glaisne had expected as the new leader. "Anluan," he asked, "I understand this land is known for its cattle. Are the herds being sheltered early on the high pastures?"

Anluan looked down, embarrassed. "The warriors demanded payment. At first my father gave them gold, but that soon ran out." Anluan's voice grew quieter. "The only way he could retain them was to pay them in cattle. And once the siege of Crimthann's fort was underway, the men had to be fed."

"Are there none left?" Ruadh's asked, incredulous.

"We have a few. We sent them to the summer pastures early because we have no fodder." He did not meet their eyes.

"Anluan," said Ruadh, lowering his voice. "I don't understand. If there wasn't enough gold or cattle to pay for an army, why would Canoc press the campaign? Were there no objections from the flaith? His recklessness put everyone's life in danger!"

"It was the priests. They goaded him. And mother. They said our warriors fought for the new God, Isu, and were bound to be victorious, while Crimthann's men were Pagani worshiping false Gods. They told our men that if they fought valiantly and died in battle, they would go to the Cristaidi Otherworld. Once there, your troubles end and forever is a soft spring day. Father and mother believed them."

"And the warriors?"

"I can't say, Ruadh. I know they wanted gold and cattle. Now, we have barely enough to feed ourselves, even if we hunt wild game." Anluan put his face in his hands.

"These priests have nearly destroyed our clann and the villages," said Ruadh.

"Tomorrow we will mend the weir and see to the fields."

"This is what always comes of war," added Glaisne. "The Druid teach that war brings desecration and rends the land. A war fought for religion brings the hardest ruin."

Glaisne called for a council meeting the next evening. The flaith who were within easy riding distance and some of the wealthier boaire came, along with their wives and kin, to meet the new king. Canoc's great hall had once been hung with foreign tapestries and decorated with gold. The trestle table had held gold plates, cups and candlesticks and bronze braziers with golden animals soldered onto their handles and rims. Piece by piece the furnishings had disappeared, given to the warriors' kin. The walls of the hall were now bare and the candlesticks were of iron, hastily made by the smiths of Canoc's rath.

As the ornaments of her home disappeared, Fithir had tried to maintain a royal household, sweeping floors, strewing fresh scented rushes, polishing tables and benches to a high gloss. Following the advice of the Abbot, she left financial arrangements to her husband and to her son, as was proper for a Roman style Cristaide wife and mother. She never thought that Canoc would die; such a thought would lack faith. At the assembly, she sat on a bench to one side of the dais, wrapped in a dark woolen shawl paying scant attention to the meeting.

"Mother" said Ruadh gently, "would you like to open the council as is your right?"

Fithir made no reply, but sat staring vaguely.

"Very well then," offered Ruadh. "I will do it."

Glaisne sat on the dais, but according to tradition, would not be first to speak.

With no Druid present, Ruadh assumed the right to invoke the ancestor's blessings. "In the name of Land, Sea and Sky," he began.

"Young man!" A voice interrupted from one side of the chamber. "Do you invoke the Pagani deities in this house? This is a house of the one God and of his son, Isu!"

Ruadh raised his voice again. "I ask that every person in this hall respect the ancient laws of assembly and not interrupt until the meeting is properly opened." Albinus strode forward and planted himself before the throne, facing Glaisne.

"This is a Cristaidi house and there will be no Pagani invocations here. *I* will open the meeting with a prayer to the one true God."

Glaisne pointed to the priest before him. "Guards, seize this man and escort him from the hall. We meet in peace. Ruadh, proceed with your opening prayer."

A clutch of warriors closed in on Albinus, forcing him towards the door.

"You are damned! God will pour his wrath upon you!" screamed the priest, resisting as he was swept away between strong arms.

With order restored, the local nobles presented their swords to the new king, and their wives made discreet inquiries of his marital status, wealth and family connections.

Fithir remained remote and silent. Anluan's face was wooden, concealing the wounds to his heart and pride.

Ruadh, trying to draw his brother out, asked; "I wonder at the change in mother. I know she is grieving, but this is her home and she should properly welcome the new king. She is the former Rígain with powers and rights, yet she says nothing." This behavior was so unlike a tribal queen that Ruadh suspected she had gone mad.

Ruadh sought out his mother repeatedly after that, gently reminding her of his childhood when she had taught him to use his sword. How often as not she would end the day playing a spirited game with the children of the rath, with sticks and a leather ball. He reminded her of her laughter and high spirits as she taught them to dance in the cow barn, preparing for royal functions.

"That was worthless, childish frivolity." was all she would say, her mind dulled by grief over Canoc's death, and occupied with the religious instruction Albinus imposed.

# 37

Albinus walked briskly down the hill towards Germanus and the group of monks waiting for him by the weir.

"It is intolerable!" shouted Albinus as he approached the small group. "The new king of this province is a Paganus. He threw me out of the assembly!"

"You force too much on them all at once," said Germanus.

"I'm *not* going to let my years of hard work go to waste. They have rejected the one true God, and have set a woman on the high throne of the Island despite all my teachings!"

Brother Ardal spoke. "I hear they severed Canoc's head after the battle was over and his army defeated. They decapitated other dead warriors too."

"Our work here is far from over," said Germanus. "Be not impatient. We won't allow the Island to fall back into Pagani ways. We will be as constant as the wind and as strong. Even the trees and rocks give way when the wind bears upon them. So shall it be here. Our word will spread over the country and the *true* faith will take hold."

The monks fell to their knees as Germanus led them in prayer in the dust of the road. "Go forth and spread your wisdom to those with ears to hear. The Kingdom of God is at hand and the kingdom of Ethne the Rígain is a fleck on the wind."

"Amen," the monks intoned.

At the rath of Ethne, preparations were underway for Beltaine, the great festival of summer. This Beltaine was to be particularly memorable, as it would celebrate peace, the new queen's reign *and* the beginning of the light half of the year. Only the great festival of Samain at the end of the year held equal significance. The thoughts and intentions of the participants in both rites determined the outcome of the next half of the yearly cycle. Ethne took great interest in the details of preparation.

"We need nine men from nine families to bring nine sacred woods for the ritual fires," she announced at the morning council. "When they bring the wood, it will be their job to light the pyres. I want everything to be fresh and new for this occasion, no old fires will be used to kindle the flames."

In the days before the feast, the young people of In Medon also made preparations. After being blessed by the fires they would follow the cattle up to the hills to spend the summer guarding the herds and sporting with each other. Many fertile unions began in those hills and babies conceived at Beltaine were said to be especially fortunate.

When the day of the festival dawned, everyone was up before sunrise to watch as the two huge pyres that stood outside the gates of the rath were lit. Nine men had spent the night working their fire drills to kindle the small fires from which the central fires would be sparked. Even the great fire at the center of the Nemed had been put out so that it too could be re-lit from the new flames.

The cattle that survived the siege were herded together and now stood in a group, a small sea of shaggy brown bodies just inside the gates of the dun. Behind them the sheep, pigs and horses waited to be led through the gates and between the flames in an act of ritual purification. Gaine intoned the ancient blessings of Beltaine upon the assembly:

*Hail Summer, season of light and life! Blessed are those who stand here today, witness to the ancient rite. To everyone who passes between the flames, whether human or beast, may health and prosperity come!*

*May the Fires bring us fields of ripe corn. May the Fires bring us streams of white milk, and fruit in abundance!*

*May the Fires bring us freedom from conquest, fair justice and righteous law, comfort in every home.*

*May the fires bring us rivers of fish; forests filled with every variety of strong wood, clean water for drinking, shining, strong weapons; ornaments of gold and silver; healthy soil for abundant crops; sheep with fine fleece; fat pigs and healthy cattle!*

*May the fires bring us respect for the elderly, care for the sick, and duty to fathers and mothers. May all Druid be honored. May craftsmen be well compensated for their art and may every person be valued according to their honor price.*

*May the kindling of these fires bring health to the ailing, to the kingdom and to our queen, and all blessings of peace on the people, near and far!*

Gaine raised up a stick wrapped in linen and soaked in oil and bees wax. Touching it to a small fire, she lit each of the great fires in turn. Finally she handed the torch to Damán who ran with it to the Nemed, to rekindle the Fire Altar.

The folk of the rath cheered as the first cows pushed through. It would be midday before all the cattle, sheep, horses and people had walked between the pyres, those who were too feeble or sick to walk were carried. Runners from every corner of the Island appeared at intervals throughout the day to dip their torches into the flames and carry fire to outlying districts. Hilltop by hilltop fires flared as village after village purified their herds and people in preparation for summer.

As Ethne walked between the twin pyres, the baby turned restlessly in her belly.

"Rest easy and be still, little one," she whispered. "Your time will come soon enough."

Ruadh's continuing absence was a trial for Ethne. She waited eagerly for messages he would send by runner. He missed her greatly, but was preoccupied restoring his family's lands to prosperity. Without gold or cattle, Oirthir's situation was desperate.

All afternoon farmers, craftsmen, farmers, and the mogae picnicked in the grass, in sight of the twin fires. Ethne, the senior Druid, the warriors and flaith dined in the great hall and then danced late into the night. Gaine retired early and remained in seclusion in the Nemed, sitting close by the central Fire Altar, scrying into its brightness for omens of the season to come.

"Ethne's child should be born during the corn harvest, if what I hear is true," said Germanus to Albinus. They were traveling on foot towards a village in Irardacht, having made a circuit of the Eastern lands to consolidate their gains among the recent converts.

"From what I hear she and that Fennid, Ruadh, are partnered, and messages fly from one to the other. If she bears a son, we will *never* be rid of them. Crimthann's son Daire is Druid-trained and hers will be, too."

The Abbot's pace slowed, and Albinus waited as Germanus formulated his thoughts. He recognized the way the older man folded his hands within the deep folds of his sleeves.

"My aim is to disrupt the succession," continued Germanus. "Crimthann and Ruadh are . . . or were . . . champions of the Fennidi and heroes of the people. A child sired by either would be a strong candidate for the throne. Both children are tainted by the Druid and will be difficult to convert to the cause of the Christus. The immediate problem is to persuade the queen. She threatens everything we work for."

"Yes," answered Albinus. "The queen and the children are a hindrance."

"The Lord gives us obstacles to test our faith, Albinus. We must be persistent, carrying the Word into every corner of this Island and gathering those who would listen into an army of believers."

"But, Germanus," interrupted Albinus, "We have lost our strongest adherent in Canoc. How can we hope to rekindle followers if Rome's gold did not buy us victory?"

"Brother Albinus, we must look for other ways to win this land to our way. God will open a path for us. Now, leave me to my prayers." Albinus walked ahead, his head bowed in meditation, murmuring passages on the sufferings of the Christus.

Albinus let himself fall behind, and he too sank into a kind of meditation, but his heart was not filled with prayer. His mind worked over the recent conversation seeing images of Ethne as ruler and mother. Germanus had agreed that this woman and her unborn child were standing in God's way. Albinus sought to solve the dilemma.

As he walked, the task became clearer, to be rid of the child and the mother. But to achieve both would bring chaos and suspicion. He walked on, scuffing stones underfoot.

He nearly collided with Germanus, when he began pointing excitedly to a windwracked tree. Above it a wren was circling and diving, screaming and stabbing at a falcon, which zigzagged and sped off, a bit of fuzz clutched in its talons.

"A sign!" said Albinus.

"Mother love," said Germanus.

"What?"

"There is no fiercer bond." said the old man.

Germanus bowed his head again and walked on, leaving Albinus staring in wonder at the sky, the image of the wren, the falcon and the crumpled chick filling his imagination.

# 38

Ethne was past the nausea of early pregnancy and her energy had rebounded. Her face was round with a milky bloom as her skin took on a radiant sheen. She was filled with high spirits and a desire to be physically active.

"Gaine, I have not made a circuit of the central province since I became Rígain. I feel wonderfully strong. Let's take a cart and two guards and visit the nearby settlements. I want a change of scenery."

"Are you forgetting your duties at court? What about the petitioners who come daily, seeking the queen's justice?"

"The Brehons can manage for a few weeks. They have ancient precedents to follow and if something difficult arises, it can wait until I return, or they can send for me."

"Well, you look strong, and it *is* traditional for a new ruler to inspect her lands. I'll alert the Brehons and you can announce it at tomorrow's assembly."

"Wonderful!" Ethne clapped her hands.

Besides her increasing energy and stamina, Ethne already felt trapped in her routine, the same feeling that had propelled Crimthann into late night excursions to the Stone Circle. Ethne's swollen belly made such ramblings impossible, so she devised this more overt escape.

It was mid-summer and the local crops, though planted late, were finally poking their green heads out of the fields. There had been enough of both wet and fine weather that they would be able to harvest enough spelt, oats and barley for the coming winter. Ethne stood in the side garden helping the mogae to hang and beat cloth hangings and tapestries from the walls of the royal hall when a messenger appeared, followed by three warriors from the dun.

"My Lady! The eastern coast has been an invaded. The Men of the North are attacking the villages again, and I am here to ask for fighters!"

"What about the Fennidi? Aren't they mounting a defense?"

"Yes, but this time they may need our help."

"The Fennidi are our best fighters. By the time I send men, the raiders will be gone, as has happened before. You will be fed and accommodated then you can return to your people and tell them I place my full trust in the Fennidi. Ask a Fennidi contingent to come to me after the battle and give me a full report. They shall be rewarded for their service."

Ethne went back to beating a dusty tapestry with a wooden paddle, humming to herself and enjoying the sensation of exercising her arms in the warm summer sunshine.

The men accompanying the messenger were sullen but held their tongues. Only when they were out of the queen's hearing did they speak.

"Our Rígain prefers renegades and thieves to her own warriors. This is an insult!" Cadla spewed, spitting for emphasis.

"I agree," said Ronan. "She doesn't understand the path of a warrior. We sit inside this rath playing house in the soldier's quarters and practicing endlessly on each other. This is the work of boys, not fighting men. When will *we* have a chance for honor?"

The disgruntled warriors continued their complaints into the night. Of all this, the queen was ignorant as she packed her bags for the journey.

The morning dawned bright and clear. Ethne entered the assembly dressed in traveling clothes, and formally handed over decision-making responsibilities to three sober looking Brehons, a woman and two men.

"These three are charged with settling all disputes in my absence. Their word shall be law," she said, handing them her scepter and bidding them to sit on chairs before the throne. "As Brehons, you three are oath-bound to be impartial in judgment, using only ancient precedents and no personal opinions to inform your decisions."

The petitioners were satisfied with the traditional method for making judgments in a royal ruler's absence. Ethne and Gaine exited the smoky hall to join the small caravan of carts and mounted warriors waiting at the main gate. "At least she trusts us to guard her on her journey," mumbled Lorcan to Ronan whose horses walked side by side behind the carts.

Two more warriors rode behind them and another four preceded the caravan of carts. A mounted warrior guarded either side of the train.

Ethne had brought several female attendants with her as well as Gaine. The mood was festive, the carts twined with ribbons and flowers and piled high with pillows and brightly colored throws. Small barrels of mead and fion topped the food stores.

That evening they stopped in a secluded area near a waterfall and had a gay supper, telling ribald stories and tales of magical journeys under the moon. Ethne noticed that the warriors did not join the fun, keeping their distance and drinking extra portions of mead.

"Lorcan, Cadla! It is such a beautiful evening and the moon is almost full. Sit with us. These ladies would gladly have a strong shoulder to lean on!"

The women giggled invitingly at the warriors, but got little response.

"Perhaps we are interrupting their official duties!" said Ethne gaily, re-filling the women's cups and turning the conversation back to stories of romance. But she was suddenly uneasy.

The following morning they came upon the first settlement. The tuath consisted of little more than a few round houses of gray stone covered with willow thatch, a communal cooking pit for boiling meat with hot rocks and a communal fire over which an ancient cauldron bubbled, stew for the farmers when they came home. As they neared, Ethne inspected the fields, noticing the condition of the crops. Those that had been planted were doing well, but many of the fields lay fallow, covered in weeds. Elsewhere hares wandered between the crop lines, nibbling new growth. A gang of children should have been patrolling the fields, scaring away crows with sticks and pebbles.

"I don't like this silence," said Ethne to Gaine.

"Perhaps there has been a handfasting or a funeral and they are all away." Gaine ventured.

"Perhaps," said Ethne doubtfully.

Within the tiny settlement there was more to make Ethne uneasy. Small children should have be pouring from the fields and houses, breathlessly asking about the strange caravan and running to announce them to the adults. Where were the children? Two dogs greeted them, an emaciated black dog and a tiny, wiry terrier. Both barked thinly and appeared nearly starved.

"I don't like this at all," said Ethne, foreboding in her voice.

As they reached a stone bridge that spanned a small river, a toothless old woman and a dim-witted young man, her son or grandson judging by the family resemblance, raised their hands in salute.

"Welcome to our tuath, lady. We are glad to see you in these evil times," said the old woman.

"Evil times?" asked Ethne, noticing they were badly nourished and tired. Something had caused them sleepless nights. Gray circles under their eyes extended to the edges of their eye sockets, a sign of deep exhaustion.

"My lady, we have the fever here," said the old woman.

"What remedies do you try? I saw elder bushes blooming along the road and loosestrife in the ditches around the fields," said Ethne, her professional curiosity piqued.

"Ah, you are Druid-trained and a healer. Talk sense to the people of this tuath." The old woman said.

Ethne wondered what manner of fever could resist loose-strife and elder. "Old woman," she said aloud, "please take me to the sick. I want to know how the Liaig are treating them."

The old woman laughed a dry cackle of desperation. "We have no Drui here!"

"What?" asked Ethne incredulous.

"This town is Cristaidi. The Abbot sends his monks to say Mass, to baptize and to bury the dead. The monks tell the people to ignore the Druid, that they belong to the evil God, Satan. Without the Druid knowledge, the people cannot heal themselves."

"But what do you use for healing? The sweathouse? Fasting?"

The old woman cackled again. "The Bible! That is what they teach. Place it in the baby's cradle if the baby has a fever or dip a corner of it in a jug of water and give it to the sick. If the person dies they say she has been 'called to heaven to be with Isu' and you are supposed to rejoice. But *I* don't."

"Is that why there are no children in the fields or running in the road to greet us?" asked Gaine.

"Many are dead from the fever," said the old woman, shaking her head and peering into the dust of the road.

Ethne was horrified. The deaths of so many should have been reported to her.

"Old woman, why did no one tell us? I would have sent a Liaig to doctor the village!"

"Albinus told us to keep quiet. He said you would not understand, being a Heathen."

The old woman sidled closer to the cart and whispered directly into Ethne's ear, "I never gave up the our ways, my lady. But to say that might be worth your life!" She spat into the dust as if to rid herself of poison.

Ethne commanded the carts and warriors to enter the tuath. Everyone was tense and wary, the warriors suspected plague or some other dread disease and believed the queen was taking unnecessary chances. Upon reaching the center of the tribal holdings they were met by a small, silent crowd. Not a child was seen.

"Take me into your houses. I would visit the sick," said Ethne.

"My lady, is that wise?" asked Cadla, darkly.

"Cadla, I do not ask you or your men to come with me. I am a healer and will do what I can to help."

Ethne and Gaine dismounted the cart. The warriors stayed on their mounts, not wanting to walk on ground contaminated by disease. Ethne entered one of the small houses accompanied by Gaine. Inside lay a tiny child on a palette, alive but listless and burning with fever. The mother sat silently next to it, ill nourished and beyond hope.

"What have you given this child to make it well?" asked the queen gently.

"Nothing, my lady. I don't give her anything bad, just holy water from the church. I sprinkle it on her when I say my prayers."

"Did you ask for a Drui when you saw she wasn't getting better?"

"Oh no, the Druid belong to the Devil," and she crossed herself.

"Have you any elderflowers?"

"Those are herbs fit only for beasts."

"We'll see about that." Ethne's anger threatened to override her pity. "Gaine, order the others to gather elder blossoms, mints and yarrow. Have them brought here quickly."

Gaine took the queen's message to the group waiting at the carts, as Ethne ddressed the people.

"I have visited one of your sick children. She has a stomach fever, a common ailment. It is easily cured with elderflowers, yarrow and mint. Too many here have died, and I will not allow it to go on!"

That afternoon Ethne supervised the making of medicine in her own cauldron and showed the people how to dose their children and babies. She visited the sick adults and elderly of the tuath, standing by until they drank her potion. The people of the tuath watched her with fear and a shy hope. She was Rígain, a near Goddess, sent to them in their need.

"Gaine," said Ethne, wiping her forehead with her sleeve after leaving a husband and wife too weak to tend to each other. "I have not felt this useful in many months. It restores my spirit to know that I can be of help. I will assemble a cadre of Liaig to make regular circuits of every province and check the tuaths for illness. They can dispense herbs to those who need them.

Once, every tuath had its wise women and men to care for the sick. What will save this Island if the people abandon the ancient remedies? This is madness," Ethne's bewilderment and frustration mounted.

"I sense it too," answered Gaine "Coemgen worried about the people turning their backs on the trees, the green hills and the sacred rivers. In his wisdom he foresaw the disorder we find here today. Who can tell when the balance will be restored?"

The two women worked long in the center of the tuath, filling the villagers' jugs with a healing mix of leaves and flowers.

# 39

In the weeks that followed, a pattern emerged. Those communities where Druid remained had healthy crops and herb gardens. Those villages without Druid influence were left on their own to heal the sick.

"Why can't they see the pattern?" wondered Ethne. "Does it *really* take a Drui to see where this new way is headed?"

The small caravan developed a routine, picking healing herbs and digging medicinal roots where they could. At each tuath, Ethne assessed the medical needs and handed out healing plants to those who could be trusted to dispense them with care. Her presence was often enough to re-kindle the faith in the Land Spirits, but some were obdurate, trusting to the salvation promised by the priests, an end to the perpetual round of reincarnation.

Upon their return to the royal dun, Ethne assigned Liaig to travel in twos or threes to every part of the Island, to tend the sick and report to her district by district.

A week later, Ruadh arrived for a brief visit. Ethne's belly was huge, her mood vacillating between pride and impatience as she anticipated the birth. No longer could she hide her desire for Ruadh, and she no longer cared if they were seen together. Ruadh, putting aside the clothing of the Fian, dressed in princely garb, his torque polished and shining.

Erc, Buan, Fidach, Colchu and Corc came from the coast to report on the latest battle with The Men of the North. Ragnall had been killed by a raider's spear, and Erc and Miadach were handfasted. Ethne called for a victory celebration in the great hall, but many of the rath's warriors abstained from the feast. They found it hard to sit with the Fian at table, and wondered at the sight of the Rígain and her favorite, both in their noble garb, entertaining a rabble of forest-dwellers.

Ethne gifted the Fennidi with six horses. She also indicated a selection of iron household implements and tartan cloths as gifts for Miadach. After the feast, Ethne and Ruadh walked to the gates to see them off and stole a private moment.

"There will be a handfasting soon," Clothru murmured to Damán, watching as the pair disappeared behind the bough of an apple tree.

The first fruits of the harvest were in and though sparser than past years, the Lugnasad celebration was joyous. Ethne insisted on the traditional horse race, and the warriors urged their chargers on, whooping and clapping each other on the back as the horses ran around the hill of the stone circle. Many bets were won and lost that day. A fat, squealing pig was the winner's prize, and everyone laughed as it wriggled free and started another race, this time led by the children.

At the holy well, the Druid petitioned Danann and Lug to bring good weather and abundance in the harvest. Several of the local boaire were handfast that day, walking into the well by twos to be "reborn" in its waters.

At dawn members of the rath gathered the first sheaf of the harvest, which they placed in the sun to dry. That evening the sheaf was set on fire to burn off the chaff then winnowed, ground in a quern, kneaded on a sheepskin and baked into a large bannock on a ruadán twig fire. Ethne, her belly round as the harvest moon, broke the bannock into small pieces and distributed it to the people for luck. The younger folk danced sunwise around the fire all evening, enjoying ripe blueberries and sweet mead. The flaith retired to the royal rath for a formal harvest banquet.

Ethne sat watching the dancing and laughing with Gaine at the clowning men, and admiring the women's plaited hair. Ruadh stood near, clapping in time to the drums and filling Ethne's cup with mead when it ran low. At a break in the music he bent to her.

"I must leave for a short time to help my clann with the harvest. Anluan and my mother will accept Glaisne more readily if I am there to support him as Chief when the crops are brought in and the cattle feed prepared for winter."

"Tell Fithir I send her joy of the harvest and a warm winter by the fire," answered Ethne. "I hope Anluan's grief at your father's death has softened so that he may take his own place as a clann leader." She smiled up at him and he lifted her hand and kissed it.

"I won't be gone long. This baby will take its place in the sun very soon."

"Don't worry, Ruadh, my time is after the last of the harvest. Go and be safe." She rested her head on his arm briefly, then let him go.

In the following days Ethne woke earlier than she had for several months and enjoyed sorting linen, bundling small bunches of herbs, and preparing dried seeds and blossoms for the drawers in the storeroom . She stitched small garments which she embroidered with spirals or edged with braided threads. If her own company gave her pleasure, the company of the women tested her patience, every woman she encountered had words of advice. In the kitchens or in the great hall, she was counseled on motherhood and childbirth:

"My lady, if you would keep your child from the colic, don't eat cabbage or turnips."

"My lady, drink strong ale after the birth. It will make your milk flow."

"My lady, poultice your breasts with knit-bone, mashed, warmed and spread on a linen cloth to avoid soreness after the baby feeds."

"My lady, eat berries by the handful to keep from binding up."

"I am a *healer*!" Ethne said to Gaine, exasperated as they sat cutting the stems from wild mushrooms. "Do they think I don't know how to care for my own body?"

"Before you were a priestess and a queen, unapproachable. Now you are a woman just like them. They mean it as kindness."

"Of course, you are right, but I grow so irritable at times, wanting this baby to myself."

"No woman has a baby all to herself, Ethne, and especially not a queen. Come; let's walk in the sun before the shadows grow together."

The two women ambled into the fresh air and let their feet guide them where they would. Soon they found themselves halfway up the hill of stones. As Ethne climbed a few steps further, a spasm gripped her lower back. She sat down slowly and Gaine came to her side. "What is it, Ethne?" Then Gaine saw that Ethne's gown was soaked. The two women looked at one another and Ethne's eyes grew wide.

"I think my water has broken!"

Gaine smiled and nodded. "It would seem so. Can you make it to the House of Healing? Your time has begun."

They walked with careful steps to the hut where clean linens and sheepskins had long been prepared. Gaine sent a runner to fetch a midwife from a house near the rath who arrived quickly with her apprentice and a store of pain-killing balms. The midwife felt Ethne's swollen belly and massaged her back, asked her when she had last eaten and made her drink clear water.

"Now you must walk, dear. Slowly and steadily. You may even walk outside as long as you don't go far from this hut. Let your legs and back carry you and let your mind float. Go."

She dismissed Ethne to stroll in the inner yard while she arranged her herbs and tools. For several hours Ethne moved about the yard, stopping occasionally to lean on a fence or on Gaine's arm when a contraction coiled up across her belly. But after one particularly wrenching contraction, Gaine suggested they return to the hut. There, Ethne continued her perambulations, but soon, even within this small space, the effort of walking was too much. The contractions surged up and over her now, overtaking her breath and her focus. She put her attention on the point between her eyes, trying to still her fear and distance herself from the pain.

"Sit, dear. Lean back on these cushions and let the pull take you," the midwife advised.

Ethne lowered herself to the cot, reclining on the piled cushions. She had seen many women give birth and knew that each found her own way through the mounting pain. She called on her own Spirits to guide her and began to breathe in rhythm as if she were moving on an ocean's current. As a contraction swept over her, she would breathe out a deep, low growl, like a sea creature fighting its way for shore.

In the Nemed, Gaine busied herself making offerings to Brighid, Goddess of motherhood and Airmid, Goddess of herbal healers. She walked sun-wise around the Fire Altar pouring butter and oils into the flames:

> *Brighid! Great Goddess of healing,*
> *spread your cloak of strength and protection*
> *on Ethne as she enters her time of travail.*
> *Spread your cloak upon the little one*
> *who prepares to pass from one life to the next.*
> *Airmid send strength to the plants*
> *That comfort the mother and child.*

Next she moved to the Cauldron of Sea and poured waters into it, visualizing the passage from one Ocean of Being to another, from life to life.

> *Like a half moon he is,*
> *outside one world and barely in the other,*
> *a spirit moving from the womb of one existence*

*into the open door of the next.*
*Make his passage smooth, his way easy*
*as he dies to the Otherworld.*
*Open wide the gates of this world*
*that we may soon see his face,*
*the prince who comes. Blessed Airmid, make it so!*

And finally, she walked to the sacred Ash, placing her left hand upon it:

*Sister tree, Spirit who moves between the worlds,*
*from the above to the below*
*and from the below to the above,*
*root to branch, branch to root,*
*help guide this child*
*as he moves from one world to the next.*
*Send him strength and fortify his life!*

Gaine's inner sight showed her that the child was a boy, but the vision was troubling. It would not be an easy passage for the child or the mother. She made her way to the men at the gates. "Go to Ruadh, now! Bring him back quickly!"

A day passed and still the child did not come. Ethne no longer made occasional turns around the room. The midwife brought a wooden birthing stool to help support her. From time to time the women urged her to her feet, and, as she leaned on them, they guided her across the room. The apprentice made a strong spikenard brew.

"It's a bane to the fleas but brings on a woman's courses," said the midwife, encouraging Ethne to drink. "The only better remedy is the love of the one that put that child in there."

Stepping outside the hut, the midwife confided to Gaine. "She is wearing down, though she has her courage. I have seen some continue like this for another night, but often neither the infant nor the mother lives."

"Thank you for your honesty," Gaine answered. "I will do all I can to aid them." She ran to the Nemed to craft a birthing spell with Damán and Clothru.

As the sun set, Ethne felt the shadows growing long even though she could only see the change in light under the leather door covering. The muscles in her legs felt knotted and her back was a constant fire of pain. She no longer could tell when one contraction ended and another began. The midwife gave her sips of water from the coldest well. More and more no matter how hard she worked at bringing her focus back within the room, her mind drifted and floated above the rath.

Ethne knew she was failing. A powerful contraction gripped her and she screamed as the swell rose and clamped her body. "Let me go," she panted as her legs went limp and her body shivered beyond her control.

At that moment, Ruadh appeared. His mouth went slack as he saw her strained body, soaked with sweat and breathing in great gulping gasps.

He froze. "Is there nothing I can do?"

"Get behind her and hold her up," commanded the midwife.

Without question, Ruadh kneeled on the bed and raised Ethne in his arms.

"Sit behind her so she is lying against your chest. Hold her steady, gently. Talk to her. Tell her she needs to be strong."

The midwife bared her arm. She placed her hand between Ethne's legs and felt cautiously for the baby's head. Frowning, she reached further and felt instead a round knob of shoulder. Bracing herself, the midwife made a scoop with her hand, cupped the shoulder, and slid it back into Ethne's womb. Ethne gave out a shrill cry and began to shake. The midwife slid her hand in a small arc within Ethne and found the baby's head crooked to the side. She cradled the head in her hand, getting leverage on the base of the skull and pulled firmly, slowly. "Push, girl! Push with everything you have left! Push this baby into the light. Push!"

"Aaaaahhhhhhiiiii!!!!" Ethne's voice filled the hut and carried beyond, villagers tending the night fires and keeping watch turned with awe at the sound.

"Ethne you are the storm wind, you are the mighty sea," Ruadh spoke into her ear.

"You are the earth that opens for the great trees to grow."

"*Push now!*" yelled the midwife and with a gush, the baby slid whole and quivering into her waiting hands. With a quick slice, she cut the chord and tied it neatly on the baby's belly. She stood and placed the still-wet child on Ethne's stomach.

"You have a prince, my queen," whispered Ruadh, rocking both his loves in his arms. He brushed the hair back from Ethne's face and kissed her at the corner of her mouth. Tears ran down his face. Ethne raised the baby to her breast and drew a corner of the blanket around him, tracing his nose, his ear, his chin with her finger.

"I have never seen anything so perfect," she breathed and closed her eyes to let sleep drown her exhaustion.

The midwife came to the bed and took the child from Ethne's sleeping arms, gesturing Ruadh to follow her. She placed herself on one side of the central hearth and pointed to Ruadh to stand on the other. Then she handed the child to him and he returned the baby three times, passing the baby over the flames.

"*May you be blessed all your days by holy fire,*" she intoned.

She walked three times, sun-wise, around the hearth bearing the baby.

"*May you be blessed all your days by the shining Sun.*"

She carried the infant to a wooden bath that held a golden coin, token of his status as prince and symbolic of the Sun, pouring wavelets over his body nine times.

*In the name of Brighid, nine blessings of water upon you.*
*A blessing on your form, that it be strong*
*and beautiful to behold,*

*a blessing on your voice, that it be melodious,*
*a blessing on your speech, that it be eloquent,*
*a blessing on your means, that you may never want,*
*a blessing on your generosity, that you be always hospitable,*
*a blessing on your appetite, that it be hale,*
*a blessing on your wealth, that you be prosperous,*
*a blessing on your life, that it be long,*
*a blessing on your health, that it be constant.*

Following these words she put three drops of water on the child's brow.

*No seed of Faery, nor human foe may best you.*
*No evil eye nor envy nor malice disturb thy sleep.*
*May the loving arms of Brighid surround you*
*and shield you, this night and every night.*

The midwife roused Ethne, pulled the sheets from the bed and helped her out of her bloody shift, replacing it with the brightly embroidered nightgown she had worn on the eve of her marriage to Crimthann. Ethne drank a strong cup of lady's mantle to staunch internal bleeding, after which she and Ruadh shared a beaker of dark ale. "To build your strength and bring down your milk," said the midwife.

The apprentice took the placenta to the Nemed where Gaine and the Druid buried it with ceremony under the Sacred Ash, and the Druid made offerings of thanks to the Fire Altar. Word of the new prince made its way like an evening moth from hut to hut and the people rejoiced.

Ruadh handed the baby, swaddled in the softest white wool, back to Ethne and lowered himself beside them. He held them and let his breathing slow to match theirs.

The world was complete within the small hut, within the compass of his arms.

"What shall we name him?" Ruadh asked as Ethne nursed the infant. They were still resident in the House of Healing, attended only by midwives and Druid. It was an effort to shelter Ethne and the baby from the daily petitioners.

Ethne cradled the baby to her and nosed his feathery hair. "He smells like life itself," she murmured and kissed him softly on his temple.

She loved the feel of his round bottom and the weight of his little head against her arm. She looked up at Ruadh who was watching them intently. "Let us name him Ruadán, he has flame-colored hair and it is a fitting name for your son."

"Ruadán it is," answered Ruadh. "A vigorous name for a hearty boy and one that mirrors my own."

The baby dropped off to sleep, his mouth still in an "o." Ruadh reached down and lifted him from Ethne's arms and began a slow, swaying walk around the hut. Ethne stretched her arms and back, straightened her gown, and sat with her head on one hand watching her tiny son, nestled in Ruadh's powerful arms. Her contentment rose and broke over her like the first warm breezes of spring. She wanted to put a spell on the door, to bar the world from intruding, but Gaine stepped in followed by a midwife with fresh linens.

"Everyone is rejoicing at the prince's birth," she announced. "They are planning a festival in his honor as soon as you and he are strong enough."

Ethne smiled politely. "How do the people fare in my absence? Are there any pressing matters I must hear?"

"Only the usual complaints of straying cattle and someone dug a deer-pit in the middle of a field that was intended for turnips. We settled that with a fine of two fat ewes."

Ethne nodded her head and waited. She knew there was more by the way Gaine grasped one hand in the other. She had seen that gesture too often before. Gaine began again, "What concerns me most is the attitude of the warriors, they grow bolder in their complaints about the Fennidi. They are jealous of their success against Canoc and of the welcome you gave them after their recent battle with the Men of the North."

"Gaine, there is more to it than that." Ethne stood and began pacing. "I am a woman, a healer Druid-trained. I am no battle-lord who would lead them to greater glory and a chance to win the hero's portion at the feast. They think I don't understand what it means to be a warrior, what it means to lead this Island. I must show them that they are wrong."

Ruadh placed the baby in his cradle and voiced his thoughts. "If glory is what they seek, then let's offer it. Why not build a royal outpost on the coast where battlehungry men can sit and wait for the northern wolves in their ships. Then they will have the action they desire."

Ethne nodded, warming to the idea. "Perhaps it would be best if we put these warriors on one coast and kept the Fennidi on the other," she added. "And I would like you, Ruadh, to be in charge of building the outpost against the raiders. You have experience and will be respected for it. I don't know if it will heal the rift between the warriors and the Fennidi, but it will show everyone that I depend on you in important matters. They will soon accept that we rule together."

"It is a sound plan, Ethne," beamed Gaine. "You show the makings of a fine queen."

After Gaine left, Ruadh said with a rueful smile, "I used to chafe at the responsibilities of running the farm. Now, here I am responsible for a kingdom!"

"Our destiny is in the hands of the Gods, Ruadh. If we honor them, our responsibilities come as welcomed kin."

# 40

━━━━━━

Albinus appeared one morning at the assembly, bearing gifts and asking to meet the prince. "My lord Ruadh and lady Ethne, I come in the name of peace, to welcome the young prince into this world."

He opened a cloth bundle and placed it at the foot of the dais. Those who could see murmured praise. On the cloth lay a solid gold rattle, a tiny torque of gold and a small sword, complete with a beautifully worked, green leather scabbard and belt.

"Abbot Germanus wishes everyone to know that we recognize this child as the prince of the realm, a king in his own right one day!" Albinus beamed at the parents and the assembly.

"Whether he will be a king in his time," Ethne responded, "is a matter for the people to decide. Please tell the Abbot that we accept his gifts in gratitude and friendship."

Ethne was grateful for the Abbot's generosity. Perhaps this could be a sign of peace between the religions of the Island. "Please tell the Abbot he is welcome here, should he wish to visit the prince," said Ethne. Albinus bowed graciously and exited the hall.

A young woman stepped out of the crowd before the throne, shy and embarrassed, with eyes cast down, her hair tightly bound and covered with a kerchief, her clothes of sober hue. Ethne gestured for her to speak.

"I am Orla. I lost my own child to a fever, three days ago and the people of the tuath thought it would be a kindness to me and to you, your highness, if I could serve you as a wet-nurse. That would free you to rule more effectively, and it would ease my own pain."

Ethne looked from Ruadh to Gaine. Ethne suckled her own child, but with the new fort being built on the coast, and the other business of rulership, a nurse to watch over the baby would be a help.

"I welcome you, Orla, into our household, and many thanks to the kind villagers who sent you. Please take her to my private quarters where prince Ruadán is sleeping," said Ethne, relief and unease mixing together within her.

Ethne watched Orla for the first few days to see what sort of woman would spend time with her newborn child. She suppressed pangs of jealousy each time she saw Orla leave with the prince in her arms, when she turned her attention to the day's duties and the needs of the Island. In truth, she did find Orla's presence a help. They worked out a system, where the prince stayed with Ethne in the gardens or the assembly until he cried. If he could not be comforted quickly or needed to have his clothes changed, Orla was there to take him to another room, out of earshot. Ethne came to depend upon her.

"I could not do without her services even if I wanted to," Ethne confided to Gaine. "It is so much easier now to concentrate on matters of policy and law."

"It is for the best, Ethne. You are Rígain, not a farm wife, noble mistress or Ban-Drui. Prince Ruadán is healthy and well, and your kingdom is prosperous and happy."

"By the Gods may it remain so," answered Ethne.

A few evenings later, after Ruadán was asleep, Ruadh asked, "What do you think of Orla?"

"She is very helpful, but there is one thing I find strange," said Ethne.

"What is it, love?"

"She is so shy and quiet. She never asks questions or tells stories about what Ruadán has done that day. She seldom laughs, and she only speaks when I speak to her first or ask her something directly."

"She is in awe of you, Ethne. She comes from a simple farm family."

"No, it is something more. I can't quite put my finger on it." Ruadh thought for a moment. "She does remind me of my mother."

"Your mother?" Ethne leaned up on one elbow.

"Since my mother became a Cristaide. She used to be talkative and forceful in her way, a Rígain of the tribes. Now she sits in silence, with her head covered by a dark cloth, as if her spirit were deflated. It is more than my father's death and the loss of the kingdom. She has her home and her clann, but she behaves differently with everyone now."

"Do you think Orla has been influenced by Albinus?"

"Possibly. Her silence is most troubling."

"I would make a poor Cristaide then!" laughed Ethne.

"You certainly would!" agreed Ruadh, pulling her close and kissing her neck and shoulders. "Having a wet-nurse means I have you to myself," he added, kissing her breasts and cupping her bottom to pull her close in the dark.

Ethne dispatched a troop of warriors to the coast to help build the fort. Ruadh went with them to advise on its placement and construction and to teach the men some secrets of the Fian. Convincing the warriors to work in unison was difficult. The guiding philosophy of the warrior class was to gain personal glory and be praised by the people. Their ultimate achievement was to have songs and poems composed about their individual exploits.

Ruadh tried to instill new ideas in them. "Among the Fennidi, the success of the individual is measured by the success of the group. It is the honor and reputation of the Fian that counts, far more than the reputation of any individual warrior. The Fennidi operate as small independent units that are very successful due to stealth and creative use of resources.

You warriors of the flaith look for personal glory in battle. When the Men of the North come swinging their axes, you must stand together and use your combined cunning. In the Fian we learn to be a fly on a leaf or a salmon hidden in the pool. We learn to strike in the night, unseen, and use the element of surprise."

The warriors respected him for his skill but did not adapt fully to his training.

"Why should we listen to *him*? He knows only quick skirmishes, not full battle attack." said Cadla, speaking out of Ruadh's hearing.

# 40

Samain came and went. The kings of the four provinces were present for the all night vigil, and Ethne was glad to have Orla's help. It was a blessing not to worry about tending a baby during this most solemn ritual. The cows, brought down from the hills, brought joy as everyone saw that the herd had increased over the summer. The harvest was bountiful, the granaries and root cellars nearly as full as in previous years. Carts of grain and vegetables trundled to outlying villages where there had been sickness and famine.

"Gaine, what do you think of a marriage feast during the waxing moon?" asked Ethne, enjoying a rare afternoon in the Nemed garden with her son. She had Ruadán all to herself, and carried him everywhere to look at the flowers, nuzzling the soft skin of his neck. He made her laugh even when changing his soiled cloths. Ruadán chortled and gurgled as she lifted him into the air, whirling in a circle around the herb garden.

"Whee! Ruadán flies like an eagle!" Ethne laughed. It was an achingly clear day, the sun bright and the sky a cloudless blue. Gaine was picking asters to decorate the feasting hall and the two women had asters in their braids, and little clumps of aster flowers, purple and white, littered the walkway where they had fallen out of Gaine's basket.

"You must wear blue this time, for luck. The Doini Sidi favor blue."

"Yes, I want all the little traditional details I missed before because the ceremony was so grand. I want a simple ceremony this time, salt in our pockets and silver in our shoes. We can clasp hands in the river, we don't have to go all the way to the well."

"Is this what Ruadh wants? It is his wedding, too."

"With us it is a formality. It's as if we have always been married." Said Ethne, looking past Gaine towards the hill of stones.

Gaine searched Ethne's face then dropped her gaze. "Even if the ceremony is simple, there will be many details, guest lists and so on. We should begin right away. Send for Ruadh" she said.

The next few weeks were filled with preparations. One difficulty was sending messengers to the tuaths and kingdoms of the Island, getting their replies and coordinating a hosting for each. Three kinds of meat had to be available every day for a fortnight for every guest, and gallons of mead and fion would need to be procured.

With most of the warriors away building the fort, the few that were left were occupied with riding in and out bearing messages. Many residents of the rath were away on merchanting expeditions, bartering for supplies for the wedding feast. The royal dun was occupied mostly by women, children, Druid and a small skeleton force of guards who stayed to care for the horses and defend the gates.

Orla sent messages to Albinus via her younger brother, Duald. She secretly reported on the prince's health, his whereabouts and the goings on at the dun. As preparations for the royal wedding gathered momentum, Ethne relied more and more on Orla to attend to Ruadán. Sometimes, as on this day, she would wait until late morning or early afternoon before calling for the baby. Ethne stood next to Gaine holding material for a wedding dress when the mog she had sent returned alone.

"What do you mean you can't find them? *Someone* must know where they are."

Ethne's hand poised in mid-air, about to cut a piece of cloth. "Have you searched the Nemed gardens? Sometimes Orla walks there with Ruadán."

The mog shook his head and moved from one foot to the other. "We have looked everywhere within the rath, lady."

Ethne faced him squarely. "I will go and look myself."

Before Gaine or the ladies could protest, she had swept out of the room into the watery sunlight of the rath. She went to Orla's hut and saw her shift hanging behind the door and at the baby clothes she had stitched, still clean and folded on top of the chest.

She went to the neighbors and from their answers walked along the pathway to the gate. After a few words with the guards, she quickened her pace and left the rath, following the track that led around a small hill. As she rounded the base of the hill, her hopes rose, thinking she would see Orla strolling in her languid way with Ruadán slung before her in a striped cloth. But her eyes found only the space between the trees and the stillness of an afternoon.

"Orla! *Orla!*" Ethne turned and spun as she ran, "Orla, are you there?"

A few birds startled and fluttered away. Ethne looked up the hill, but it was a steep mound, covered with briers. She ran further along the track, her heart stiff in her chest. Faster she went, calling first "Orla" then "Ruadán! Ruadán!" until her voice cracked. She swung every which way trying to make them appear from behind a rise, from beside the stones. All at once she caught a glimpse of red, of dark hair and her joy bounded, she ran towards the color only to find a villager with a bundle of wood on his back coming around the bend.

"Have you seen a woman? A young woman with a baby in these last hours?" Ethne panted.

"Yes, lady. Not long after I sat to have my midday bread and cheese. They were right here on this path."

"Did you see where she went?"

"She walked the way I've just come, lady. She walked past without a 'Gods be with you.' She hurried and the baby was crying. I did not recognize her."

Ethne swallowed hard. "What do you mean?"

"She was no villager, lady. She was not one I ever knew."

Ethne stood dumb, frozen as a black pit gaped before her. She turned from the man and half ran half walked further down the track. Suddenly Gaine and a few guards were there. The guards questioned the man, and Gaine tried to put her arms around Ethne and soothe her.

"NOOO!!!! NOOO!!!" Ethne's screams tore the air. "Don't tell me he is gone!" She raised her fists and shrieked. "I will find him. I will go down every track, through every forest path and walk the stones of the shore until I find him. He is not gone!" She clawed at Gaine to let her go and there was nothing the older woman could do to hold her. Gaine conferred with the guards and sent them in every direction in search of Ruadán, instructing one guard to stay with Ethne, to do as the queen asked, to keep her safe. Gaine returned to the Nemed to gather the Druid.

For days that had no shape or color, Ethne asked everywhere of her child. Women reached out their arms to her and filled their eyes with sympathy. Men offered to join the search, but never did she hear one word that told her Ruadán was within her reach.

Late one afternoon Father Per found Ethne at the edge of the Nemed. He touched her sleeve and she knew he had news. With blanched face, she stood and heard him.

"I overheard Albinus," Per began. He stepped close, pitching his voice to undercut her panic and grief. "A woman brought a child to the monks. She said he was left alone after fever had taken both his mother and father. I fear the monks have carried him away to be sent to a Cristaidi monastery, somewhere in Kernow." Father Per knew comfort was useless.

Ethne collapsed as a dull, dark weight settled upon her. She was carried to her private chamber and tended by Gaine and other ladies of the court. She stayed mute, staring blankly at the walls.

# 42

════════════

Ruadh came to the door of the royal bedchamber and halted. He had ridden his horse until it nearly collapsed under him, but now that he was about to face Ethne, his courage failed. He willed himself to push the oak panel open, and what he saw nearly brought him to his knees.

Ethne sat like a carved image in a chair. Her eyes, like stones, gave back no light, no warmth. With quiet steps Ruadh went to her and crouched next to her chair. Without a sound he put his arms about her and began to rock her. When she did not resist, he held her more firmly and placed her head on his shoulder. They sat thus for a long time, he rocking and trying to hold her from shattering beyond his reach. As the day darkened, Ethne moaned, a slight, faint sound that carried her despair like winter sleet. A jagged sob tore through Ruadh and he shook as convulsive cries rose and poured from him. His mouth was a grimace of agony and tears teemed down his face. He buried himself in Ethne's hair and held her so tight she gasped for breath. She raised her hands to break his grip and found his wet, pleading eyes. With a choking cry she turned to him and began to scream.

"Give him back! Ruadán! Ruadán! *Give him back*!" She banged her fists against Ruadh's head, his arms, his chest. She clawed at him, pulled his hair and screamed. "Ruadán! My child!" The tears came in hot, coursing, gulping sobs that gripped her heart and wrung out of her like demon spirits.

Ruadh held her, let her pummel him, let her scratch and fight her grief and anger to a size she could hold everyday. He heard his son's name as it ripped from her voice and sent his prayers with it. He could do no more than be the rock against which she battered her sorrow and her loss. Finally, her hair tangled and wet, her shift torn and face swollen, she collapsed against him and they clung together, weeping. He picked her up and brought her to the bed where they lay through the long hours of the night, letting their tears mingle and surrendering the joy of their son.

In the following days, Ruadh managed to coax Ethne to drink a little and take bites from the food Gaine brought. He dressed her, brushed her hair, bathed her face and sat by her as slow tears made their way down her cheeks. He convinced her to walk a little way around the dun. She looked upon the people of the rath, the animals in their pens, the birds that fluttered and pecked at the ground as objects with no meaning. She did not respond when villagers paid their respects, feeling her loss as theirs.

Gaine, in the meantime, upheld the laws and traditions at court. The Druid scryed into the flames and the waters for a vision, but none came. "All I can say for certain is that Ruadán still lives," said Damán, who had seen an image of the child reflected in the waters of the Cauldron of Sea. One day, as they walked their usual circuit of the dun, Ethne faced Ruadh. "Take me to the hill of stones."

Ruadh complied, helping her climb the hill and sitting next to her as she lowered herself to lean against one of the ancient menhirs. "I am no longer Ard-Rígain," Ethne said of a sudden. "I cannot lead the people. I can't even live inside my own skin!"

"The people understand your sorrow, Ethne," answered Ruadh. "You aren't alone. *I* will never leave you and Gaine is ever at your side."

"The warriors need a battle queen, not a grieving mother." Her tears came again and Ruadh held her to him. But gradually, slowly, her outpouring of emotion calmed as the cool earth of the hill and the strength of the stones worked their magic.

"I will call a council meeting for tomorrow morning. The business of the kingdom must go forward. The Gods have put me here and I must summon all my courage to carry on."

He dried her face with his sleeve, seeing a hint of the old sparkle in her eyes.

"You have only to try for a day. And each day will follow the next. Things will get easier, I promise."

While Ethne and Ruadh sat talking on the hill of stones, a small leather ship left the shores of the Island, bound for Kernow and a monastery on its shore. The ship was scheduled to continue south to Armorica to a friary known for its teaching brothers and library. Orla, Duald and Ruadán were on board along with three sturdy sailors. They carried baggage and gifts for the monks.

Ruadán would be educated in the new religion and one-day return to In Medon, knowing his parentage, and armed with the Cristaidi religion. Albinus had dispatched the craft, despite the sailors' warnings. A red dawn indicated approaching bad weather, and the experienced mariners had tried in vain to persuade the priest to postpone the voyage.

"Let us pray to the Christus for safe passage." Albinus knelt, recited a Latin prayer and sprinkled the ship's prow with holy water. "The Lord has aided our plans," he added as he watched it depart, drawing the sign of the cross in the air.

As the sun lowered to the horizon a squall blew up, knocking the vessel sideways and spilling nearly all its contents into the cold sea. A few days later, a fishing family found clothes and foodstuffs washed up on shore still wrapped in tight bundles. They marveled at the richness of the materials, but said nothing to their neighbors. It would be almost a year before a messenger appeared at the abbey to inform Albinus that the expected travelers had not reached Kernow.

That night a bright patch of moonlight stretched across Ethne's face and Ruadh's as they slept fitfully, the kind of sleep that causes the mind to remember the images and emotions of dreams. Attuned as they were to each other, they had entered each other's dreaming.

Ethne was in a forest, searching. She felt a terrible anxiety at not finding something precious she had lost. Her feet were bogged in deep mud that was dotted with poisonous and evil smelling worts. Around her were twisted and gnarled branches of old apple trees. She peered closely at one and discovered it was abloom with perfect, pink blossoms in the midst of all that dankness. A huge black bird scrabbled onto a branch and viciously picked off the sweet flowers.

In Ruadh's dream he too was mired in the mud of a dark, damp forest. He was searching for Ethne. When he finally caught a glimpse of her she was caught in an old tree, her hair tangled hopelessly in its branches, her feet held fast by the slime.

"I am coming, Ethne!" he cried. But his feet would not move.

Ethne's dream shifted. In the distance she saw a clearing more beautiful than any patch of forest she had ever seen. "It must be the Land of Faery," she thought.

The plants in the clearing were a pale, translucent green, the shade of new leaves in earliest spring. The stones were covered in brightly colored mosses, each a different hue and blooming with tiny red and orange flowers. Bright red, pink and orange mushrooms popped from between rocks. Dense fir trees and elegant gray beeches spread their branches, each covered with dew-speckled greenery. White birches, so noble and bright they were almost painful to look at, swayed amongst the evergreens. A brown hawk flew soundlessly before her. "He is pointing the way," and without knowing how, she was out of the mud, her feet on a path strewn with beech leaves and pine cones. She followed the path with her eyes and saw in the distance, flooded with sunlight and surrounded by apple trees in full bloom, bluebells, larkspur and bright white yarrow, her house in the forest.

In Ruadh's dream he found himself nestled in the feathers of a great bird, a hawk judging from its cry. The bird carried him to a sunlit clearing within the forest where he saw Ethne; barefoot and clothed in the simple gown she had worn when he first knew her. She threw her arms about him as he slid off of the bird's back.

"What took you so long?" she asked.

"I didn't know how to follow you."

They woke, turning to each other, conscious and alert.

"You were in my dream," said Ethne, excitedly.

"You were in mine." "We were in a forest."

"There was a clearing."

"It was so beautiful."

"It was the Forest House."

"Yes."

They lay soundless, holding the dream, feeling joy and gazing into each other's eyes. And then Ruadán was between them, their loss separating them, settling with the crush of an anvil, lodged.

Ethne drew a ragged breath and whispered, "The Gods have been kind. It was a healing dream, sent to lift our hearts and spirits."

"It was a glimpse of the Faery realm in the midst of our sorrow," said Ruadh.

"Give thanks to Brighid for the gift. I will place an offering into the Fire Altar in Her name," Ethne murmured into the darkness.

They clung to each other, searching to lighten the other's burden, neither able to recapture that momentary grace.

# 43

Gaine opened the assembly, shaking the golden chain and invoking the Gods: "In the name of Land, Sea and Sky; in the name of Danann, Mother of the Gods and of In Dagdae, I declare this assembly open. May Oghma bless us with eloquence of speech and Brighid bring us inspiration. May we each leave with lightened burdens and clear directions."

Gaine sat down in her accustomed place behind the throne. Ethne and Ruadh sat side by side, Ruadh on a large oaken chair only a bit smaller and less elaborate than Ethne's. The oak tree and eagle carvings on the wall behind the throne pulsed in the thick tension of the room. The wolf and boar heads mounted on the walls came alive as every clann invoked its totem animal. The loss of the prince was a terrible omen for the people, animals and land. It was a judgment from the Gods.

Cadla came forward. "I speak for my clann, the warriors, and myself. We believe that the disappearance of the prince is a judgment on Ethne's fitness to rule. Since Crimthann's death the warriors have lacked confidence in her leadership. This queen is not battle-tested nor is she wise in the ways of strategy. We call for an election."

The crowd murmured approval. Ruadh rose to speak in Ethne's defense. "The queen suffers a great grief. As her chosen consort I stand beside her. I am a tested warrior and battle leader."

"We don't want a weeping Rígain!" came a cry from the back of the hall. It was Ronan, red-faced and angry. "We don't want a *Drui* sitting on the throne. We want a strong war leader we can trust!"

Lorcan spoke from one side of the hall, surrounded by his male kin. "I am not a Drui, and I can't say I understand the ways of religion, but are we praying to the wrong Gods? Albinus says this happened because we did not accept the God of the Cristaidi. He said the Roman emperor conquered his enemies by painting the Cristaidi cross on his shields and banners. This misfortune has come on us because we ignore this God!"

A chorus of "Aye!" came from many in the hall.

Albinus pushed his way forward from the edge, with several warriors at his back, ready to defend Lorcan. "My friends! You are beginning to see the light! God does not want a woman to rule, nor does he want you to follow the old religion! The disappearance of the prince is a sign. The time of Druid rule is over! It is time for a new way!"

Cadla jumped up on the dais in front of Ethne and Ruadh. "I call for an election now! Who is with me?"

Gaine, to mitigate the chaos and disrespect, deliberately placed herself in front of Cadla. She banged the butt end of her thick oaken staff on the floor three times. "This assembly is closed!" she roared. "You will all leave, now!"

A Drui had spoken in anger! The people, conditioned from birth to accept the word of a Drui as sacred, responded immediately. Even the cries of Albinus could not prevent their going. For now, the upset and shock were over. Gaine had said so. They would meet again tomorrow when tempers had cooled.

But they did not meet on the next day, or the next. Gaine, after conferring with the senior Druid, decided an interval was needed to assess the attitudes of the clanns and to strengthen ties with the tuaths. As if mirroring the emotions seething across the landscape, the fall rains set in. They began one evening with a gradual obscuring of the stars followed by a shrinking corona around the moon. Farmers and herders saw it and hastened to cover their stores of peat and wood.

The days grew unremittingly soggy. Salt left in little pots on the high table hardened into clumps. Doors swelled and stuck. The rheumatic elderly took to their beds or would not move from the fire. Everyone's hair curled and thickened, sheep and dogs grew extra thickness in their pelts. The air was so heavy and damp that it magnified sounds. Distant barking or wood chopping carried on the moisture-laden atmosphere until it was impossible to tell if it was near or far. Earth, mud, and cattle dung smells were amplified in the wet. Shoes, clothing and hair stayed damp. Everyone's temper was foul.

The hall of the Ard-Rígain was sodden. Little rivulets of rain found their way down the roof pillars and gathered into puddles on the floor. Drops of water seeped through the willow thatching and hissed as they fell onto braziers. The women's quarters, supposed to be the sunniest in the building, were dark and close. Even the music of the household bard failed to lift the sagging spirits of Ethne and her ladies as they worked the loom and dealt with sheared wool, packed into thick piles in baskets on the floor.

"It's so very strange," said Ethne to Gaine in a somber mood as they carded.

"When I lived in the Forest House, the rain never depressed me. I sat by the fire and waited out the storms. Sometimes I deliberately went out to watch the raindrops as they hit the stream. It was so very beautiful. I would go into trance and have visions by watching the bubbles on the surface of the water."

"What did you see?"

"Sometimes I could see a water Spirit. She appeared as an old woman with flowing locks, gazing up at me from between the stones."

"Ah yes, I have seen Her, the ancient Earth Mother. They say She is older than the Gods of our people, that She was here before the Free People arrived on these shores."

"I gave Her offerings of honey and fish."

"Ethne, you are smiling!"

"I suppose I am. Thinking of that place brings me joy."
Ethne sighed deeply and gazed into the fire.

"That strange little house in the woods means so much to
you?" asked Gaine.

"It does. It is a living thing in my memory, and in Ruadh's."

Gaine said nothing, but watched Ethne, a woman with a
throne, a kingdom, power and wealth, yet longing for a stone hut
in the wilderness. Gaine remembered the words of her old teacher:
"*When you reduce things down to a paradox, you know you are on
the right track, for two opposites will reveal a third way.*" She continued with the carding, knowing that something was unfolding. But
what exactly the Gods intended, she was not yet certain.

The sun, for days invisible behind thick banks of clouds,
broke wanly through the curtained sky, its corona growing
brighter as the morning wore on. By midday its light was reflected in the puddles scattered across the open spaces of the
dun. The warriors emerged from their damp quarters to begin anew the endless drills and competitions that kept them in
fighting shape. Cadla requested that Ethne, Gaine and Ruadh
be guarded by two men at all times. Ruadh reluctantly agreed.
Ethne and Gaine refused the escorts but accepted the increased
guard should they leave the gates.

"My lady, if you do not allow us to protect you, we can't
guarantee your safety."

"I am shielded by the Gods I have served all my life. Are
you questioning *their* ability to protect me?"

Cadla became more and more frustrated with the obstinate
queen. He was annoyed that she did not heed his advice and
was resentful at being dismissed by a woman.

Albinus appeared at the gates daily, through wind and rain.
The guards led him into the warriors' quarters to speak to the
bored and housebound men. They were glad of the diversion
brought by Albinus's biblical tales and delighted in hearing the
stories of Constantine's victories under the sign of the cross.

"That sign is powerful magic. If it worked for an emperor, perhaps it will work for us," said Lorcan.

"We'll never know," Ronan responded dryly. "The Rígain and her prince are Pagani, sworn to the old Gods and none other. As long as they're in power, there is little chance for us to worship the new God Isu."

Cadla agreed. "If we just added the God Isu to the official pantheon we would be made stronger for it! This Isu can lend his battle magic to the Morrigu!"

And so it continued. Day after day more men were swayed by Albinus' tales of power and victory under the sign of the cross. By Solstice Eve nearly all the warriors were convinced that the God Isu should be worshipped in the dun, alongside the sacred warrior and protector Gods of the tribes. A contingent of warriors went to the assembly one morning when the frost sparkled on the still green grass. Albinus was with them and Cadla led the pack.

"It is time for the Christus Mass. It is fitting to honor this God within the enclosure of the dun." Cadla announced.

"I will pass judgment on this later, after I speak with the Druid," said Ethne firmly.

Her face was pinched and her voice harsh when she conferred with the Druid. "I hear Albinus holds late night meetings in the warriors' quarters. He goes in and out of the dun at all hours."

"We are a free people, Ethne," said Gaine. "We can't stop them from learning about or even worshipping this God. It would go against everything we teach and believe." It was her final opinion on the matter. The Druid reluctantly agreed to let the matter take its course, while they petitioned the Island Gods and Goddesses for aid.

In the assembly next morning Ethne looked at the faces before her. Most were warriors. The few Druid and villagers in the crowd looked anxious. "The warriors have found a common cause," thought Ethne. She knew they would not back down, no more than would a boar, once it had a mind to charge. They were united in their determination to bring the new God into the royal enclosure just a few yards from the Nemed; the shrine of the Fire Altar, the Sacred Ash and the Cauldron of Sea.

"Very well," she announced. "Tell Albinus that he may celebrate the rituals of the God Isu in the warriors' quarters. We are a free people. No Drui or Rígain will prevent you from following the Gods you choose."

A cheer went up. A few men clapped each other on the back and one or two crossed themselves. Albinus knelt, clasping his hands in prayer and uttering thanks to his God. Ethne's heart sank. She looked at Gaine and saw defeat written on her face. Ruadh was grim before the determination of the warriors. He too understood they were not to be denied. The warriors poured from the royal hall into the frosty air, rejoining Albinus for an impromptu service of prayer. The Mass, Albinus determined, would be held at dawn on the morning of Saturnalia, the ancient Roman winter festival. "Next we will build a church, here within the walls of the dun!" cried Albinus, exulting. He hurried through the gates to bring the news to Germanus. On his way he met Father Per, a basket of warm bread on his arm.

"Peace be with you," said Per.

"You will find no peace, Father, after your betrayal. Didn't you think I would learn that you told the queen about her son? You're a heretic, Per, and the Roman Church wants no more of you. Your followers now hear Mass with our monks."

"I will pray for you and for all the people of this kingdom. May God show us mercy." Father Per walked on, his loaves cooling in the chill air.

On Solstice Eve the villagers lit their bonfires on the surrounding hills, welcoming the first spark of the Fires of Life as the Sun began Her cycle to fullness. They drank mead and ate sweet meats, dancing in circles around the fires, lending the Sun strength and passion to hasten Her renewal.

"The Goddess Grian waxes and wanes just like Her sister the Moon, only in longer cycles," explained Gaine to the children in the Nemed. "The growing and waning Moon and Sun are repeated in women's bodies. A woman with child waxes full, her body large and streaming with milk. Later she wanes once again. The Land follows the same pattern; pouring forth life during one half of the year and shrinking back in the other.

Man's job is to foster and support life in women and the land. This is the divine pattern in the heavens and on earth."

"Why don't the Cristaidi honor these cycles?" asked Daire, who was older than his years.

"Wisdom waxes and wanes just like the seasons and the planets and the Land," said Gaine. "We are entering a time when the eyes of the people are veiled to What Is. They are fixing their minds on one God, denying nature's balance. This new philosophy will wax and grow full and in its course will wane again, as do all things. Our job as Druid, as wise ones, is to keep knowledge alive so that it may be rekindled when the cycle comes full course.

The Cristaidi are like children; playing with new ideas, not knowing where their philosophy will lead. Our ways are old, tested by time. We must be patient, allow them to err and comfort them when they fall." Gaine had the look of prophecy such as the Fili had when making their utterances. "Woman and man, earth and sky, queen and king, water and fire, dark and light, death and life. All things are held in balance to maintain the pattern. Honor is due to each. Reverence and care. Respect for the Truth of what is."

The children and Druid were spellbound. Gaine's words transformed the Druid from unquestioned rulers and decision makers of society to the caretakers of ancient wisdom. Like all prophecies her words directed them forward with no clear indication where they might lead.

# 44

Cadla's demands became insistent. He paced the dun with his admiring followers. When he spoke in the assembly they backed him. On the morning the results of the tax gathering were announced, everyone listened anxiously. When the final tallies were recited, Cadla boomed over the hall. "This is ridiculous! The provinces yield only half what they are supposed to. In Medon can't be maintained this way!"

"Cadla, what would you have me do?" asked Ethne. "Should I force the people to comply by threats of violence? You forget that the tribes are recovering from war, sickness and famine."

"Maintaining an army takes precedence. The Men of the North or Roman forces could attack us at any time. Where would the people be then? It's better they tighten their belts and give In Medon its due."

"I will not send troops against my own people, Cadla!"

"You are weaker than I *thought*!" Cadla stormed out of the assembly, followed by his men.

Ethne soberly addressed those remaining. "The rules of sacred sovereignty state that the best ruler is the one to whom the people willingly give their due. I trust that my people gave what they could in a very difficult year. I will hear no more talk of violence and coercion."

When the hall cleared Ethne conferred privately with Gaine. "Whatever position I take on an issue Cadla takes the opposite. We are locked in a contest of wills and can no longer find agreement in politics, religion or even the order of warriors at table.

Those that Cadla honors are ones with the greatest physical skill. I honor the most intelligent, the cleverest strategists."

"Cadla seeks to usurp the throne," Gaine replied simply. "He gathers more and more of the warriors around him. It is now the fashion for the fighting men to wear the Latin cross, though many are careful to wear the Druid Sun symbol too. Some have combined them into one, with the circle of the Sun superimposed on the cross of the Latins. It is an affront to your leadership as a Druid queen."

"But the common folk continue their rituals: well blessings, bonfires and offerings to fire and water," mused Ethne. "They are unaware of the tension within the flaith; Druid versus Cristaide, our ways versus the new. It is unbearable, Gaine. I grit my teeth at night until my jaws hurt. I have headaches when I think of Cadla."

"This is leadership, Ethne. You will not change the nature of those around you. Try to re-arrange your internal perception of what is occurring. Treat this as a passing show and look to the larger play of time."

"If this is to be my lot for the rest of this life, I fear I shall go mad."

"Take it to the Gods, Ethne. Sit under the Sacred Ash or by the Fire Altar. Listen to the voices in the embers and the rustling of the leaves. The Gods will send you a message if there is something you need to hear." Gaine rose and Ethne walked out of the hall to find comfort within the bare branches, dried leaves and dry stalks of the Nemed garden.

With hooded eyes and softened vision, Ethne gazed into the embers of the Fire Altar. At first familiar signs appeared: animals totems of the clans with whom she was bound by mutual obligation gaped and sang among the burning oak logs. Some were larger and more prominent, others receded. Had she been in need of political advice on how to manage the families she might have taken careful notice. Then the air pulsed faintly as the fire swayed and shimmered with currents of power, the atmosphere thrumming like a myriad of insect wings. Ethne felt her body transform into a feathery weightlessness.

As she fixed her gaze on the center of the flames, a blue tongue shot up and a figure appeared, a woman of fire, her face yellow, her long hair orange tendrils of flame. The base of her gown blazed blue and green gradually blending to gold towards her bodice and shoulders. Her outstretched arms, neck and torso were entwined with living coils of red jewels, which moved with separate will and life. They were serpents of fire, some slithering dessel, others tuathamail. They twined in opposite spirals up each arm to her face and then reversed direction, twining back down to her hands. Sparks flew from her eyes, and the center of each palm held a steady flame. A column of flame rose from the top of her head.

With a voice as deep as the sea, the vision spoke, "My daughter, sadness sits on you. Your thoughts travel steadily down a well-worn stream. It need not be so. The Fires of Life fill you with infinite possibilities. Listen to the words of the fire: "Move on. Move on!"" The Lady of Flame smiled and stretched forth her arms, blessing Ethne with her fingers. As she touched the queen, she began to fade, the blue dress gradually disappearing, followed by the golden bodice and snake entwined arms, until all that were left were her laughing eyes and ecstatic smile. These too dissolved in a puff of sparks.

It took a few heartbeats for Ethne to regain her senses. Feeling faint, she backed away from the edge of the Fire Altar to find a cool spot on a bench, needing to lie down and close her eyes. When she reopened them, Gaine was there, as were Clothru and Damán. They hovered anxiously, wondering.

"Ethne, are you ill?" asked Gaine.

"No, overwhelmed. I have met a Goddess."

"Which one? What did She look like?" asked Clothru, who longed passionately for such an encounter.

"I believe it was the blessed Brighid herself."

"Did She bring a message?" asked Gaine.

"She reminded me that life holds infinite possibilities for change and that I have been stuck in my thinking. She urged me to find new channels for my thoughts."

"That's all?" asked Clothru, confused.

"The Gods don't give explicit orders or tell us what to do," said Gaine. "They inspire us to be greater than we imagine. They ask us to imitate their confidence and strength, not be their servants."

"I know what I must do now," said Ethne. "But I will discuss it with Ruadh first."

"We await your decision," said Gaine, cautioning Clothru and Damán against more questions. "An encounter with Deity is powerful and will have repercussions. The queen must come to understand it in her own time."

The Druid moved off, leaving Ethne to recover her sense of the present. Gaine watched from a distance, making sure that Ethne was fully back in this world.

# 45

———

Ruadh was near the warrior's quarters, practicing feints and parries with the warriors of the flaith. Ethne approached quietly from the Nemed, not wanting to distract him lest he be injured by a sharp blade. Ruadh's opponent saw her first and immediately dropped his sword and bowed. When Ruadh moved to greet her, the ever-present guards fell in behind.

"Please leave us for a moment" said Ethne sternly. Her preoccupation with the vision made her sharp. The men retreated reluctantly, unsure whether to honor Ethne's command or Cadla's. Cadla had ordered them to stay with Ruadh no matter what.

"What a relief!" exclaimed Ruadh. "You are the only person in the rath they will listen to since Cadla created his special guard. It is unbearable. I can't even relieve myself in peace!"

"Sweetheart, walk with me to the royal hall. I want to discuss something in private."

They made their way to their chamber behind the throne. Ethne called for fion and a simple supper while Ruadh lit the fire.

"I had a vision," Ethne began. "The blessed Brighid appeared to me at the Fire Altar in the Nemed."

"What did She say?"

"Very little, actually. She told me to follow my heart and reminded me that life is ever changeable."

Ruadh made no comment and poked at the logs with iron tongs. He knew Ethne was leading up to something important.

"I no longer wish to be Rígain."

A small grunt of air came out of Ruadh and he sat back. "Are you giving in to Cadla and his followers?"

"Not giving in, no. I hear an insistent song in my blood, a wild song. I am of the forest, the waters, trees and wild places. I miss offering fresh-picked herbs to the Spirits. I miss listening to the voices in the streams. I miss the way the birds alert me to danger and sing what is happening in the world."

"I miss those things too, but our duty is here."

"I thought so too. But I see now that Cadla and those like him will win out in the end. He wants power, and with Roman backing it is only a matter of time before he gets it. The Cristaidi will stop at nothing to get what they want, and I no longer have the will to oppose them."

"But the laws, the throne!"

"I will give up what Coemgen and Gaine forced me to accept. I give away none of my power. After the vision of Brighid, I fell asleep and I was given a dream. I saw the Druid hiding away, maybe for centuries. But the cycle will come round and we will emerge to restore the balance of the world. We must go while we still have our teachings and our ways. If we can hide, we will survive, like wild animals do. If we stay in the open, we will hunted in a ruthless world."

"Will you again be Ban-Drui?"

"Yes, it is the noblest title I aspire to. In my dream I saw us all – you, me, Gaine, Damán, Clothru, Daire and the others – living as Forest Druid. I saw us teaching and dwelling in simplicity. I saw our young ones dispersing to the four directions, carrying our teachings and lineage into secret places in the hills of the Island and beyond, preserving the our ways for a future time. This battle may be lost but the war is far from over. We will preserve the truth by hiding it away. Brighid herself sent me this vision and I will honor it."

"My heart is lighter just hearing you speak. Life at court is suffocating. Cadla's men follow me everywhere waiting for the chance to do me harm. Going back to the forest is what I want also."

Ethne put a hand on his face. "I will tell Gaine and the Druid tomorrow, and then I will call for an election. I've no doubt who will win. Cadla and Albinus have been campaigning against me for months."

"Ethne, a weight has lifted. I feel the rightness of this."

"I will send a messenger to Labraid, the healer who now maintains the Forest House. He can choose if he wants to stay or return to court, or to his clann."

The mogae brought their supper. Ethne and Ruadh ate, talking over plans and sharing thoughts of how a Forest Druid community could be organized. As they sat before the fire, Ethne thought of the cave where they had first made love. Ruadh knew all her scars now and some were deeper than she could ever have thought possible. "Ethne, you cannot! You will undo all our plans!" Gaine's face was white with shock and anger.

"Gaine, I have always given you my deference and respect, but now I bow to a higher authority – Brighid and my own heart!"

"You are a willful woman! How *dare* you oppose the Ban-Ard-Drui? The world is going insane! This is too far!"

"Ruadh and I will address the assembly today. We ask you to join us in our new direction, but if you can't, I'm sure they will allow some Druid at court. Cadla and Albinus know your value. You can live comfortably in the Nemed, surrounded by mogae and those Druid who choose to remain."

Gaine had a vision of her future life: she felt the mantle of authority and respect, hers by right of title, growing thinner. With a Cristaide king she would be a symbolic figure, tolerated, but no longer a decision-making voice. Her chin came up and she said, "*I* will honor my vows. I will hear the complaints of local women and farmers. I will hold my position at court. I will not be forced away!"

Gaine stormed out of Ethne's chamber and took her place beside the throne. She was filled with fury, betraying none of it in her expression but for a blanched face. The gathered petitioners saw only the familiar proud figure of the Ban-Ard-Drui waiting for the sovereign to enter. Ruadh waited patiently before his oaken throne. The people stood in silence anticipating Ethne's arrival.

Ethne dressed carefully, first bathing in purifying herbs: lavender, vervain and powdered young oak leaves because this morning was an initiation, a new beginning. She wore her simplest white gown and a triskellion instead of her golden torque. On her head she placed a garland of dried oak leaves, in place of of her crown. A golden sickle hung at her waist, symbolic of her rank as Ban-Drui and a reminder of her role as healer and Liaig.

The audience drew in their breath when she appeared. Gaine fumed, but betrayed nothing. Ruadh grinned at her audacity.

Gaine addressed the council. "According to the ancient traditions and by the precedents set by our ancestors, I declare this assembly open." She banged her oaken staff three times on the platform of the dais and then took a seat behind the thrones.

Ethne spoke, "My people, I come today to address you and ask that you take this message far and wide, to all the tuaths. I call for an election this Spring, at the feast of Imbolc, before the roads turn too muddy for passage."

Cadla's men pricked up their ears. One of them excitedly pushed his way through the crowd and out the door, to take the news to his master.

"I feel strong currents of change moving across this land," continued Ethne. "It is change that goes against everything I believe. The ancient ways tell us to honor the Spirits of the land. We are taught to make offerings to trees, fire and rivers, to give thanks for the herbs we use for our sicknesses, and to the green growing things and animals we use for food. Now there are those among us who teach that it is wrong to honor these things. They say we lack faith by thanking the land for remedies and sustenance.

The ancient ways honor both the feminine and masculine, Goddesses and Gods, women and men. Another way has come to the Island that gives men authority over women and says the female must be controlled, even beaten into submission. This way goes against the ways of nature and will lead to great sadness.

Our Island has always welcomed strangers; merchants, traders and philosophers. Throughout the ages these travelers have brought new ideas and religions to our shores, and we were glad to learn from them, honoring them as they honored our traditions and us. Never before has a religion condemned all others as evil, as depraved. This religion is overtaking our ways, tuath by tuath, family by family. I see this change and I want no part of it.

I respectfully ask you to elect a new ruler, one who will flourish within this upheaval. I will retreat to the forest from which I came almost two years ago. There I will abide simply and live my life the best way I know, as I was taught by the Druid elders. Any who wish to dedicate themselves anew to the our ways are free to join me. Ruadh and I will go to with those Druid who support us."

Some of those listening wept openly. The Druid and villagers heard the power and truth of her words. Many felt the emptiness of loss, knowing that something sacred was passing from their lives.

Ethne remained on her throne, hearing petitions into the morning. When the last villager left, she retreated to the Nemed to meditate and make offerings to the Sacred Ash, the Fire Altar and the Cauldron of Sea.

Cadla rode out of the dun with his retinue to secure the votes of the petty kings and the warriors whose fealty they owned. Albinus came and went from the rath daily.

Like a wolf smelling blood and sensing weakness in its prey, he began an all out offensive against the native religion and its traditions. One night, after a Cristaidi prayer session outside the gates of the rath, Albinus asked the Christus to purify the dun from demons. Afterwards, village men took an axe to the ancient Bíle, the oak that had stood for a thousand years before the gates. Able to only make a gash, they lit a fire that threatened to finish the damage, but guards emerged to quench the flames. Then the Druid came, placing herbs of healing and consecration around the base to assuage the offended Spirits.

"Fools! By attacking the tree they only attack themselves!" wailed Clothru. "The Bíle holds the ancestors' Spirits, Spirits that would help us!" Tears streamed down her face as she surveyed the damage.

"You and Damán, go to the forest and collect pine pitch," instructed Ethne.

"Smear it on the wounds of the Bíle to prevent infection and heal the burns."

Damán and Clothru did as instructed, followed by guards to protect them. Nearly every day now some insult was directed against the Druid or the holy places of the ancient faith.

"Ethne, you are partly responsible for this," Gaine declared. "If you had not abdicated, the Cristaidi would not be so bold."

"Gaine, you have heard the reports as well as I. These desecrations are happening in Albu, Caledonia, Armorica and Gaul. History has turned against us. But the cycle will turn again. Life is change, as the Goddess reminded me."

Gaine could say nothing. She walked to the Bíle, put her arms around her old, dear friend, and let her sorrow cover them both.

# 46

Ethne and Ruadh spent mornings in the assembly, hearing petitions and approving the judgments of the Brehons. Afternoons they devoted to gathering equipment and supplies they would need for life in the forest. Ethne went through every basket and drawer in the royal storehouse seeking roots, resins, herbs and seeds she would not find near her old hut. She selected crockery, linens, blankets and plaids; for no longer would the royal dun keep her supplied. She collected kegs of The Waters of Life, essential for healing, and an assortment of cauldrons, needles, and spools of fine thread.

Ruadh commissioned swords and dirks, saws, hammers, and metal arrowheads from the blacksmiths of the rath. He asked the royal wood wrights to fashion ax handles, barrels and other wooden implements. Master carpenters built a huge wooden cart to carry their belongings, and Ruadh carved numerous arrows and bows out of ash wood and yew.

Imbolc came all too quickly. The rath mobilized to feed and house the flaith of the kingdoms, and the local boaire hosted those of their rank in their houses and barns. The smoke of roasting cows filled the air and hung like a fine veil over the dun. Cadla and the warriors anticipated their victory every night: drinking, singing and dancing into a stupor. Cadla gave generous gifts of mead to garner still more votes.

The mood in the Nemed contrasted sharply. Each Drui faced the decision to follow the queen to a sacred community of the old ways or to remain in the difficult atmosphere of the rath where they would serve the aging Ban-Ard-Drui and help the remaining faithful. The choice was painful, not easily made.

Visitors from the local tuaths, mostly old women, paid their respects to Gaine or visited Coemgen's grave. They brought small gifts of flowers, a woolen blanket or choice foods for the Druid. Some, sensing the profound change that was coming over the kingdom, went to the heart of the Nemed to pray and place a pat of butter in the Sacred Fire, or anoint themselves with water from the Cauldron of Sea. Tears came to Gaine's eyes as she watched them. She sensed this was the last generation that would be free to openly show its devotion, the new ways were descending like a dark tide.

The children of the Nemed, like all children, eagerly anticipated the adventures a new life would bring. Daire, Crimthann's son, was the children's leader. He had his father's good looks, easy charm, physical agility and intelligence. Ethne looked to him with pride and imagined days when she would walk the fields or along the stream with this quick inquisitive boy.

On the low hill beyond the rath Father Per doused his fire and swept the floor of his hut. He placed his folded cloak, his worn prayer book and a rough wooden cross into a cloth bag. Facing the dun, he raised his right hand and said, "May the good folk of this land find peace; May the Lord keep them from evil." He touched the stones where the children had told their stories and began his journey to the islands in the Western Sea.

The morning of the election, Gaine stood to open the assembly. Before she could shake the golden chain to call for silence, Germanus approached the dais.

"I mean no disrespect," he began. "But as many of these folk are now Cristaidi, I will share the authority of this assembly."

Gaine stared mutely. All the history of her people, all the years of her training, drowned in the quiet sureness of this man's presence. She looked into his eyes and saw the future. She shook the bells and opened her hand to let him begin.

He, in turn, lifted his hands in the orans position, invoking the blessings of the God Isu. His prayer came before Gaine's, his God took precedence. Many of the people dropped to their knees as he spoke. The Druid stood in their dignity and silence.

"This is the way it will be," Ethne whispered to Ruadh, as they waited for Germanus to finish.

"We will be the hidden ones, the secret ones," Ruadh replied. "That will be our survival."

When the Abbot had finished his prayer, Gaine intoned a short blessing of her own, calling on the spirits of Land, Sea and Sky and the Gods to bless the proceedings.

She called to the Blessed Brighid because She had insti-gated Ethne's abdication, and because Gaine knew a feminine deity would irk Germanus. It gave her a small tingle of pleasure.

Petty kings and warriors began their speeches to vie for the throne. The kings of the four outer kingdoms; Rochad, Conaire, Marcan and Glaisne, were the candidates running against Cadla and each had his supporters. Rochad, Conaire and Marcan were evenly matched; Glaisne was a virtual stranger in Oirthir and had little backing. Cadla, however, had won the hearts and minds of the troops in In Medon and, like Crimthann before him, stood the best chance with the majority of the people.

"Age and wisdom count for little with most of the folk. Give them a trim body, thick hair and a strong sword arm and they will follow," said Gaine.

"At least the past warrior-kings had Brehons and Druid to make sure they didn't become greedy. Without the Druid wis-dom, I fear for the future of the kingdoms," said Ethne ruefully.

Gaine's face took on the look of prophecy. "My Imbas tells me that the kingdoms will enter a dark time. The warrior-kings will rule with weapons, without the guiding hand of the Druid. The people will suffer for many generations."

"I see it, too," said Ethne, her eyes clouded.

The Feast of Imbolc dawned crisp with a sky of eggshell blue. Those who lived inside and around the rath assembled in the courtyard of the dun, wrapped against the chill, their faces holding a pinched expectancy that had nothing to do with the cold. They shuffled and jostled each other as they crowded to gain warmth. Voices called to one another as those from outlying areas greeted clann members they had not seen since the harvest.

The crowd quieted as the Druid led a group of maidens dressed in white, in a procession around the gathered throng and then brought them into the middle. The people applauded the girls. These were their daughters, sisters, nieces, and friends. Each girl carried a candle and a small bunch of flowers, which she presented to the Rígain who stood on the steps of the great hall.

"These girls are the Fires of Life. They are the future of our people," Ethne called to the crowd. "Show them all honor on this day sacred to the blessed Brighid."

She smiled on the young faces turned up to her and thought how beautiful and strong they looked. Her inner sight told her that their lives would not be easy and she grieved for them. They were about to begin a way of life that held them in little regard. She watched as the girls proceeded to the royal hall for the ceremonial meal of milk, cheeses and honey cakes. No warriors attended this ritual, only the mogae, a few Druid and some of the old women of the tuaths had come to serve them. Ethne followed them in and sat on her throne. She listened to the girls' laughter and watched their shining eyes and busy hands as they ate.

"I pray to Brighid, this day," she said, "to keep the Spirits of the Land strong within these girls." She looked directly at each one. "May you hear the songs of the restless seas, may you know the stories in the wind curling about the hills, may you feed the people always as the crops give their bounty, may you see in your children's eyes in the stars of the night. May you hold within you ever the Sith of this land, yours because you are Island-born."

The girls looked on her with wonder. No one had told them the queen would give them a special blessing. They saw in each other something more than they had seen when they entered the hall. When the meal was finished, the Druid led the girls out, back to the gathered clanns.

Ethne emerged from the hall and again stood on the steps overlooking the crowd.

"You have come to choose your leader," she said. "I ask those who wish to lead to stand at the corners of the yard. Now, will those who back each candidate please stand with your chosen candidate."

If the election had been hotly contested there might have been a single combat to determine the winner. As it was, the people sorted themselves quickly into tight groups around the inner yard. No one was surprised to see that Cadla had the support of most, including most of the warriors. Some started to cheer, but it faltered and died, as Ethne and the Druid looked on but did not join in. Many of the people stood uncertainly, looking to the Druid to lead them in the proper response. But the Druid stood silent. They too were in a new reality where the next steps were unknown. Cadla received a few congratulatory thumps on the back, and then strode towards the great hall and up the steps. He stood beside Ethne, who stepped back, granting him the right of place.

"People of In Medon and beyond" he called, "You are witness to a new beginning! You have chosen me as your leader, and I will bring you prosperity and protection." All faces turned to him, listening. "We are no longer just the people of this small land. We join with those from Gaul, Albu and Rome to become people of a larger world. A world of power and riches!" A cheer went up and some of the warriors banged their shields. "I call for a celebration! For three days and three nights there will be mead and fion and vats of the Waters of Life for all. We will have singing, dancing and bonfires upon the hills!" The crowd roared their approval and the warriors gave their battle cries. Cadla raised his fists in the air, beaming his triumph.

Ethne retreated into the great hall. She looked at the table where the maidens had honored Brighid. Half-eaten honey cakes and a spilled bowl of milk lay in the silence. She passed them by and went to her chamber to finish gathering her belongings. She began folding a blanket, and then lowered it slowly. Before her she saw her days and nights in this room and felt the weight of all she had gained by coming to the Nemed, so many years before in her girlhood. More, she felt the weight of all she had lost. She took a breath and began again to fold the cloth. Ruadh came in behind her. "We are free, Ethne," he said, helping her to stack their belongings so they could be bundled and crated.

She turned to him, biting her lip to hold back a cry. "I am going to find Gaine," she said finally, her voice under control.

Ethne walked out the main gate of the rath, and up the grassy knoll to the hill of stones. A keen wind bit her face and hands as she walked sunwise, visiting each stone and murmuring a prayer, saying goodbye to old friends. Her face was calm when she turned toward the center and saw Gaine standing there, her familiar graying hair with sprigs of evergreen tucked into the braids.

The older woman put out her hands, and with a sob, Ethne ran to her. They held each other and let their tears mingle as Gaine pressed her cheek to Ethne's. "You are the child of these stones, dearest Ethne. You are *my* child," Gaine whispered. "Go with my love and blessings. Hold our ways in safekeeping. You are the trust we have in another day." Gaine kissed Ethne on the forehead and smiled at her.

"Don't be sad, child. My days are not so long now, and we will meet on the Western Shore. Then you will tell me how the Forest House remembers the voices of the Land and how the Spirits speak to those who dwell there."

She took Ethne by the hand and led her down the hill toward the cart where Ruadh, several Druid and a few families and individuals of the rath waited. Before they reached the gathering Gaine paused. "I would have you carry the Cauldron of Sea into safe keeping." When Ethne began to protest, Gaine shook her head and continued, "It is fitting that you should take it. It is the heart of the Nemed, as are you. Let the waters within it nourish the spirit of our ways in all who follow you."

Ethne's throat burned and her eyes drowned in the love she felt for this woman who had shown her a mother's care. Gaine saw her struggle and smiled, "Shhh, now, it's none so sad." Ethne threw her arms around Gaine in one more embrace then quickly turned to Ruadh and the cart.

Members of the tuath were there to pay their respects, shedding tears and offering gifts for the journey. Bards sang of leave-taking as Ruadh gave the command to turn their faces toward the road. As they walked, villagers tossed branches of green before them.

Ethne stooped, picked up a holly sprig and tucked it into her braid.

When they cleared the gates of the dun, all looked back and gave a final wave to the villagers and the Druid on the ramparts. Ethne caught sight of Gaine's many-colored cloak billowing around her. She raised her hand to wave, but cried out. All looked where she pointed. On the field before the palisade, the Bíle lay prostrate, its ancient trunk severed, its branches hacked and splintered.

Ethne set her mind towards the forest. The caravan of Druid, two horses, a cart and twenty people on foot wound slowly into the hills beyond the royal enclosure. The day kept clear with the promise of a frosty night, and the dirt road held firm. They passed sheep pastures and barley fields ready for plowing. They passed the low stone chapel and ovens of Father Per and walked on. Soon they reached the forest that stretched unbroken from Oirthir to Murthracht. Delving ever deeper into its fastness, they felt safer and lighter of spirit. By night-fall they were camped near a small waterfall that sprayed onto frost-blanched yellow ferns and mosses.

After dinner, Ethne gathered the children around the fire for their evening lesson. A woodlark sang from a nearby bush as the smell of roasted fish and fresh bannocks lingered in the still, cold air. Laughter drifted from downstream where Clothru and Damán scrubbed pans with sand and shave-grass. Ruadh and others strung nets to snare trout for the morning meal.

"This way is our way from now on," said Ethne. "You are the future of our tradition and you will be taught everything I and the other Druid know. You in your turn will pass on the teachings to your own students. We will keep our ways hidden and safe until a new cycle begins."

"How long will it take for us to learn it all?" asked Aífe of the golden curls.

"You will not see the end of your learning for many life-times," said Ethne. "So now, let us begin . . ."

# Epilogue

W hile specific events and characters of this story are fictional, the following are of relevance, and historically accurate.

The Fians of Ireland were abolished according to legend, when they were defeated at the battle of Gabra in 280 CE, but the institution of a band of free men with no inheritance who supported themselves by raiding and a generally nomadic existence lasted into the 9th century. Clerical condemnations of their activities continued until that time with heated propaganda campaigns being directed against them calling them the "Devil's men," and other such names.

In "The Colloquy of the Old Men," Caoilte, a Fennid, answers Saint Patrick's question: "Who or what was it that maintained you so in your life?" And Caoilte's answer was, "Truth that was in our hearts, and strength in our arms, and fulfillment in our tongues."

Friesian pirates were plying the coasts of Europe as early as the second century, long before the more famous Viking raiders began their looting.

The "Cain Adamanan," of the 697 Synod of Tara, made it illegal to "force" women into physical combat. The fact that such laws were enacted periodically indicates that there must have been problems with compliance.

According to Latin sources, the ancient Druid were priests, prophets, astrologers, and teachers of the sons of nobles. Oaths were sworn in their presence and they belonged to the very highest strata of society. By the 7th century the advance of Christianity reduced their status to sorcerer or witch doctor. They, along with satirists and brigands, were entitled to sick-maintenance only to the level of a cow farmer (boaire).

Saint Kevin, 6th century abbot and founder of the Glendaloch monastery in Wicklow, Ireland, was famous for his virtue. He threw a woman over a cliff (and to her death) because he was sexually attracted to her, and sought to remain pure.

The Coptic Church had a strong influence in Ireland, where monks sought to imitate the Egyptian habit of retreating into the wilderness to find isolation and closeness to God. In Ireland this isolation was achieved on islands and in religious communities at the fringes of the sea. The famous Madonna and Child plate from the Book of Kells is painted in a Coptic Egyptian style.

One method of mass conversion in Britain, and on the continent, was for a missionary to offer gold to a local ruler in exchange for that ruler's people being considered instantly converted. Churchmen were then satisfied to term the area "Christian," even if the ruler and his circle might represent only a tiny element in the midst of a still-Pagan majority.

The conversion of the Pagan peoples generally involved centuries of further missionary activity, destruction or adaptation of local shrines, enhanced career options and education via the church, exemption from taxes and military service for clergy, and sometimes military force against those who resisted. The religious tolerance of Pagans only hastened Paganism's decline.

Druidism is a rapidly growing religion in the world today, with many thousands of adherents.

# Further Reading

## Historical Resources

Nora Chadwick, THE CELTS Penguin, Middlesex, 1985

Barry Cunliffe, THE CELTIC WORLD An Illustrated History of the Celtic Race, Their Culture, Customs and Legends, Greenwich House, NY, 1986

Miranda Green, THE WORLD OF THE DRUIDS Thames and Hudson, New York, NY, 1997

Fergus Kelly, A GUIDE TO EARLY IRISH LAW A Guide to Early Irish Law Dublin Institute for Advanced Studies, Dublin, 1991

Fergus Kelly, EARLY IRISH FARMING Dublin Institute for Advanced Studies, Dublin, 1997

Bruce Lincoln, DEATH, WAR AND SACRIFICE University of Chicago Press, Chicago, IL, 1991

Alwyn and Brinley Rees, CELTIC HERITAGE Ancient Tradition in Ireland And Wales Thames and Hudson, NY, 1994

Anne Ross, PAGAN CELTIC BRITAIN STUDIES IN ICONOGRAPHY AND TRADITION Routledge & Kegan Paul, London, 1967 (reprinted 1994)

Marie-Louise Sjoestedt, GODS AND HEROES OF THE ANCIENT CELTS, Dover Publications, NY, 2000

Peter, Wells, BEYOND CELTS, GERMANS, AND SCYTHIANS: Archaeology and Identity in Iron Age Europe, Gerald Duckworth & Co., Ltd, London, 2002

## AIDS TO CREATING DRUID RITUALS

Janet and Colin Bord, EARTH RITES: Fertility Practices in Pre-Industrial Britain, Granada Publishing Limited, London, 1983

Janet and Colin Bord, SACRED WATERS, Paladin Grafton Books, London 1986

Alexander Carmichael, CARMINA GADELICA Hymns and Incantations, Floris Books, Edinburgh, 1992

Cross and Slover, ANCIENT IRISH TALES Barnes and Noble, Totowa, NJ, 1988 (reprint of the 1936 edition)

Ellen Evert Hopman, A DRUID'S HERBAL FOR THE SACRED EARTH YEAR Destiny Books, Rochester, VT, 1995

Ellen Evert Hopman, TREE MEDICINE – TREE MAGIC, Pendraig Publishing Inc, Green Valley Lake, CA, 2017

Alexei Kondratiev, CELTIC RITUALS: AN AUTHENTIC GUIDE TO ANCIENT CELTIC SPIRITUALITY New Celtic Publishing, Scotland, 1999

## FOR INFORMATION ABOUT MODERN DRUIDS

Tribe of the Oak www.tribeoftheoak.com

# About the Author

Ellen Evert Hopman has been a teacher of herbalism since 1983 and is a professional member of the American Herbalists Guild. She is the author of a number of books on Celtic history, Herbalism and lore. A Druidic initiate since 1984, she is the Arch Druid of Tribe of the Oak www.tribeoftheoak.com, a founding member and former Co-Chief of The Order of the White Oak (Ord Na Darach Gile), a Bard of the Gorsedd of Caer Abiri, an ArchDruidess of the Druid Clan of Dana, and was Vice President of the Henge of Keltria for nine years. She is a member of the Grey Council of Mages and Sages and taught at the Grey School of Wizardry for several years. Hopman lives in New England. Find her books and blog at www.elleneverthopman.com.

# Interview with Ellen Evert Hopman, author of *Priestess of the Forest*

---

*Q: In Priestess of the Forest, you write about what ancient Druids might have done in their rites and rituals. Where does this information come from? Is it historically accurate, or a romantic vision of what might have been?*

We don't know exactly what the ancient Druids did in their rituals because they did not believe in writing things down that they considered truly sacred. They did this to keep their teachings pure and to make sure the teachings were handed down intact from teacher to student. We know that the ancient Druids trained for about twenty years and that it was a path for intellectuals and poets, usually passed down within Druidic families. We also know that Druids were herbalists, lawyers, ambassadors, judges, historians and philosophers, teachers of the children of the nobility, astronomers, sacred story tellers and genealogists. Their various grades included seers, ritualists and magicians and they were both male and female.

Every king or queen had to have a Druid at their side. The Druids knew the laws and precedents without which no king could pass judgment. This pairing was described by the ancients as the "two kidneys" of a tribe.

In the novel I have developed rituals based on actual Celtic cosmology. For example, the rites done by the Druids in the *Nemed* are based on the concept of the "Three Worlds" of Land,

Sea and Sky. The Cauldron of Sea represents the Underworld and the realm of the ancestors, the Fairies, and the wisdom that can be brought from that realm via trance and meditation. The ancient Celts understood that water was the gateway to the ancestors and to the Fairy realm which is why they made offerings to sacred wells, pools, lakes, and rivers. The Fire Altar represents the Sky World because fire and smoke travel upwards, bearing messages to the Gods via prayers and offerings that are put into the flames. The Sacred Ash is the mediating principle between the worlds. Trees have the ability to reach down to the Underworld via their roots and up to the Sky World of the Gods and Goddesses via their branches. They span all three worlds, including the middle world of the humans, animals and nature spirits.

We know, of course that the Druids considered trees to be sacred beings and that they designated certain trees such as Yew, Rowan, Hawthorn, Willow, Ash and Oak to be especially magical. Yew trees were associated with death, rebirth and immortality and Yew wood was used to make bows for warriors, and bowls for the feast. Yew was poisonous but it could also heal when it was used by a trained herbalist. Rowan was a tree that repelled all evil. Branches of Rowan could be put in the house, the barn, the cradle, and so forth, to protect the family. Rowan berries are full of Vitamin C and powerful healing agents in their own right. Hawthorn was sacred to the Fairies. It was said that a solitary Hawthorn on a hill marked an entrance to the Land of Fairy. Hawthorns were often associated with healing wells, and Hawthorn berries, leaves and flowers were a valuable medicine for the heart. Ash was a noble wood that gave the most constant heat when burned and also made stout thrones, tools and weapons. Oak was very sacred; it could draw lightning and survive the blast and it would sometimes host the magical healing herb Mistletoe. It was associated with all the highest Gods of thunder and lightning. Oak leaves and bark were valuable to heal wounds and the acorns were an important food for pigs, deer, and people. Willow was used to make Bardic harps; it was a tree sacred to the poets.

Trees have been used by shamans and magical practitioners in many cultures as vehicles for travel between the worlds; down through their roots, and up through their branches.

In my opinion unless you have a tree, a fire, and a sacred well or body of water in which to make offerings, you can't really do a Druidic ritual. Those are the most basic elements of Celtic ritual form. I used my own *Iomas* or inner inspiration to create the rites you see in this book. I also felt the voices of the Gods at my back as I wrote.

I have been a Druid Priestess for over thirty years. This book was conceived as a teaching tool for potential Druid dedicants and is written in such a way that there is a ritual for just about every life passage and seasonal festival somewhere within it. It is my hope that aspiring Druids will use these rites as templates to create their own Druidic ceremonies.

### Q: Are there still Druids today? Who are they and where do they gather? Are there different types of Druidism?

Yes, there are still Druids today and there are different kinds of Druids. But this doesn't mean that there is an unbroken Druidic tradition handed down from antiquity. In modern times different groups and individuals have worked to re-create the Druid religion, according to their own interpretation of it.

One such group is the English Romantic Revival Druids who look to traditions from the last few centuries and meld them into their own idea of Druidism. Many of the early English Romantic Revival Druids of the eighteenth century were Masons and thus their rituals derive from Masonic tradition. Some famous Druids of that type were the poet William Blake and Prime Minister Winston Churchill. Many of these English Romantic Revival Druids were and are Christians though these days more and more of them are Pagans. Originally, they were all men but many of these groups now accept women.

In Wales there are Druids who are mostly Christians and who primarily engage in poetry and language competitions, seeking to keep their native language alive. I am proud to say that they are succeeding! The current Archbishop of Canterbury, Dr. Rowan Williams, is a Druid of this type. He is the first Druid to be head of the Church of England.

Ireland is home to the Forest Druid tradition where Pagan Druids are seeking to keep the ancient woods wisdom alive. They are working to re-create the foods, medicines, and ancient rites that were once performed by pre-Christian forest dwellers. The Forest Druids of Ireland are a main source of inspiration for this book.

My own tradition is called Celtic Reconstructionist Druidism or "CR" for short. The Order I belong to and of which I am presently Arch Druid is called Tribe of the Oak (*Tuatha na Dara*). We base our teachings on ancient Irish manuscripts from the seventh century. These documents were in the oral tradition before then and were first written down when Christian monks sought to preserve the stories and poems in writing (for which we are grateful). We also study the archaeological and historical records to try and understand who the ancient Celts and Druids really were. Our initiates are both men and women and our training program takes several years to complete. As far as I am aware, we are all Pagans.

*Q: What do modern day Druids believe in, and how do they practice their faith? What does Druidism offer to modern men and women?*

All Druids honor the Earth and Her creatures. We recognize that there are sacred plants, sacred trees, sacred animals, and sacred landscape features all around us. For us the Earth is alive. We see rivers as beings in their own right and know that stones have an indwelling soul. The fire speaks to us and the clouds sing to us. We respect the nobility of the great trees and of the animals of the forest. We find the sacred in everything we touch and see.

We value courage and integrity and look to the ancient *Brehon* laws (the old tribal laws) for guidance. The ancient laws show us that Celtic society was a place of rules, respect, and mutual obligations. We admire people of truth who are stable and giving, hospitable and kind.

Our path helps us to reconnect with our ancestral traditions. We celebrate the ancient European agricultural festivals and honor the cycles of nature. Our religion is in many ways the spiritual arm of the ecological movement. You can get an idea of the types of rituals we do by studying and hopefully performing some of the rituals encoded in this book.

Here is an overview of basic Druidic beliefs and practices that I wrote for the US Military Chaplain's Handbook (which was being rewritten at the time).

1.  Holidays: all Druids celebrate the major Fire Festivals which are:

    *Samhain* (may be celebrated October/31/November 1 to November 11/12);

    *Imbolc* (may be celebrated February 1/2 to February 15 approximately, depending on the time of the annual thaw and when the local sheep are lactating);
    *Beltaine* (may be celebrated the last week of April to the first week of May); and

*Lughnasad* (may be celebrated any time from the last week of July to the second week of August depending on when the harvest is ready).

Some Druids celebrate the Solstices and Equinoxes as well.

2. Tools: common tools include a staff, a sickle (a curved reaping hook), crystals for healing work, one or more cauldrons, a bell-branch (a tree branch with nine bells attached), a wand, and one or more containers for sacramental drinks and offerings.

3. Ritual space: the ideal ritual space will have a fire, a water source (such as a stream, lake, pond, the ocean, or a cauldron of water), and a tree. Sometimes one or more large rocks are used to mark a sacred circle. Circles of trees are special places for Druids or one old tree might become a ritual focus.

4. On formal ritual occasions a Druid will likely want to wear a ritual robe, a kilt, or other Celtic garb.

5. Druids may worship alone or in a "Grove," which is the term for a congregation of Druids.

6. Modern Druids offer fruits, vegetables, herbs, poetry, music, song, artwork and crafts to their Gods. Living animals are not harmed in any way.

7. Burial customs: a Druid may be buried by any means he or she has chosen, either by internment in the ground or by cremation. American Druid Orders have voted for the tri-line "Awen" symbol to be placed on military markers and graves (we are currently petitioning the Veteran's Administration to allow this). Most Druids believe in reincarnation.

8.  Common symbols that Druids may wear include the Triskel or Triskellion, a triple spiral design, oak leaves and acorns, the tri-line "Awen" symbol, and the "Druid Sigil" which is a circle with two lines through it.

9.  Deities - Druids may be polytheist, monotheist, duo-theist, deist, pantheist, animist, panentheist, or any combination of the above. Most Druids pick a Patron God or Patroness Goddess to work with. Some deities that Druids work with include; *Brighid, Lugh, In Daghda, The Morrigan, Anu, Danu, Diancecht, Miach, Airmid, Goibniu*, and many others. Druids believe in the inherent divinity of nature, and by extension the inherent sacredness of all natural features, plants, trees, animals, and people. Druids believe in the Otherworld and seek to form a close familiarity with the Spirits and departed ancestors from that realm of existence.

10. Some Druids sing or recite prayers in Gaelic or in some other Celtic language.

11. Druids may be male or female.

12. Druids perform divinations using *Ogham* sticks, *Ogham* stones, and by other methods.

13. Most Druids have a profound respect for and love of history, intellectual growth, artistic creativity, and the pursuit of truth and justice.

14. Dietary restrictions: none unless the individual Druid is under a *geas* (spiritual/magical prohibition) to not eat a certain food.

*Q: If someone were drawn to the Druid path after reading "Priestess of the Forest," where would you suggest they start? Are there any helpful books to read or organizations to contact?*

Tribe of the Oak has a basic reading list that you will find on our website www.tribeoftheoak.com. Once you have read all the books you may apply to our mailing list (which is by invitation only). We have Groves and individual members scattered all over the planet. On the website you will also find links to our virtual shrines, dedicated to many different Celtic deities.

*Q: Do you believe one can be Christian and still follow the Druid path?*

Absolutely! It is interesting that the *Fili*, the highest grade of sacred poets who were so advanced that they would utter prophecy, gradually assumed the Christian faith and became the priests of the new religion. Druids have nothing against Jesus. We value him and his teachings because he was a great prophet of peace and forgiveness. However, we also honor and respect the old Gods and Goddesses and form close bonds with them. For us they are not mutually exclusive.

That said the religion that most closely parallels Druidism is the Hindu faith. The Celtic and Hindu religions both have a common root – the ancient Indo-European Vedic tradition. Both paths have triple deities, sacred fire and sacred water, three worlds, and many other commonalities. Modern Druids often read Vedic texts such as the Rig Veda and the Upanishads and study Brahminic ritual forms as part of their training.

*Q: What do you think Druidism offers for the future of our culture?*

As the era of oil draws to a close people will spend more time growing food locally. They won't be able to afford to buy gourmet food items from around the world because they will be too costly, both to ship and in terms of the carbon emissions caused by their transport and packaging. As people begin to grow their own food again, and tend their own animals, they will naturally seek to honor the Earth and Her cycles. They will once again look to the old ways for how to organize their lives. Our faith provides a beautiful template for how to honor the Earth and Her rhythms.

19095178R00268